THORNS of a REFORMATION ROSE

Jeanne Messick Loidolt

XULON PRESS

Xulon Press
2301 Lucien Way #415
Maitland, FL 32751
407.339.4217
www.xulonpress.com

Unless otherwise indicated, Scripture taken from the NEW AMERCAN STANDARD BIBLE, © 1960, 1962, 1963, 1968, 1971, 1972, 1973, 1975, 1977 by the Lockman foundation. Used by permission.

Printed in the United States of America.

ISBN-13: 978-1-54564-748-6

Table of Contents

Introduction

I find writing an historical novel exciting because the author can explore a character within three-dimensional perspectives: inside, outside and long range. Initially an author considers how the character sees himself, his actions and feelings from his private standpoint against history. Second, how his friends, strangers and loved ones view him, his actions and feelings by the influence and impact on their individual lives. Thirdly, how a character has affected the historical progression and changes as a result of having lived and influenced the friends, loved ones and fellow travelers along the road of life amid the greater flow of consequential historical events of all mankind.

We, as individual persons, cannot imagine or appreciate the influences we leave behind us when we cease our toil on this earth. We have no perspective to follow the ripples and currents that flow outward from us as we make our journey.

As an artist labors over a masterpiece, applying paint strokes of happiness, joy, adversity, and tribulations, some strokes are bold and impactful while others may be conciliatory and connecting; some define and others detail, with little understanding of the finished product — until the artist steps back to view the picture as a whole with all the highlights and shadows in their proper places. Only then can the masterpiece be seen in its full impact.

Even so, an historical novel paints a picture of a character that includes a completed aspect of a life, its influences and long-reaching consequences. My personal journey of learning more about the characters, heroes and common folk among my ancestors has led me down a fascinating path leading to the Queen of Navarre.

Her historical notations beckoned me to step into the shoes of the historical figure and to look through her eyes at her world. It has been quite an adventure. I hope that you see a full image of a courageous woman who stood strong in the face of deadly persecutions from every aspect of her immoral century, relying on her faith in her Lord Jesus Christ alone, in spite of the religious currents of her day. Her life has inspired me to stand strong within the trials of my personal journey, resting in Christ Jesus my Lord.

The life and faith of the Queen of Navarre impacted three noble families of France in the province of Languedoc who were devoted and strong Protestants embroiled in the Reformation. They risked their lives, abandoned their rightful estates and lost their fortunes to stay dedicated to the truth of their faith. The Straboos (Trabues), Guerrants and de Podios (DuPuys) endured great trials to escape the religious persecutions of Reformation France and travel to America where they established the community of Mannekin Town (now Richmond) at the mouth of the York and the Rappahannock rivers in Virginia, the site of a village abandoned by Monacan Indians. I am proud to be a descendant of these devoted giants and have seen the reflection of their strengths in my own beautiful paternal grandmother who was swept along in the flood of pioneers moving west.

The facts and events of Jeanne d'Albret's life are historical and well documented. I have created fictional characters and relationships to round out the forces which shaped the strong traits and character of Princess Jeanne on her journey to become Queen. The tribulations and challenges she endured in her life remain real and active in our current society. They wear the same faces of deceit, immorality, jealousy, and self-gratification that attempt to manipulate each individual toward the eternal destruction of their mortal souls. Jeanne's weapons of warfare against these unseen forces were established through her knowledge and study of the truth of the Word of God. I pray that the unfolding of her character, strength, and perseverance will edify and encourage each of my readers as they encounter personal challenges in their own lives. God bless you all with the knowledge of His merciful love and faithful guidance.

Dedication

To those descendants who follow after strong ancestors: those builders who continue to pass on their strengths of character, faith, intellect, thirst for freedom and the embodiment of human compassion and goodness.

Acknowledgements

To my Lord and Savior Jesus Christ, who has walked with me through this journey, given me inspiration and words and who put this book in my heart; who has been my Encourager, my fountain of knowledge and living water and my constant Companion and Friend.

To my beloved husband, Dick Loidolt, who has supported, encouraged and endured my writing distractions without complaint, including mental desertion and great lack of house cleaning and cooking. Without your faithful love I would never have found my voice.

To my four children for their constant support and encouragement: Chris and wife, Christine; Russ, who has labored in love to improve my internet knowledge and communication skills, and Colleen, his sweet wife and my precious 'daughter,' for her infinite encouragement; Stephen and his dear wife, Shauna for their experience in blogging; and my only daughter, Lisa and her husband Wes, for their daily encouragement amidst my highs and lows, and hesitations.

To my sister, Joanie and husband David Cruz, the "wind beneath my wings".

To my dear friends and spiritual leaders, Bruce and Brenda Smith. I treasure your constant encouragements and could not have completed this endeavor without your critical editing skills.

To Pastors Brenda and Kelvin Copeland for giving me that initial push; and Jake for his inspiration.

River of Life

Lord, You set the appointed moment of my beginning,
You formed me in the deep places of Your creation.
You chose my course and set the boundary of my flow.
From my beginning I have been nourished
by attributes and traits of forbearers;
sustained with qualities of progenitors before
my given time.
I am a silent force springing to life by Your purpose;
Bubbling across the rocks and pebbles in my course
With joy and laughter;
Increasing in strength by Your great power.
My thunderous turbulence pounds
Against unexpected, immovable objects;
Booming, precipitous falls loom in my path
Roaring to declare the strength and power of Your presence.
May sunbeams glistening off my surface be a reflection
of Your face and light.
May my deep pools be a quiet, peaceful haven of Your love.
May the melody of my journey resonate with sweet refrain, rising
to proclaim Your infinite mercy and grace.
May my small streams and tributaries flow continuously forward,
growing with strength and love to merge into
the future of Your eternal Son.

Jeanne Messick Loidolt

Book 1. THE ROSE

"Afflictions are often the black settings in which God places the jewels of His children's graces to make them shine brighter."

Charles H. Spurgeon

1. Despair

"I will never desert you nor will I ever forsake you"

Deuteronomy 31:6, 8/Hebrews 13:5 (NASB)

The bleak light crept through long, narrow windows high in the stone walls and nudged Jeanne's swollen eyelids. She squinched her eyes tightly closed and burrowed deeper into the warmth of her blankets to shut out the beginning of a new day. Her body ached. Exhaustion and crushing emotions overwhelmed her. Normally, five-year-old Jeanne d'Albret, Princess of Navarre, would have bounced from her bed in anticipation of new adventures. Today, she didn't want to live.

Regardless of the growing light, she fought to hold the doors of her mind against memories pushing into her conscious thought. New tears puddled behind her swollen eyelids as the reality of her emptiness poured over her. She was so devastatingly lonely.

Just a few days ago on January 7, 1533,[i] she had danced around the elaborate preparations for her fifth birthday, intoxicated with anticipation and full to overflowing with giggles and suspense. She was the center of everyone's love and attention throughout the castle. Her father, Henri d'Albret II, King of Navarre, had spared no expense in honoring his daughter and only child. Even the guards of the realm and the castle floor-sweepers had smiled as she pirouetted through the hallways and great rooms. Not only were the birthday preparations beyond her wildest imagination, this would be an extra-special celebration since her most loved Uncle Francis would also be attending.

Her mother's brother, the King of France, had cradled her after birth, showered her with presents on his every visit, focused his total attention on her small tales, secrets, and hurts, while willingly allowing her to wrap his heart around her little finger. No other living person was permitted the same free access, out-spoken opinion, or bold arrogance with the King of France. Her mother, Marguerite d'Angoulême, Queen of Navarre, and sister of the King, chastised Jeanne frequently for the impudence she displayed while in the presence of the King of France. Jeanne didn't pay attention. She loved her uncle, and he loved her back. She knew that to the core of her soul.

When the pandemonium of celebration had diminished to a dull roar, Jeanne was exhausted from the excitement of presents, pony-rides, and well-wishers and was bedded down in her cozy bed for the night.

Downstairs, behind the closed doors of the d'Albret throne room, an intense discussion was taking place. Soon it turned into an argument and shouting. The unsuspecting subject of these discussions slumbered secure and undisturbed, dancing through dreams of happiness.

The following day, Jeanne was called from playing with birthday presents in the late morning to take a walk with her favorite uncle, before he returned to his royal palace at Fontainebleau. She was not prepared for the impact this conversation would have on her life.

Jeanne's maids had wrapped her in furs from head to toe against the bitter winds howling around the corners of the castle. With her small leather glove enfolded in the warmth of Uncle Francis's large fingers, Jeanne tipped her face upward to hear his every word before the January winds whipped them away. Uncle Francis stopped to sit on a bench and pulled her onto his lap to be sure she did not miss hearing a single word. She did not understand everything he explained to her, but she did grasp the enormity of his statements.

Before day's end, Jeanne would travel many miles across France toward a castle located within the realm of King Francis I. The Castle of Château de Plessis-lez-Tours had been the home of French King Louis XI in 1463 during the late years of his reign. There Jeanne was to be hidden away, alone, (with accompanying maids and necessary guards, cooks, and keepers, of course), secluded from seeking eyes of rival regents seeking to form alliances by finalizing a political negotiation sweetened by marriage of a sweet young bride for an eligible prince or reigning king. Jeanne was his favorite, Uncle Francis reassured her, and she must be prepared for the role of a future Queen of renown. Her frozen face and stiff back were not a result of the bitter wind.

King Francis would personally oversee her care, education and companions, orchestrating her tutors, ladies-in-waiting, training in court etiquette and grooming in fashion and beauty. What the King did not tell her was his fear of rumors that Emperor Charles V of Spain, and Ferdinand the Catholic, a representative of the Pope, were intent on making the kingdom of Navarre a part of Spain. If they succeeded Jeanne would lose the right of accession to the throne of Navarre. King Francis I also did not share his suspicions that Henri d'Albret, might make a secret alliance with Spain's Emperor Charles V to marry Jeanne to his son, Prince Philip. The jealousy and distrust between the King of France and his brother-in-law, Henri d'Albret, caused King Francis to remove Princess Jeanne at age five from the influence and fellowship of her royal parents by essentially holding her captive at the Château Plessis.

On returning to the warmth of the castle of Nérac, Princess Jeanne was led to her room to sit before a warm fire. The bustle and confusion surrounding her, as necessary belongings and bedchamber trappings were bundled to be piled on carts for immediate departure, did not penetrate her thoughts or distract her shock.

She sat unmoving, replaying the words that had crumbled her foundation; the flames she sat before seemed to gobble up everything that had been her joy and security. The warmth of the fire could not reach the cold, frozen core of her being. She had no desire to seek human kindness or understanding. Who could fathom the depth of abandonment or betrayal gripping her heart? She had no one to turn to and no recourse. She had received the King's Edict from the King himself, and he made it plain there would be no avoidance of his plans. His orders required immediate departure.

Whispers among the servants slipped through the fog in her mind and revealed that her mother who had retired in seclusion to her apartments when Princess Jeanne left the castle to walk with her Uncle, provided instructions not to be disturbed. The King's orders would be followed to the letter and she recognized all pleading or wailing would be futile. Soon after their return, she had been vaguely aware of the clatter of horses and wagons and knew the King had escaped any further discussion by returning to his palace at Fontainebleau.

Minette, Jeanne's sweet nursemaid, grasped her little Princess quickly in an embrace of farewell. She whispered words in haste against Jeanne's ear, saying she would see her Princess when she returned home to visit her mother.

Jeanne received the embrace and endearment as woodenly as a small statue; however, an ember of dim hope landed amid her inner core of grief and numbing despair. It smoldered, a spark of survival waiting to be fanned into a flickering glow in a deep recess of her subconscious mind. The coach jostled along the dark, cold road of blind destination among a line of wagons, pack horses and soldiers lumbering along the trails as rapidly as possible.

Irrepressible tears soaked the fox fur coat and white rabbit muff of the forsaken little Princess hidden in the dark corner of her sumptuous coach. The coach was drawn by twelve horses, their staccato hoof-beats beating a steady rhythm through miles and miles of mountainous forest road and winding valley plains in the black night. No sound could be heard over the cacophony of the traveling party; especially not the small, weeping grief and suffering of the heart-broken child confined there. Only muted sobs, sniffles and hiccups disclosed the depth of her wretched anguish.

The grueling journey of three hundred miles lasted nearly ten days through the rough terrain of Gascony to Bordeaux; skirting the coast before turning again toward central France and north to the Loire Valley, with only occasional breaks to change horses and stop for food and drink. The stern traveling companion assigned as a chaperone for Jeanne had no interest in engaging the little royal, never perceiving the pain borne by the lonely child. A bitter woman, she fixated on her own discomfort of painful arthritis, dwelling instead on the jolting movements of the ride. She had no thought, time or heart for little Princess Jeanne.

From the depths of her inconsolable, broken little heart, waves of conviction overwhelmed Jeanne that no one in the whole world cared about her feelings. She was right: her personal reactions and despair were given no consideration by the strong political winds generated by forces beyond her insignificant influence.

2. Rush to the Future

"But we have this treasure in earthen vessels, that
the surpassing greatness of the power may be of God
and not from ourselves; we are afflicted in every
way, but not crushed; perplexed, but not despairing;
persecuted, but not forsaken; struck down, but not
destroyed; always carrying about in the body the dying
of Jesus, that the life of Jesus also may be manifested in
our body."

2 Corinthians 4:7-10 (NASB)

The thin winter light invading an immense chamber on the morning of January 18, 1533, promised no increasing warmth in the day to come. The traveling party had reached its destination late in the dark of the night before. The destitute heart of the little Princess could find no impetus to welcome the breaking dawn. Only the quavering ember of hope and survival deep in the recesses of her unconscious mind compelled her to continue living. That tiny glow within, along with the stubborn assault of light upon her little eyelids initiated a flutter of her lashes. Then, in surrender, she peeked.

As her little head poked out of the pile of comforters and fur blankets, muffled whispers of movement and activity beyond the brocade curtains of her bed joined the campaign to bring her fully awake. Suddenly the rustling was right there beside the bed, and she found herself staring into two smiling, bright eyes through a small opening framed by the curtain. Forgotten memories stirred and she knew she remembered these eyes. The curtain parted further to reveal a petite nose with a bright smile accompanied by creases framing laughing eyes. Thin strands of grey hair peeked out of a delicate linen cap on the head attached to the sweet face. A gentle voice spoke, "My Lady, God has blessed you with another glorious day!" and Jeanne knew this was Aymée de la Fayette, the kind, gentle attendant and friend of her mother's confinement for her birth and a constant companion during Jeanne's own tender years as an infant and toddler.

When the memory released a crowd of feelings of shattered security and lost affection, unbidden tears stung her eyes and threatened to overwhelm her.

"Now, now, my sweet Lady, greet the breaking day with new strength after a long and painful ordeal," Aymée spoke quietly with a light caress, not wanting to be overheard by other maids in the room.

"You are in a new home with new adventures to be revealed. Remember your sweet mother and know that she would have you be brave."

Allowing no alternative, Aymée tugged the toasty comforters off the small body, wrapped Jeanne in her warmest dressing gown and gathered her into stout arms. The Princess allowed herself to be ushered near one of the three roaring fireplaces around the great room. Aymée seated her on a cushioned settee and massaged her arms and shoulders to generate increased body warmth. It was a familiar routine of what seemed to Jeanne had happened eternities ago in her childhood memory.

Looking about her, Jeanne took in the massive room with a raised dais in the center for her bed. Servants were hurrying everywhere, brushing away cobwebs and cleaning corners in the stone wall. She shrank from the cold, impersonal space. A shiver of distaste and despair shook her as she thought, "Where are the cozy rooms of Nérac? It is cold, and I want my mother!"

Thoughts flooded her mind of the gracious apartments of the Queen of Navarre at Nérac with visions of light and music, warmth, and happy conversation.

Bitterly, Aymée's little Princess made a mental note to demand candles and oil lamps be installed as soon as conceivable. She decided she would require any lady-in-waiting assigned to her attendance be schooled in music, singing, and instruments. Lady Jeanne, Princess of Navarre and ward of the King of France, had always been a willful and stubborn child, twisting her uncle's will to her desires. Unbidden, the King's own words came to her mind of how, for the sake of his kingdom, his necessary order had also caused him pain and guilt. A perception began to grow in her young mind; she realized she might hold in her own small hands the power to define her royal identity and shape who she was to become.

Unconsciously her spine stiffened, and her shoulders drew back in response to the weight of responsibility and opportunity that dawned upon her consciousness. It was almost imperceptible; however, Aymée, who was busy with the ministrations of bathing and dressing the little Princess, sensed a change in the royal mind. With an inward chuckle, Aymée sped a small prayer of request with wings of love to the Throne of Grace. He was the one who set leaders and kings in their places and supervised their comings and goings. She knew without a doubt 'Who' was in charge of this dramatic change in the life of her little Princess, and it was not King Francis.

Princess Jeanne sat silent and unmoving, enduring the brushing of tangles, curling and pulling of her abundant hair while Aymée's experienced fingers quickly arranged a stylish coiffure of braids and upswept layers of curls on her childish head. Jeanne's mind had sped back to the birthday celebrations and love that were no longer a part of her life. Aymée recognized the sudden loss of the princess's childhood and this forced rush to adulthood. In defiance, Aymée allowed a few locks and ringlets to escape the severity of trapped strands to tumble around the small face and neck. The effect was lovely.

Jeanne remained silent, lost in her own private thoughts. Aymée admired the natural beauty revealed as she gazed at the enchanting eyes of her little Princess. Her eyes were blue at first glance, but not only blue, alive with lights and movement of purple mixed with multi-layered shades of vibrant, deep navy blues, now flashing with flecks of gold over inscrutable pools, encircled with a dark, almost-black, royal blue. Recognition of the task God had placed in her hands dawned on Aymée as she studied Jeanne's small face.

She had faithfully served scores of small aristocrats in the imperial house of King Francis but never had she been impressed that the task put before her could very well result in influences that would challenge all of France.

Aymée was privy to the knowledge of negotiations by the Emperor Charles of Spain to wed his son Philip to this little Princess. Such a union would allow the monarch of Spain to unite the Kingdom of Navarre with Spain through marriage and would position Princess Jeanne in an influential role as consort of the future King of Spain. Aymée was much opposed to such a betrothal as she was well aware of the devious machinations of the Emperor of Spain against the King of France to undermine his power.

Aymée grasped the small hands of Princess Jeanne and pulled her to her feet. The dress the little Princess wore was dark blue velvet with an upside-down v-front panel of pinch-pleated satin; a royal blue velvet cape was attached at the shoulder and fell to just a few inches above the floor. The sleeves of the dress were padded to the elbow, and inside the bell-shaped sleeve from elbow to wrist additional pinched-pleated satin peeked out from the bottom before tightening around her wrist. On her head, a matching crown of blue velvet was lined with pearls. Aymée was pleased with the way the elegant royal blue velvet brought out the blue in her eyes; and the cape, abundance of petticoats and long sleeves would provide warm comfort in the drafty castle. She moved the Princess to the massive door of her chamber and reached out to pull the handle and open it. She was struck with the smallness of the Princess against the massive oak of the door, seeming to represent the over-whelming obstacles that awaited her on its other side.

Jeanne's hand lightly touched Aymée's wrist. Startled, she glanced quickly at Princess Jeanne who was staring straight ahead. The little Princess narrowed her concentration against everything in her path, taking a deep breath to readjust her thoughts and composure before proceeding. Aymée wondered if, at that very moment, Princess Jeanne of Navarre dropped her grip on childhood and shouldered the responsibility of her future. Natural majesty had been bred into the child by her environment and royal blood coursed through her veins. Aymée was convinced that what God ordained for this child would be accomplished. Aymée's job would be to build a foundation of prayer. She trembled at the enormity of her part in this undertaking.

Princess Jeanne lifted her fingers from Aymée's wrist, permitting the heavy door to be opened, and the two of them stepped forward to face the future.

3. Chateau de Plessis

*"For momentary, light affliction is producing for us
an eternal weight of glory far beyond all comparison,
while we look not at the things which are seen, but at
the things which are not seen; for the things which are
seen are temporal, but the things which are not seen
are eternal."*

2 Corinthians 4:17-18 (NASB)

The door closed behind them, and the two companions moved down the hallway toward the wide, winding staircase located around the next corner. Just before the stair there was a small alcove bare of furniture, and suddenly Aymée pulled her Princess aside and spoke urgently in a low tone willing Jeanne to understand the seriousness of her words.

"My Lady," she said, "at the foot of the stairs the Chamberlain of the castle, Sir Arnauld Duquesse who has been appointed by King Francis, will be waiting. You must understand that he will be in control of every detail of all that will take place in the castle. He reports to His Majesty and will be the eyes and ears for the King."

Aymée's comments might be viewed by many, including the waiting Chamberlain, as insubordination. At this moment, the only thought in Aymée's mind was to prepare her five-year-old Princess for the encounter at the foot of the stairs. She would leave any negative repercussions for her warning in the lap of God.

Her passionate words had an impact on the little Princess as memories filled her mind of her mother, Queen of Navarre, descending stairs in the castle of Nérac to greet ambassadors, kings, Cardinals, bishops, and scholars who came to seek her royal favor. Unconsciously, Jeanne arranged her demeanor to match the example of her mother and moved to the stairs with an air of royalty, with her heart beating loudly in her ears.

At the foot of the stairs, Sir Arnauld Duquesse waited impatiently, shifting his weight from one foot to the other. He was not happy that his King had appointed him to this remote, forsaken castle to serve, of all people, a five-year-old girl. He was not a babysitter and was intent to find a course of escape to an assignment more congenial to his social nature.

Stewing with resentment, the disgruntled Chamberlain became aware of rustle and movement at the head of the stairs. He arranged his posture into the characteristic pose of a supplicant in the service of royalty and glanced up at the child moving toward him. Surprised at the majestic bearing, poise, and somber face of the little Princess, his inner thoughts struggled to comprehend that what he was seeing was diametrically opposed to what he had expected. This was no capricious child to be controlled and disciplined.

The diminutive young lady, followed by her governess, stopped on the stair step which aligned her eyes just a few inches above his gaze. She regally held out her fingers to allow him to take her hand. This movement declared in a moment that she was his superior and would not suffer him to disrespect her. Without conscious thought, by mimicking her mother's actions, the Princess laid the responsibility of this encounter squarely on his shoulders as it gave him the opportunity to take her hand and bow deferentially to kiss the fingers of his monarch. His automatic response to her royalty was a surprise to the chamberlain.

After releasing her hand, he raised his eyes and found himself scrutinized. In the expressions that moved through the changing colors of her eyes, he saw kindness, compassion, and sympathy for his position with an invitation for the possibility of friendship. These mesmerizing eyes enhanced the impact of the royal carriage and demeanor of this beautiful child. Most of all, she was remarkably discerning with an inexplicable inner glow.

He had frequently been at court at Fontainebleau and had seen the Queen of Navarre, sister of King Francis, who often acted as official hostess and mediator. She was known throughout France for her beauty, wit, and wisdom. Marguerite d'Albret de Navarre's young daughter promised all that the mother was known for; also, strangely for this young age, she displayed confidence that only emerged in one who has survived tribulation. What Jeanne saw in Sir Duquesse's returning gaze was respect. He yielded to her service.

Aymée watched this interchange with satisfaction. It was an auspicious beginning. It seemed the prayers she had not yet spoken were already being answered. Her hand moved unconsciously over her heart in thanksgiving.

Sir Duquesse offered Princess Jeanne his hand to walk with her to a circle of chairs by the fire. It was an enormous hearth with massive tree trunks and smaller logs burning with raging flames in the center of the hall. Smoke from the burning logs drifted upward in a pillar toward the far recesses three stories above them. The enormity of the room offered a strange sort of privacy as the immense boulders with which the castle was built absorbed the various sounds bouncing off their surfaces.

Many wagons bringing furniture and supplies from the palace of Fontainebleau had begun arriving. Sounds of coming and going deliveries, arrivals of servants, military personnel, esquires and gardeners bearing their required tools blended into a dull background roar.

Sir Arnauld Duquesse automatically proceeded to dispense of his duties, and he and Princess Jeanne bent their heads together in deep conversation. He relayed to her a quick assessment of his plans to decorate and furnish the empty castle. A summary followed concerning plans for her educational development. She listened intently, and Arnauld was astounded at how she grasped the matters he presented; the corresponding questions she offered showed the depth of her perception. She was like no other five-year-old he had ever encountered.

Soon Sir Duquesse detected a wandering of Jeanne's attention and evidence of weariness around her eyes. He suggested they stroll around the castle and he would enlighten her about some of the castle's history.

As he signaled a waiting attendant to order lunch upon their return, Jeanne exhaled a deep breath in relief. It had been a great deal of information to absorb. She glanced at Aymée who had positioned herself just at the edge of hearing, waiting for any sign from her Princess if she might be needed. A weary little smile sent the message of her appreciation for Aymée's support and her hope that Aymée would remember much of the conversation later so they could talk about it.

Suddenly the child realized how fatigued she felt. A cup of steaming hot chocolate with a small plate of warm almond cookies was offered to Princess Jeanne. The imports of cocoa beans from Spain had only recently been introduced in France, and the newly discovered flavor resulting from crushing the beans and mixing sugar and cream to prepare a hot beverage was rarely seen except in royal circles. It was a new, novel delicacy and Princess Jeanne sipped timidly from the cup and found it delicious. She smiled broadly and gratefully acknowledged her pleasure. Nibbling on the cookies relieved her wilting energy even though the ordeal of crushing emotional disillusionments and a ten-day journey were beginning to take their toll.

When Sir Duquesse returned to her side, she managed a smile and rose to explore this isolated, drafty, stone edifice that was to be her home. She had no concept of how long her enforced seclusion would last, but along with her decision to be the mistress of her identity, she was determined to command her environment in whatever manner she could. Glancing casually over her shoulder, Jeanne confirmed that Aymée continued to accompany them at a discreet distance.

4. Legacy of King Louis XI

"Trust in the Lord with all your heart, and do not lean on your own understanding. In all your ways acknowledge Him, and He will make your paths straight."

Proverbs 3:5-6 (NASB)

Jeanne's Chamberlain was a handsome young man about twenty years of age with light brown sun-streaked hair. He carried himself with a natural ease that complimented his athletic build. It was evident that he enjoyed spending time outside and Princess Jeanne suspected he was proficient at hunting and riding horses. His face was pleasant with a gentle smile and friendly eyes. The Chamberlain, being tall, towered over Jeanne's small frame. Although she had to bend her neck up so very far to speak with him or to listen to what he said, she felt comfortable immediately. As though suddenly aware of what a discomfort it must be to look up to him, he quickly bent over, making sure he could look the Princess in her eyes to avoid causing her pain. The six-foot frame of Duquesse bending toward the three and one-half foot little Princess was an almost comic caricature of his submission to her authority. The movement of Jeanne's short legs betrayed evidence of her fatigue, and Sir Duquesse had to shorten his gait to little, mincing steps. He began relating the story of the previous resident of the castle as they crossed the immense space of the great room toward a corridor in the south wall.

The castle of Plessis had been built several centuries earlier before King Louis XI made it his home.[ii] It was built in a square with a massive courtyard in the center. It was a vast, enormous castle, overwhelmingly empty. At his remark of King Louis XI, Arnauld cast a sideways glance at Jeanne to judge how he should proceed. She was pale and appeared exhausted, so he determined to keep this initial tour brief.

He disliked the place. It was filled with a disturbed spirit along with many immoveable reminders of the fear and torment the former tenant had generated here. He must keep himself from permitting his reactions to creep into his conversation.

He kept his dissertation to a summary of how young Louis XI had submitted in obedience to the diplomatic arrangement by his father, France's King Charles, for Louis' marriage at age thirteen to eleven-year-old Margaret of Scotland.

"Louis' marriage with Margaret resulted from the nature of medieval royal diplomacy and the precarious financial position of the French monarchy. The wedding ceremony, very plain by standards of that day took place on a June afternoon in 1436 and was presided over by the Archbishop of Reims. The thirteen-year-old Louis looked more mature than his eleven-year-old bride, who was said to resemble a beautiful doll. King Charles of France attended the wedding wearing grey riding pants and did not even bother to remove his spurs. The Scottish guests and family of the bride were quickly hustled out after the wedding reception, as the French royal court was quite impoverished at this time. They could not afford an extravagant ceremony or to host their Scottish guests for any longer than they did. The Scots, however, saw this behavior as an insult to their small, but proud, country. Louis had grown up aware of the continuing financial weakness of the French nation and hated his father for it.

"Following the wedding ceremony, Margaret continued her studies, and Louis went on a military tour with his father to loyal areas of the kingdom. It was on that trip Louis was named Dauphin of France, as was traditional for the eldest son of the king and expected heir to the throne. Margaret was highly regarded at the court of France, but her marriage to Louis was not a happy one, in part because of his strained relations with his father. She died childless in 1445 at the age of twenty.

"Louis, when age sixteen, took part in an uprising which sought to install him as regent of France in his father's place. A strong-minded boy, he found he could not carry off his intentions by mere bluster. Louis never forgot this lesson. The rebellion failed, and Louis was forced to submit to the king, who chose to forgive him. However, he still quarreled with his father and his offensive scheming and disrespectful behavior caused him to be ordered out of court and sent to his province of Dauphiné where Louis ruled as king in all but name. Despite frequent summons by King Charles, the two would never meet again.

"Without King Charles' consent, Louis, who had been widowed for six years, made a strategic marriage to Charlotte of Savoy. The groom was twenty-seven years old, and the bride was nine. This marriage had long-ranging effects on foreign policy, involving France in future disputes and political affairs in Italy. The couple had eight children though only three lived. Louis neglected his bride as he continued his plots against his father. Louis had Charlotte and her household kept secluded at the Château of Amboise, where she was so deprived of his attention that it was rumored she dressed like an ordinary country farm-girl.

"Finally, King Charles sent an army against his son. Louis fled to Burgundy seeking refuge with his father's most hated enemy. In his haste to escape, Louis abandoned Charlotte to her own devices, and she was required to beg for a mode of transportation from acquaintances to flee with her children to join Louis.

"When Louis learned that his father was dying, he hurried to Reims to be crowned in case his brother, Charles, Duke of Berry, would try to do the same. Louis XI became King of France on 25 July 1461.

"Louis XI reigned with tools of war, cunning, and sheer guile to overcome France's rebellious feudal lords. At the time of his death he had united France and laid the foundations of a strong monarchy though he was a secretive, reclusive man, and few would mourn his death. He spent the latter years of his reign alone, isolated at Château de Plessis-lez-Tours, where he spun webs of political intrigue and earned the nickname of 'Universal Spider.' He resented the obstacles he had to overcome, continuing to blame his father. His isolation at Château de Plessis-lez-Tours only increased his suspicious paranoias, so he also included plans of defense against real and imagined adversaries to protect himself in the castle. He ordered huge moats to surround the castle, with mazes ending in dead-end walls throughout the grounds. Yawning pits and long, deep ditches are hidden among the trees and gardens. The castle itself borders the wide River Loire, creating a natural defensive barrier and its rushing currents carried away enemies spotted by the many archers that maintained the battlements."[iii]

Sir Duquesse, lost in his knowledge of this depressing castle's history, spoke as though building to a climax. Jeanne's thoughts had centered on how young Louis' wives were when he married them and how miserable the king must have been in his self-imposed isolation. She imagined the strong soldiers who may have been killed in the skirmishes around the castle walls of her new home.

Sir Duquesse stopped suddenly as the three moved into the doorway of a dark and ominous hall. Princess Jeanne peered at him in dread before moving cautiously forward. The voice of the Chamberlain faded. If Sir Duquesse had said more than his short comment, "This was King Louis XI's torture chamber," the Princess did not hear it. Her wide eyes fixed on a multitude of cages hanging from the far distant ceiling, large enough that her small stature would have fit, but too small for a man any larger than herself to stand up in or to spread his legs to full length if sitting. Jeanne's eyes had become adjusted to the dim light and her gaze traveled around the walls hung with various terrible tools used for torment. She was suddenly assaulted with visions of the unimaginable pain and terror that occurred here in her castle.

Aymée, behind her, gasped in horror. Anger welled up in the governess' body until she was shaking with rage. Her precious child should never have been exposed to this woeful, ominous display! She anxiously contemplated Jeanne's demeanor, ready to pounce should the impact of this exposure cause her little miss to swoon.

For his part, Sir Duquesse also scrutinized Princess Jeanne. What a blunder he had made! He had spoken to her as an adult, and he now realized his error. Regardless of her grace and poise, she was, after all, five-years-old and more than likely equipped with a child's vivid imagination. He stood immobile in confusion and wondered what he should do. King Francis had given his precious niece into Arnauld's care and this unthinking moment could be the undoing of any benefits he hoped to gain from the assignment. He was afraid to look at Aymée because he could feel the rage radiating off of her. Both Arnauld and Aymée watched as Jeanne pivoted slowly and, disregarding their stares, pronounced she would be grateful to retire to her apartments for a rest.

At the foot of the broad, winding staircase to her quarters, Princess Jeanne faced them and offered her hand to her Chamberlain.

Her low voice drew them both near as she said, "I thank you, sir, for your report of the castle and what King Francis has decided for my education. I need to think about all you have told me. I want to meet you again an hour before dinner. May I now be served lunch in my apartment?"

As Sir Duquesse bent to kiss her hand, a mischievous smile played across Jeanne's face, and she remarked meaningfully, "You and I must find something to do with those awful cages; fill them with birds perhaps?" Turning then to begin ascending the stairway, Jeanne missed the astounded, gawking stare of Sir Arnauld Duquesse at her departure. She was too busy counting the stairs as she climbed.

5. Worldly Pleasures

*"Things which eye has not seen and ear has not heard,
and which have not entered the heart of man, all that
God has prepared for those who love Him"*

1 Corinthians 2:9 (NASB)

Jeanne entered her apartments and stopped short. Clearly, King Francis meant to keep his promise to provide everything in his power to make her as physically comfortable as possible. The apartment had been completely refinished with every possible feminine luxury and appointment any woman could desire. The stone floors were strewn with thick, soft fur rugs and on the cold walls hung artistically woven and stitched landscapes of mountains, streams, and fields of flowers. The walls were lined with heavy carved dressers, wooden chests, and tallboys, containing dresses, coats, capes and linen lacy undergarments.

Pillows, cushions and heavy, fur-lined comforters were scattered in abundance, especially around the hearths of the three fireplaces. To Jeanne's delight, candles and lamps glowed in profusion everywhere! The heavily padded chairs and couches were paired with large pots of greenery, poinsettias and winter petunias.

In one of the small rooms that opened onto the greater bedchamber was a delicate, fragile-looking desk complete with feathered writing utensils and a small ink pot. Shelves lined the wall of the little area, with a few small, bound volumes already in place.

Next to the large oak door, an area with a narrow bed was equally equipped. It could be closed off with beautiful linen screens that would spread across the opening. This was Aymée's accommodations since she would be in constant attendance to Jeanne and well-deserved her modest privacy.

Jeanne turned and caught her breath at an alcove of small chairs next to a harp, pianoforte, and small musical instruments including a flute, piccolo, and mandolin. Someone had been reading her mind!

Even the 'water closet' had received attention, with small conveniences that indicated thoughtful consideration. She suspected the touches of her mother, the Queen, in cooperation with the King and was suddenly overwhelmed with the depth of her fatigue and loneliness as tears threatened to disarm her completely – she sought solace from Aymée.

Aymée had also been profoundly pleased with the efforts of King Francis for she had never seen this level of luxury. Privately, she was delighted that the King had included her in his generous penance to Princess Jeanne. The only thought that disturbed her was the realization that absolutely nothing in this gorgeous apartment was directed to the interests of a child. Jeanne's childhood was being ripped away with velvet gloves! Apparently, King Francis felt an urgency to prepare this five-year-old child for instant adult responsibilities. Aymée grieved in her heart for such a betrayal. Immediately conscious of Jeanne's dismayed look, concern jarred her back to her own immediate responsibility to this child.

When Jeanne had been fed lunch, disrobed and tucked into her bed, Aymée held her in her arms until the tension in the small frame released, and her breathing maintained a steady rhythm. She slipped from the bed and prepared for the rest of this long day. Laying out an appropriate dress and cape along with ribbons and sparkling diamond pins to hold Jeanne's hair in place, Aymée stopped to recharge with her own neglected lunch.

Then she retired to her private space and dropped to her knees. This promised to be a long conversation with her Holy God. She needed divine help to cope with the revelations that had occurred and the challenges facing her until bedtime. Aymée wanted help. Requiring discernment and wisdom, she implored her God for all the help He could provide on Jeanne's behalf. They were facing a long battle against unknown forces, and she knew where strength lay. This battle was the Lord's.

6. History is Important

"Be anxious for nothing, but in everything by prayer
and supplication with thanksgiving let your requests be
made known to God."

Philippians 4:6 (NASB)

When it came time to rouse Jeanne later that afternoon and prepare her for dinner and meeting with the Chamberlain, Aymée
spoke gently, knowing that it would take the child a while to separate dreams (or nightmares) from reality and to adjust her mind
again to her new surroundings. Aymée repeated the routine of the
morning and soon had Jeanne wrapped in a silk dressing gown, sitting silently on the settee, unconscious of Aymée's busy hands in
her hair. Aymée's thoughts and memories traveled back to the time
she had spent with Marguerite d'Albret of Angoulême, Duchess of
Alençon. Aymée de la Fayette was a favorite at court and was one
of Marguerite's closest companions. They had known each other as
very young women although intervening marriages had sometimes
kept them separated for several years. Aymée, when widowed, had
been a stalwart comfort to Marguerite during her sixteen years of
a loveless and childless marriage.

The arrangement for Marguerite's first marriage to Charles,
Duke of Alençon, at age seventeen had been a political maneuver
of Louis XII while then King of France. The avaricious Louis XII
was able to retain possession of the county of Armagnac and its

revenues by arranging the marriage of the Duke of Alençon to Marguerite, as the bride would receive the county, plus 60,000 crowns, as her dowry.

The Duke of Alençon had been considered a worthy husband for Marguerite since he was a direct descendant from Charles, Count d'Valois, Count of Alencon. Charles d'Valois was a brother to Philip the Fair, who became King of France in 1285 and by marriage, King of Navarre. However, Charles, Duke of Alencon was far from being a suitable mate for the intelligent, quick-witted, liberally educated Marguerite. She had been a companion with her brother Francis during the years of their education. Her superior intelligence had surpassed even the gifted intellectual pursuits of her brother.

Duke Charles was a dull, melancholic man with a mean, quick-tempered disposition. He was absent from his bride and home for extended periods spent abroad to fight in battles on the frontiers of France with Louis XII. When Francis I was crowned king in 1515, the Duke fought under his brother-in-law, expecting to receive prestigious positions in the military, although as a soldier and a leader he was regarded as unreliable. To escape her lonely life in Alençon, Marguerite made frequent visits to court in response to the demands of her brother. It was during this time her acquaintance with Aymée developed into loyal support and joy. In her private times of loneliness, and disappointment in her marriage, Marguerite turned to religion.

During the years when France engaged in battles in Spain, Alençon had fought alongside his King where he had acquitted himself well enough. In the heat of the battlefield at Pavia, King Francis had given Alençon the critical command of the vanguard. As the Spanish forces turned the battle toward victory over the French troops, Alencon abandoned his post and fled to avoid capture.

This failure to carry out his command successfully in support of the King led to the king's capture by the Emperor Charles V of Spain. As Duke d'Alençon made his way home to Marguerite, taunts of "deserter" followed him. He arrived at the end of March, desperately ill with pneumonia and shame. Feeling only contempt for his disgrace at the battle of Pavia as well as resentment for the capture of her beloved brother, Marguerite nevertheless was moved to pity and nursed him until his death the following month.

Marguerite, now a thirty-three-year-old widow and still childless after sixteen years of marriage, became the King's most faithful subject and ambassador. Concern for the captive King deepened when word arrived he was gravely ill with no sign of his release. A decision was made that Marguerite should go to Spain offering her proven nursing skills to Francis and employ her diplomatic skills to those already working in Madrid for the King's release. Aymée, in loyal service and loving companionship, accompanied her friend on this perilous four-month trip.

Marguerite set out on a journey which was hazardous, strenuous, and grueling in the heat of the summer. Traveling down the river Rhône by barge, Marguerite was delayed for an additional two weeks waiting for permission of safe-conduct from the Spanish emperor, Charles V. The consent arrived with stipulations that she would not be allowed to engage in diplomatic means to secure Francis' release and secondly, that she was limited to a stay of three months.

Arriving at their destination of Palamos, in Catalonia, Marguerite learned her brother had been moved to Madrid, requiring additional days of travel that would shorten her limited stay. When she finally arrived at his bedside in prison, Francis was very ill with a high fever. When Francis did not recognize her, Marguerite became distraught, remaining at his side praying for several days. The abscess in his head causing the fever suddenly burst, and he regained consciousness and began to recover. Francis declared that Marguerite had saved his life. She devoted herself solely to the nursing and care of Francis and made no diplomatic efforts to seek an audience with the Emperor.

Marguerite learned that Charles V planned to arrest her if she stayed longer than the permitted three months. With Aymée, she dashed for the border, traveling twelve hours a day on horseback for speed, and reached Narbonne, France, on Christmas Day, the last day of her allotted time. The Madrid treaty was finalized in the New Year, and Francis left captivity on February 21, 1526, arriving in March at the border where he was exchanged for his two young sons, who Emperor Charles V insisted must now become the hostages of Spain as demanded by the conditions of the treaty. Back in France, Marguerite received praise for her efforts to save the King. She now directed her energies to secure the release of her nephews, whose condition in prison worsened as efforts were slowly made to raise the money for their ransom. The boys were eventually returned in 1530 after four miserable years as prisoners.

On her return from Madrid, Marguerite joined her mother, Louise of Savoy, acting regent of France in the absence of her son Francis, at her castle in Lyons. Henri II d'Albret, King of Navarre, was captured with Francis and imprisoned in the palace of Pavia. He dressed as a page and was able to escape. Upon his escape from captivity, Henri made his way to Lyons to offer his loyalty and services to the king's regent.

Marguerite and Henri d'Albret were mutually attracted. He saw a beautiful, accomplished woman, pale and dignified in her mourning and acclaimed by the people of France for saving the king's life. "I have found my pearl and placed it in my heart," the King of Navarre said about Marguerite.

To Marguerite, Henri d'Albret completed those emotional longings so neglected in the barren sixteen years of marriage to the Duke d'Alencon. His courage and intelligence were suitably equivalent to her own and he displayed a devotion to the arts and showed sympathies to the reform movement that had captured Marguerite's devotion; and they shared a mutual hatred for the Emperor Charles V. Marguerite believed she had found her knight in shining armor though Henri was eleven years younger than Marguerite.

Henri admired her diplomatic skills and believed her attributes would contribute greatly to the kingdom of Navarre as his Queen. Francis gave his consent, and they were married on January 24, 1527, at St. Germain-sur-Laye. The festivities and tournaments lasted for eight days.

Early January of the following year, Marguerite traveled to Fontainebleau for her impending lying-in for the birth of her first child. She arrived in a condition of poor health and suffered from a persistent cough that seemed to be beyond the skill of palace doctors. The attentiveness of King Francis had been constant on his sister as he, with their mother, Louise de Savoy, spent hours together discussing matters of state with her. Then the King was summoned to another conflict on the border with Spain as a result of the Madrid Treaty he had signed two years previously to obtain his release from captivity by the powerful Emperor Charles V.

The devotion that Marguerite had for her brother was grounded in their constant companionship as children and in Francis' dependence on her after he became King. Marguerite was older than Francis and excelled in intelligence, able to evaluate and assess political ambiguities. Her marriage to the Duke of Alençon was disappointing, and she was disgusted and mortified at his betrayal of Francis, Her disappointment in the Duke profoundly strengthened the bond between Marguerite and the King. The despair and grief at his capture, his illness and ill-treatment she had witnessed in Madrid, so intensely reinforced Marguerite's love and loyalty that eventually her devotion to the King surmounted all other obligations in her life. After King Francis left Fontainebleau for the disturbances on the border with Spain, she sank into a deep depression at his absence, imagining that she would not survive if Francis were not close by when the child arrived.[iv] Her mother remained in Lyons to support Francis, leaving Marguerite alone at the Palace of Fontainebleau during January.

Henri had joined Francis in Spain because that conflict was significant in determining the future of the kingdom of Navarre, and he was intent that politics in Spain would not overtake his throne. He did send word from Bourges of his joy at receiving news that his wife and child had endured the ordeal safely. Aymée wondered at the time if affection and jealousy for his sister and her child had delayed Francis from considering Henri's political petitions and requests to be united to his wife. When Henri, disappointed at Francis' inactivity on his behalf, returned to Fontainebleau occasionally, rumors spread that he had been keeping company with one of the enchanting ladies at court to ease his frustration. Aymée remembered Henri had never appeared at the bedside of his wife.

Two months after Jeanne's birth, Marguerite had pleaded that Aymée take the infant to her family's castle in Lonray, near Alençon, and to raise Jeanne among her children, away from the restrictions, homage, and constant attention of the multitudes of unprincipled and unreliable courtiers within the royal household at Fontainebleau. It had been a precious two years for Aymée as Jeanne played contentedly with her children and grew to be active and healthy with a frolicsome spirit. Jeanne's courage and happy disposition were astonishing to everyone blessed to enjoy her presence.

During those years, Aymée had spoken often to Jeanne of the affection and care Marguerite had for her child and of the goodness of her royal mother who caused the people of France to adore her for her devoted efforts to obtain the release of Francis. On the rare occasions Marguerite could arrange a visit to Alençon, Jeanne would bound with wild delight into the arms of her beautiful and gifted mother. Suddenly, soon after Jeanne turned two years old, Henri of Navarre had appeared at Alençon to reclaim his daughter.

Aymée commiserated with the circumstances that had pressed against the couple, wondering if those two years were evidence of a tumultuous marriage, or possibly the result of Henri's neglect of his beautiful wife while he sought desperately to ensure the future of Navarre. Marguerite had, in turn, devoted her attention to the demands of King Francis' political goals. The marriage that had begun so well appeared to falter. Trials and sorrow plagued them when several months after Jeanne returned to the home of her parents, her brother, little Jean, was born in August 1530[v] but never thrived, and then died on Christmas Day of that year. Marguerite never fully recovered from the effects of her ordeals endured on her trip to Madrid or the serious illness she suffered before Jeanne's birth. Her tender emotions and weak physical condition magnified her sorrow and disappointment of not producing a male heir. Losing her precious little boy and future heir of the throne of Navarre after five months had been a devastating blow. As she turned to the study of her faith and her love of poetry for comfort, Marguerite had little emotional reserve for a rambunctious child. Being desperate for a relationship with her mother, Jeanne had clung to every opportunity to spend time in her presence, playing nearby in lonely silence. There were few appropriate playmates available for Jeanne except an occasional arranged time with one of the daughters of the Queen's ladies-in-waiting. There had been no playful childhood during Jeanne's three years at Nérac, adding to her sense of being alone. It was no wonder that Jeanne's unfulfilling relationship with her royal mother had been complicated and strained.

As she finished securing the ribbons she had braided through Jeanne's hair and attached sparkling diamond pins across her brow like a tiara against the braids, Aymée cut short her wandering thoughts. It was painfully obvious what had been absent from Jeanne's last five years; however, that was not Aymée's concern. She must follow God's direction and deal with what the Princess needed now, at this moment!

7. Dealing with a Dilemma

*"I am the light of the world; he who follows Me shall not
walk in the darkness, but shall have the light of life."*

John 8:12 (NASB)

Princess Jeanne looked up at her governess with an intent gaze.
She had been replaying the events of her morning and wanted
to talk about them.

"Aymée?" she said, hesitantly.

After keeping so still for such a long time waiting for Aymée
to finish her hair, Jeanne jumped to her feet and walked to the fireplace, staring at the flames as she formed her questions. Aymée sat
down in an adjoining chair and waited.

"Do you think that Uncle Francis has been planning this move
for me for a long time?" She asked, turning to face Aymée. "Why
do you think I had to come so far away? All this stuff," she gestured around the room with a sweeping arc of her arm, "had to take
a long time to reach this castle."

Hidden beneath her questions was a pleading need to know
why all this was happening to her at such a young age. Aymée had
no response and Jeanne rushed on with new thoughts crowding
into her mind.

"I have suddenly become the mistress of this strange, enormous
castle, and the Chamberlain Uncle Francis appointed is asking me
to agree with him and his decisions. I have no way to answer his

questions! What a terrible place I have come to! How long must I stay? Why? How could the King and Queen, my mother and father, agree to this? You must help me," she pleaded and her face crumpled. "Did you see that horrible room? How can I stay here? I feel so abandoned and alone; you are my only comfort." Jeanne's determined demeanor wilted and tears shone in her eyes.

Aymée rushed to Jeanne's side and flung her arms around her.

"Oh my darling," she murmured, "you have landed in a very puzzling place and have been so incredibly brave. I cannot answer why this is happening or how so much can be expected of you at such a young age. What I do know is that you faced this morning's surprises with amazing courage. I am so proud of you! With God's help, we will figure out together how to make it through this misfortune and find a way to live here. I do know that your Chamberlain was selected because he can do his job well. This morning I saw Sir Duquesse come to admire and respect you and I believe he will be as loyal to you as King Francis will allow. We must face each problem and difficulty bravely, together."

Jeanne stared into Aymée's eyes. The realization that Aymée could not save her or change anything was a cruel disappointment; there was no way out of her dilemma. Nearly overwhelmed by helpless desperation, Jeanne grasped for any small hope to survive.

She could see Aymée was sincere in her devotion and the Princess sensed her love. In itself, that was a very new feeling in her little life. It was not Aymée's fault she was trapped here. A rising determination again rose within her. She must not allow herself to be defeated. She must do something to make this sojourn in a cold, horrible castle acceptable.

Even though her royal parents had little time for her, the familiar warmth and safety provided by the castle of Nérac had been her security. Though demonstrations of love and affection had lacked in the upbringing of the Princess of Navarre, she had replaced her empty longings with the satisfaction of familiarity and a stalwart, growing independence. King Francis' wholehearted fondness for her had become her foundation. Deeply feeling her uncle's betrayal, Jeanne clung to Aymée's love like a drowning swimmer.

While at Nérac, Jeanne had been permitted to play quietly alone in the corners of the Queen's apartments entertaining herself. She had listened intently to the conversations taking place around her. It was amazing how much her little mind had absorbed as scholars debated with her mother and various artists who sought the Queen's favor had showered the room with a song or expounded about renowned art. Even the bishops and Cardinals of the Church had wheedled and bombarded their Queen with doctrine and theology. Frequently after the departure of these pillars of knowledge, the Queen and her ladies discussed their opinions of such high-minded sentiments. At times these discussions caught her attention and were even understandable to Jeanne. The most advantageous benefit resulted from hours of Bible reading by her mother with studies of the New Testament while Jeanne bent quietly over her dolls.

Resolve replaced the tears in Jeanne's eyes. Moving out of Aymée's embrace and continuing to pace in front of the fire, Jeanne cried out in frustration, "What must we do now?"

Aymée rose to her feet, seeking her Lord for guidance. She fought to organize her whirling thoughts. Jeanne was right; they must prepare to respond with wisdom to Sir Duquesse's report of this morning and formulate a plan to pursue Jeanne's well-being during the rigorous education designed to instruct for her role as a Queen.

"Let's make a list of all the points Sir Duquesse relayed and discuss each one, deciding if you agree or disagree," Aymée suggested. "I am afraid we cannot remove that horrible room or its contents so we must think about whether you would desire Sir Duquesse to lock it up or do something with it."

Purposefully, Jeanne moved toward the small alcove of her desk and sat, looking hesitantly at Aymée, who had followed and sat across from the Princess. Aymée knew it would be difficult tempering her personal opinions while helping Jeanne form her thoughts. She breathed a prayer for help to God who was her rock and fortress. After several minutes of conversation, they had whittled the mountain of information down to specific items Jeanne wanted to tackle with her Chamberlain. She would leave the subject of that horrible room until a later time when she would be more confident in her trust of Sir Duquesse. Such a formidable problem required much more study than time remained before her meeting.

Both felt the weight of the task had lightened, and Aymée asked Jeanne if she would be willing to join in prayer. It would be a new experience for the Princess, as this kind of prayer had not ever been a part of her young life. She sensed the inner strength and peace that was so ingrained in Aymée and longed for that consolation in her own life. She shyly bowed her head and peered at Aymée through tear-laden lashes.

Aymée spoke as if another person was standing in the room and she was talking directly to Him. As Aymée petitioned for courage, wisdom, and comfort, Jeanne wondered if anyone was listening. Aymée thanked God for the help He had already bestowed on them and glorified Him for His faithful attention to their lives. Giving God thanksgiving that He had united them in the center of distress, Aymée asked for strength to see it through. Her humble, "In Jesus name I pray," signified the end of her prayer and Jeanne raised her head. She sat, momentarily contemplating the sense of relief that replaced her desperation. She was not alone after all, and her discovery of Aymée's dependable compassion and love had released the tight knot of fear which had plagued her through the last several days of her lonely ordeals.

Aymée offered the dress of embroidered swirls and velvet accents to slip it over Jeanne's head and quickly buttoned the tiny buttons from the back of the neck to her waist. She set soft, matching leather slippers at Jeanne's feet and promptly rearranged any wayward locks of hair that had slipped out of the carefully positioned braids sitting like a crown on Jeanne's head. Long curls flowed down her back. She held the ankle-length, sleeveless, mink cape for Jeanne to put her arms through and settled it on her shoulders. The satin lining rustled with any movement and would announce her presence, wherever Jeanne went. Aymée admired the beautiful coral gown and dark brown mink cape. Everything in the bulging wardrobes had come from Fontainebleau and Aymée suspected Marguerite's involvement. The outfit brought out the profound beauty of Jeanne's eyes and warmed the color of her skin. Her dark brown hair shimmered with reflections of light and amber highlights. Aymée's heart flooded again with overwhelming love for this brave little girl. This morning, her forceful personality had been evident in her eyes, regardless that they had been a bit dull and dazed. Now displaying newfound determination, her eyes had begun to show fresh sparkle.

It was a remarkable recovery from the desperate pleas she had made earlier. Aymée was convicted that this strength of character would be a lasting benefit to Jeanne and would indeed set her apart and above many others throughout her life.

Princess Jeanne turned toward the doors, prepared to meet with Chamberlain Duquesse.

8. Inward Contemplations

"If I glorify myself, My glory is nothing; it is My Father
who glorifies me, of whom you say, 'He is our God.'"

John 8:54 (NASB)

Arnauld Duquesse had spent the afternoon at his desk in deep thought. Unfinished scraps of lunch remained at his elbow waiting for removal. Outside his office, sounds of cleaning, scrapes of furniture across the stone floors and rattling of scaffolding along the high walls gave evidence of the hordes of servants and workers going about the business of renewing the old palace. It was a monstrous task; however, at the moment his thoughts were nowhere near the efforts taking place outside, or the bills of lading and shipment list piling up on his desk. This endeavor had been years in preparation and under his watchful eye, was proceeding as planned. Ironically, the small victories that were evidenced by the busy commotion had lost their luster and, instead, seemed to be bringing about an uncomfortable, hard lump in his belly.

Arnauld came from a long line of renowned chamberlains who had been in the service of nearly every royal, count and Duke in French aristocracy. He had been trained well during years of apprenticeship. He knew the range of duties shouldered by a man in his position and was efficiently capable of carrying the keys to the palace of Château de Plessis-lez-Tours with pride. He was competent to supervise the household furnishing, upkeep, and repair of the castle and grounds, supervision of the servants, as well as taking charge of the financial books, keeping an eagle eye on the budget coming directly from the King of France, until the steward arrived. It was a daunting task, and he had tackled it with enthusiasm.

When King Francis had first contacted him through an emissary from the King's cabinet, he had been deeply flattered. After the King laid out the scope of the position, he had jumped at the chance offered him. The pride that he, among all possible candidates, had been selected swelled his ego to an enormous size. Multitudes of chamberlains before him had taken a similar road to achieve positions of influence and become councilors for the French aristocracy throughout centuries. Moving in such circles of power offered opportunities to marry into families of renown and join the higher classes who then would seek to employ younger ambitious chamberlains.

In preparation for his post, he had researched the castle and studied its history, along with all the dismal information about its former occupant. He had visited the castle several times, delighted with the size of his generous expense allowance. He had inspected the grounds and assessed the crumbling walls with an eye to minute detail. What an exciting adventure it had been to formulate his visions of grandeur and prepare extensive plans to present to the King for approval with a significant allowance to complete them.

Arnauld twirled the leather cord that held the palace keys and contemplated the path into his current position. He now realized that he had discussed the restoration of the palace with the King many times, but there was no mention of who would be residing here. For two years the King had been scheming, keeping secret the heart of Francis' motives until just a month ago. It was at that point Arnauld realized he had believed this would be a leap up the ladder of his career, fantasizing that perhaps even the King himself would be his resident, and had cooperated fully in the charade. He grudgingly admitted that no experienced, respectable chamberlain would have considered accepting this post without more information. At twenty years of age, he had been swept away on his vain imaginings and dreams of lofty influence and power. Now, disappointment and bitterness at being isolated in this forsaken old palace were in danger of consuming him.

This morning, when the dreaded moment arrived to meet the object of his humiliation and assume the duties he would be required to perform, everything turned topsy-turvy. The child was a remarkable study, so far from his expectations! He realized that not only had she captured the King's affections to a surprising degree but her little body housed wisdom and grace that stretched far beyond the benefits of breeding and environment.

Uncharacteristically, she was not even aware of her radiant command and inner beauty. Arnauld had been overwhelmed at how focused she remained as he reported on the condition of the palace and plans for her education. She had listened intently with those astonishing eyes never leaving his. Even when she was obviously exhausted from concentrating so long, she never complained. Her gracious appreciation for the small snack he offered her disarmed him. He was aware that the grueling travel she had so recently endured would have disabled a healthy adult; however, she met her obligations wordlessly.

Guilt washed over Arnauld as he remembered his thoughtless lengthy dissertation of historical facts. He realized with horror that his presentation of that ghastly room grew from his bitter anger of being trapped here. He wondered how Jeanne could have possibly been capable of enduring that moment when she was so incredibly vulnerable herself. He puzzled to distinguish the unnamable characteristic so prevalent in her responses. He struggled to identify what it was . . . Ahh, yes, mercy! That must be a significant part of it! She harbored no animosity in her little body for previous treatment or current mistakes of others.

Arnauld sat upright in his chair and stood to pace the floor of his ample office. The staggering perception began to grow that the incredible strength of spirit which blessed this child could, perhaps, move governments and nations to her will. An unrecognized and overwhelming fatherly instinct rose up and thrust through him in a tremendous surge of protective emotions. He laughed at himself, feeling foolish to think she might 'move' nations.

The future lay clouded in mystery, but he vowed to protect and serve this incredible little Princess to the best of his ability. It was an entirely unfamiliar devotion absent of all selfish motivation. If Jeanne d'Albret could face the future in this gloomy palace, he would do everything in his power to enable her growth and development. Replacing the key about his neck in a small gesture of commitment, he pulled the bell rope to call for a servant to clear the dishes and strode out of the office intent on the varied tasks waiting for his attention. Heading toward the workmen, he chuckled to himself at the memory of Jeanne's parting comment before she retired to her room. Birds might just be the answer.

9. Planning Together

*"The Spirit Himself bears witness with our spirit that
we are children of God, and if children, heirs also,
heirs of God and fellow heirs with Christ, if indeed we
suffer with Him in order that we may also be glorified
with Him."*

Romans 8:16-17 (NASB)

Later Arnauld pored through the pile of statements and receipts cluttering his desk. When he heard a rustling at his door, he glanced up and immediately leaped to his feet. Bowing low, he murmured his appreciation that her Majesty would bestow her presence on his small office. Princess Jeanne acknowledged his remarks with a slight nod of her head and a sweet smile. She was beautifully attired. He gestured to a plump settee and waited for Jeanne to sit comfortably with a pillow behind her back.

His attention to detail in preparing for this meeting was evident with a crystal pitcher filled with chilled apple cider, three crystal goblets and a silver tray of canapés. He had chosen to forego his bottle of Bordeaux wine in deference to the young age of the Princess. He glanced at Aymée who was sitting behind Princess Jeanne, and she smiled in appreciation. Children in France had been drinking watered-down wine from very young ages. His choice had honored the importance of the meeting, how fatigued his Princess must surely be after her long journey, and the clarity needed for both of them. He had struck the perfect note. Arnauld sat down, waiting for the Princess to speak.

Princess Jeanne began by commenting on the improvements that had occurred since this morning. Her eyes shone with pleasure as she thanked him for the comfortable items of beauty and light that transformed her apartments.

She noted the long, beautiful, gleaming wooden table that she passed in the Great Hall, laden with flower arrangements and sparkling crystal candlesticks in full flame. The clusters of chairs, couches, and fragile looking end-tables were quite inviting, scattered in intimate groups throughout the Great Hall. Beautiful works of art, decorative screens and wall hangings spaced carefully at intervals warmed the atmosphere of the cold castle walls. Sconces, candelabras, and vases of flowers were scattered among the chairs and small tables. It delighted her to see such a happy room.

Arnauld warmed with pleasure at her remarks and gave a slight nod to acknowledge her compliments. So many more empty rooms awaited attention, and the Princess spoke that she looked forward to seeing his intended results, which she expected the King of France had assisted in planning.

Jeanne shifted the subject to her education and asked Sir Duquesse to go over each area slowly. Arnauld took a deep breath and reached for a folder on the upper corner of his desk. The King had taken a very active interest in these plans and had been adamant that Arnauld fulfill them to the letter.

The poet, Nicholas de Bourbon, received the appointment of preceptor to Jeanne.[v] It was his duty to teach the Princess her letters, history, languages, and poetry; King Francis appointed two chaplains to instruct his niece in her religious duties and theological doctrine. They were to establish residences in her household, placed under the oversight of Pierre du Châtel, bishop of Tulle and Mâcon.[vi]

Aymée would singularly be responsible for the instruction of manners, etiquette and appropriate court interactions. Aymée's close relationship with Marguerite who was the epitome of courtly graces and wisdom would give her intimate insight into the goal of Jeanne's instruction. Having been herself a popular favorite and

friend of many courtiers and ladies, Aymée was uniquely quali-
fied to prepare the young maiden for the unavoidable pressures of
self-seeking, immoral, and vindictive personalities always on the
prowl in court life.

M. d'Izernay[vii] was appointed the steward of Princess Jeanne's
household. Beside oversight of the castle finances, it would be
his domain to organize and implement any ceremonious events
required when orders came from the Royal Throne for coming
visits by the King.

The ladies-in-waiting to be attendants in Jeanne's apartments
would be interviewed and selected by Aymée, along with laundry
maids, wardrobe maids, and housemaids.

Jeanne asked for a few minor considerations. "Sir Duquesse, I
would like to learn Latin so someday I can read the Bible myself.
Would M. de Bourbon teach me Latin along with my program of
French, English and Spanish languages? I also want to learn to
write well. My mother writes beautifully."

Sir Duquesse had been scribbling notes on the journal he kept
with him at all times for a reminder of what needed his attention.
Jeanne waited for a moment until he paused, and then continued.

"I especially want to learn about the history of France. I hope
my ladies-in-waiting will also be able to play musical instruments
and sing. I would like to learn too." Jeanne peeked at Aymée to
recruit her support.

Inwardly Arnauld was amazed. Here again, she had gone directly
to the heart of the matter and requested items most important to her
advancement. Her choices demonstrated wise insights into capaci-
ties that would be required of her in the future.

Sir Duquesse made additional notes in his journal and inquired
if Jeanne had other questions or subjects she would like to cover.
She demurred, and he stood to assist her from the settee.

"Are you agreeable that we should tackle the problem of cages
and birds at a later date?" he asked, seriously.

A huge smile spread across Jeanne's face, and she replied som-
berly, "I do believe it would be better to prepare for those who will
be arriving here to teach me. I am sure the cages will still be here
several months from now."

The beautiful eyes of the little Princess sparkled mischievously.

"I believe dinner is waiting for us, Princess." Sir Duquesse offered his arm and Jeanne placed her small hand on his wrist. They were both smiling at each other as they walked out of the office.

Aymée was having a difficult time to keep from laughing out loud. "Thank you, Lord," she whispered.

While Princess Jeanne occasionally had, but rarely, been included at dinners at the table of King Henri and Queen Marguerite in their castle at Nérac, she was schooled in all the proper manners and behavior expected of her. The three years preceding her departure to Château Plessis had included training in etiquette, even when dining in her room, alone with only her nursemaid.

Proper display of manners was drilled into Jeanne because all members of the aristocracy, and especially those who strove to be counted in that elite group, imposed strict adherence on themselves. Manners established the division between them and the common people. Table manners of the upper class raised them above the "pig trough" habits of the lower class.

Manners for Royalty and Aristocratic Classes[viii]

"The eye has a claim upon you for so much of beauty in form, color, arrangement, position, and movement as you are able to present to it. It is the duty of a pretty woman to look pretty. It is the duty of all women, and all men too, to look and behave just as well as they can, and whoever fails in this, fails in good manners and duty.

"The ear demands agreeable tones and harmonious combinations of tones—pleasant words and sweet songs. If you indulge in loud talking, in boisterous and untimely laughter, or in profane or vulgar language, or sing out of tune, you violate its rights and offend good manners.

"The sense of smell requires pleasant odors for its enjoyment. A fragrance is its proper element. To bring the fetid odor of unwashed feet or filthy garments, or the stench of bad tobacco or worse whiskey, or the offensive scent of onions or garlic within its sphere, is an act of impoliteness.

"The sense of taste asks for agreeable flavors and has a right to the best we can give in the way of delicious foods and drinks.

"The sense of feeling, though less cultivated and not so sensitive as the others, has its rights too and is offended by too great coarseness, roughness, and hardness. It has a claim on us for higher culture."

"In a group dining situation, it is considered impolite to begin eating before all the group have been served their food and are ready to start.

"Napkins should be placed on the lap and not tucked into clothing. They should not be used for anything other than wiping your mouth and should be placed unfolded on the seat of your chair should you need to leave the table during the meal or placed unfolded on the table when the meal is finished.

"The fork is held with the left hand and the knife held with the right. The fork is held generally with the tines down, using the knife to cut food or help guide food on to the fork. When no knife is being used, the fork can be held with the tines up. With the tines up, the fork balances on the side of the index finger, held in place with the thumb and index finger. Under no circumstances should the fork be held like a shovel, with all fingers wrapped around the base. A single mouthful of food should be lifted on the fork, and you should not chew or bite food from the fork. The knife should be held with the base into the palm of the hand, not like a pen with the base resting between the thumb and forefinger. The knife must never enter the mouth or be licked.

"When eating soup, the spoon is held in the right hand, and the bowl tipped away from the diner, scooping the soup in outward movements. The soup spoon should never be put into the mouth, and soup should be sipped from the side of the spoon, not the end.

"Food should always be chewed with the mouth closed. Talking with food in one's mouth is seen as very rude. Licking one's fingers and eating slowly can also be considered impolite. Food should always be tasted before salt and pepper are added. Applying condiments or seasoning before the food is tasted is viewed as an insult to the cook, as it shows a lack of faith in the cook's ability to prepare a meal.

"Butter should be cut, not scraped, from the butter dish using a butter knife or side plate knife and put onto a side plate, not spread directly on to the bread. This prevents the butter in the dish from gathering bread crumbs as it is passed around. Bread rolls should be torn with the hands into mouth-sized pieces and buttered individually, from the butter placed on the side plate, using a knife. Bread should not be used to dip into soup or sauces. As with butter, cheese should be cut and placed on your plate before eating.

"Only white wine or rosé is held by the stem of the glass; red by the bowl. Pouring one's drink when eating with other people is acceptable, but it is more polite to offer to pour drinks to the people sitting on either side. Wine bottles should not be upturned in an ice bucket when empty.

"It is impolite to reach over someone to pick up food or other items. Diners should always ask for items to be passed along the table to them. In the same vein, diners should pass those items directly to the person who asked. It is also rude to slurp food, eat noisily or make noise with cutlery.

"Elbows should remain off the table.

"When one has finished eating, this should be communicated to other diners and wait-staff by placing the knife and fork together on the plate, at approximately 6 o'clock position, with the fork tines facing upwards.

"At family meals, children are often expected to ask permission to leave the table at the end of the meal. Children should be seen and not heard."

As Sir Duquesse seated her at the head of the table, she looked at the beautifully-set table with pride and some consternation. She was painfully aware of the responsibility she had observed her mother play out so often. Her stomach fluttered with butterflies while her little legs swung rapidly back and forth under her chair. Her leg movement under the table was the only evidence that she realized the weight of absolute dominance she carried in her first role as the hostess of the Château. Her royal behavior had been bred and ingrained deeply so now she comprehended the etiquette required to be Mistress of her royal table nearly unconsciously. The

Princess had often observed her mother as she ruled over the service of the table and, as a matchless hostess, was adept at guiding a genial conversation to include every guest; while deftly changing subjects at the first hint of dispute and now even though she knew what was required it was quite another task to carry it off.

At the table presided by Princess Jeanne, there was no lack of subject matter for conversation. Her inquisitive nature and forthright curiosity, so typical of a five-year-old child, was undoubtedly enhanced since here she was the center of attention and her questions and remarks were of consequence to everyone in her captivated audience. Accustomed to being admonished for any childish disruption, Jeanne had always assumed the role of the invisible listener. Her tendency to listen intently to another's point or explanation without interruption became a hallmark of Queenly graces all her life.

Discussion centered on the apparent improvements of immediate surroundings. The Princess exclaimed over her delightful apartments and had many questions regarding the arrival of her private domestics and attendants. After Sir Duquesse explained the process and timeline for filling these appointments, Jeanne hurried on with questions about others who would be concerned with her education. She wondered when the chaplains Uncle Francis had selected to lead her religious studies would be coming and were their cloistered lodgings arranged? Jeanne asked if the chapel of the castle had any needed implements and supplies or if the chaplains would be bringing everything? When would she be able to go and see the chapel? She wondered if Sir Duquesse would take her as soon as possible.

Also, she asked, "Are the horses that brought me here still in the stables or have they returned to Fontainebleau? Will we be having a Great Ecuyer, (head stable master), or is the castle not large enough to need one? I shall not be traveling much, as the King does not wish me to leave the castle; however, won't others need horses and carriages?"

There was a short pause to gather her thoughts, and then Jeanne asked, "Is it snowing outside? Are there paths I can explore? What about gardens? Are they overgrown? Have they been tended all this time without someone living here?"

She asked, with a pensive look; "May I have a dog? Will there be hunting dogs? Will there be hunts if the King comes to visit? Will there be a Grand Veneur to direct the royal stag hunts? Do you think we will also have a Grand Falconer or a Louvetier to hunt wolves and boar?" Her imagination was boundless as many of her inquiries regarded activities she would not be likely to participate in but had observed at Nérac or Fontainebleau. She had been fascinated watching the Grand Falconer and his birds of prey with her father.

Before Sir Duquesse could open his mouth, let alone speak, Jeanne was contemplating the possibility of her uncle visiting.

"Do you think the King will come to visit me?"

Sir Duquesse threw his head back and laughed heartily. Now, this was what he would expect of a five-year-old. However, Jeanne was so sincere and polite in her questions with a real goal of getting answers that he could not find fault or scold her.

"My sweet Princess!" he exclaimed. "You do not give me time to collect my thoughts between questions! I will do my best to answer all of them. Some of your questions I can answer, some I will have to check with others for additional information. Some, I am not informed yet as to what will be expected in the future."

Jeanne was looking at him expectantly as if waiting for him to tackle answering all that he could. He said, "I will report to you tomorrow when I have answers to all that I am able, and I will let you know why I do not have answers to some now. I will, as well, take you to see the chapel area after dinner."

He took a deep breath and studied the Princess as if gauging how tired she might be.

"If you agree to bring to our morning meeting one question you would like to ask at dinner, I will do my best to prepare a complete answer. I will keep you generally updated at our daily meeting. I hope that will be sufficient.

"When we are ready to leave the table, I have arranged for you to meet the members of the household domestics. Now let us enjoy our dessert and discuss what manner of weather may be occurring outside."

Aymée would have been embarrassed at this barrage of questions if she had not felt that Princess Jeanne deserved to have answers to every one of them. She could understand Sir Duquesse being a bit put off with such an attack. Thankfully, he had handled everything quite well. Aymée was aware that a person seeking the position of Chamberlain, historically, had to have achieved knighthood to qualify. The code of a Knight was evidently why Sir Duquesse exhibited impeccable gentlemanly manners and a capacity for diplomatic negotiations. He displayed excellent wisdom and had a quick grasp on all means of problem-solving. So far, Aymée believed King Francis had made an outstanding choice and vowed to take the first opportunity to write of her conclusions and observations to the Queen of Navarre and the King of France.

After dessert, Sir Duquesse signaled the First Butler and spoke instructions quietly to him. Soon after, a parade of household domestics lined up near the dining table. It was incredible to Princess Jeanne that such a large number of people would be required to provide service for herself, Aymée, and Sir Duquesse. She had grown up in the castle of her parents and was just as at home at Fontainebleau, the palace of the King. Of course, in both châteaus these domestic positions were everywhere, maintaining the smooth operations and upkeep of the castle and producing meals, banquets and ceremonial events so efficiently they were almost invisible.

One of the most vital functions of the medieval household was the procuration, storage, and preparation of food; both in feeding the occupants of the residence daily and in preparing more substantial feasts for guests.

First in the line of La Bouches du Roi to be introduced to Princess Jeanne and Aymée was the Premier Maître d'hôtel (Chief Butler) who ruled all aspects of meal service in the castle.

Princess Jeanne rose from her chair to offer the Chief Butler her hand in welcome. She looked deeply into his eyes, discerning all she could from the eyes gazing back at her. Similar to the reaction Sir Duquesse had experienced, the Chief Butler was overwhelmed with the inner beauty her eyes reflected, as well as her desire to know and appreciate him and his duties.

All the way down the line of wait-staff, Princess Jeanne gave each person the same courtesy and searching scrutiny she had begun with the Chief Butler. They all were proud to be serving in one of the households of the King of France, and now, as one, they were smitten with the gracious beauty of their small Princess. A deep loyalty to her began to rise within each.

This process took a significant amount of time, and when she finally moved to the last person in the line, she felt very weary. Any monarch had to accept the rigors of long, exhausting reception lines. Jeanne was extraordinarily young for such a task however, her desire that each person should receive her appreciation over-powered her impulse to run away. Sir Duquesse was impressed by her resolve to see it through to the end. Aymée was swelling with pride, recognizing an unconscious appearance of the grace of the Queen of Navarre, who was well-known throughout France for her gentle, caring ways.

Sir Duquesse gently touched the Princess's elbow and directed her to a sitting area beside the Great Hearth. Here he told her that many of the remaining departments of the castle would similarly have as many individuals involved in the furtherance of the responsibilities of so large a castle, especially considering it was the abode of royalty. He felt it would be prudent to spread those introductions over several days as there was such a substantial number.

Asking Princess Jeanne if she would prefer to delay seeing the chapel area, he reminded her occupants would not be arriving for perhaps a week or more. Many preparations for private quarters and other accommodations were still in progress. Jeanne looked at him with relief and appreciation.

He then said, "Instead of going to the chapel, may I ask you to accompany me to a secret chamber I have prepared for you that was completed this very afternoon?"

Aymée thought, "How clever—he has maneuvered Jeanne out of weary obligation and offered her what every five-year-old child desires – a secret present!"

Rising from their chairs, Sir Duquesse led them up the staircase to the door of Jeanne's apartment. Pausing at the door, he asked her permission to enter. Puzzled, Jeanne nodded enthusiastically.

Moving across the apartment, on the opposite wall from the entry door Sir Duquesse pressed against a hidden, polished, wooden panel and a door opened silently inward. Picking up a lantern glowing on a nearby table, he beckoned for the Princess to proceed ahead of him. The light of the lantern revealed a small stone staircase. In fascination, Jeanne climbed up the seven or eight stairs that curved upward, ending in an open doorway. Jeanne stepped into the room. It was enclosed by the circular tower that connected the South and East walls of the castle battlements, several stories above. Windows filled the outside walls. Jeanne gasped in wonder for the surrounding landscape was covered in the white of newly fallen snow reflecting the bright light of a full moon.

Sir Duquesse said, "This is your very own retreat where you can come to think, pray, and read to your heart's content."

He smiled broadly at her reaction. She looked around the room, furnished with a relaxing couch, chairs, and window seats. A small coal-burning grate waited in preparation of setting it aflame.

"Oh, Sir Duquesse, it is wonderful! Thank you! Thank you!" and she flung her arms around his waist and buried her small face in the warmth of his velvet dinner jacket.

Sir Duquesse bowed low and asked leave of her Majesty. He backed quietly from the room and left Princess Jeanne and Aymée alone. Enchantment overpowered the quiet room with snow falling against the window panes. The two remained motionless in the absolute silence. Aymée stood quietly, overwhelmed with the responsibilities Jeanne had recently assumed so naturally. She was very young, yet she had slipped into her appointed role seamlessly.

Then Jeanne rubbed her arms and shivered. It was cold. In a whisper, not wanting to spoil the magic of the moment, Aymée asked Jeanne if she would like to change to warmer clothes or if she desired to light the fire? "It is getting late. It has certainly been a challenging day with so many highs and lows of emotion."

Reluctantly, Jeanne admitted to herself that she was exhausted. Aymée saw her shoulders droop and pulled the Princess into a warm embrace. "Come here child, let us pray and then sleep." Locked in Aymée's arms, Jeanne gave herself up to the One who holds us all. As Aymée's prayer washed over her, she welcomed the peace that covered her, much like the snow falling outside the window.

10. Reflections and Discovery

"But if we hope for what we do not see, with perseverance we wait eagerly for it."

Romans 8:25 (NASB)

When Jeanne woke on a cold, frigid morning at the end of January, she jumped out of bed, searched for slippers and a warm wrapper, and headed straight for her secret room. Merry flames crackled in the grate and a warm room greeted her. She crawled up on the cushioned window box and feasted her eyes on the glistening landscape spread before her. The trees of the forest surrounding the castle nearly blocked out the view of the river Loire beyond them. Branches were laden with tall caps of snow, and any bare, ice-covered branches sparkled like diamonds.

Jeanne considered the beautiful room she just left. What a change from when she first woke up there! The passing days had given her Aymée whom she so needed. Meeting Sir Duquesse had been scary, and now she looked forward to meeting with him. She felt he was beginning to like her, too.

Aymée had read Isaiah 49:16 to her, "See, I have inscribed you on the palms of My hands." She marveled at that. Not only had Jeanne been close to God's heart, but He also carried her in His hand. Aymée said when He inscribed her on His palms He didn't just write her name there. He carved it. This concept drew her in, much like a warm fire does a cold soul.

In Jeanne's short life, her parents remained royally remote, and now Aymée insisted that God cared about her so much, He carried her close, in the palm of His hand. These thoughts caused her to wonder at how God could know her and care about her little life! She breathed a silent prayer, "Lord, thank You for loving me. Please help me today! I am just a child. I promise I will do the best I can."

Jeanne sat watching the changes taking place outside the window as the sun began to warm and some of the piles of snow on boughs began melting and then, all through the forest, plops of snow started dropping beneath the trees. Too soon, she heard Aymée's voice calling up the stairway.

"I'm coming," Jeanne answered and reluctantly left the room.

Her bath waited, and clothes had been laid out on her carefully-made bed. Aymée selected a wool dress decorated with beautiful small stitches around the neck and wrists. A long coat matching the purple stitching completed the outfit. She wore soft cashmere wool stockings to keep her legs warm. Instead of layers of cotton petticoats, her undergarments were made of heavy muslin with a smaller bustle so the drafts from the cold castle stone floor would not find so many opportunities to seep up through the layers of fabric. Purple, soft suede leather boots would provide warmth when walking around the drafty, stone floors of the castle.

She finished her bath and dressed, and Aymée braided parts of her hair to hang down her back on top of the long curls. She then placed her wimple crowned with a purple head-dress resplendent with purple gems on her head. The purple attire reflected in her eyes caused the violet-blue to pop out with vivid beauty.

When she finished, Aymée said, "I have received word that Nicholas de Bourbon, preceptor of your education, will be arriving sometime this morning. You must be ready to welcome him. Your breakfast will be coming soon, and then if you like, you can spend more time in your room."

Jeanne looked at her with delight, immediately grateful for something new to discover that would overshadow the gloomy feelings of loneliness that hovered overwhelmingly in the corners of her mind. She had sensed during her meditations in her secret room that the new day might offer new joys. She asked, "Would you come and read the Bible to me until then?"

As her breakfast was brought in on a silver tray, she excitedly asked if Aymée had met M. Bourbon and if she knew anything about him?

"No, I have not met him yet, but I heard a great deal about him before we came to Château de Plessis. He has a wide reputation for being an excellent teacher and has served in many noble houses for several years. I understand he comes from the village Vendœuvres and his father was a master blacksmith at Langres. As a young poet, he was regarded as unusually talented by many powerful patrons. Your mother, Queen Marguerite, became acquainted with him at Fontainebleau when King Francis appointed him to a post about the palace. He is not young, but then I don't believe he is so very old. I would guess he is middle aged. Now eat your breakfast so you will have a sharp mind when you meet him."

Monsieur Bourbon was young-looking with dark, wavy, hair that curled behind his ears. Sprinkles of grey peppered his temples and streaks of grey hair were beginning to show among his long curls. When he took Princess Jeanne's hand in greeting, she noticed his well-groomed nails and the softness of his hands. He was undoubtedly a man who had never needed to do hard labor and was more preoccupied with reading and study than an outdoor activity. He looked into her eyes as if to weigh how devoted she would be to her studies.

She smiled at him, thinking, "I hope he is a good teacher. There is so much I want to learn."

At that moment Sir Duquesse appeared at Princess Jeanne's elbow and asked if he might show them to the room prepared for her education. He offered Princess Jeanne his arm and laying her hand lightly on it she stepped eagerly forward. She had no idea where they were going, so she tried to pace her steps to keep up with Sir Duquesse's long legs. They walked around the Great Hearth to the hallway of the Southeast wall. They entered a double door from the Great Hall and stepped into a large room rising two stories. Books lined the wall from floor to ceiling with attached ladders to enable access to the books. Stairways could reach the second story balcony on either side of the door. The eastern wall was the only wall not covered by books. It had wide, tall windows with heavy maroon curtains drawn back in the middle and attached to the intermediate walls. Paintings of landscapes and portraits of kings of France adorned each of the spaces between the windows.

Centered in the wall of windows was a large fireplace, its heat emanating fiercely to overcome the chill of the windows. A large, round, carved, oak table was the centerpiece of the room and appeared to anchor the books rising so high up the walls. Near the windows, comfortable chairs were placed to get the most benefit of the light streaming in the window panes. The windows opened onto a snow-covered garden with dwarf yaupons and boxwoods lining a garden path. Ornamental, straight-backed chairs surrounded the table and a small desk, set off to the side of the table, held an ink pot, stacks of parchment, vellum, and quill pens. Several large chandeliers hung from the high ceiling and sparkled with bright light.

Princess Jeanne clapped her hands with delight. At the sound, M. Bourbon started with surprise and considered the little Princess whose eyes sparkled with anticipation. Her face was animated and glowing. Jeanne turned to Sir Duquesse, "How wonderful it is! You have thought of everything! Thank you!"

She ran lightly to the table and climbed onto one of the chairs. She was ready and did not want to wait another moment. M. Bourbon strolled to the desk, his wide eyes watching Jeanne in amazement.

Sir Duquesse smiled, bowed and, followed by Aymée, made his exit from the Library. A feeling of pleasure satisfied Sir Duquesse that he had pleased the Princess.

M. Bourbon was a bit confused about how to start. He usually had several hours to prepare his approach after meeting the students he would teach. He had only just arrived at the castle and had not yet settled into his living quarters. The only teaching tools he had unpacked were tucked under his arm.

This little girl, only five-years-old, was the first student he could remember who waited impatiently to begin lessons. His mind was turning rapidly through the starting programs he had established in previous educational efforts. He selected his Bible from the books stacked under his arm and turned to Psalm 23. Picking up a stack of vellum, an inkpot and quill pens, he walked to the table and set them down.

"Your majesty," he started hesitantly, "we are in an unusual position with you a niece of the King and me, just a humble teacher. I beg you to understand that when I give you direction I am not presuming on your excellence. It is the normal procedure for teacher and student. When I ask you to complete a sum or an assignment, you must obey so we can make progress together. Are you agreed?"

Princess Jeanne looked at him impatiently and said, "Of course! May we start?"

"Immediately, Your Highness. We will begin with learning your letters. I will be asking you to copy scriptures from the Bible and in that way we will be accomplishing three goals; first to learn to write, second to read, and third to become acquainted with the Scriptures."

He laid the 23rd Psalm open at her elbow and arranged the quill pen, a sheet of vellum and inkpot before her. She was to copy the first line of the verse. He would read the beginning line and then after she copied the first word he asked her to speak it out loud. For such a young scholar, it was tedious work requiring intense concentration. Since it was her first experience of learning letters, writing them and then reading each word she began with great determination to make her letters look just like the small printed words in the Bible. In the quiet library, only the crackling of the fire could be heard over the scratching sound of her quill, interrupted when she spoke each letter, and M. Bourbon read the word. She kept at it without pause until Aymée quietly knocked at the door and brought in a tray of fig and date fritters and a goblet of milk. Jeanne leaned back in her chair and took a deep breath while selecting a fritter.

Gratefully accepting the hot cup of tea Aymée offered him, M. Bourbon looked at her quizzically and shook his head as if in disbelief. He was amazed at the concentration expended by his young student. She did not need teaching, only guidance, at least now. As they enjoyed their snack, M. Bourbon picked up her paper. He read, "The Lord is my....." Though her letters were not level on the line, and some were larger than others, he saw how she carefully copied them. Excellent work up to this point was M. Bourbon's assessment. Aymée nodded approvingly and patted Jeanne on the shoulder. Jeanne smiled up at her with a milk mustache above her mouth. Offering Jeanne a napkin she asked, "Can you read it to me?" and eagerly Jeanne read, "The Lord is my…"

Aymée slipped out of the door to leave the Princess to deliberate on her work. Jeanne laid the vellum on the table and picked up her quill. Immediately her concentration was focused on copying the next word.

When she completed writing 'Shepherd,' M. Bourbon asked her to read the complete sentence to him. He knew by that time that she had almost memorized the phrase, so it was doubtful she was reading; however, she had written well, and it was indeed readable. He commended her for such a productive effort. It was getting close to lunch time, and M. Bourbon asked if she would like to go for a walk in the snowy garden.

"Oh yes, I would like that."

M. Bourbon pulled a cord by the door. Aymée soon entered to accompany Jeanne to her apartment for a coat.

When Jeanne slipped into the fur coat and white rabbit muff, her mind flew back to the horrible ride from Nérac to Château de Plessis. Her desperate loneliness flooded over her. It was only a week or so from that excruciating trip, and she was still numb with profound loneliness. Today had offered a new beginning, and she had been somewhat distracted by her many activities. Now her demeanor sobered, and even with anticipation of spending some time outside stomping in the snow, she suffered deep sorrow. Her steps were slow as she returned to M. Bourbon's side and followed him to the door that opened on the small enclosed garden.

She was vaguely aware that two of the castle guards followed after them out the door. Were they there to keep her from running away or to protect her from being snatched from the grounds by someone wanting to harm King Francis?

That cruel question closed in around her, and she had a difficult time responding to M. Bourbon when he asked her if she would like to hear something about the countryside surrounding the Château. She mumbled a low affirmative, and they walked about the garden with M. Bourbon rambling on about the nearby town of Tours and what the agriculture of the countryside contributed to the operations of the Château.

Eventually, Jeanne listened more closely as M. Bourbon described how the castle offered opportunities for the villagers to work and by buying goods from the local community the Château helped the economy of the area prosper. She knew he spoke from his own life's experience as a son of a master blacksmith. It was a serious subject to M. Bourbon, and Jeanne listened eagerly to understand the economic benefits of kings and castles to France.

It was cold outside, and even though the sun was melting the snow, a brisk wind blowing all the snow off the branches was seeping up her sleeves and down her collar. The cold air was invigorating, causing Jeanne to wish for a companion to throw snowballs with or knock the snow piles off the yaupons. Jeanne appreciated M. Bourbon's willingness to get some exercise while outside, but she soon became bored, and her pent-up sorrows and feelings of isolation weighed heavily on her. After a couple of turns on the path around the garden, they turned toward the door to the castle. A lunch of rich, hot, soup and freshly-baked bread with cheese waited for them to come to the large table. Jeanne was grateful for the heat from the massive fire and rubbed her hands together to get the blood circulating in her fingers.

After a satisfying lunch, M. Bourbon led them back to the Library. Aymée accompanied them, carrying her bag of needlework with her. She would evaluate when the Princess began showing weariness and needed to go to the apartment to rest. She had noticed how somber and quiet Jeanne had been at lunch and knew her despondency was from remembering the grueling trip and painful separation from her royal parents. Fatigue would not help her shake her unhappiness.

M. Bourbon addressed Jeanne enthusiastically as they entered the Library, "Princess Jeanne, how would you like to play a game of chess with me?"

In a challenging tone, Jeanne tipped her head to the side and said, "I don't know how!"

Not fazed, M. Bourbon moved to a chess table in the corner of the library and began setting the chess pieces in order on the table.

"Come and sit down; I will teach you."

Princess Jeanne walked to the opposite chair and waited. M. Bourbon began describing each piece and explaining the rules that applied to each of them. Very quickly, Jeanne was interested in the court pieces and was listening intently. As the game progressed, Jeanne became absorbed in learning each piece and its possible moves. M. Bourbon was impressed with her ability to remember so much of what he told her and to ask questions about the strategy of each movement. After an hour of intense concentration, Aymée stepped forward and suggested it was time for the Princess to rest before dinner.

11. Life Does Go On

*"And we know that God causes all things to work
together for good to those who love God, to those who
are called according to His purpose."*

Romans 8:28 (NASB)

As the days passed, Jeanne began to fall into a routine. Time in
her secret room started her day. She was trying to memorize the
23rd Psalm as she wrote it out to learn her letters and Jeanne spent
time each morning reading what she had written, over and over.
After breakfast, she went to the Library and continued her studies.
She was learning her letters in French, Spanish, Latin, and English.
M. Bourbon was patiently helping her to read in each of the languages. Before lunch, they would go for a stroll in the garden.
The weather continued to be frigid with heavy snow at times. In
the afternoon they played chess together, and as Jeanne removed
each of the chess pieces from the board, she learned to count. She
enjoyed chess and had shown M. Bourbon her grasp of it on several occasions. She had not won, but her tutor chuckled and often
said she almost had him.

Mid-afternoon Aymée would remind her it was time for a rest.
Resting and spending more time in her secret room revived her to
make it through dinner and the evening hours. The chaplains had
still not arrived, and Jeanne began to wonder how she would fit religious instruction into her schedule. She longed to be at Nérac to sit

quietly in her mother's apartments listening to music and playing with dolls while gentle conversation floated softly over her head. At times, memories came of how her father carried her as a small princess to the stables to pet and talk to the beautiful horses there. She did not even know if there were horses at Château Plessis. She must remember to ask Sir Duquesse about horses at their regular morning meeting. She would like to get acquainted with them, so when the weather warmed up, she might be able to learn to ride.

More and more her thoughts seemed to wander through those happy times at Nérac and then she would feel very sad for a long time. Questions would plague her, "Why, oh why must I be isolated in this unhappy castle?" "Why did Uncle Francis have to send me here?" "How long must I stay?"

These questions tormented her upon waking, when she ate her meals, while walking in the garden, or sitting by the fire in the evening. Many nights she stared into the darkness trying to remember the happiness at Nérac and would mull over her memories as though counting and re-counting the precious stones on a necklace. She often woke up sobbing, reliving the long, lonely ride from Nérac, seemingly drowning in her desolate sense of abandonment. "Why?" she would silently cry out, and "When will I not feel so alone?" As activities filled up her days, nights brought crushing revelations that nothing would ever change; that she would be desperately alone all of her days.

By mid-February three of Jeanne's ladies-in-waiting had arrived and were getting settled. Aymée seemed always to be correcting or instructing to mold them to her expectations. They had previously been trained at other castles however Jeanne found it awkward having them around in addition to Aymée. She hoped, as time passed, they would become more familiar. What Jeanne sorely missed was having someone near her age.

Almost a week later the chaplains arrived. There were spiritual needs to care for, and a chapel was a natural part of every large household in France. The country was dominantly devoted to the faith of the Catholic Church. These household chapels were staffed by varying numbers of clerics, chaplains, confessors, and almoners.

Earlier that morning Sir Duquesse had taken Princess Jeanne to view the chapel and the rooms for the clergy. The chapel in the castle was intended to be used by all members of the castle household for worship services and prayer. It was accessible from the Great Hall, on the opposite wall from the stairway to Princess Jeanne's apartments. It was two stories high with the nave divided horizontally. The royal family and dignitaries sat in the upper part, and the servants occupied the lower part of the chapel. There was an attached Oratory intended for use as a private chapel for prayer by the royal family.

It was an exciting day. M. Bourbon canceled lessons. Confusion and uproar at the arrival of the clergy set the entire castle to frantic pandemonium. With accommodations prepared, and fresh bedding fetched, boxes full of richly decorated books for prayers, music, and Old and New Testament readings, needed to be unpacked. Because of their sacred purpose, liturgical objects crafted of the most precious materials, Eucharistic vessels and hundreds of other vessels and furnishings made of pure gold embedded with pearls and precious stones required careful handling. Kneeling benches, boxes of music, instruments, crosses for the altar, crosses to be carried in procession, censers for the burning of incense, lighting devices for the sanctuary, boxes and boxes of candles, all had to be unpacked and cleaned. Then baths must be drawn for the travel-weary pilgrims and lunch offered.

The bishop and two lead chaplains would be joining them for dinner from now on. The table, with the addition of the clergy and M. Bourbon, grew more crowded. The conversation was more diverse and less focused on Princess Jeanne.

At dinner that evening came an announcement by Sir Duquesse that the following week some pages-in-training would join her in receiving instruction. These young boys were eight and ten-years-old. They were the sons of aristocratic families from estates near the castle and were being prepared, hopefully, to serve in court and eventually rise through the ranks at court to be available for marriage to a Princess or duchess. Jeanne was thrilled that she would have others near her age learning with her.

The next week passed very slowly. Jeanne's day now began in the Chapel Oratory for devotions before going to the Library. The bishop started her religious instructions and encouraged her to attend confession. Jeanne weighed this suggestion in her mind for several days. She finally decided that she was not guilty of sin, only of bitterness and anger against those who had sinned against her and had hurtfully used her. Her tender feelings were a subject she often discussed with God in the privacy of her secret room and felt that He had done more to help her through her dark moments than a stranger ever could by repeating rehearsed words over and over. However, in obedience, she arranged what she thought acceptable into apologetic words about her bitter feelings and loneliness.

Around the castle, she was allowed more freedom to walk to the Library and Chapel by herself. Aymée had pulled back from her vigilant overwatch, agreeing that Princess Jeanne was well acquainted with the castle and would be safe since guards were posted everywhere. The ever-present attendance of guards near her had ceased to cause Jeanne anxiety. Admittedly she was in the line of sight of Aymée, or one of her ladies-in-waiting, every waking moment; nevertheless, she dismissed her awareness of them and felt she was free to go wherever she needed. She had asked about the ever-present guards in meetings with Chamberlain Duquesse. He explained that not only was the castle her home; it was also a part of the King's defensive military position with troops garrisoned there in the event of any aggression by hostile kingdoms, their charge of her protection was a definite benefit. These guard units were well trained and kept at the ready in the event their forces would be needed anywhere along the Loire valley.

Even Jeanne's morning walks turned out to be solitary as M. Bourbon admitted he was not fond of walking in the cold weather or sleeting rain. The guards, of course, still followed her, staying far enough behind to be almost undetected. When she played chess with M. Bourbon, she was free to linger longer to study the board or to solve a sum that had stumped her. M. Bourbon was pleased with her rapid progress and pushed her as far as time would allow, convinced she would be able to hold her own with the boys.

Finally, the day arrived when Fauzio and Raymond entered the Library when M. Bourbon was lecturing Princess Jeanne on the history of France. She was listening intently since this was a subject she had great interest to know. Jeanne had often heard her father, Henri II of Navarre, heatedly discuss the disposition of the kingdom of Navarre as Spain and France disputed over which country had rights to its taxes and revenues.

Fauzio was the older of the two boys, and it was apparent Raymond looked up to him. During introductions, they gazed around the Library and barely acknowledged M. Bourbon or the Princess. Angered by this disregard for the benefits provided to them by the castle, Jeanne's abrupt nod expressed her displeasure. Her demeanor stiffened further on seeing the indifference they showed to M. Bourbon. He had been an excellent instructor, and she simmered with indignation in his defense. She immediately concluded that they were ungrateful, with a weak character.

The boys knew that the purpose of education and training as a page was to accomplish the goal of attracting a young lady for marriage. With Princess Jeanne, they had no aspirations. Just a little girl, she was an aggravation to them as they settled into a study routine.

Most irritating to Jeanne were their boisterous interruptions of M. Bourbon. They refused to stay on subject, instead, asking distracting questions and then veering off to something unrelated and unimportant. Jeanne staunchly insisted that they return to M. Bourbon's chosen teaching, and eventually tension began to develop between them.

M. Bourbon challenged their thinking by posing controversial questions and allowing them free discussion. Jeanne was tenacious and forthright in her thought processes and refused to be moved by emotional or frivolous points in an argument. M. Bourbon could see her thorough independent study to be informed of the subjects they discussed. Her foundation of a dispute was established on truthfulness and fact. The boys argued heatedly, widely casting thoughts afar, substituting truth with assumptions and personal perspective. It was not the quantity of Jeanne's knowledge that impressed M. Bourbon. He was astounded at her ability to discover the crucial kernel at the center of the debate and defend it without wavering.

M. Bourbon's most significant challenge was to control the emotional atmosphere of the Library. He admonished Jeanne to temper her adamant disgust against the opposing side who insisted on expressing a failed argument. She sharply rebuked their thought processes and inability to defend their position. Jeanne could hold her own against their weak attacks when she was resolute about the truth of her personal opinion.

This little Princess stood firm, ignoring any possibility of punishment for her sharp, incisive presentation. Placing her insistence of truth above any threat of personal discipline, regardless if that might result from her determined, tenacious proclamations until the opposite side yielded. Before many months passed, Princess Jeanne ruled the classroom in both strength of personality and intellectual pursuit.

12. A Joyful Surprise

The warming winds of late March and rains of April blew in on wings of spring. Aymée walked in the budding garden with Jeanne one day as the warming sun brightened their spirits. Aymée did not usually leave her duties to take a walk with the Princess. Today, however, she had news she looked forward to sharing with Jeanne.

When they were making a turn around the corner furthest from the castle, Aymée said, "I received correspondence from your mother announcing she plans to visit us. She will arrive the day after tomorrow and will be here for a week, after which she has matters to attend to at Alençon."

The joy on Jeanne's face was overwhelming! Tears filled Aymée's eyes, seeing her happiness. It was nearly five months since Jeanne left Nérac and the sadness plaguing her had been increasing each month exponentially. The news was a tremendous blessing for Jeanne, and she could hardly contain her excitement.

The joy that had overcome the Princess was contagious. Her beaming face was infectious, and she chattered non-stop to anyone that would listen, from M. Bourbon to chambermaids, door attendants to gardeners, milkmaids, and valets. Everyone must know and share Jeanne's excitement. The topic of conversation throughout the kitchen, buttery, and pantry was the happiness of sweet Princess Jeanne. She praised her mother's qualities and beauty to any ear that would listen, although the Queen of Navarre was well regarded and loved by everyone in the region already.

After two dreadfully long days of anticipation, Marguerite d' Angoulême, Queen of Navarre, finally arrived. Jeanne flew to her mother and trapped her in a lengthy embrace. Marguerite held Jeanne close and then gently pushed her away to look at her.

"My dear child, you have grown quite rapidly these five months," she said. "I believe your care and instruction have been of great benefit."

She smiled at Aymée over Jeanne's head and then turned away from the coach, leading Jeanne and Aymée into the castle. Inside the door, the Queen of Navarre graciously greeted M. Izvernay, Chamberlain Duquesse, and the Chief Butler. Speaking in low tones to the Steward, she asked that her maids be shown to her room and a bath drawn immediately. Jeanne glued herself to her mother's right side like a limpet. Even though she was well aware of how fatigued her mother was following her travel, Jeanne could not bear to leave her.

Slipping her arm around Jeanne, the Queen said, "My sweet Jeanne, you are developing into a beautiful young lady, and I have missed you! Leave me now, for I must refresh after such a long trip and later would like to speak with the Bishop and M. Bourbon regarding your advancement. I will have one of my maids come to you before the dinner hour and bring you to me."

They were standing by a stairway just to the north of the stairs to Jeanne's apartments. Jeanne had never explored that stair because there was always something blocking it. Now she realized that her mother was occupying apartments prepared for her arrival with great care. A line of housemaids and servants were scurrying up and down the stairs to assist in settling their Queen in her luxurious apartment. Jeanne remained standing at the bottom of the stairs observing all the action as if she wished she could be among the servants, to be closer to her mother.

After some time, M. Bourbon, who had been watching her from across the Great Hall, appeared before her.

"Are you up to a game of chess until your mother summons one of us?"

He looked at the Princess with grave concern and believed he had a small idea of what she was suffering. He wanted to distract her before thoughts of abandonment and rejection overwhelmed her. For a moment Jeanne looked at him blankly and then, realizing he was offering a distraction to pass the time, she smiled and nodded.

13. A Life Gift

"Finally, be strong in the Lord, and in the strength of His might."

Ephesians 6:10 (NASB)

Jeanne was distracted during their first game of chess. M. Bourbon beat her soundly and quickly. As she absent-mindedly replaced her chess pieces back on the chess board, M. Bourbon watched her movements. Her mind was so far away from the focus the game of chess required and deserved; it was evident continuing to play was a waste of time.

M. Bourbon sat patiently waiting until Princess Jeanne finally raised her eyes to his when she noticed that his hands had not yet moved over the chess board. Her eyes glistened with tears, and she quickly looked back at the board. With a sniffle, and taking a deep breath, she managed to ask, in a coarse, ragged voice, "Do you want to continue playing?"

M. Bourbon moved forward in his chair and covered her trembling hand with his well-manicured fingers.

"Princess, this is a tough time for you, and I understand how your thoughts can be so disorganized and full of emotions from the past and the Queen's present visit. As your loyal and faithful servant regarding your education, I would ask your permission to share my thoughts with you. Are you willing to give me your undivided attention?"

M. Bourbon produced a handkerchief from the depths of an inner pocket in his jacket. Princess Jeanne dabbed her eyes, blew her nose and gripping the hanky in her lap, she looked directly at M. Bourbon.

He continued, "Princess Jeanne, because of your position of royalty your future holds many mountains and valleys of despair and disappointment. These disappointments come to all humans who have the responsibility of ruling over lands and people."

M. Bourbon paused to be sure she was following what he was saying.

"Your future lies before you. You will succeed if you view all the coming days of your life as a 'chessboard' requiring planning and strategy to avoid the perilous pitfalls and defeats that will inevitably come if you just stumble through your days in reaction to unexpected forces and events."

Jeanne listened intently, and he could tell she saw an imaginary chessboard in her own mind.

"Your past fear and despair were the result of unknown forces moving against your world. Formidable powers have used your dear loved ones as pieces in their game. As a result, you now find yourself a pawn of influences driving the direction of significant players who genuinely care for you.

"However, you are a Queen on your chessboard, and you have the mind and gifted wisdom to prepare for and influence the moves that will be coming against you. At this moment, you are feeling victimized and mistreated. You do not know how to right what you see as wrong in your life. As the Queen of this castle, you must seek to understand and learn the positions and objectives of each piece on the board. That will allow you to form your strategy and manage each challenge as it presents itself.

"Chess is all about anticipating the intentions and purposes of your opponents as they make moves to achieve their chosen goal. How do you diagnose your potential move in a regular game of chess?

"These are the skills you must sharpen to adopt them as a natural reaction to every situation you will face. Going forward, when you are Queen, you will negotiate with people of state, discern military needs for future wars or battles, or determine who you can trust in your life. These skills will be extremely valuable.

"All who live here in the Château Plessis love you and will serve you loyally. However, you will not always live here. There is no way to guess when you will leave and move on to the rest of your life, away from such a loyal and faithful environment. Prepare yourself, your Highness, for what will come."

Jeanne sat immobile, her eyes never leaving those of M. Bourbon. When he paused, she shifted her gaze to the flames of the fire not far from where they sat. M. Bourbon watched the amazing colors of her eyes move, deepen, widen, and reflect flashes of azure as she concentrated on his thoughts. Then as she gazed at the fire in deep concentration, her eyes became deep pools of dark blue and purple. He waited and watched her intently.

No tears or storm clouds threatened the horizon of her eyes. As he believed she would, her mind weighed the value and truth of her tutor's words and then adopted the ideas and stored them in her heart.

With a quick movement, Jeanne sat up straight in her chair and challenged him,

"Monsieur Bourbon, would you like to play another game? This time, I will be France, and you can be Spain. The Kingdom of Navarre goes to the winner!"

M. Bourbon laughed heartily. Absolutely!" he exclaimed and began to place his pieces on the board.

This game took much, much longer and the only sound in the Library was the crackle of the flames. Jeanne was so intent and focused that she sat for many minutes studying each action before moving any of her pieces. It was an intense game. Jeanne was fighting for her homeland and M. Bourbon exercised his sharpest and most competitive skills, not willing to give her any quarter, for to do so would have invalidated the lesson he needed to impart.

Finally, exhausted, Jeanne announced "checkmate" in a low, relieved voice. She had played well and planned her moves by analyzing every possible resulting counter-move. M. Bourbon had fought her to the best of his ability; she knew that without question.

He sat across from her with a pleased expression on his face and a chuckle in his eyes.

"Princess, you have learned your lesson well. I commend you," he said. "Never again will you play another chess game with no thought to your goal." Princess Jeanne grinned back at him, sharing his pleasure.

The door had silently opened and Aymée stood quietly watching the last minutes of the game. When Marguerite had finished conversing with her about Jeanne's development, the Queen requested that she ask M. Bourbon to join the Queen in her apartments. Aymée had seen Princess Jeanne's face as she longingly watched her mother disappear at the top of the stairs to her apartment. Well aware of the feelings that tormented Jeanne, Aymée felt helpless to give her the support she needed. The victorious look on Jeanne's face and her pleased giggle at M. Bourbon's remark brought into focus again the unusual strength of her spirit. Knowing Marguerite as well as she did, Aymée was sure that this strength had been passed down from mother to daughter.

Stepping forward, Aymée relayed her message to M. Bourbon and then pulled the bell cord to summon refreshment for herself and Jeanne. Jeanne left her chair and joined Aymée at the chairs by the windows. She smiled as she took her seat and quietly said that she had soundly defeated M. Bourbon at their game of chess. Aymée invited Jeanne to tell her about their game; however, the Princess waved her off and asked if she had just left the Queen.

"Yes, Princess," she answered, "I have had a delightful visit with your dear mother. She is very pleased with everything I was able to share with her and has only positive remarks about what she has seen and heard. The difficulties of your absence and the demands that have been made on her to serve France and the King have caused her great distress. No doubt, your ability to successfully adapt to the changes forced upon you has lifted her spirits and brought you joy. She is deeply concerned about your religious development and has brought you volumes of the writings of Lefever, Roussel, and Erasmus. As you know, these are some of her favorite individual writers as well as loyal friends. When you are ready, she would like you to spend some time getting acquainted with their thoughts."

The refreshments arrived, and they sat companionably watching the antics of a small blue bird industriously collecting sticks and leaves to build a nest in the boxwoods outside the window.

"What are your thoughts, Princess?" Aymée asked.

She had expected to find Princess Jeanne a bundle of emotions and frustrations. She was well aware that spending time with her mother was the most intense desire of Jeanne's heart. To find her concentrating so intensely on a chess game and seeming to be satisfied to wait her turn to return to Marguerite's side was puzzling, as well as a relief. Aymée wondered what had brought about this unexpected self-possession and incredible adaptation to a less-than-desired rank in her mother's priorities.

Princess Jeanne spent time thinking over her response. She was not aware the change in her inner attitude had resulted in an outward display of strength. Her thoughts centered on assessing the purpose of the Queen's visit and how she, as daughter and Princess, could best help her mother accomplish that purpose and still satisfy the deep hunger to spend every possible moment with her mother. It would not be in the interest of her mother or herself if her emotions were allowed to spill all over this visit.

Jeanne wanted to have happy memories to hold on to after her mother's departure. She asked the time of the evening meal and if her mother would have time for some rest. Whether or not Jeanne spent time with her mother today or this evening, she knew it would be more enjoyable if they were both rested. Aymée sat in astounded silence before answering.

Queen Marguerite was finishing her conversation with M. Bourbon and was relieved to get his report that Jeanne was progressing rapidly in every area of his program. She inquired at length of the difficulty of tempering Jeanne's willful and determined manner, especially regarding persuading everyone to adopt her point of view in a discussion. M. Bourbon was most complimentary on Jeanne's ability to get to the heart of the truth of any debate and to unswervingly adopt her position in support of it. Her distinctive attack mode against any opposing her point of view was obvious. Secretly, M. Bourbon believed it was this very instinct that would undergird her success as a reigning Queen in the future. He realized, however, that at this time in her life it was not what her mother desired to see in Jeanne's development. Determined not to emphasize that side of the Princess's education, he would instead continue to support Jeanne in learning to be effective in analyzing her most influential position. If this resulted in Jeanne's arrogant refusal to be dominated and used by others wishing to control the direction of her life, well, so be it.

The interview ended on a positive note, and M. Bourbon was satisfied that he had pleased the Queen by meeting her expectations. What he did not admit to himself was that his loyalties belonged entirely to the Princess, no matter what the Kings and Queens in his life wanted.

14. Honor and Respect

"Children, obey your parents in the Lord, for this is right. Honor you father and mother (which is the first commandment with a promise), that it may be well with you, and that you may live long on the earth."

Ephesians 6:1-4 (NASB)

The week of Marguerite's visit to Château d'Plessis seemed to be over in just a few moments. Jeanne was respectful of the duties that weighed upon the Queen in both the areas of her duchies at Alençon and Armagnac and also in her constant correspondence with her brother, Francis.

Princess Jeanne continued her routine going to the Chapel, Library, meeting with Chamberlain Duquesse and Steward d'Izernay, and walking in the garden each morning. Fauzio and Raymond had been given the week as a vacation. Jeanne was glad to study with M. Bourbon without their distractions. After lunch, she attended her mother in the Queen's apartments. Often Aymée joined them, and together they shared news from the court of Francis. Marguerite confided her opinions of the many antics and adventures of the King, as well as the ladies of the court that were perpetually surrounding his presence.

Jeanne sat quietly and listened, delighted that she was allowed in her mother's presence and included to hear these stories of a life she had never been privy to before. She stared at her mother, memorizing every feature of her beautiful face and graceful manners, laughter and intent skills of listening. The Queen had clear, pale skin and wide violet eyes that crinkled at the edges when she was amused. Her laugh was a lilting, low tone that rippled from her lips with contagious joy.

Her long brown hair had a few streaks of grey that remained hidden under her jeweled headdress shaped like a crown and the wimple flowing down her back nearly to the floor. Regardless that she had endured three pregnancies and led a mostly sedentary lifestyle, ensconced with her books and writing materials, Marguerite had a lovely, slender figure that displayed supple, elegant, grace when she moved. She dispensed her attentions in order of their importance to her; her brother, the King of France; her husband, King Henri II of Navarre; her faith; Jeanne and the people of Béarn.

Marguerite told of when the Kingdom of France had struggled to recover from five years of famine, sickness, and infection resulting from the unending and extraordinary heat suffered year-round at that time. Béarn and the location of the castle of Nérac had been severely affected. The unusual warmth in January and February had caused the trees to form fruit which withered. The new ears turned brown too soon in the fields. Only a slight frost lasting two days was seen in all of France. In the southern counties, swarms of insects devoured vegetation. A fatal epidemic followed famine. Provisions were so scarce that peasants of the land resorted to eating cakes composed of fern leaves, acorns, and beechnuts. The Queen of Navarre was so distressed by the conditions of her people that she petitioned the King for some relief to see the Béarnois through their hardship. All of France cried for help.

Jeanne hung on every word about her mother's life, breathless to hear anything that would give her insight into Marguerite's heart and duties. Marguerite turned and spoke directly to her daughter to attempt to help her understand the complicated forces at work in France. Politics and religion were inseparable in France, as most citizens embraced the Catholic faith of their forefathers. Royal families obtained legitimacy of divine right to rule through sanction by the Church.

In the distant past, a small tremor started to disturb the set traditions of the Church with the exposure of cracks at the foundations of the faith. The invention of the Guttenberg printing press
at that time made Bibles for the common man possible. A devoted
Augustinian priest in Werms, Germany, educated as a lawyer before
his call to the priesthood, labored to translate the original Greek
manuscripts of the Bible into the German language. Working in
seclusion and with the blessing of the Catholic Church, his detailed
efforts revealed errors and abuses that had occurred within the
church for centuries. This revelation of the truth of practices condoned and observed in direct departure from the actual word of God
brought anguish to the devoted and gentle spirit of Martin Luther.
[ix] Seeking to urge renewal and reform, Luther hoped to impel the
Catholic Church to explore the need for change when he courageously posted his 95 points on the church door on October 31,
1517. This act created a schism affecting every social, political and
religious institution in existence across Europe. The movement
gained momentum when, in Geneva, John Calvin made a complete
break from the Catholic traditions and organized the Protestants
who believed in the divine truths of the Bible, but not the adoration
of Mary, worship of saints, or the intercession of priests between
God and sinful man.

The Catholic Church in France relied on the judgments and
edicts proclaimed by the ecclesiastical powers of the appointed
Council of the Faculties of Paris at Sorbonne University. The
Council was formed to defend the religious doctrines observed
in the Church for 1500 years. The University of Sorbonne was
a hotbed of demonstrations against the perceived heresies of the
reform movement. Leaders of that council, Cardinals de Tournon,
and Duprat, fostering a strong spirit of intolerance and persecution,
attacked vehemently any preaching in Paris supporting the need
for reform in the Catholic Church.

Meeting together in the Queen's apartments included shared
memories of the harrowing journey to Madrid when Marguerite and
Aymée traveled there to nurse the ailing King Francis during his captivity. These were tales of events entirely unknown for Jeanne. She
was appalled at the treatment her mother and Aymée experienced,

as well as the terror of the illness of her dear Uncle Francis. The desperate flight of these two ladies on horseback through the countryside of Spain to escape arrest by Emperor Charles V left her breathless, and she adopted as her own the suspicious distrust the Queen and Aymée held against the Emperor of Spain.

The account of travel and experiences during those three months of their journey led to discussions of Marguerite's continuing and persistent illness that had plagued the Queen on her return and during the time of Jeanne's birth. Jeanne discovered new respect and awe for the versatility, tenacious courage and inner strength of her mother. Jeanne determined to strive to be as faithful and courageous as the example set by her mother.

One of these afternoons was spent leisurely strolling among the trees and pathways of the forest surrounding the Château d'Plessis. Aymée arranged to place blankets and comfortable lawn chairs beneath the towering trees near the bank of the river Loire, with a bevy of baskets of refreshments, fruits, and cheeses to be waiting for them when they grew tired. After a long, leisurely walk, Marguerite said she was ready to relax in the shade of the towering trees and enjoy the peaceful movement of the waters and the cooling breeze off the Loire. Aymée settled into her chair, and Jeanne brought the baskets near where they reposed.

Marguerite had extended her visit into June to take advantage of the mild weather in the North of France, as well as to continue to develop the budding relationship with her daughter. Jeanne had exhibited the desired obedience, submission and respect toward her mother with such devotion that she had indeed captured Marguerite's heart. The Queen was delighted to enjoy Jeanne's company and the attending eagerness with which she listened to all of Marguerite's tales. Companionship and renewal of her friendship with Aymée had so lifted Marguerite's spirits and contributed to her increasing good health that she was reluctant to move on to obligations waiting for her at the duchies.

As the three relaxed by the river and shared the goodies in the baskets, Marguerite began to relate one of her many adventures in service to the King. She wanted Princess Jeanne to understand how her grandmother had contributed to the history of France and their family. It was important that Jeanne learn much of the conflicts between King Francis and the Emperor and King of Spain, Charles V.

Conflicts between the two leading sovereigns in Europe had included wars, disputes, and battles, accompanied with bitter exchanges between the royal courts of Emperor Charles V and Francis I, resulting in devastation, famine, and illness in each country. Both monarchies were strapped to the extreme financially, with counselors and advisors from both sides urging efforts toward peace. Ambassadors shuffled between the two kings laboring to bring them both to a negotiation.

Emperor Charles agreed to send his aunt, Archduchess Marguerite of Austria, the widow of Philibert II, Duke of Savoy, and Regent of the Low Countries. Marguerite of Austria was Charles V's aunt and representative of the interests of Spain. Francis's mother, Louise d'Savoy, Duchess of Angoulême, who had served as regent of France during the King's captivity in Spain represented France. Marguerite of Austria and Louise d'Savoy were sisters-in-law before Philibert II, Duke of Savoy died. Marguerite affectionately referred to her mother as Madame.

The King and Queen of Navarre and other chief nobles of France accompanied Madame to Cambray for the negotiations.

The Duchess of Angoulême and Archduchess Marguerite were experienced and tough negotiators. The talks proceeded with many messages carried back and forth to the opposing kings. Neither of the sides was willing to budge on the terms demanded by their negotiators, and for many days the talks faltered and withered in the oppressive heat of July. The singular point of contention surrounded the release of Francis's two sons who had been exchanged for Francis and taken in his place to captivity, according to the agreement signed in Madrid. Francis had continually offered a large sum to pay ransom for them, and the Emperor had refused unless the payment was accompanied with Francis' surrender to be retaken into captivity. Finally, the King of France had enough. He expressed to his mother that God was on the side of France and that the Emperor had no goal other than to destroy the nation of France. He urged Madame to return home immediately.

Madame, instead, continued in secret meetings with the Archduchess Marguerite and eventually reached an agreement which stipulated that Francis would pay the Emperor two million golden crowns as a ransom for his sons, and also agreed to marry Queen Eleanor of Austria, Emperor Charles V's sister. The treaty was signed late at night on July 24, 1529, and was ever after referred to as the Paix des Dames, or the Agreement of the Royal Ladies. The very existence of France depended on these negotiations for peace. Madame's completion of this treaty took place when Jeanne was a year-and-a-half old and in the care of Aymée at her castle of Lonray.

Aymée asked many questions about the activities of the nobles and their wives and ladies during the sojourn in Cambray and what manner of fashion they exhibited there. They laughed together at Marguerite's humorous tales of the occupations and pastimes of the noble class along with the pursuits and leisure endeavors of acquaintances known to both. Marguerite admitted that the travel, events, and ceremonies had taken a toll on her physical well-being as she was still recovering from the birth of Jeanne and she had been plagued with severe fatigue in the months following.

These hours of conversation and exposure to the trials and challenges in her mother's life deepened respect and devotion in Jeanne, as well as compassion for the duties and difficulties that had separated Jeanne from constant companionship with her parents. She began to grasp the perspective demanded of a sovereign in response to the needs of their subjects, even at the expense of their family relationships.

When the day eventually arrived for Marguerite's departure to journey on to other destinations, Jeanne clung to her mother fiercely and then reluctantly released her to persist in her Queenly duties. She had resolved herself to accept her abandonment and isolation as necessary for the advancement of the kingdom. It was not agreeable but, Jeanne acknowledged, a necessity. She realized that her current place in this game of thrones was in the position of a pawn; however, she would direct her efforts toward becoming a more significant player in the game.

Unavoidably, feelings of abandonment deepened and periods of loneliness and depression continued to torment her as the months passed. She treasured the memories of the time with her mother and longed to enjoy her fellowship again.

15. Distractions

*"Set your mind on the things above, not on the things
that are on the earth."*

Colossians 3:2 (NASB)

In October of 1533, King Francis stopped at the Château de Plessis to see Jeanne. Jeanne's arrogance and outspoken nature exposed her feelings of abandonment and hurt during every encounter with her uncle. He responded by emphasizing that his decisions had been made for the benefit of Jeanne and her future; and joined with his traveling companions in joyful pursuit of a stag through the forest surrounding the castle.

The King was pleased with the reports of M. Bourbon, M. d'Izvernay, Bishop du Châtel and Chamberlain Duquesse. As a reward to Jeanne for her progress, he presented her with a beautiful Weimaraner puppy. She was delighted and immediately named him Sir Ami (Sir Friend). The puppy was nearly as tall as Jeanne and showed his love by promptly licking her face and lying down at her feet. The King also presented a new stable groom who would be tasked to teach her to ride a horse and learn to hunt on horseback. It would be a marvelous way to be sure Sir Ami received necessary exercise and training to go along on the hunt.

The kitchens of Château d'Plessis were at their height of industry and exertions. Although the King had brought his own army of chefs and assistants with him, the Château kitchen staff had increased energies to provide the utmost honor and reverence to their Princess and the King.

The royal table had expanded and now seated nearly twenty people at the evening meal. Several other tables were placed near the royal table in the Grand Hall to accommodate the royal guard and other attendants and nobles that accompanied the King. Every aspect of formality and decorum was observed. Jeanne, feeling overwhelmed, assumed her role of a silent listener. She was required by correct manners to converse with the individuals at her sides and those who sat opposite to her across the table.

The King demanded that she sit at his left hand at every meal. She repeatedly requested that Aymée, M. Bourbon or Sir Duquesse be seated on her other side. It was a relief to Jeanne that King Francis carried the conversation in jovial remarks to all, even shouting to be heard by those seated at the far ends of the table.

Occasionally Francis would engage Princess Jeanne in private conversation, asking her opinion on much of the discussion taking place. He developed a growing appreciation for her ability to analyze and discern the critical points as her keen mind consistently probed each point, searching for the truth of the matter. The King soon saw that if she had no opinion to share, it was because she needed additional information of the facts in dispute.

At dinner one evening, Bishop du Châtel announced he would be saying High Mass for the King in the Chapel of Château de Plessis-lez-Tours and looked forward to the attendance of every member of the castle staff, as well as many aristocratic nobles of the town and countryside.

The day for High Mass began normally, however after the noon meal Aymée directed Jeanne to return to her apartment. The next four afternoon hours were spent in an agonizing process to prepare the Princess for her appearance at the King's side for the royal procession to the Chapel. It seemed ludicrous to Jeanne to bathe and wash her hair in the midday, though that was only the beginning of the ordeal. Doused with moisturizing ointments, perfumes, and powders that preceded the long process of curling, braiding and piling her long, dark hair into a beautiful nest on her head studded with diamond pins throughout. Aymée certainly exhibited her talented expertise while Jeanne sat patiently, listening to the beautiful voices and music of her ladies-in-waiting.

Then came the dressing; she donned several layers of linen and lace underthings, ruffled petticoats, then a large hoop under-skirt, topped with more petticoats.

Sitting, at this point, appeared to be impossible. Jeanne could imagine herself trying to sit down, only to be catapulted onto her back with her feet over her head. Since she would be sitting during Mass, her attendants showed her how to maneuver her skirts aside to straddle a stool similar to one that would be in the balcony just for her.

After she mastered that little move, she practiced lifting her skirts at just the right position to keep from tripping on her petticoats when stepping upstairs. The process was going to be much more difficult than she had imagined.

All her attendants, including Aymée, helped lift her beautiful, satin, royal-purple gown over her head and petticoats. Three rows of diamonds about her neck and wrists reflected every source of light. Jeanne shuffled about, trying to walk in the vast skirts of her dress.

"Glide," said Aymée.

Jeanne laughed and responded, "Glide? I feel more like a turtle crawling along trying to keep from flipping on to my back!"

Moving toward the door and soon arriving at the top of the stairs, she gasped. She couldn't see her feet. How was she going to walk down all those stairs?! As she hesitated, she saw Sir Duquesse suddenly leave his spot at the foot of the stair to leap up the steps, three at a time, and offer his hand to her.

"Go slowly, Princess, and slide your feet until you can feel the edge of the step. Don't look down! Just look at me and you will be fine!"

It was fine; by the time she stood at the bottom, she had mastered gliding without a tumble. Sir Duquesse escorted her to the rear entrance of the Chapel, and she began to feel more comfortable walking with her arm outstretched to reach his wrist. She was grateful he knew his part and was sure he had done this before, but with someone older and taller.

When the King arrived beside Princess Jeanne, he bent near and kissed her cheek, then held his arm out to her. As they moved up to the back of the Chapel, Jeanne realized the aisle was only broad enough for her full skirt. She panicked and looked at Uncle Francis for some guidance. He never looked at her, he kept his head forward, so naturally positioning himself just a step behind the most expansive portion of her skirt that they moved gracefully together without a struggle. She giggled at herself: of course, a king must do this all the time!

It was a splendorous affair as the King of France and contingent arrived in full finery and magnificence. At the side of King Francis I, Princess Jeanne walked with her small hand on his arm. The procession down the center aisle of the Chapel, up the winding staircase into the second-floor nave of the Chapel was an impressive spectacle of stateliness and majesty. The Princess sparkled brightly as the diamonds around the neck of her dress and her diamond tiara and hairpins reflected the lights of the candelabras.

Such a sensation of grandeur was a very new experience for Princess Jeanne. The Chapel filled with servants and inhabitants of the Château who bowed low at their appearance. She marveled that so many faces she moved among on a daily basis who had become friends were there, beaming with pride at her glory. Even the nobles from Tours and the countryside appeared in force to support the King and their Princess. A new lesson nestled into her subconscious that such an impressive display lifted the confidence and devotion of subjects for their monarch. The Bishop had elevated the celebration of Mass to match the splendidness of his royal congregation. The entire event left a lasting impression on Jeanne.

After the King's departure, Jeanne added her lessons in riding to her daily schedule. She enjoyed the time and was pleased with her progress. She liked riding side-saddle and was soon quite proficient. The opportunities to ride out in the late afternoons with her groom and Sir Ami alongside were exhilarating.

As her riding skills improved, it was most tempting to shout, "Come," to Sir Ami and gallop down the forest paths in an attempt to leave her guards and groom far behind. Each week her lead increased. She would imagine that the soldiers of Spain were pursuing her, as they had her mother. Arriving back at the stable, when the soldiers were dismounting, they had to pay up for bets which they made with stable-hands whether they could keep up with her or not. Eventually, her groom ceased to accompany her unless he was teaching her hunting skills.

As the brilliant fall colors of the forest turned to bare branches; chill winds blew through the castle. Jeanne strangely seemed drawn to the castle torture chamber, contemplating its cages and implements of torture. With Sir Ami close on her heels, she stood forlornly gazing around the room as though seeking to feel the torment and pain suffered there. Her daily walks expanded from the castle gardens to the woods that led to the banks of the Loire. Too often, she would stumble upon the yawning pits that had been placed everywhere as a part of defenses established by King Louis XI. She barely avoided falling into many of the holes herself, warned by Sir Ami's frantic barking. This near brush with death increased her fearful identification with the young men caught in Louis' evil nets. She became obsessed with attempting to feel their fear and terror. Her imaginations wandered through the battles and skirmishes that had taken place and envisioned the bodies hanging from the tree limbs, or floating down the Loire pierced with arrows. The images settled in her mind, a constant background playing through all her activities

She sought out gardeners and serving maids who were residents in the employ of the castle to inquire relentlessly about their memories of the history of the castle. Aymée was relieved to see the loyal devotion of Sir Ami who accompanied Jeanne wherever she went. Concern grew in Aymée's mind that Jeanne was withdrawing more and more into her private obsession with the torture that had taken place in the castle and on its grounds.

Bitter cold and biting winds drove her inside by the fire to play chess with M. Bourbon. Many evenings she sat for long periods alone, staring into the flames of the fireplace in the Library or her apartments. Late in the dark of night, she would wake abruptly, breathing heavily after a terrible dream of people around her in great pain, writhing and suffering among the torture devices. Fleeing to her secret room, she curled up on the couch with her arms around Sir Ami. She could be found in the early mornings sitting in her secret room with the Bible on her lap and Sir Ami snoring by her side.

Aymée asked if she had any questions about what she was reading and Jeanne would shake her head without a response, her large eyes glistening with tears. Aymée devoted more time on her knees asking God for wisdom to understand and help her Princess find her way through these emotional, intellectual struggles. Eventually, Aymée spoke with Chamberlain Duquesse to ask if his meetings with Jeanne could shed any light on her thoughts.

"Princess Jeanne is always very attentive and often asks questions pertinent to our conversation. I appreciate her view on many subjects. We have not approached the torture chamber issue since our first meeting. It is a subject that hangs in the middle of our meetings and is never brought up. I have judged it must be her choice to discuss. Since the King left, the Princess has been less animated; however she is always courteous and considerate," he responded. Aymée was not sure if she felt better or worse with his report.

In the midst of Aymée's agonizing worry over Jeanne's growing depression, a letter arrived from Queen Marguerite. For some time Aymée debated over the wisdom of reading it to Jeanne, then decided any word from her mother might break through the gloom of her loneliness. Sitting with Jeanne in her secret room, Aymée read the letter.

Previously that year, on a morning in October 1534, Paris, a city in great turmoil, had awakened to a deluge of reform placards posted about the city to make public the errors and abuses in the church.[ix] These placards accused the Catholic Hierarchy of robbing and misleading their congregations, particularly in the areas of indulgences, confession, and forgiveness of sins by priests, bishops, and deacons, within the Papal system. These practices were the very backbone of the enormous wealth collected by the Catholic hierarchy. To direct government policy and control the loyalties and behavior of the common man depended on the ongoing grip of papal power on the souls of men.

In the distant past, a small tremor started to disturb the set traditions of the Church with the exposure of cracks at the foundations of the faith. The invention of the Guttenberg printing press
at that time made Bibles for the common man possible. A devoted
Augustinian priest in Werms, Germany, educated as a lawyer before
his call to the priesthood, labored to translate the original Greek
manuscripts of the Bible into the German language.

Working in seclusion and with the blessing of the Catholic
Church, his efforts revealed errors and abuses that had occurred
within the church for centuries. This revelation of the truth of practices condoned and observed in direct departure from the correct
word of God brought anguish to the devoted and gentle spirit of
Martin Luther.[x] Seeking to urge renewal and reform, Luther hoped
to impel the Catholic Church to explore the need for change when
he courageously posted his 95 points on the church door on October
31, 1517. This act created a schism affecting every social, political
and religious institution in existence across Europe. The movement
gained momentum when, in Geneva, John Calvin made a complete
break from the Catholic traditions and organized the Protestants
who believed in the divine truths of the Bible, but not the adoration
of Mary, worship of saints, or the intercession of priests between
God and sinful man. The Catholic Church in France relied on the
judgments and edicts proclaimed by the ecclesiastical powers of the
appointed Council of the Faculties of Paris at Sorbonne University.
The Council was formed to defend the religious doctrines observed
in the Church for 1500 years. The University of Sorbonne was
a hotbed of demonstrations against the perceived heresies of the
reform movement. Leaders of that council, Cardinals de Tournon,
and Duprat, fostering a strong spirit of intolerance and persecution,
attacked vehemently any preaching in Paris supporting the need
for reform in the Catholic Church.

Cardinal de Tournon initiated insurgent attacks against the
Queen of Navarre for her provision of refuge in Béarn to Gerard
Roussel, Erasmus, and Lefever. Cardinal Tournon believed they
were the leaders of the reform movement in France. Rumors implied
that Marguerite, the Queen of Navarre, had initiated the placards.

An effort to diminish the influence of Marguerite on King Francis was initiated by challenging his protection of her. These two Cardinals pressed the King and whispered deceitful suggestions that the King's tolerance of her heresies would eventually bring the fall of his royal authority. They whispered that his tolerance of Marguerite demonstrated his lack of love for Christ. Angered, the King, whose primary interest in the reform movement was whether it threatened his royal prerogative to govern, declared by proclamation all reform preachers in Paris be arrested. Persecutions were rampant, and any hint of heresy led to the loss of liberty and, too often, even death at the stakes.

Among those arrested were particular friends of Marguerite's, Gerard Roussel and his two chaplains taken for preaching in Paris.

Viewing the King's edict support of their cause, the theologians in Paris broadcast their fanatic denunciations loudly against Marguerite. Without actually using her name, their crafty insinuations implicated her as privy to conspiracies to assassinate numerous Catholic priests on a specified date throughout the city of Paris. The faction at the Sorbonne viciously represented this rumor as fact, and carried out, with increasing severity, persecutions on every manner of heresy, including burning six unfortunate Lutheran preachers and a naive schoolmistress at the stake. With Marguerite isolated in Béarn, the Cardinals triumphantly believed their whispers to the King would soon eliminate the Queen of Navarre's obnoxious influences on the King.

King Francis, so beset with internal political chaos and opposing perspectives, had sorely missed his sister's quiet counsel and wisdom.

In a surprising move, Francis called on Marguerite to return to his court to appear before the theologians of Paris to answer the charges. Marguerite responded immediately and arrived in Paris not long after. Although Duprat and Tournon had readily attacked the character of Marguerite while she was at a distance; they had no desire to encounter her in person, knowing that her intelligent rebuttal of their lies would expose the truth and also would effectively turn the King against them.

Marguerite's presence in Paris hampered the activities of the Cardinals and their allies of the council, as her influence was so profound. Never happy at being separated from her, the King considered the two of them were of one mind; her presence again by his side diminished his confusion.

The King's coldness toward those who had accused her of despicable motives removed any possible renewal of the charges. Marguerite convinced the King that her efforts were only to increase the purity of the faith by encouraging the priesthood to abandon the erroneous doctrine and superstitious practices that threatened the beauty of the rituals of the Catholic Church. When Francis insisted he would not leave the Roman Catholic faith, she reassured him her efforts were only to unite the faith by eliminating the dogmas which threatened it. Using her gifted diplomatic talents, her intercession in the trial of Roussel and the two monks obtained a complete acquittal which allowed them to return to Béarn.

King Francis opposed the reform movement. Cardinal Duprat, Archbishop of Sens, and the King's mother, Louise d'Savoy, Duchess of Angoulême, persuaded Francis that the reform movement would eventually result in the decline of the royal dynasty and undermine the divine right of kings. Francis I would not risk his position of wealth and power.

Marguerite did not presume to voice opposition to the King's stance; however, she did write letters seeking intercession from him for her friends. Although Marguerite did not publicly declare her support for the reform movement throughout France, she did provide refuge and friendship to the leaders. When home in Nérac, Queen Marguerite spent long hours in conversations with the scholar Gérard Roussel, a refugee who sought to escape the persecutions against the reform advocates in Paris by fleeing to Béarn.

Cardinal Duprat was the King's appointed Finance Councilor of France, a position that gave continued access to the King's ear. He continually urged the King to take more severe measures against the reform movement. He knew the King loved the ceremony, acclaim and wealth of being king, so he exaggerated reports of the zeal and destructive activity of the reformers, describing their actions as that of heretical rebels.

This Cardinal Chancellor's dedication to the church with a deceitful zeal for the purity of the faith camouflaged his arrogant indignation toward any person who could hold opinions which he condemned. His outrage against the reform movement grew from his dishonest massing of personal wealth by filling his pockets with the abundance of the offerings, favors, and payments for salvation. Incensed at the King's hesitation to stamp out the dangerous reformers, his maneuvers to press the King to action against reform included calling on the University of Sorbonne's Council to declare its disapproval of any of the professors of the Sorbonne who were supporters of the Lutheran movement.

One particular scholar, Louis de Berquin, was determined to expose the corruption of the Council of Sorbonne through his writings. His treatise drew the attention of the Council who focused on his heretical leanings and targeted him for the wrath and persecution of the Catholic Church and its supporters. Persuaded by his friends and fellow supporters of reform to seek asylum at the castle in Béarn under the protection of the Queen of Navarre, Berquin hesitated too long, and an Inquisition council was formed in Paris which tried and sentenced him to be burned at the stake. The Queen of Navarre had begged the King to intercede in the sentence but to no avail. This first Inquisition council began the intense persecution of reformers and Huguenots in France. The Huguenots were so called because of the influence of one of their leaders, Bezanson Hugues who was a follower of John Calvin's writings in Geneva, Switzerland.

Jeanne listened intently to this accounting by her mother, sensing that the Queen was deeply emotional regarding the country's treatment against the seekers of truth in religion as she was apparently in agreement with their beliefs. The Princess burned with resentment that her mother had been so maligned. She was also sensitive to Aymée's conformity with the Queen in these matters. Jeanne meditated upon this subject in her times of seclusion in her secret room. She had her own experiences witnessing Aymée's deep faith and dependence on her personal savior Jesus Christ. It had been evident to Jeanne in these past months that the strengths and comforts of her governess came from her relationship with

Jesus and had nothing to do with the ceremonies and practices being taught by the bishop and chaplains at the Chapel. So far, the dogmas of her catechism lessons had provided little correlation or comfort to her circumstances and challenges. She wanted to find out who Jesus was in her own life.

Hearing from her mother about the bravery and courageous stand she had made for her beliefs, Jeanne longed, even more, to be in her mother's presence. Aymée worried whether sharing the Queen's letter brought light into Jeanne's dark thoughts or made it worse.

December came and passed. Christmas decorations embellished the castle and Jeanne attended Christmas Eve Mass by herself. Her demeanor did not change, and she seemed oblivious to the festivities around her. January blew in with frigid winds and little snow. There was no recognition or reference to Jeanne's sixth birthday from anyone outside of the castle, and she did not seem to care; expressing appreciation for the gift Aymée gave her, but not much interest in celebration. Aymée grieved to see her precious girl withdraw farther behind the walls she was building.

Princess Jeanne continued at her studies and attended her religious instructions, often asking questions about salvation that puzzled the chaplains and revealed her deep theological searching.

The months rolled by and another lonely Christmas season and another year were gone with Jeanne's seventh birthday passing unnoticed.

Spring again made its appearance in 1535. Jeanne labored over writing letters to her mother and on occasion received one in return. Marguerite wrote she was recovering from her illness; however, she continued to fight off residual symptoms of coughing and depleted energy. Her letter concentrated primarily on the declining health of Madame. Jeanne had not had occasion in her lifetime to meet and become acquainted with her maternal grandmother, but she could empathize with her mother's sense of sadness. When Jeanne received word that Madame had died, she was deeply moved with sympathy for her mother who had nursed Madame faithfully until her death. Her letters were a brave effort to be supportive of her mother's feelings of mourning and loss of companionship.

Though Jeanne continued to progress in her education and training as Aymée, Sir Duquesse and M. Bourbon had been charged to implement by King Francis, and her mentors shared a corporate concern for the withdrawal evident in the Princess's despondency. They met together to share their common concerns and seek an avenue to combat Jeanne's downward spiral.

Sir Duquesse suggested an occasional outing to the town of Tours as a change of perspective. The King's express orders had adamantly insisted that Jeanne not be allowed to leave the protective grounds of the Château without his majesty's permission. The three agreed that Duquesse should immediately inquire for the King's approval so the arrangements would be ready as soon as the weather was mild. So they dispatched a courier with a request for a response at the King's earliest opportunity. The letter was carefully worded by Jeanne's supporters to present the idea in the best possible light, without a hint of their reason for the request.

They waited impatiently for the King's response. As weeks passed, they disappointedly watched Jeanne's mood duplicate the dreary, heavy rains of April. At the onset of the stormy season, Jeanne walked with Sir Ami to the river, in spite of the weather. Stubbornly refusing to wear protection from the rain, on her return, her sodden hair lay in tangles around her face. Aymée was frantic that she might become deathly ill.

Her increasing lethargy in the mounting heat of May and June brought her supporters discouragement, with still no word from the King.

When they met in July, M. Bourbon was pleased to report that Jeanne was quite proficient in reading, writing, and languages; Sir Duquesse also indicated the Princess was expressing some interest in the gardens and landscaping efforts around the castle. Aymée, however, did not share any good news. Jeanne increasingly refused Aymée's efforts of grooming, preferring to let her hair hang limp and loose about her shoulders. She insisted on wearing her oldest, more comfortable clothes. Aymée was confused about how to approach her lady and encourage a more diligent effort toward her appearance. Her moods disheartened all of her supporters.

When the King's permission finally came, it included stipulations that the carriage must have castle troops on guard. The three conspirators had fully expected the King's demand that the Princess not be allowed to travel farther than Tours; however, they wondered if adding the heavy guard might create a more significant problem than the one they hoped to alleviate. Regardless of their many misgivings, they made plans to arrange an opportunity for the outing.

An unusual day dawned with blue skies and cool breezes. Temperatures had dipped lower than the typical July heat, and with hope, the plan was put in action. Sir Duquesse asked Jeanne at their daily meeting if she would like to accompany him on an errand he must make to Tours. Her melancholy face never changed as she debated in her mind if she had the desire or energy to say yes. Finally, she met his eyes and nodded in agreement. He was profoundly disappointed by the absence of her former animation and sparkle. They would leave immediately after their noonday meal, and he diffidently suggested that she dress appropriately to be seen by her subjects.

Jeanne and Sir Ami walked to the river after her meeting with the Chamberlain. Silently she watched the water flow by, imagining that her own life was slipping away in the current of a river of loneliness. Her thoughts were a jumbled mess. She felt lost in a forest of tangled confusion and emptiness and seemed to be standing on a shifting foundation with no purpose or goal that she could see.

Sighing, she resigned herself to return to the castle and ask Aymée's help for preparation to present herself to the townspeople.

16. New Adventure

"For I am confident of this very thing, that He who began a good work in you will perfect it until the day of Christ Jesus."

Philippians 1:6 (NASB)

Jeanne accompanied Sir Duquesse to the stables, petting the horses until the carriage was hitched to the team. Her riding lessons had improved her confidence around the horses, and she was especially fond of the mount that she was learning to ride. Sir Ami sat obediently at her feet displaying the lessons he had also received about his behavior around the stables.

Sir Duquesse bowed before Jeanne and offered his hand as she stepped into the carriage, allowing Sir Ami to follow to sit beside her. Then Sir Duquesse sat across from her and gave instructions to the driver. When the castle guards on horseback who would accompany them surrounded the carriage, the Princess raised her eyebrows and looked at the Chamberlain questioningly. She had not expected such a display, but when Sir Duquesse made no explanation, she shifted her gaze to the countryside

It was invigorating. Sir Ami amused her as he sat leaning into the breeze, his ears blowing back like flapping flags and his tongue waving in the wind. Jeanne's giggle startled Sir Duquesse. The carriage moved into a gallop, and with the guard thundering all around them Jeanne had to admit it was exciting. She determined to ignore the confusions that plagued her and just enjoy the moment. As the joy of the day overcame her, she lifted a silent prayer to the Father she had ignored for months and gave thanks for the beauty of the day.

Before long, the carriage slowed to a walk, and they began to pass farmers on the roads bearing loads of produce to the markets in Tours. Jeanne looked as curiously at them as they did her. She had been so isolated for much of her life that these scenes were not familiar. As they approached the town, the roads became increasingly congested with people moving in every direction. As the castle guard came into view, the people would flee to the shoulder of the gravel roadway in a panic. The carriage emerged in the midst of the soldiers and caused the teeming crowd to crane their necks and push against the other gawkers for a view of the young Princess and her dog. She had never made a public appearance before, although some of the citizens had attended the Christmas Mass and many had friends or relatives employed at the castle.

Princess Jeanne was an unending subject of conversation throughout the town for all the months she had been in residence at the Château de Plessis. They followed her life and accomplishments as closely as the gossip from the castle would allow. All were equally sympathetic to the miseries and difficulties she must be suffering from stories her loyal representatives of the castle staff were too willing to impart. They wished only the best for the little Princess as they would for their own child for, as a whole, the town had adopted her as their own.

Jeanne had no knowledge of the worship and interest that followed her through the streets. Displaying the joyous response of a child, she waved to them as she went along. The noise of cheers and applause followed them until it reached a crescendo the moment the carriage stopped in front of the offices of the city officials. Sir Duquesse was astounded as he stood to step from the carriage. It was impossible for him to proceed as the roar subsided and the crowds formed an orderly line alongside the carriage, bowing and smiling at the Princess and her regal dog. Jeanne stood in response and nodded to each person on both sides of the carriage until the lines began to dwindle, and the crowds dispersed and went about their previous responsibilities. The guards had arranged themselves around the carriage in a defensive position with swords drawn, held across their chests. They took care not to block the view of the Princess to see the faces of the crowds.

Sir Duquesse asked the Princess if she would care to accompany him to the offices of the mayor.

She replied, "I would prefer to wait here if possible. Seeing all of the people has tired me. I shall go with you if you think it necessary."

Sir Duquesse debated his answer and then determined that it would be more appropriate for the Mayor to come to the Princess rather than vice versa. Somehow his familiarity with her at the castle had clouded his grasp of her majesty, and he scolded himself for nearly allowing such an error in protocol.

He bowed to the Princess and said, "As you wish, your Majesty."

Speaking a low warning and instruction to the commander of the guard, Sir Duquesse left the carriage and proceeded to enter the nearby building.

As the Princess sat thinking about the responses of the crowds, a movement in the corner of her vision caused her to glance to the side of the building, past some piles of trash. A slight girl about her age was peeking out to stare at the Princess, her dog, the guards, and carriage.

Princess Jeanne smiled brightly and said, "Hi!"

The face of the girl disappeared behind the trash pile momentarily, and then she peered at Jeanne again. In response, Jeanne motioned to her to come closer. When the girl only took a few steps forward, Jeanne called, "Please, do come closer."

When the guard nearest to the girl stiffened, and Sir Ami muttered a low growl, Jeanne stood and placed her hand on the dog's head, then commanded the guard to let the girl who had frozen in place come closer to the carriage. She again smiled and beckoned to the girl with a friendly wave.

The little girl hesitantly moved forward and reached out to stroke the carved rose on the side of the beautiful carriage. She lifted her eyes to meet Jeanne's and they filled with wonder and awe. Jeanne looked back and studied the girl, her own eyes registering her various emotions in a rapid display of changing purple, blue and sparkling azure. The Princess noted the scraggly hair and sallow complexion of the girl with bony shoulders, thin arms and ragged clothes hanging off a skeletal frame.

The girl stared at the perfectly arranged braids and curls topped with a perky little, feathered cap that had kept the Princess's hair from blowing in the wind. Her wonder increased at the gorgeous clothes of satin trimmed in velvet with pearls attached all over the bodice. The Princess held out her gloved hand to the girl and said, "My name is Jeanne, what is yours?"

The girl whispered, "Antoinette. You are very beautiful."

Jeanne laughed and replied, "So are you! Your eyes are such a vibrant blue. Do you have any brothers and sisters?"

"No," replied Antoinette, "only a baby at home but he is not well. My mother's milk has stopped, and he is too young to eat solid food. He will probably die as all the rest have."

"Well, we are much alike then, for I have no brothers or sisters either and my baby brother died when he was only five months old. It was very sad, and I cried a great deal," Jeanne responded. "Are you terribly lonely, too?"

Antoinette thought about that a while and then said, "No, not so much. I have my mother and father at home; however they are sad all the time, and my father is angry a lot because he cannot find work. I also have friends who live near me, and when I want to get away from the arguments at home, I go to play with them. They were here with me, watching as you came up, but they ran home to tell their parents you were here. I think they walked by in the crowd."

Suddenly, Sir Duquesse emerged from the offices, accompanied by the mayor. Antoinette gasped, turned quickly and ran away. Jeanne had hardly blinked, and she was gone. Turning to watch the approach of Sir Duquesse and the mayor, Jeanne felt a deep sense of loss. After formal introductions, immediately the mayor bobbed in repeated bows, apologizing profusely that the Princess had been approached and bothered by one of the urchins of their citizens. He assured her that the culprit would immediately be apprehended and dealt with harshly.

Jeanne responded in shock, saying severely, "Don't you dare! I invited her, and she offered me her friendship. Out of the hundreds of people that walked by my carriage, Antoinette was the only person to show interest in me, not the grandeur that surrounds me. I will appreciate your concern if you will find where she lives and provide me with that information, but you must not punish her at all. I consider her my friend and will not allow you to offend her or her family in any way!"

Sir Duquesse, who had questioned the commander of the guards and threatened to discipline him for his lax in the protection of the Princess, heard the last of this conversation between the mayor and Her Majesty. He waved the guard away and stepped over to stand next to the mayor.

He looked quizzically at them both and watched as Jeanne extended her hand to the mayor and said graciously, "Thank you, Monsieur Mayor. I will look forward to receiving the information I have requested of you."

Turning to Duquesse, she said, "Are you ready to go? I believe Sir Ami would enjoy a short walk in the park if we have the time."

"Of course, Your Highness." Sir Duquesse said, and bowed before stepping into the carriage, nodded to the mayor, and after the Princess was comfortably seated, touched the shoulder of the driver.

They stopped at a nearby grassy park, and one of the soldiers took Sir Ami for a short run. On the way back to the castle, Jeanne appeared lost in deep thought. Sir Duquesse studied her carefully, wondering if she had lost all the joy and excitement of the incoming trip. He pondered how he would explain the events of this confusing trip. Jeanne did not show any response as the carriage rushed along at a gallop.

Sir Ami leaned into the wind, ears flapping, and tongue slapping against his cheeks, trembling in anticipation of rabbits and squirrels hiding among the trees along the way.

17. Hopeless

"... and hope does not disappoint, because the love of
God has been poured out within our hearts through the
Holy Spirit who was given to us."

Romans 5:5 (NASB)

When the man with the Princess came back to the carriage, Antoinette had run home as quickly as she could; she was fast, winning races with the neighborhood boys all the time. Afraid that the bailiff would come looking for her to take her to jail for bothering the Princess of the Château de Plessis, she hid, terrified, behind the laundry baskets in the back of her house. The baby was screaming with hunger though Mumsie was trying to quiet him while she labored over the tubs of wash she took in to earn what little bit she could to buy food. The baby had been such a distraction that Mumsie was far behind in her task. Normally Antoinette helped Mumsie lift the heavy clothes out of the boiling pot of rinse water, however that day Mumsie had sent her to dig among the trash heaps in search of something that could be boiled to make a broth for the baby; a last resort since all of them knew the babe could not live much longer without something to eat. Then she had talked with the Princess. Antoinette was trembling with fear and muttered a constant prayer for Jesus to help her as she hid. If she was taken by the bailiff, Antoinette was sure it would be the breaking point for Mumsie and Dads.

99

Not only was Dads deeply depressed because no one wanted to employ a one-armed man, he blamed himself for not being able to feed his family. Now he would be faced with seeing his daughter go to jail. She knew he would feel it his fault for not being able to bail her out. Antoinette knew she had really messed up.

It was a common problem among the very poor. When kids had to beg, steal and scavenge food it was common for them to get caught and be stuck in jail for months. The boys she played with didn't care because most were glad to get at least one meal a day while they were in the lockup. She knew it would kill her father if that happened to her. She had been very careful not to cross the law when she went hunting for food. Antoinette was sure that talking to the Princess was the worst thing she had ever done, and now she didn't know if the other three members of her family would still be alive when her release from lock-up eventually came.

Finally, when no one showed up to arrest her after a couple of hours, she crawled out from her hiding place and admitted to Mumsie what she had done. All Mumsie could do was cover her mouth with her hand and hug Antoinette tightly. Then she stopped her laundry work and helped Antoinette make a little hiding place among the baskets, warning Antoinette that if anyone came down the path to their home, she must hide quickly. Mumsie said she would not let anyone find her. Later, after dark, Mumsie went, in her place, to find scraps on the waste heaps from dinners in the big houses across town. She would not risk Antoinette going back outside for fear she might be seen.

Antoinette stood at the back door, close to the crowded baskets, watching Dads wearily return to the house. He rummaged in the kitchen but there was not even a dry crust of bread for him. He sat down at the table holding his head in his hands. He did not see Antoinette in the half-light of the doorway. When the baby started crying again after waking from a restless nap, Dads' shoulders heaved with huge sobs. Antoinette backed quietly away from the lighted doorway and sat among the baskets in the dark. She wished Mumsie would come back soon. Her parents had often fought over Mumsie being out on the streets after dark and she had heard Dads shout that he could not live if something happened to Mumsie.

When the baby finally cried himself to sleep again, Antoinette curled up on the floor, anxiously listening for footsteps in the lane. "Please Jesus, let it be Mumsie and not the bailiff," she prayed.

18 Emotional Response

"... Remember the poor ..."

Galatians 2:10 (NASB)

J eanne rushed to her apartments when they arrived back at the castle. The conspirators huddled in the Great Hall to discuss and evaluate what impact the outing to town had made on the Princess. None were encouraged at the report and disappointedly agreed they must continue to observe her.

Aymée sped to Jeanne's apartments in fear of finding her in an emotional tailspin. Bursting through the door to Jeanne's rooms, she did not see what she expected. The Princess was standing before her wardrobes adding to a mounting pile of clothes behind her. Her maids-in-waiting huddled nearby whispering together in confusion.

Aymée moved to Jeanne's side, and with a firm grip that blocked her arm from reaching into the wardrobe again, she said, "What are you doing?"

The Princess looked at Aymée quickly and then shaking off her hand, turned back to reach again into the wardrobe. She spoke with an authority that Aymée had not heard before, saying, "I am so pleased that you are here to help me Aymée for I have much to do! Please ask the maids to help you fold these old clothes of mine to be carried into Tours. They are good, beautiful clothes, however, I have been growing lately and can no longer wear them. My friend, Antoinette, needs them."

Aymée stood immobile, trying to piece together the threads of what she had heard in Sir Duquesse's report and what was happening in front of her.

Jeanne whipped around and said, "Please Aymée, help me!"

At this point, Aymée wrapped her arms tightly around Jeanne and replied, "You wonderful child! Your heart is bigger than you are! Come and sit with me and tell me all about your new friend, Antoinette. The maids can fold the garments as we talk and then you and I can work together to determine what will be appropriate for her."

Aymée led her Princess to the chairs by the empty fireplace, leaving the maids to take over folding the garments in a pile. Jeanne excitedly began to share what had happened that day in Tours.

"Aymée, the people in Tours are very loving and shouted and cheered as we rode by. Then they walked by the carriage one by one and honored me. I am only seven-years-old, and yet they bowed before me as though I was King Francis. I was so surprised and could hardly wrap my mind around what was happening. Sir Ami was so good! He never moved a muscle as the crowd closed in, and when he growled at Antoinette, he was only protecting me! He stopped immediately, and the guards listened when I told them to let her come close to my carriage.

"Oh, Aymée, she is pretty with such beautiful blue eyes, but very hungry; her baby brother is dying because he has no food, and his mother has no milk for him. Antoinette says her father cannot find work and sometimes her parents fight. I must do something to help her! She admired my dress, and hers was all torn and ripped. Surely something in this pile of clothes will fit her!"

The words tumbled out so rapidly that it took a moment for Aymée to sort them out. At last, she laid her hand on Jeanne's arm and said, "Of course we must do something, and I will help you in every way I can. Let's approach this as you would a game of chess and figure out how to help her, but not hurt her. We will study the circumstances and see how the chessboard sits and what moves will achieve your goal. You are right to want to give out of your abundance, so be sure your moves will reach the right goal. Do you think to give her your dresses to play in the streets with other children, who are as poor as she is, will help her? Or will it expose her to teasing and rejection? Every action of yours results in a counter move. We must think it all through to avoid pitfalls."

Jeanne stared at Aymée; it took her a moment to readjust her thinking to what she had just seen. She could see the truth of these remarks and was grateful that she had received such wise advice.

"Oh Aymée, we must do something quickly! How should we go about helping her best?" Jeanne asked earnestly.

At this Aymée retrieved a paper and pen from the desk and wrote at the top of the page: 'Plan to Help.' Together they decided on topics to accomplish immediately; plus some long-term plans that might be helpful.

First, they would carefully choose a few dresses that would hold up to the play and living conditions of Antoinette's environment.

Secondly, Jeanne would speak to kitchen staff to see if there was any food available, along with something the baby could consume, to pack up and take to Antoinette and her family.

Thirdly, she would consult with Sir Duquesse and M. d'Izernay to see if there might be a need somewhere at the castle for Antoinette's father to be employed.

Fourthly, Jeanne hoped to help Antoinette learn to read and write.

Last, Jeanne would inquire if Fauzio and Raymond, as well as other attendants at the castle, had some outgrown boys' clothes which would allow Jeanne to include all of Antoinette's friends in the bounty she hoped to bestow on the neighborhood.

Aymée impressed on Jeanne that her efforts must proceed carefully and wisely, so as not to offend with her gifts. Hurting someone by giving a gift had not occurred to Princess Jeanne. She could not imagine how there would be any reason for her generosity to be offensive. Jeanne could see that they should explore longer-lasting solutions than just returning this evening with a pile of her clothes. A plan of long-term goals needed to be created. That was a frustration, but she determined to see it through the right way.

19. Wise Counsel

"And the King will answer and say to them, 'Truly, I say to you, to the extent that you did it to one of these brothers of Mine, even the least of them, you did it to Me.'"

Matthew 25:40 (NASB)

Aymée insisted that Jeanne write notes asking Sir Duquesse, Steward Izvernay and M. Bourbon to meet with her in the Library before their evening meal.

"Jeanne," she said, "this plan will require their contribution and support. Listen to their reactions and try to understand any objections they may have, otherwise you will not be informed enough to form your own response."

Of course, Aymée was right, but Jeanne did not see how they could argue against what she wanted to do, because it was right. How could she not help Antoinette and her family?

When everyone had arrived in the Library, Jeanne hesitated, looking to Aymée to share their plan. Aymée shook her head 'no' and motioned for Jeanne to do it herself. Taking a deep breath, she started by sharing how she had decided she wanted Antoinette as her friend. Then she described what she had learned about her friend's poor family, and presented the list of plans she and Aymée had prepared. When she finished, everyone sat silently, continuing to look at her.

Her royal hackles raised and she demanded, "Well, what are your thoughts?"

Aymée thought, "There is that tone again. Jeanne has recognized who she is in this household."

Sir Duquesse cringed, thinking "What have I begun here with just one trip into town?"

Steward d'Izernay wanted to shout, "That is not the way we employ people to serve in the castle. They must have a letter of recommendation."

M. Bourbon just sat with his mouth open, like a turtle refusing to be drawn out of his shell fearing throngs of dirty urchins yelling and running in circles with no interest in an education.

They stared back at the Princess, respecting her command, however no one began to speak.

"Oh dear" Jeanne thought. "If no one will say anything, how can I know what they are thinking?" She watched the adults before her and could perceive their misgivings.

"So I must force them to at least play a pawn on their side of the board."

Studying each face, she finally settled on Sir Duquesse as her most reliable friend outside of Aymée. So she peered intently at Sir Duquesse and asked again, "Tell me what your thoughts are, Sir Duquesse, so I can cooperate with you in working out any problems."

His answer was short and direct. "Princess, what you observed on your trip to Tours was something very new to you. When the crowds cheered and recognized you, did you look closely at them? Did you see how varied they were dressed, as some were definitely poor, some were well dressed, and some were ragged and dirty? Do you remember?"

The Princess thought back to when the carriage first stopped in front of the mayor's offices, remembering the mass of people who had gathered there, nodded in agreement and said, "There were so many it all became a blur, except for Antoinette because I saw her up close and talked with her."

"Correct," said Sir Duquesse. "I must ask you to take time to fix your memory closely on what you saw and tell me if you could say that Tours is a great mixture of all sorts of people; many of them desperately poor. We are charged by King Francis, whose greatest desire is for your safety and wellbeing, to see every person as a threat. Granted, there may be only one bad apple in the whole town, or maybe not even that. Especially, after your conversation with Antoinette, I believe, with you, that she would not dream to hurt you."

At this point, the slight frown on Jeanne's face disappeared and her shoulders relaxed.

"My concern demands that I learn more about her parents, their circumstances and neighborhood, before I can even begin to allow you to make another trip into Tours. I do not disagree with your heart, Princess Jeanne, however King Francis is my ruler, and I could not consider even following up on your request without consulting the King for his permission. Can you possibly see the awkward position your plans will place me in?"

Jeanne listened intently, her exquisite eyes changing colors rapidly and then settling into a dark pool that could not be fathomed. The Library was very quiet as she considered all that he said. Eventually, she turned her eyes to her steward, M. d'Izernay, and pinned him to the chair with her gaze.

"M. d'Izernay, tell me what you think." Jeanne said.

She could see the steward's Adam's apple moving up and down rapidly as he swallowed several times before speaking.

Trying to sound in favor of the Princess's ideas without giving an inch of his grip on how he felt his position must be exercised, the steward cleared his throat and shifted in his chair.

"Your highness, we are committed here in the castle to take the utmost care in hiring people that are trustworthy, well-trained and are able to meet our high expectations. It is only because of that, we are so diligent in who we consider. Our employees come with multiple recommendations that are assiduously checked and reconfirmed. To offer Antoinette's father a post, simply because he is her father, will not maintain our high standards. At this time, I am not aware of any needs for more help anywhere about the castle."

A shadow crossed his eyes and he blinked several times, remembering that only this morning he had heard that both the kennel keeper and stable master had requested more help. He looked away from Jeanne's penetrating gaze and wondered to himself how dangerous it would be for him to consider the possibility of either of these posts. They were both low level positions, dealing mostly with cleaning up the refuse in the kennels and stables. He decided to keep it a secret, in case he found himself backed into a corner. In order to stay in the good graces of the King, M. d'Izernay had demanded that every position thus far, even the pooper-scoopers, required a recommendation. He had come from the staff at Fontainebleau and had conveniently dipped from the pool of employees there to fill many posts at Château Plessis. Only a few came from the surrounding countryside, and they had all worked for previous occupants of the castle and had existing documentation of their work records. He vowed he would not allow this child to manipulate his methodology.

"Not much chance she would be the one fired by the King!"

Jeanne had been observing the shadows and reactions of his thoughts as they passed across his eyes. She then saw that flicker of defiance. M. d'Izernay had always been respectful in an aloof, superior kind of way. His cooperation might be difficult but she would tackle it somehow.

Coming to M. Bourbon, the Princess looked at him fondly. They had been partners in the effort to educate her above normal expectations, which had been made difficult with the addition of Fauzio and Raymond.

She asked him gently, "M. Bourbon, my most excellent teacher, can we at least discuss possibilities for me to share the gift you have given me so generously with Antoinette? If only we could prepare her to be in a position to serve as a ladies maid in some way. Adding just one additional student, at least for now, to see how it goes?"

M. Bourbon smiled at her and responded, "I will be happy to explore that possibility with you, Princess."

With relief, Jeanne turned to Aymée who had an encouraging smile on her face. She spoke without being prompted and said, "Princess, I admire how you have listened closely to what each person has said to you. As you can see, there are many wrinkles we must iron out before proceeding. It is my responsibility to inform your mother, the Queen, and wait to receive her counsel and direction in this matter. She has much experience and wisdom in such efforts and I would encourage you to also seek her thoughts on what you have set your heart to do. However, I do not believe we would be committing any wrongdoing if we spoke to the Premier Chef after dinner. We should ask if there are any morsels left from dinner that could be sent home with a servant boy from Tours, to be delivered to Antoinette and her family, as a small gift for your conversation today.

"I must remind you that jealousy is a strong and often evil emotion that can result in unfortunate reactions. So I also must ask that you be patient in your desire to give away your dresses. You must choose carefully only one dress to send with the food packet tonight until we understand more about the circumstances Antoinette lives in. People can be most unpredictable when receiving gifts from someone who has abundance when they have so little. It is your responsibility to give freely and wisely. Your heart would break if the dress you choose would cause someone to think less of Antoinette if she wears it."

Immediately Jeanne remembered the pile of dresses full of satin and lace that she had pulled from her wardrobe. They were very pretty and she would love to see Antoinette in one of them; all of them, for that matter. She could understand how someone who played in the streets with the boys would be a little out of place in one of those dresses. After all, the streets of Tours were not clean and trim as were the paths and roads of Château Plessis. Jeanne recalled the mud and pile of trash; it was only one of many about the town. She then remembered seeing Antoinette out of the corner of her eye, digging in that trash as though looking for something. Her skin crawled and she shivered, realizing that if someone were hungry enough, they might be looking through another's waste to find food.

Aymée was absolutely right; she must send what would be most valuable to Antoinette and her family: food, something for the baby, and a plain dress for play for Antoinette. She grasped more clearly how a long term solution would fit the need so much better than frilly dresses.

She would write to her mother before bed, and also, a note to Antoinette even if she could not read it. She must see that food was sent after dinner. She reminded herself to also ask the Premier Chef to give the servant boy some provision for his own family so he would not be tempted to steal Antoinette's food.

20. Resentments

"And this I pray, that your love may abound still more
and more in real knowledge and all discernment, so
that you may approve the things that are excellent,
in order to be sincere and blameless until the day of
Christ; having been filled with the fruit of righteousness
which comes through Jesus Christ to the glory and
praise of God."

Philippians 1:9-11 (NASB)

Before dinner, Jeanne had a short bit of time to run up to her apartments and try to sort through the piles of satin and lace to find a dress from last summer, a cool cotton with little decoration. Finally, she found what she was looking for. It was sky blue with a pinched bodice and a ribbon around the waist to tie a bow in the back. It had short, puffed sleeves and two rows of ribbon binding around the bottom of the puffs. One ribbon was a creamy vanilla and the other a brighter blue that matched the ribbon around the waist. It had been among her clothes when they arrived from Nérac so she had worn it when she was only five years old. She was sure it would fit Antoinette and would not require tearing off any fancy frills. It had been one of her own favorites, and would be such a beautiful match to Antoinette's eyes. Jeanne laid it carefully on the bed so she could show it to Aymée for her approval. Then she dashed back down the stairs to join the others at the table.

Dinner conversation continued discussion about possibilities of helping citizens in need in Tours. Not many suggestions that were made survived the subsequent discussions.

Aymée went with her to see the Premier Chef. He was confused, at first, as to why Jeanne wanted the left-over food. Eventually, he understood; he then explained that the castle procedure normally used left-overs to prepare meals for the kitchen staff after dinner was served at the formal table. Finally, the Chef agreed to hold out enough for the family of three, plus some portions for the boy who would carry the meal to Antoinette's family. Jeanne began to see that the Chef was adept at allowing as little waste as possible to occur in the castle kitchens. Apparently his priority was to provide abundantly for those who were employed by the castle with what came from preparations for the royal table. That was a good policy for the castle. Sending emergency food and some clothes would only be a short term bandage.

Most of all, Antoinette's father needed a job. She must challenge M. d'Izernay again to find a place for him. Before leaving the Premier Chef, she reminded him of a need for something for the baby. He nodded and said he would send a boy out immediately to the barn to milk a goat.

Princess Jeanne then asked Aymée to help her find Sir Duquesse, and talk with him. She insisted that she needed to do everything she could to find Antoinette's father a job. Aymée agreed that Sir Duquesse would be the best to persuade M. d'Izernay to help. As they approached the Chamberlain's office, they could hear both Duquesse and d'Izernay in a heated discussion behind the closed door. Apparently, the subject was about Jeanne's request. When they knocked, the voices stopped abruptly. Sir Duquesse opened the door. His face was flushed, with bright pink spots on his cheekbones. Opening the door wide, the Chamberlain invited them into his office. M. d'Izernay was standing with his back toward them, breathing heavily.

Sir Duquesse said graciously, "Come in, your Highness. M. d'Izernay has just informed me that we may possibly have a job to offer Antoinette's father. It will require further inquiry into his work record and loyalties, which we will begin tomorrow."

M. d'Izernay turned slowly and bowed his head in agreement. He did not raise his eyes to look directly at the Princess. She could tell that he only acquiesced because he had no other choice. It was confusing to see that one member of her household might not be fully aligned with her. A warning registered in her heart to be more careful to discern the hearts of those around her.

Aymée and Princess Jeanne sat together in Jeanne's secret room before getting ready for bed that night. Jeanne shared with Aymée her confusion that M. d'Izernay seemed to be against helping Antoinette and her family.

Aymée listened closely and then said, "You must understand that many people care more about their own comfort and power and have little regard for others. M. d'Izernay wants to be in charge of his own job and resents any interference from someone else. People are often so caught up in their own selfish desires that they ignore others. Selfishness is a powerful force for evil. As with anyone in your service you must be aware of all that M. d'Izernay is doing by listening closely to his opinions and reports at your weekly meetings, just as a king must be aware of everyone in his castle and their motives, in case one of them desires to do harm to the King or his kingdom. Your Highness, because you are young does not mean you can ignore the signs around you. Be wise, be cautious, and be aware."

Jeanne shared with Aymée her desire to begin an opportunity for the children of the town to receive an education. She wished all the children could be brought to the castle for classes. Aymée applauded her thoughts but she doubted such an accommodation would be possible because it would require a considerable number of permissions from King Francis. Disappointed, Jeanne recognized that she might not be able to make a big difference in the lives of the children of Tours; at least not at this time.

Aymée happily approved Jeanne's choice of the blue dress so they wrapped it to be protected when the boy delivered it with the food. Jeanne asked Aymée to pray that the dress would be accepted for the friendship she offered and the food would be a blessing to the family. Knowing it would probably be a very long time before she would be allowed to go to Tours again, she wondered if Antoinette might be allowed to visit the castle, instead.

Jeanne could hardly settle down to sleep, she was so excited to hear how Antoinette and her family would receive the packets from the castle, and if the father would be able to come to the castle to work. Her mind was reeling with ideas and plans to see more of Antoinette.

As the various chores and duties were accomplished about the castle that evening, M. d'Izernay went about his nightly routine in the Great Hall and adjoining areas, checking that all candles had been snuffed and rooms were in order, before retiring for the night. Almost at each step, he thought of a new reason to argue against hiring a new man for the stables or kennels without following the usual procedures he had adopted for all prospective employees. How could he be asked to make such a decision without going through the proper channels? If push came to shove, he would see that this person, about whom he knew nothing, would fail. Then he could go through his normal process and hire someone properly. When M. d'Izernay had finished his rounds and returned to his private quarters, he immediately sat at his desk to write a letter to King Francis explaining what this willful child was asking him to do. He would nip this encroachment on his territory in the bud and show her who was in charge of the castle.

Aymée slipped down the stairs in search of Sir Duquesse after seeing that Jeanne was comfortably in bed. She wanted him to know how Jeanne had her heart set on seeing that Antoinette's father was employed. Her personal observation of M. d'Izernay's reluctance to consider finding an available position filled her with misgivings. It had not occurred to her before that he might hold some unreadable bitterness or resentment. She wanted to hear the Chamberlain's perspective on the matter.

Aymée found Sir Duquesse doing paperwork in his office. It was getting quite late and he was weary from the stresses of the day. Aymée waited patiently for him to finish the item in front of him and then she asked what had happened with his tense conversation with M. d'Izernay. She admitted her own misgivings that had surfaced that day.

Sir Duquesse rubbed his eyes with both hands and took a deep breath. He told Aymée that he had been quite surprised with M. d'Izernay's obstinate disapproval to even explore the subject. The steward had admitted a couple of positions, probably the most disagreeable jobs in the castle, had been brought to his attention that morning. Sir Duquesse had not been able to determine why he was so adamantly opposed to even consider the father.

He shook his head and said, "It was very confusing and we finally reached a hostile agreement to look into it tomorrow morning together. I plan to write the King and seek his approval for Princess Jeanne to go again into Tours and perhaps we can visit the girl together to see how true her story is. The packet was sent this evening and I am anxious to hear the report from the servant boy who delivered the items, before we leave in the morning. I am hoping this entire episode can be settled without repercussions and we can continue in our normal routine."

Aymée left the Chamberlain's office a bit discouraged for it seemed such a simple solution to hire the man to sweep out the stables. However, if this became a sore point of contention for the steward, she would not like to see an increase in his resentment against the Princess. She began to explore other possibilities in her mind of alternate ways to help the family. Aymée could understand the Princess's desire to offer, not just Antoinette's family, but all the very poor of Tours, a way to help them out of poverty. Before climbing into bed, she prayed for wisdom to find a solution to all the different issues that had come about. Aymée also gave thanks that Jeanne's focus had been redirected to another's need and not her own depression.

21. Deliverance

*"Casting all your anxiety upon Him, because He
cares for you."*

1 Peter 5:7 (NASB)

Lying in the dark, Antoinette dozed fitfully until she heard footsteps. Many footsteps it seemed; at least, she was sure it was
more than one person. She crawled deep into her hiding place as
silently as she could. It didn't help that her stomach was growling
so loud it sounded like thunder in her ears. Now it was apparent
someone was running up to their door. Antoinette shut her eyes
and curled up into a tight ball, as small as she could be, hoping the
dark would keep her from being discovered. Suddenly, the baskets
went helter-skelter, tossed aside, and when she opened her eyes a
crack, cringing against a possible blow, she saw her Mumsie's face.
She was smiling!

Mumsie pulled Antoinette out into the light and laughed and
cried at the same time as she explained that a servant boy from the
Château had brought a package to their house and said the Princess
was sending a thank you for Antoinette showing her friendship.

Mumsie wiped tears from her face and tore into the package
of food. First, she removed the container of goat's milk, and then
the small packets filled with roast pheasant, potatoes, carrots, and
herbs. It was a meal fit for a king, and here it was, on their very own
table. There was a whole loaf of bread wrapped separately, with

several pats of butter in a small bowl. The bread was still warm, freshly baked, with a fragrance that permeated the entire room. Last, a wrapper with several slices of chocolate cake. Mumsie just stared at the pieces of cake in disbelief, slowly reaching out to scoop a bit of frosting and touch it to her tongue.

Then Mumsie noticed that another packet, flatter than the first, was under the paper wrapping the food. It was written very plainly on the outside, "For Antoinette."

Antoinette was afraid to take it; she could not imagine what might be in this package for her. Encouraged by the servant boy from the castle, and Mumsie and Dads, she began to peel back the paper revealing the most beautiful blue dress she had ever seen. She stared down at her ragged clothes and then back to the lovely dress. Antoinette hugged the dress to her breast as tears began running down her face, streaking the smudges of dirt on her cheeks.

There was a small note sitting on top of the dress. Dads could read. He had learned at his other job, before the accident, so she handed it to him.

He read, "Thank you for talking to me today. I thought you might like this color of blue because it matches your beautiful eyes. Your friend, Princess Jeanne d'Albret of Navarre."

Mumsie turned to hug the young boy from the castle and thanked him again. Dads shook his hand and slapped him on the back and said, "You are a fine young boy, and we are most grateful for the generosity of the castle! Please tell them of our sincere thanks." Dads kept pumping the boy's hand as he walked him from the house. The boy headed down the path to his home while Dads just kept saying "Thank you!" over and over until the boy was out of sight.

When he returned to the kitchen, Mumsie was warming the goat's milk at the stove. She flew to Dads and clasped his hands laughing and swinging about the kitchen.

Antoinette stared, not knowing what to think, but the aroma of the freshly baked bread made her mouth water and her stomach growl again. At last, Mumsie pulled plates from the kitchen cabinet and began dividing up the food among four plates. They always shared whatever food they found with the widow lady next door.

Mrs. Croix was quite elderly and depended on their generosity to eat. Antoinette knew that Dads had sometimes given his portion to Mrs. Croix so she would have a more substantial share. He always said he was thankful to give to someone less fortunate than he was.

Antoinette returned from delivering the plate to the Widow Croix. Before the family sat down to eat, Mumsie cut the loaf of bread and rewarded Antoinette with the first buttered slice. Dads bowed his head to pray a thanksgiving over the food they were about to eat. Each of their hearts was genuinely humbled, knowing God had indeed placed this food before them in answer to their pleas. There was more than enough to satisfy their hunger. They ate the cake very slowly, savoring each bite of the precious chocolate. Mumsie cleared the table, carefully wrapped up any leftovers and stored them away. She handled the fresh bread as if it were gold, wrapping it in several layers of paper and stored it in the cabinet so their hunger would be delayed, at least for tomorrow.

The baby had gulped the warmed goat's milk hungrily, and after watching him closely for some time, they all agreed that his stomach had taken it well. After a bit of time, Mumsie fed him again. She laughed softly and nuzzled his downy hair, delighted that he might sleep through the night with a full tummy. Even Dads smiled as they sat at the table, marveling at their good fortune and asking Antoinette to repeat her encounter with the Princess again and again.

Antoinette and her parents stared in wonder at the blue dress for a long time. Antoinette was a friend of the Princess. It was amazing. Then Antoinette asked, "Mumsie, may I take a bath and wash my hair before I see if it will fit me? I can use the leftover rinse water from the laundry."

"Absolutely not," Dads exclaimed. "I will haul fresh water myself for the friend of the Princess."

Immediately, he jumped up and raced to get the bucket. Antoinette could see tears on his cheeks. She was still so shocked and amazed at this turn-around in her day she couldn't move. Then Mumsie turned to Antoinette and said, "Come here, my little friend of the Princess, and let me hold your dress while you get ready for your bath."

Of course, the dress fit, needing only a few tucks here and there to make it just right. Mumsie hunted for her needle and thread and had it sewn right up. It was beautiful on Antoinette, bringing out the brilliant blue of her eyes.

22. Encouragement

"If therefore there is any encouragement in Christ,
if there is any consolation of love, if there is
any fellowship of the Spirit, if any affection and
compassion, make my joy complete by being of the
same mind, maintaining the same love, united in
spirit, intent on one purpose."

Philippians 2:1-2 (NASB)

T he report brought by the servant boy was favorable. The family was surprised and overwhelmed by the delivery of food. When Antoinette opened the packet with the dress, everyone had looked at him in wide-eyed disbelief and could not believe the beautiful Princess had sent her such a wonderful gift. They profusely thanked the boy over and over. Antoinette had hugged the dress to her breast and had tears streaming down her cheeks when the boy left.

Sir Duquesse and M. d'Izernay left the castle to go into Tours about mid-morning. While Princess Jeanne worked in the Library on her lessons, Aymée walked to the stables to speak with the stable master. She needed to discuss with him what he expected from the person who would be hired to help at the stables. She also wanted to alert him that he would more than likely be approached by Princess Jeanne later when she came for riding lessons. It seemed only fair to give him a full accounting of how he had suddenly become an essential part of the decision to be made.

Pierre, the stable master, was in his middle-fifties and had spent his entire life caring for the King's horses at Fontainebleau. His love of horses drew him to work at the stables when still a young man. The skill gained from so many years of caring for horses and keeping them healthy moved him to the honored position of stable master. Pierre was a quiet, mild-mannered man whose whole world centered on his horses. Aymée hoped to reveal the heart of the Princess to him, so he would be receptive to the introduction of a man who may not even have experience with horses, into his stable. Pierre just chuckled, deep in his chest with a low rumble, and said he had started in that same position many years ago.

23. Salvage

*"Let not your heart be troubled; believe in God, believe
also in Me."*

John 14:1 (NASB)

Two men and three castle guards made their way through the
winding streets of the poor section of town. M. d'Izernay had
pulled a handkerchief from his pocket and covered his nose to alleviate the stench from the trash heaps and puddles of muddy water.
He walked with his head down, picking his way among the mud
holes and litter that lay everywhere. Tip-toeing to keep his polished
shoes from the mud, he looked as though he were a silly ballerina.
Sir Duquesse and the guards wore boots and strode ahead with purpose. The noise of their feet preceded their arrival at Antoinette's
home. Mumsie was standing at the front door, holding the baby;
however, Antoinette was nowhere to be seen. This house was different from the rest, with windows washed and the yard and step
swept clean. Even a straggled wildflower was struggling to stay
alive in a cracked pot on the doorstep.

Mumsie's eyes were wide with fear, and she stood in front
of the door as if blocking any entry. Sir Duquesse swept his hat
off and bowed low in greeting. He had seen the fear in the woman's eyes and did not want to prolong her anxiety. M. d'Izernay
was several yards behind, still picking his way down the path. Sir
Duquesse proceeded to introduce both of them, regardless that M.

d'Izernay was not beside him yet. Then he asked if the man of the house were present.

Mumsie's eyes shifted from one to the other, and then to where the guards were standing. Turning back to Sir Duquesse, she said, "My husband is out looking for work at one of the large homes across Tours. If he is not successful," and here Mumsie took a deep breath and lowered her head, "he will most likely make his way back here for some lunch. We are so grateful to the Princess and the castle for the generous provisions we received last night; we can never begin to say how much."

Sir Duquesse nodded in response. As M. d'Izernay finally appeared at his side, the Chamberlain asked, "Is there hope that Mademoiselle Antoinette is here? Princess Jeanne will be most anxious to hear that we have found her friend and can report she is doing well."

Mumsie hesitated a moment, looking back and forth at the two men, weighing the possibility they might grab Antoinette and take her in custody. Then she turned toward the house and in a low voice, called for Antoinette to come to her.

Antoinette crawled from her hiding place and cautiously walked to her mother, who immediately put her arm protectively around Antoinette's shoulders. The girl kept her eyes lowered, afraid to look up at the men. Dressed in ragged, but clean clothes, her golden hair glistened in the morning sunlight. Mumsie had braided it that morning, and the long braid fell over Antoinette's shoulder and almost reached her waist.

Sir Duquesse took a step closer and extended his hand, saying "The Princess was quite right, you are a beautiful girl and just the right age to be a friend." As Antoinette reached out her hand, she looked up at Sir Duquesse and gave him an embarrassed smile. She did have the most beautiful, bright, blue eyes.

At this remark, Mumsie asked if they would please come inside for a cup of tea. The confusion of her emotions had caused her to forget her manners. The baby was sleeping in her arms, so she laid him in his cradle as she entered the house. Antoinette followed closely behind her and ran to the kitchen to pull the tea kettle from the back of the stove onto the heat. The room was small, with few chairs, so Mumsie offered the three around the table so they might sit down.

Sir Duquesse looked about the room, trying to get an understanding of what kind of man lived there. Mumsie kept her home immaculate although the small size did not offer much storage, so there were makeshift boxes about that had been converted to household furniture. Through the door on the other side of the wood-burning stove, there were several baskets, and a clothesline hung with dozens of drying clothes. Apparently, from the appearance of such a variety of sizes and styles, these clothes did not belong to the family. Mumsie must be taking in laundry to make money for food. That was a good sign.

M. d'Izernay was still trying not to touch anything as if he were afraid he might catch something. He held himself tightly and stood stiffly in the middle of the small room. Suddenly he said, "Do you think your husband will return soon?" Mumsie looked at him as if he were daft as she had just explained that she was not sure when her husband would return. "Soon, I hope," she replied.

The kettle began to sing, and Mumsie pulled the tea box from the shelf, along with the teapot. She dumped the contents of the tea box into the teapot. It was not much. They had carefully rationed the remaining tea, loathe to see it disappear as there was no money to buy more. This pot would be very weak tea, and she was embarrassed to serve it to guests. She was also disconcerted because now there would be no tea for Dads when he finally came home tonight. It was the one luxury they both treasured because it gave them hope that someday they would not have to live so meagerly. As she poured hot water into the teapot, she apologized in her heart to Dads that she would have no tea for him tonight. Then she hunted through her cabinet in search of sugar. Nothing there. She called Antoinette and whispered for her to ask if the Widow Croix had any sugar. Antoinette ran out the back door while Mumsie heated a bit of the precious goat's milk if someone wanted milk for their tea.

Antoinette returned a few moments later with a small, half-full container of the Widow's prized sugar. Whispering to her mother, Antoinette said that all the neighbors were peering out their windows at the guards in front of their house and the Widow Croix had tried to find out what was happening before she gave up her sugar. Mumsie nodded; she was certain no one was more curious about the reason for this visit than she and Antoinette were.

Setting the teacups and teapot on the table, Mumsie asked Antoinette to bring the container of sugar and a pitcher of milk. Antoinette stood at her shoulder, and M. d'Izernay reluctantly sat in the only remaining chair, perched like an anxious bird on a window sill. Mumsie was facing the door at the front of the house and saw Dads running down the path toward her. She whispered to Antoinette to bring another cup to the table. Smiling, Mumsie said she could see her husband coming. It would be a relief, she thought, to be able to share the burden of being hospitable to these strangers.

As the soldiers and men from the castle first made their way down the street to the Abérnois house, boys from the neighborhood had run as fast as they could to find him in the work line, waiting and hoping his name would be called. When they told him two men from the castle were at his house, he had come at once. As Dads burst through the door, he stopped at the sight of the men sitting at his table. Seeing the guards outside had raised his fears another level. Was there a problem with receiving the packets the night before? What other trouble could be camping at their doorstep now?

His hair was falling in his eyes, and he was sweating from running so far. He had not shaved for several days because he got up so early in the dark morning to be at the front of the work line. This morning he had been determined to have a chance to work. He had vowed that never would he let his family get so hungry again. They had tasted real food last night, and his heart had broken that he had allowed them to reach such a point of starvation. His face was puffy and red from all the tears he had shed during the night, and he was out of breath from running.

The men at the table looked at him, and he could see the disgust in the eyes of one at his appearance. It is obvious, he thought, these men had no concept of what could bring a man so low when circumstances sped out of control. Squaring his shoulders, he extended his hand and welcomed the men to his humble home.

Sir Duquesse was a bit dismayed at the appearance of the man approaching; however, he certainly deserved credit for having the courtesy to greet them politely. It was immediately clear that he had an injured arm as his left hand hung lifelessly at his side. M. d'Izernay merely nodded and did not shake the man's hand. His glance said it all; he saw the lifeless arm and unkempt appearance and gloated that he saw just what he had expected, a beggar and a bum.

Sir Duquesse rose to his feet, asked the man his name and suggested they step outside for a conversation. Leaving the front door, the Chamberlain intentionally chose the muddiest spot on the path to stop and turn to M. Abérnois to talk. M. d'Izernay stood farther away in order not to dirty his shoes.

With the small amount of privacy that was afforded by this arrangement, Sir Duquesse spoke quietly and asked some pertinent questions about his ability to work and if he felt he could journey from Tours to the castle every day if there were a position for him there. M. Abérnois humbly said he thought he could and would do any job that might be available and would not mind the three to four-mile walk every morning and evening. Many of the townspeople did just that. His heart was beating so fast at the possibility of finally going to work; he could not breathe. How had this even happened? The food last night and then this visit this morning coming out of the blue; overcome with apprehension that everything would evaporate if he blinked his eyes, he forced himself to breathe slowly.

M. d'Izernay selected spots on the path that were a bit drier than the rest to move up closer to hear the conversation. When he heard Sir Duquesse ask if M. Abérnois would be agreeable to coming back to the castle to visit with the stable master about the job of a stable hand, M. d'Izernay angrily spoke up in disagreement. He insisted on the importance of contacting work references before this man could set foot on the castle grounds.

Sir Duquesse dismissed the steward's remarks with a wave of his hand and suggested they make their way to the carriage waiting outside the neighborhood. M. Abérnois stepped to the front door of his house to tell Mumsie what he was doing. She slipped a small wrapped package of leftovers in his pants pocket since she

knew he had not eaten at all that morning. Cold pheasant and potatoes would still be edible even if he couldn't eat it until walking
home that night. She softly caressed Dads' face to encourage him
before he left.

Turning to Antoinette, Mumsie said, "Hurry Sis, we must get as
much of the laundry done as possible so I can return it to its owners.
Perhaps someone might agree to let me have some of their oldest
pieces so Dads will be better dressed to work at the castle. Oh Lord,
I beg you to let this opportunity come to fruit."

In the carriage on the way to the castle, M. d'Izernay angrily
stared at the passing countryside and composed in his mind
another letter he would most definitely send to the King about the
Chamberlain's refusal to allow him to interview this man properly.
Who was in charge of castle staff after all?

After lunch, as Jeanne prepared to go to the stables for her afternoon riding lessons, the sound of the carriage returning from town
could be heard outside. Jeanne finished pulling on her riding boots
and dashed down the stairs, nearly tripping on Sir Ami as he raced
alongside her. She was most anxious to hear how the morning had
gone for Sir Duquesse and M. d'Izernay. She nearly collided with
M. d'Izernay as he barged through the door of the castle leading
to the stables. He only acknowledged that he had almost knocked
her down with a quick bow and then turned quickly to continue
moving toward his office. Jeanne watched his back disappearing
down the hall and considered he was either very angry or perhaps
feeling sick. That was not a promising omen.

Approaching the stables, Jeanne saw a man standing beside
Sir Duquesse, talking with the stable master. She slowed her steps
and strolled up to the group, listening intently to the conversation taking place. The men turned toward her as she moved nearer,
each, in turn, making a bow to acknowledge her presence. She
nodded in return and looked inquiringly at Sir Duquesse. At the
same time, she saw that the stranger had a mangled left arm that
appeared to have recently healed without regaining strength. No
wonder Antoinette's family was in such discouraging conditions.

Princess Jeanne held out her hand, expecting an introduction.
Sir Duquesse stepped forward and said, "Princess Jeanne, this is

Monsieur Abérnois, Mademoiselle Antoinette's father. He is here to discuss a possible position with the stable master."

The wide smile of the Princess revealed her approval. As the Princess inquired how the baby was doing and if the dress had fit Antoinette, M. Abérnois bowed and expressed his profound appreciation for his family, and yes, the baby had been able to digest the goat's milk and was quite greedy for more.

Leaving M. Abérnois and Pierre to finish their conversation, Sir Duquesse, Princess Jeanne and Sir Ami moved into the stable where her mount was saddled. The Princess motioned for Sir Duquesse to bend nearer and whispered, "Don't you think we should send the goat home with M. Abérnois so the baby will have enough milk all the time?"

Sir Duquesse was startled by the suggestion and agreed it should be done. He chided himself that he hadn't come up with the idea.

He answered, "I will inquire immediately if that will be possible. It will depend on the needs of the castle concerning the production of that particular goat. I agree it is a good idea and will most certainly look into it immediately."

Jeanne mounted the saddle of her horse, waved to M. Abérnois and Pierre, and called to Sir Ami to come along as she rode out to the forest path. The guards were waiting and followed after her.

Pierre asked M. Abérnois if he believed his left arm would be strong enough to shovel the dirty straw out of the horse stalls. M. Abérnois answered that he was sure he was strong enough to do the job and was dependable and trustworthy. Pierre clapped him on the back and told him where to find the shovel, broom, pitchfork, and the fresh straw.

As Pierre turned to leave, M. Abérnois dropped to his knees and bent his head in prayer. Pierre glanced back and felt that his thankfulness was an excellent sign. The dependability and trustworthiness would say volumes about his character, as would the actions and attitudes of the horses in the stable. Pierre felt the horses would have the final say about whether the new man would be allowed to stay. Horses had a keen sense of the heart of a man and were excellent judges of a man's inner spirit.

Pierre went about his duties, watching M. Abérnois out of the corner of his eye. He had some difficulty balancing the first few shovels of the dirty straw. Eventually, with repeated efforts, he mastered the right angle of his arm to support the shovel.

He appeared to be a hard worker and went from stall to stall without stopping to lean against the side of the stall gate and gaze around the barn at the horses. He did not walk to the bucket for a drink of water or to find some conversation. Pierre watched as he finished the stalls and found a broom to sweep out the rest of the barn. As he passed the stalls, checking over the sides, Pierre was pleased to see what a competent job he had done. Also, observing M. Abérnois' way of working around the horses, he noticed how kindly and gently he petted and spoke to each one. Pierre felt sure that M. Abérnois had previous experience around horses, but had not spoken of it. Perhaps, Abérnois did not believe what he had done before his injury was essential to the job he had now. He had little to say about the accident that had injured his arm so severely; only that he had been working for one of the noble families in the area and had been careless. That had been several months before as his recovery had been long and debilitating.

When Princess Jeanne returned from her afternoon ride, Abérnois stopped what he was doing and helped with brushing down her horse. The Princess whistled as she turned toward the castle and Sir Ami leaped to join her.

As he watched the girl and her dog return to the castle, M. Abérnois was overwhelmed with gratitude for her unassuming desire to give him a second chance to begin his life again. He would devote himself to her in any way he could and felt it was an honor to serve her by just cleaning out the stables. His arm throbbed with the unaccustomed activity. He rubbed the muscles and looked around to see if there was something else he could find to do. He decided, after seeing the beautiful dog that accompanied the Princess, that he would walk over to the kennels to see the King's hunting hounds.

M. d'Izernay continued to stew in his office after returning from Tours. He had posted his message to the King earlier and now replayed in his mind the arguments he could have presented against the hiring of the one-armed man. It was too bad he had not known about that injury before writing to the King. It would have been an additional point to bolster his arguments. Sir Duquesse had pulled a fast one on him by arranging for Pierre to meet the beggar without consulting him first. Now, he could just imagine that the soft-hearted stable master would give the man a chance, even with that injured arm. Disgusted with the whole affair, M. d'Izernay began to shuffle the papers on his desk attempting to find something else to occupy his thoughts. A soft knock on the door caused his hands to freeze above the documents. That knock meant only one thing – the Princess was outside his door!

Princess Jeanne entered the steward's office and began thanking him profusely for giving M. Abérnois a chance. She complimented him for his excellent judgment in allowing Pierre to evaluate his capabilities given his damaged arm. The Princess was extremely proud that so many individuals in the castle had given their help and heartfelt support to accomplish her desire to help this family in need. She also told him she planned to write to her uncle, King Francis, how helpful and willing her steward had been to accomplish the opportunity for M. Abérnois to work to support his family adequately.

M. d'Izernay did not say a word, knowing that he had not agreed with the Princess' desire to help lift this man out of poverty. He merely bowed low and thanked the Princess for an opportunity to assist. He just wanted her to leave his office. His knowledge that his intentions had been such a contrast to her compliments made him increasingly uncomfortable.

Sir Duquesse was in the kitchen asking the Premier Chef about arranging for M. Abérnois to take the milk goat home with him to Tours. The Chef was reluctant as he used goat's milk in his gourmet dishes. Eventually, after speaking directly with the goat herder for the Château, it was decided that M. Abérnois should milk the goat before going home each night to bring his family, especially the baby, fresh milk, but leave the goat at the castle. Sir Duquesse had determined in his mind that he would not say anything to M. d'Izernay. He was sure the steward would consider the milk a legitimate deduction in M. Abérnois' salary. Such pernicious accounting procedures were beneath the tradition of a royal palace.

Sir Duquesse was already in conflict with M. d'Izernay over hiring this stable hand and there most certainly would be aggravation if the steward heard M. Abérnois was receiving special considerations. This matter had created a hazardous split in castle staff with M. d'Izernay in opposition with everyone else. It was a dangerous situation, and Sir Duquesse was familiar with how hard feelings could evolve. He made a note to discuss the conflict with Aymée and M. Bourbon; he intended to keep the Premier Chef aware of any possible contradicting orders from the steward. It required a delicate touch to avoid deepening the divide to a chasm of argument and disagreement. Duquesse had heard of other castles with similar conflicts and had lost too many staff members to continue to operate. It could become equivalent to a civil war within one household. What a disaster that would be for his career, and for the successful position of Princess Jeanne as mistress of Château de Plessis lez Tours representing the King of France,

Sir Duquesse laid out his dilemma to Aymée and M. Bourbon. They both had similarly been surprised with Steward d'Izernay's responses to Princess Jeanne's wishes. An agreement was immediate to explore every possible effort to reassure M. d'Izernay of the successful accomplishments of his duties and, at the same time, to encourage him to join in support of Princess Jeanne's efforts to meet the needs of the citizens in Tours.

24. Conclusions

"Do not merely look out for your own personal interests,
but also for the interests of others."

Philippians 2:4 (NASB)

K ing Francis sat in his private quarters at the Castle of
Fontainebleau. His desk sat beside the open casement windows
leading onto the balcony. The King loved these early morning hours
when the breeze was fresh and the pastel colors of the dawn of a new
day spread across the vast garden below. It was the King's custom
to have his breakfast on the balcony and then to read incoming
correspondence in preparation for planning the course of his day.

Resting on the desk before him were two letters, both of vital
interest to him. One was a letter from the steward at Château de
Plessis lez Tours describing what appeared to be rebellious thoughts
toward Princess Jeanne's oversight of his responsibilities in the
hiring of a stable grunt, admittedly the lowest position of castle
staff. The King was irritated that the steward considered such an
ignominious position even a subject of debate, much less a need
for the King's attention.

The other message was written carefully in a most beautiful
script from the hand of his adored niece, Princess Jeanne. This
message expressed compliments and appreciation for the assistance of her castle steward in helping a man she had brought to his
attention for a lowly job at the stables. The two letters were such

a contrast that the King pondered what hidden meaning might be brewing behind the apparent subjects of each.

As the King turned the contents of the letters over in his mind, he remembered permitting Sir Duquesse to take the Princess on an outing to Tours. He had heard nothing more until these letters came on the same day. It was a surprising turn of events, and his curiosity was aroused about what caused the conflict. It had been too long since he had visited Château de Plessis and decided to take a trip soon and see for himself how the matter was indeed evolving. Plus, his royal antennae sensed difficulty from this matter projecting into similar disputes regarding Jeanne's accession to the throne of Navarre. That could undermine his plans for her life. First, however, he must write to this pompous steward and remind him that his continuing occupation as steward of the Château de Plessis depended on the loyalty and service he provided to the Princess. He would tolerate no objection to the wishes of Princess Jeanne, at least in any aspect of the Princess' representation of the King. In this case, Princess Jeanne was caring for the citizens of France, and that was indeed representing the King of France. As he wrote, the King determined this steward should consider the King's response as notice of a probation period of his employment.

Upon finishing that bit of correspondence, the King signaled his Chamberlain to begin calling in the individual supplicants waiting in the antechamber for an audience with the King.

25. Consequences

"Yet those who wait for the Lord will gain new strength."

Isaiah 40:31 (NASB)

M. d'Izernay's position as steward required his evaluation of how well M. Abérnois completed the requirements of a stable hand and his salary. Usually, the steward would consult with Pierre for his opinion, as the stable master was overseer of anyone associated with the stables. He trusted Pierre's opinion and seldom found the reason to go further than what he heard from the stable master. This time, however, he listened to such glowing reports that M. d'Izernay determined to see for himself how the half-cripple could be adequately accomplishing what he was expected to do.

M. d'Izernay took a leisurely walk about the grounds of the castle to gaze casually at the gardens, the pig pens, and goat enclosures; he talked briefly with the sheepherder and inspected the ewes coming into lambing season, then, walked over to the hunting dog kennels. Here he stopped, impressed with the cleanliness of the kennels, the dog yards, and the well-groomed hunting hounds. He certainly had not seen this area in such orderly shape since the animals had arrived. Why, he wondered, had the kennel master requested additional help? He had everything in tip-top condition.

Then he strolled toward the stables. Every stall had clean, fresh straw and full feed bins. Most stalls were empty because this was the time of morning when the horses exercised in the round arena outside the back of the barn. He looked into the tack room where no dust had gathered on the work table, and every harness and saddle hung in order under placards of the names of the horses. The saddles gleamed with polish as the dust mites danced in the sunbeams pouring through the windows. The walkways around the barn were swept; buckets and implements hung in the proper places.

Continuing out of the back of the barn, he found Pierre and M. Abérnois brushing down a horse recently washed for grooming. Of the horses in the roundabout, many appeared to have previously been groomed, with others waiting their turn.

M. d'Izernay cocked a raised eyebrow and asked Pierre if he could speak to him privately a moment. M. Abérnois continued brushing the horse's mane after a respectful nod at the steward. Running his eyes up and down the man, M. d'Izernay realized why he looked so different. The man had bathed, shaved and had his hair cut. He was wearing worn, but clean clothes without the rips and holes of the day of his hiring. He was whistling and humming as he brushed the horse. There was such a dramatic difference in his current demeanor of a hard worker who was enjoying his job, compared to that first day when he had ridden with them from Tours, a ragged, dirty, ungroomed and shifty-eyed beggar. M. d'Izernay stared; this man did not even look disabled. He handled his right hand so efficiently his left hand was not noticeably unusable. He braced against the horse with his left shoulder as adequately as any man did with a whole arm.

Pierre cleared his throat to call the steward's attention back to his initial purpose of the visit. They walked into the stable master's small office. A steaming pot, ready for tea, was bubbling on the small brazier by the open window. The heat and steam were wafting into the outside breeze. As Pierre prepared two cups of tea, he asked the steward what brought him to the stables?

M. d'Izernay formed his words carefully and asked, "Are the improvements I see around the barn and stables a result of hiring M. Abérnois?"

Pierre responded, "I have given you reports almost every day. He is diligent, trustworthy, hardworking, and goes about his tasks as if he considers the barn his responsibility. This man works well with others and is eager to assist in every job. When he can find no other work to do, he doesn't nap on the hay bales; he goes to the dog kennels and sweeps, picks up the dog refuse and washes the dogs. I don't believe I have ever seen a hired man who is so willing to do the dirtiest or most difficult job required, regardless of his disability. Best worker I ever had."

M. d'Izernay sat silently sipping his tea, mulling over what he was hearing. So, this man was a good hire, even without all those recommendations he thought were necessary. He thanked Pierre for his time and walked back to his office. There he made notes of what he had observed.

26. Dismissed

"That He would grant you, according to the riches of His glory, to be strengthened with power through His Spirit in the inner man;"

Ephesians 3:16 (NASB)

Leaves on the trees began to turn red and orange indicating the arrival of autumn. Princess Jeanne watched for her Uncle Francis, the King of France, to make a trip to hunt in the forests around the Château de Plessis. He loved a challenging stag hunt and would use the excuse to organize a hunt after he inquired about the Princess. As years passed, Jeanne, approaching eight years of age, began to develop an awareness of her Uncle's motives and goals. He doted on anyone who showed their love for him. As King, he also planned and schemed how someone who was loyal and loved him could be used to further his personal goals.

Princess Jeanne knew that her uncle truly loved her, nearly as much as he did his devoted sister, Jeanne's mother. Unfortunately, Bishop du Châtel shared his personal opinion with Aymée when thinking his remarks could not be heard, saying "the King of France views Jeanne as an excellent political tool in negotiating with foreign powers. She is on the auction block as a marriageable virgin, if the right country desires to select her as consort to a royal heir."

The Bishop's words were a wound in her heart as she stepped back in the Library to allow them to finish their conversation. "Is that what I am here for?' Jeanne asked herself. The story of King Louis XI's nine-year-old bride was never far from her thoughts. Questions crowded through her mind. "Have I endured so much pain to then be sold like chattel? How could Uncle Francis care for me and use me just for that purpose? What is love that it can harm someone for the benefit of someone stronger?" In a deep place in her heart, she knew it was possible, and she instinctively rebelled. Drawing the walls of self-protection more firmly around her, she determined to express her refusal in any way she could.

Going immediately upstairs to her secret room, she pondered how to live with that knowledge and still maintain her old relationship with her uncle, wanting desperately to believe that he genuinely did care for her.

Jeanne wanted to share with the King about her efforts in Tours. Aymée and her ladies-in-waiting, together, had worked hard to reconstruct all of Jeanne's outgrown garments, by stripping lace, pearls and velvet trims from dresses of sturdy fabric to pass them out among the little girls in the poorer sections of Tours. It became evident that the King had other matters on his mind and for his enjoyment. He was pleased Jeanne had found productive activities to fill her days.

Regardless of her uncle's lack of interest, Jeanne lavishly provided many dresses to be given to Antoinette although she was not allowed to return to Tours to see her in person. When the castle staff heard what she was doing, many had donated their clothes, bringing handfuls of garments for boys, men, and ladies, as well.

Jeanne had even learned to sew to be able to help with the mending and trimming. Many evenings were spent in her apartments, entertained by listening to the ladies-in-waiting gossip about the romances brewing in the castle or what they recently heard from town. She became better acquainted with Phoebe, Maddie, and Chloe as they told their stories.

Widowed at an early age, Phoebe now was in her mid-twenties. Accomplished at playing the pianoforte, she had a pleasant alto voice.

Maddie was a big-boned, big breasted Dutch girl who had worked in many different castles. Her background was somewhat foggy as she preferred not to speak about it. Almost twenty-nine years old, men had misused her at other villas and she came to Château de Plessis seeking safety and steady work. It seemed that the ladies of those other castles had dismissed her immediately on discovering their man's indiscretions. Quiet and shy, Maddie played the flute so beautifully that Jeanne was sure she found an outlet for her emotions in the music.

Chloe had come from Tuscany, brought up at the castle where her mother was employed. She was very petite with a clear olive complexion. Her versatile, strong voice was pitch-perfect. She loved to sing, accompanying herself on the mandolin.

As they tired of the sewing, they gathered in the corner to play and sing softly. Jeanne remembered her mother's apartments at Nérac, and her thoughts swept her away in loneliness.

Jeanne knew that Antoinette's family was well provided. She often exchanged messages with Antoinette by passing her notes to M. Abérnois when she went riding in the warm October days. It had been almost three months since she had met Antoinette and tried, in every way she could suggest, either her to be allowed to visit Antoinette in Tours or enable Antoinette to come to the castle occasionally. No one considered her requests possible.

King Francis had written that he wanted her to accompany him on some of the hunts when he arrived in the fall, so her riding and hunting lessons had been stepped up, to be ready when he came.

She loved galloping through the crisp fall weather where on occasion she would see a majestic stag standing still in the trees before dashing away; sometimes seemingly becoming invisible as quickly as a blink of her eyes. It seemed to her that the stunning animal belonged in the woods more than she did. He was master of the forest and she an intruder. She could not imagine killing such a magnificent creature just for fun. In that regard, she was a woman. She preferred to let the men in her life provide meat for the table. Though it was beautiful to enjoy eating the bounty of the hunt; she was not interested in participating in the gory killing of it.

When King Francis had come and gone, Princess Jeanne felt lonelier than before. The whirlwind of his visit had been constant with activities every moment of the day. They hardly had time to talk together. He commended her for her efforts to help the people of Tours and remarked that she was an excellent representative for him. Disappointment dismayed Jeanne when he showed no interest in learning more about Antoinette or their friendship. He merely dismissed the thought that a Princess should have a commoner for a friend.

At one moment when they walked together to the stables, the King asked Jeanne her thoughts about the job M. d'Izernay was doing as the steward. Startled that he would ask, Princess Jeanne repeated her appreciation for his help in hiring M. Abérnois as stable hand, however when she tried to tell more about the family the King turned his attention elsewhere. The usual formal dinners abounded, and the Bishop celebrated Mass again, with all the attending ceremonies.

The Premier Chef confided to Jeanne that he had again sent leftover abundance to Tours for the Abérnois to share with their neighbors. With all the guests served in the castle, there were more leftovers than the staff could consume. They even provided a small cart to M. Abérnois to push home since he could not have carried it all.

The stag hunt was successful. When Jeanne asked the King's permission to leave when the animal was shot, he looked sternly at her and admonished her that at some point she must expect to stay until the end. He then appointed several guards to accompany her back to the castle. Jeanne knew she had disappointed the King. She tried to believe, as she grew older, she would be more willing to watch the majestic animal butchered. In her heart, she knew she would not be able to stay until the end. After all, her mother had disappointed the King for many years because she would not go hunting with him.

At their parting, Jeanne asked the King if he would allow her to travel again to Tours. She told him she would prefer to ride alone by horseback with just a couple of guards to accompany her. She felt she could represent her King better if she could move among the citizens of Tours and show a friendly, kind spirit. He held her eyes for a long moment, and then said he would write to her to let her know his decision. Then he mounted his horse and led the traveling party and all its baggage carts away.

Jeanne considered it hopeful that he had contemplated her request long enough to say he would write his answer. At least she had not received a quick, negative response. Perhaps her friendship with Antoinette would renew somehow.

27. Deterioration

*"So also we, while we were children, were held in
bondage under the elemental things of the world."*

Galatians 4:3 (NASB)

The bleak days of winter clothed the world of Château de Plessis
in icy fog and bitter winds, continuing into the dreary days after
Jeanne's eighth birthday. Jeanne lost interest in riding because of
the cold, and there was no place to go but the worn, sleet-cov-
ered paths of the forest and back again to the castle. No response
had come from the King in answer to her request. In disappointment Jeanne went out to walk to the river, mulling over disturbing
thoughts of the history of death and war surrounding her. Misery
and disappointments plagued her for months.

One evening in the summer of 1535 dinner conversation
included a discussion of the enormous wealth of the Cardinal
Duprat whose recent death had exposed his vast accumulation of
riches at the expense of many unfortunate poor and afflicted. The
Cardinal was known to be wholly worldly and addicted to pleasure. His wicked and depraved love of himself was a fact too well
known among the poorest people, while whispered rumors of it
spread among the elite classes.

These observations, when discussed freely among those
attending at Princess Jeanne's royal table, filled her mind with anxieties of death and terrible misgivings of purgatory and hell.

When more troops of the castle were suddenly called to join forces with other armies at Lyons, Jeanne's thoughts became obsessed with imaginary battles occurring on the banks of the river Loire and the advancement of Spanish troops through the forests of the castle. Everything she had heard from her mother and Aymée, along with her historical studies, created the face of a monster on not only the Emperor but also on the faces of the soldiers she imagined sneaking through the trees in the forest.

She began to pace the floor of the torture chamber, going from corner to corner, imagining the ghosts of troops hanging from the walls of the room among the evil instruments she could see and handle. Hearing in her mind their screams and moans of pain and terror, she would flee the hall of torture and fly outside with Sir Ami to walk around the grounds inspecting the trenches and battlements that had been erected by Louis XI. With her heart in her throat, she would peer into the deep holes, expecting a monstrous soldier to jump out and grab her.

The weather was quite inclement as the spring of 1536 struggled to defeat the lingering death of winter. Often the fogs would be so thick that even the substantial trunks of trees would appear and disappear with eerie movement in the chill wind. She would glance fearfully over her shoulder, startled by the sudden appearance of a dark shadow which in the movement of the wind soon emerged as a nearby bush or tree. Convinced someone should scout the riverbanks for intruders, Jeanne would run through the trees dodging here and there, imagining the many shadows which appeared were moving enemies, to then discover they were only stationary objects familiar to the forest floor. Her heart would lurch, and Sir Ami's presence alone reassured her no one was out there. Her faithful companion, he loved their excursions into the woods. The fears radiating from the Princess caused him to stay on alert and watch loyally for any dangers.

The results of her wandering among the fears of her mind were evident to everyone in the castle as she became morbidly silent, not lifting her head to look at others. She was a moving ghost among the living, locked in the dungeons of her terrifying nightmare. She longed to be released from her prison though no avenue of escape appeared. Her only comfort was the faithful Sir Ami who was persistently at her side.

More and more Jeanne walked in the castle halls to the torture chamber to stand with Sir Ami and stare around the walls, silently rehearsing the terrors that must have been committed there. At evening, only occasionally could a chess game pull her away from her inner thoughts. In her apartments, Phoebe, Maddie, and Chloe would begin singing and play the moment she came in the door, only to stop mid-song as she retreated to her secret room without a word.

In August 1536, not only had such great depression weighed heavily on the mind of the Princess, but alarming letters arrived from the court of France that her cousin, the handsome dauphin, François, Duke of Brittany, had been stricken ill under suspicious circumstances and had died at age eighteen. The Dauphin François, Duke of Brittany, and his younger brother, Henry, Duke of Orleans, had been imprisoned in the dark, dank, filthy prisons of Spain in Madrid as hostages in place of their father. The two princes, held for four years before being freed by the treaty signed in Cambray, were scarred when released to freedom. François had suffered from a lingering illness deep in his lungs. His demeanor had changed as he preferred to spend hours in seclusion reading rather than participating in the more vigorous pursuits of military training. After a tennis match, the Duke d'Brittany had asked for a drink which was brought to him by an attendant at the castle. The Duke collapsed soon after taking a drink and died days later. It happened that this servant had arrived from Spain in the troupe brought by Catherine de Medici, consort of the Duke's younger brother, Henry II, at their marriage.

Many rumors were whispered at Catherine's arrival at court about the education in the black arts Henry's new consort had received during her upbringing. These whispers made the rounds with increased fervor when the Dauphin's death placed Henry II next in line for the throne. Many believed the rumors to be true, while cooler heads insisted that the death of the Dauphin was the result of a lung disease he had contracted while a hostage in the prisons of Spain.

Grief at the loss of his favorite son plunged King Francis into a profound period of mourning, disregarding many of the responsibilities of his reign for an indefinite period. Jeanne waited anxiously to hear permission from Uncle Francis to go into Tours again, eventually realizing his attention on more pressing matters had probably pushed her request from his mind.

The days passed slowly into 1537, one dreary, bleak day after another. Months soon vanished with Jeanne merely going through the motions of school, debates with Fauzio and Raymond, devotions at the Chapel and dull meals around the table in the Great Hall. Again, Christmas had passed almost unnoticed as everyone huddled close to fireplaces all over the castle. When Aymée gave Jeanne a small gift on her ninth birthday, her only response was sudden tears in her eyes, and a whispered 'thank you.'

Every frigid day air crept up from the cold stones to freeze the bones of everyone in the castle. The fire in the Great Hall could not overcome the chill; while outdoors, no snow covered the landscape with beauty, only frozen mud and cracking sleet underfoot.

Miserable, depressed and sullen, Princess Jeanne wandered about, wondering what purpose she could have to continue living.

During her lessons, the Princess found fault with every opinion or answer her schoolmates expressed. Biting remarks and sharp comments surprised not only the two boys but M. Bourbon as well. If he reprimanded her, she merely rose from her chair and retreated to her apartments without a word. No one, not even Aymée could get her to come out of her secret room; her only response was to insist that dinner be brought to her on a tray. Most trays appeared outside the door of her secret room, hardly touched. Everyone seemed to walk as on eggshells around her, fearing the smallest remark might send her into seclusion, or more lately, tears.

Spring came very late in the year, and the dreary, cold weather continued into May. Jeanne had received a letter from her mother telling her that twin baby brothers had died at birth. Marguerite was weak but recovering, though bitterly disappointed. Jeanne wrote her back, painfully sharing grief and disappointment.

In a black corner of her mind, Jeanne wondered what impact the boys would have had on her life if they had lived. It was clear to her if her value and dowry for marriage disappeared, who would have a use for her when she was no longer heiress to the Kingdom of Navarre? Her depression deepened, and she kept to herself as much as possible.

What she did not realize was, with the passing of the years, Jeanne continued to grow more beautiful, and her stunning intelligence became increasingly apparent. She would be an excellent royal partner for the best suitor King Francis could find. Now in her ninth year, womanhood was beginning to blossom. Though not tall, her stature was graceful and appealing. The Princess's inner thought process, however, continued to feel unwanted and unloved.

28. Oppression

*"Grace to you and peace from God our Father, and
the Lord Jesus Christ, who gave Himself for our sins,
that He might deliver us out of this present evil age,
according to the will of our God and Father, to whom
be the glory forever more. Amen."*

Galatians 1:3-5 (NASB)

The terror of inquisition and punishment spread throughout France from Paris in rapid-fire search of even a hint of heresy. Insidious evil swept through the towns and countryside as clergy were compelled to protect their forms and traditions, searching out the heresy of any sort, examining every rumor and following every whispered suspicion with fanatical fervor. Friends suspiciously watched each other for signs of possible apostasy. Devoted monks and priests either turned on their parishioners to expose heretical leanings or increased their insistence of holy doctrine. Pitilessly they harangued their flock to repent of sins and pay indulgences for the salvation of their souls. The Chapel of Château de Plessis was not exempt from the storms. In devotions Jeanne attended in the Oratory, she heard sermons heavy with admonitions of original sin and the inability of humanity's choices to save himself from the grasp of Satan; offering only a fatal future for each individual to consider without hope, resulting in demands to pay the offerings for the forgiveness of sins. Jeanne's increasing knowledge of the Holy

Scriptures met with adamant dismissal from her chaplains who chose not to consider any opposing view by scolding her harshly for mouthing heresy in ignorance.

Disputes were argued openly between Jeanne, Fauzio, and Raymond, soon becoming heated and volatile. M. Bourbon patiently endeavored to impart knowledge for both sides equally; however, his sentiment leaning toward reformation was evident enough to raise the ire of Fauzio and Raymond in defense of the Church.

Raymond's parents had proposed that he might do well to seek an avenue of vocation within the Catholic Church and spent less and less time in the schoolroom and more often was seen receiving instructions from the chaplains. His declining attendance for lessons was disappointing because Jeanne missed his original thoughts and unique perspectives. She preferred arguing against them both. She felt it seemed less personal when she won.

If Raymond did attend the Library discussions, he appeared much subdued and demonstrated very little of his former enthusiasm at being in their company. Raymond was blessed with an incredibly beautiful voice and had been selected both for the Chapel boys' choir and to serve as an altar boy. Each were admirable appointments; however Jeanne could not see that he was pleased with the honor.

Fauzio, however, was always ready for a vigorous argument against the reforms of Catholic practices. Now fourteen years old, he demonstrated knowledge for the subject that could only come from discussions he had overheard at his father's dinner table. His passion prompted Jeanne to seek wisdom in the books her mother had brought to her. She selected the volume written by Gerard Roussel because her mother had mentioned how its gentle arguments had formed the basis of her faith. Jeanne sought out M. Bourbon to help her understand the points made in the book, as much was theology above her head. His explanations gave Jeanne great insight into the truths of the scriptures, and matching her studies of the Bible with M. Bourbon's teachings; she attained a decent grasp on the truth of the arguments. The activities of collecting indulgences by the priests to ensure entrance to heaven for dead relatives did not appear in the Bible. Evidence that choices made in life, good or bad, could be overturned by living relatives by paying their hard-earned money to the priests was a doctrine invented by men.

Jeanne's instinctive need to determine the truth in every dispute eventually convinced her spirit that many of the claims of the Catholic clergy were deceitful lies employed to take advantage of the ignorance of illiterate parishioners to control their thoughts and bleed their pitiful incomes to further the wealth of the Church. Her heart was persuaded to align her sympathies with the reformed movement. Being handicapped by her young age and dependence on the favor of King Francis, she adopted her mother's methods of practicing the accepted Catholic religious ceremonies. While probing the writings of leaders of that persecuted movement to be fully informed she waited until she reached the age of accountability or succession to the throne of her parents.

As the reformation persecutions mounted, the news of Gerard Roussel's arrest and imprisonment devastated Jeanne. Then when Jeanne was approaching her tenth birthday, rumors and reports of the war in the South increased Jeanne's dismay and her dark thoughts and fears deepened.

29. Forebodings

"Simon, Simon, behold, Satan has demanded permission to sift you as wheat; but I have prayed for you, that your faith may not fail; and you, when once you have turned again, strengthen your brothers."

Luke 22:31-32 (NASB)

King Francis called Marguerite to Paris in need of her counsel and discernment regarding the increasing threats of the Spanish Emperor to invade the southern regions of France. The enmity between the heads of the two countries had been ongoing since the signing of the treaty of Cambray, and both sovereigns might immediately declare war against the other at the smallest egregious move.

The recently assassinated French envoy to the court of Milan under suspicious circumstances, needed inquiries into the death that indicated a possible connection pointing to the interference of the Emperor. It was 1538, and everyone feared that war was imminent

Marguerite left Paris immediately as this looming possibility of war dramatically threatened her realm in Béarn, which among the other Southern provinces, could be the first recipients of any aggressive moves of the Emperor to invade France. The King mustered an opposing army and proceeded to move to Lyons to set military strategy in place. The King of Navarre was called to join him there, leaving Marguerite to assume the role of increasing the defensive positions of her realm.

During this time of extreme threat to the province of Béarn, Queen Marguerite was unusually energetic, traveling throughout the south of France to bolster the military fortresses in the area. The Queen was anticipating that at any point along the border with Spain, an invasion could come on them unexpectedly and allow unlimited access of the enemy to move against the King of France from his weak side. The Queen of Navarre resolved this would not happen.

Aymée had heard rumors of a possible war with Spain, and then troops currently posted at the Château de Plessis were transferred to the southern front. Then directions delivered from King Francis that Jeanne was not to be allowed to leave the castle for any reason brought fear to Château de Plessis. Aymée's thoughts became plagued by fears of spies lurking to steal Jeanne away as a bargaining point against the King of France, or that Marguerite would be in danger of involvement in a battle that could lead to her injury or even death. As Aymée considered with horror the possibilities of either of these scenarios, her fears included Jeanne's reaction to either event.

Princess Jeanne heard whispers among the servants about the occurrences in the south of France and went to the Library to study the maps there.

Reports came from Lyons that King Francis and his army were preparing to invade Milan. Eventually, however, in their dinner discussions they were surprised to hear the news that for unknown reasons, instead of war, negotiations were in process for a treaty to appoint the King's son, Henry II, Duke of Orleans and his consort, Catherine de Medici, to joint reign over Milan. A great sigh resounded throughout France, and its citizens began to shrug off the terror of war and disaster and to go about their daily existence with less anxiety. Jeanne's fear for the safety of her Uncle Francis had been so unconscious that when she received this hopeful news, she was surprised to realize she could breathe deeply again.

30. Propositions

*"It was for freedom that Christ set us free; therefore
keep standing firm and do not be subject again to a yoke
of slavery."*

Galatians 5:1 (NASB)

S everal months after Jeanne turned ten years old, in desperation, Aymée finally wrote to King Francis about her concern for Jeanne's mental state. She could no longer allow the Princess to continue her downward spiral of depression. Not even knowing what she expected the King to do, she believed it would be much worse not to make him aware.

Sooner than she expected, his return letter was immediate and concerned. King Francis did not want Princess Jeanne to assume a habitual dismal disposition, especially now, as it would not be attractive to possible suitors. Perhaps, he wrote, learning to be an ambassador for the King would be proper training. He suggested when the weather was agreeable, that she be allowed to go to Tours, by horseback if she preferred, accompanied of course, by at least six guards. He told Aymée of the request Jeanne had made on his last visit three years before.

Believing that the danger of imminent war in France had passed, Aymée asked Jeanne after breakfast on an August morning if she felt like riding into Tours to act as an ambassador for Uncle Francis by showing her kindness and caring for the citizens living in the town. Jeanne studied Aymée for a long moment, wondering what could have prompted such a question. Instead of jumping at the chance, as Aymée had expected, Jeanne's response was, "How?"

"This girl," thought Aymée, "is forever surprising me by her reactions! She is much more complicated than I realize and simple answers will not satisfy her."

Speaking directly, Aymée reminded Jeanne that the preceding years had been trying for everyone and the King had not been able to visit Jeanne or the surrounding area in a long time. He believed that Jeanne, going among the people as his representative, would bring encouragement to them to know that their King was always concerned with their welfare even in times of the threat of war.

"Perhaps," Aymée continued, "you could take Raymond with you, as your almoner. I remember how your mother, in Navarre, would send her almoner among the people to distribute small amounts of money to those in special need. I understand that Raymond is considering a future in the priesthood and he could benefit from the experience. You could, after visiting with individuals and understanding their needs, ask Raymond to bless them and give some coins to those whom you feel could benefit from a small financial gift also. If you let them know you represent their monarch and his majesty cares about them, you would be doing King Francis a good service." She paused and watched to see how Jeanne would react to this thought. Then she added, "It would also do you good to get away from the castle and perhaps to see Antoinette in the process."

Jeanne was silent. Her mind was running to and fro trying to understand how this could have happened. She had hardly dared to even think about her friendship with Antoinette as there had been such a deafening silence whenever she spoke of it. She had begun to believe that she was in fact, a prisoner in this dungeon; that she would never be allowed to be among the rest of the world again.

So her response to Aymée was repeated, "How? How have you obtained permission from my uncle or my mother to allow me to leave the castle grounds?"

Understanding began to dawn on Aymée. Jeanne must consider herself confined unwillingly to a luxurious prison cell with no way to escape. The influences of that horrid torture chamber had invaded her tender thoughts, and she had assumed the helpless role of the victims previously incarcerated there. For her, these years of imposed separation had taken on the aspect of death, or non-existence. Shocked, Aymée realized her thoughts must be devoid of hope or a future.

"Oh help me, Lord, to have the wisdom to explain the purpose of her being here; that she does have a future and a hope in You!"

Aymée rose from her chair and knelt at Jeanne's feet, taking the girl's icy hands in her own.

"My precious Princess! You have misunderstood the bonds of love cast around you to prepare you for a magnificent future. You are growing more beautiful every day. Your mind is sharp, and you have learned valuable lessons in judgment and wisdom. Your preparation to be a Queen is advancing rapidly. Confinement in this castle has not been imprisonment, only protection from evil that seeks ever to waylay a young lady's development into her potential.

"King Francis and the King and Queen of Navarre seek only your good, and to guarantee your education and advancement as a promising and valuable royal Princess capable of taking her place within majesty and royalty in her own right. The King has written to me asking that we expand your education now to learn more about the people you may someday rule.

"Can you not see that each year has been a stepping stone of preparation for you? Many of the lessons you have confronted you have accomplished because of who you naturally are; some have been difficult and a struggle to achieve; however you have undertaken them all, and you have much reason to be proud,

"This will not be a girlish adventure for your selfish enjoyment. You are being asked to take a message to the people in Tours that they are important to you and the King of France. You must get to know them and seek to understand their point of view, for King Francis may someday rely on your counsel and knowledge to help weigh a difficult future decision. The King is asking you to know the mood of the people and how they will respond. Can you do that?"

Jeanne listened to Aymée's explanation with that warning screaming in her mind of what Uncle Francis was planning for her future, and at age ten, she knew the timing of the King's goal of arranging for her to be married was now upon her. Her voice would only be strengthened in that decision if she gained as much experience as she could to bring to the bargaining table of her future. She hesitated, straddling between the need for childhood security while craving to have a decision in her adult future, this opportunity both frightened and intrigued her.

"I believe I can," Jeanne responded uncertainly. "I will listen to any suggestions. You have laid a heavy burden on me. Do you think I can do this?"

Jeanne earnestly searched Aymée's face, looking for any hint of doubt. Of course, she wanted to go to town. She wanted very much to visit Antoinette and renew their acquaintance even after several years. So much time had passed. "Would Antoinette even remember me?" Jeanne asked herself. Now, the King wanted her to be his ambassador? How would she go about doing that? Her thoughts had always been to escape this dreary castle and the many terrible memories in its history. Would she find escape and hope in Tours or just more despair as her acquaintance with the people and their troubles increased? She had learned that a few coins would not have eased Antoinette and her family's problems. Only a job for M. Abérnois had made a lasting impact. How could she begin to help so many different people with such a multitude of various needs? The thought was overwhelming!

She agreed that asking Raymond to accompany her would be a good idea. He was a gentle soul and had a genuinely caring personality. To spread a few coins around might make people like her, but she doubted it would be enough to make any progress to right the ills of so many.

Looking again at Aymée in the hope of some suggestion that might show her how even to start, Princess Jeanne realized a plan was already forming in her mind, stimulating excitement to try to meet this challenge.

Aymée had explained that she could ride alone, or with Raymond if she wanted; however, she must be accompanied by six castle guards to avoid any mishaps or trouble. Jeanne frowned at that, knowing there was nothing she could say to change the King's order.

Her heart leaped at the thought of riding horseback. To feel free and about her own business with no one to contradict her plans was a delightful concept. Raymond would be required to follow her lead and do as she commanded. She began to warm to the idea and asked Aymée to direct her ladies to lay out her best riding habit and to arrange for an appropriate bag of coins to be prepared by M. d'Izernay for Raymond to carry. She would like to leave after lunch, and before then, she needed to go to the stables to talk to M. Abérnois and then to the Chapel to see Raymond.

Aymée was delighted at Jeanne's desire to take control and make plans to go immediately. Perhaps she had listened and heard what Aymée said. Maybe her mind would become focused on the needs of others instead of solely on herself. Aymée's conviction that God would direct Jeanne's future and someday she would be a much-loved ruler whose sense of truth and justice would impact the lives of an entire kingdom deepened. This appointed task for the King would be a growing time for Jeanne. Aymée was eager to watch her decisions and reactions.

31. Approaches

*"Awake, O north wind, and come wind of the south;
make my garden breathe out fragrance, let its spices be
wafted abroad."*

Song of Solomon 4:16 (NASB)

Pierre and M. Abérnois were standing beside the circular exercise area watching the horses moving around the circle. They were speaking together quietly about their concerns about the Princess. She was very dear to them both, and her lack of enthusiasm and growing despondency had them worried. Suddenly they became aware that she was walking toward them. Respectfully bowing together, the two men turned to greet her.

They had not seen Jeanne for several months because the rumors of war had prevented her from being allowed to ride out. The King insisted, for her safety, she should not even leave the castle grounds, fearing someone might kidnap her and hold her hostage to force him to accept some disagreeable demands. Unknown to the King of France, every person in the vicinity of the Château de Plessis lez Tours had given their hearts to the Princess and would have been protectively suspicious of any stranger or untoward behavior regarding her safety. They formed circles of invisible defensive barriers from the town outward to the castle with their hearts of love and loyalty. Jeanne sank into her abyss of despondency having no idea of the feelings of the people who were proud to be her subjects. Nor did she even notice the appreciative glances Pierre and M. Abérnois exchanged at her appearance. Though her mental condition had been depressed and downhearted, her beauty became more evident as the months passed. She no longer had the look of an innocent child. Since her tenth birthday, her carriage, poise, and demeanor had developed into that of a virgin maiden with a glow of purity and eyes even more enhanced by her passion for truth and right.

Princess Jeanne made a small curtsy in response to the men and told them of her plans to ride out that afternoon to Tours. She expected to be accompanied by Raymond, who would also require a horse.

Turning then to M. Abérnois, she explained that she had been requested by King Francis to serve as his ambassador to Tours and the purpose of this outing would be to become better acquainted with the people there and to learn more about their needs. She inquired about Antoinette and wondered if a visit to her at home would be welcome. M. Abérnois assured the Princess that Antoinette would be delighted to see her again and he would provide her directions to their home. When Jeanne smiled at him and said thank you, he was sure he saw again a hint of that captivating vivacity that had won so many hearts.

As Princess Jeanne returned from the stables, she thought to seek out Raymond by walking through the garden on the path that led around the castle to the outer doors to the Chapel. The sun and shade of the garden path winding through tall, green boxwoods and patches of begonias gave a sense of seclusion as she wandered slowly, admiring the colors and small corners of floral display that seemed to sing with the glory of their beauty. Just ahead Jeanne could see a large lilac bush in full bloom. It towered overhead as she passed it. Jeanne breathed deeply of the fragrance of its flowers. The path meandered sleepily back toward the castle walls when, before her, there was a small alcove with a bench nearly hidden by honey-suckle vines and gardenia bushes.

It was such an inviting, private nook; she impulsively sat down on the partially shaded, stone seat. The Princess sat motionlessly. She closed her eyes and lifted her face to the warmth of the sun, listening to the drone of honeybees among the flowers nearby. The gentle movement of the vines in the breeze caressed her face with tendrils of cool shade. It was very quiet for there was almost no activity around the castle on that side. Peace and solitude surrounded Jeanne, embracing her as the sun and shade played across her face.

A profound sense of contentment overwhelmed her. The sun, the breeze, the occasional shade moving across her eyelids joined together like a whisper of distant chimes echoing from heaven. A sense of the source of her peace invaded her being.

God loved her. He did not demand her to love Him back. He just was, and would always be, surrounding her with His love. Settling in her mind like petals dropping from the honeysuckle, she felt this was knowledge of real love. No human love could fill her with such peace.

A thought crossed her mind that humans who love always have their agenda. They love to the best of their ability, considering that the constancy of their love may vacillate according to their desires. Her parents loved her, but distantly, as their lives had demanded they love the kingdoms of France and Navarre first; loving her much like a satellite circling around them but never joining together. Uncle Francis loved her, Jeanne knew; however, his role of King of France also demanded that he love France more. She was sure she would be asked to play a role in his love for France.

She asked herself, "Who am I to love?" She sat still in the silence as chimes echoed across her mind and again, she knew; she must love God even as He loved her. "But, how?" she asked herself. Chimes echoed softly, like a kiss against her brow, and the conviction of her heart spoke unwaveringly; she must love the people of her kingdom. She must seek them out today and love them all, the unwashed, the sick, the broken, the poor, the hard-hearted, the comfortable and the well-to-do. She would not go as an ambassador for the King of France; she would go and love them all for God, with the love she had herself experienced from Him.

The chimes ringing in her mind accompanied the song of the birds in the trees and bushes around her. Her heart lifted to the music of the birds as they belted out their songs of praise to their Creator.

Jeanne did not move. In the music of the silence, she became aware of the absolute perfect order of the living things around her. Small sounds of nearby animals drifted to her as she savored the sun and the gentle wind. Jeanne pondered a possible truth of creation and the created. God held each created thing in His hand. He alone ordained and fulfilled what sprang from His love. Her heart sang with thanksgiving, convinced her task was birthed from His love. It was a defining moment in her spirit. For so long, she felt mired in the slough of despair, and now she felt she was given an exquisite new life with a host of new beginnings. Jeanne began humming an echo of the songs of the birds with her voice, not forming words, just singing her love for life and the beauty of the gift of this day. The melody lingered in her mind, and the sweet fragrance of honeysuckle and gardenias permeated her hair and clothes. She felt encompassed by the highest Spirit of love; being clothed in an invisible garment of the fullness of God's unfathomable love.

As she rose to go on to the Chapel, she continued to softly hum the tune, not knowing that those she passed along the way caught the sweet fragrance in her passing and heard her song. The melodious refrain invaded their minds along with the fresh scent of honeysuckle, gardenias, and peace.

Turning in the large double doors of the Chapel, Jeanne stood still for a few moments, adjusting to the dark majesty of the nave and the hovering smell of incense, with only the lighted candles to see. The quiet was unbroken here, with no birdsong to interrupt; just a reverent awareness of the power of the Holy Almighty God. Jeanne responded to the sacredness of the place by dropping to one knee. Crossing herself as taught, she walked to a pew to sit about midway in the Chapel. Her thoughts continued to dwell on God and His love. She asked Jesus to guide her in the task before her and to teach her how to know what to say. The sense of His presence was profoundly real, and she desired to continue to dwell there; to never leave the peace and comfort that had settled within her.

As she prayed, she felt a person standing beside her, waiting quietly. She looked up as one of the chaplains leaned down and asked "Child, may I help you?" It took her a moment to realize that this was not Jesus, as she moved from being centered so profoundly in prayer to the reality of the dim Chapel. She was filled with peace and contentment, and disappointed to break the spell; she sighed at the interruption. She asked to speak with Raymond, and the man slipped silently away.

Soon there was Raymond, standing beside her. Recalling her reason for coming, she rose from her seat and asked Raymond to walk with her.

They came out of the Chapel into the Great Hall of the castle while Jeanne told Raymond of her task of ambassadorship in Tours and her intention to share the wealth by handing out coins to those in great need. She asked if he would like to go with her as her almoner, and that she also hoped to take some of the clothes gathered since the time she had first met Antoinette. She didn't know how many garments she would be able to carry in her saddlebags, so she asked Raymond how he would feel about carrying a large bundle on his horse. He walked with her, listening, and then for some time without saying anything. When they reached a quiet corner, he stopped and turned toward the Princess.

"Princess Jeanne," he said, "I will be honored to be your almoner. I have always considered you my dear friend, and I will most willingly go with you on this trip to Tours. I must get permission from my sponsoring chaplain, first. I have not completely made up my mind about my future with the church. I do not know if I will be allowed to wear my novice robe since so many are aware of my indecision about becoming a priest. Please know that I welcome the opportunity to accompany you whether I go as a representative of the church or as a friend. I will meet you at the stables after lunch. If you will excuse me, I will go now to confirm my sponsoring chaplain's permission."

Jeanne watched him return to the Chapel, surprised at what he had told her. She had never been sure he was happy and had observed him, identifying with his look of being trapped. She hoped they would have an opportunity to talk more as they rode; however, that would be his choice, as she had no intention of prying into his private thoughts.

As she walked to her apartments, she considered how best to make these trips yield long-term fruit instead of just being the 'good fairy,' which leaves a coin or two and then it is back to life's needs as usual. A small thought began to grow, and she wondered how she might test it without revealing her beginning plans.

Jeanne had heard the reports by Sir Duquesse and M. d'Izernay that Antoinette's mother had taken in laundry to earn extra money before M. Abérnois began working at the Château de Plessis stables. She needed to find out if any property in Tours belonged to her Uncle Francis. Jeanne knew of the piles of cast-off clothes gathered throughout the castle. Her ladies, along with other women employed at the castle, had enjoyed the companionship and social elements of working together to repair and clean the garments, so now there was quite an extensive collection of these renewed garments piling up in a castle storeroom. She wondered if she could bring all those elements together to create a way to distribute them and benefit the good of the common people.

Making a sudden detour, she decided to speak to M. d'Izernay now about her questions of a usable dwelling in Tours. The Princess knocked softly on the frame of the open door to M. d'Izernay's office. He was concentrating on the figures written in long lines down the pages of the ledger before him and at first, did not hear Jeanne at the door. She knocked again, more loudly this time and cleared her throat so he would know she was there.

M. d'Izernay jumped slightly at the sound, startled out of his deep concentration to correctly total up the sums of the columns. Upon realizing the Princess was standing at his door, he leaped to his feet, bowing deeply.

"Oh no," he thought, "What can she want now?"

It was true that M. d'Izernay still harbored a slight grudge that somehow she had won in the matter of hiring M. Abérnois and the knowledge that she had been right and he had been wrong did not sit well with him. Ever since that incident had played itself out and King Francis had reprimanded him, he had secretly considered her, maybe not an enemy, for that was too strong even for his mind, but at least someone whom he viewed with hostility and avoided crossing paths with her. Here she was at his door, and that was disturbing.

Princess Jeanne entered the Steward's office, suddenly aware that she was not welcome there.

"How strange," she thought. "Why do I feel that my Steward is not pleased to see me?"

On that small perception, Jeanne proceeded cautiously, promptly deciding she would only ask innocent, friendly questions and not discuss her entire proposal until she could understand this strange opposition.

Convinced that God impressed her to proceed diplomatically, she gave him a cheery smile and said, "Steward d'Izernay, I have a question that I believe you are better able to answer than any other. I have been asked by King Francis to be his representative and ambassador to complete a task in the town of Tours. I will be traveling to town this afternoon and would like to know if the King has a building of his own in Tours that I may use as I fulfill his request? Are you able to provide me with that information?"

Jeanne waited as her steward pondered her question with his lowered eyebrows drawn together to a crease above his nose. Such a menacing frown nearly wiped the smile off her face, and then he looked up and returned her smile.

"I believe the King has several, Mademoiselle. I will provide you with a list so you can consider which will best serve you. I will include it with the bag of coins Madame Aymée has requested for you."

With a great sense of relief, Jeanne thanked the steward and returned to seeking Aymée, making a note in her mind to pinpoint the cause of the steward's negative perspective toward her. Climbing the stairs to her apartment, she contemplated if she had ever been aware of how her mother and uncle had handled a contrary servant or subject. She did not recall knowing of a specific incident; however she believed that they had taken care to know well anyone who served them.

"I must learn more about M. d'Izernay," she thought. "If I can understand him and what he feels is most important in his own life, perhaps I can understand his reactions. Then, maybe I won't be so surprised."

Reaching the top of the stairs, she turned and looked back toward the door of M. d'Izernay's office. He had disappeared inside, and she could envision his shoulders bent over his desk, completely immersed in his figures and ledger.

"I wonder if he is lonely," she thought. "He is so dedicated to those figures that he hardly shows his face anywhere about the castle. I never see him walking in the gardens or riding a horse for either pleasure or an errand. His whole life seems confined within the walls of his office. I wonder where he finds his joy. I can't say I have ever seen him happy. With no family, he leads a very lonely life shut up in that office. I must discover a way to make him happy. I know too well how unhappy loneliness can make you feel."

Still concerned about the isolation of M. d'Izernay, Jeanne entered her apartment to look for Aymée. There she found her, talking with her ladies as they folded several of the child-sized garments to package in bundles for her saddlebags.

Aymée could always be counted on to support and encourage her. A great sense of love for Aymée engulfed her. Jeanne embraced her, laughing in delight that she could count on this woman always, without fail.

The Princess exclaimed, "Oh Aymée, how wonderful you are! I love you so much! You have never lost faith in me.

I have been in such a dark place, and still, you have been steadfastly at my side. What love you have shown me. What faithfulness you have demonstrated. Only your constancy has kept me secured in hope. Such love cannot be measured. What you have received you have given freely to me. I will never forget how you have loved me. Today, I feel God's love has set me free."

Overcome with this outburst, Aymée could see joy and confidence which she had never seen before reflected in those deep blue pools.

"My little Princess is like a small bird," Aymée mused, "perched on a high branch considering its first plunge, who, when returning on its wings to that same high branch, exults in the discovery it is no longer bound to the tiny nest of its previous habitation. From now on this little bird will fly, free to pursue her heights, uninhibited."

A mixture of joy and fear filled Aymée, realizing that this would be the beginning of the end of her responsibility to her 'becoming Queen'. Now would come the pain of letting go, coupled with the pride of watching Jeanne blossom on the wings of God's love.

"Bless her Lord with Your fullness, and guard her against evil as she soars to new heights. She has always belonged only to You, dearest Jesus, and You know I can only let go of her if she is holding Your hand. Give me strength, I pray, to let go at the right moment of Your plan."

They turned away from each other, both profoundly feeling the revelations of that moment; returning to their given tasks with increased strength of purpose. Jeanne spoke to Maddie, thanking her for her hard work on the packaged garments.

Then to Phoebe, she said, "I would like my hair in a braid when I go to town. May we do that now?"

Jeanne began softly humming the refrain from the garden, and the fragrance of honeysuckle and gardenias filled her memory. After listening a while, Aymée's contralto and Chloe's sweet soprano chimed in, humming while they assisted her as she changed into the royal blue riding habit and Phoebe braided her hair. Aymée could only see her beautiful little bluebird getting ready to make her maiden flight. As Jeanne swept out of the room to go to lunch, the four ladies continued humming together as they watched her go. Anytime they sang after that, they recalled its lingering melody, calling it the "Sweet song."

32. Disclosures

*"The things which are impossible with men are possible
with God."*

Luke 18:27 (NASB)

Sir Duquesse sat down at the table beside Princess Jeanne and
commented that in her blue riding habit she was stunning. There
was no doubt a dramatic change had occurred in the Princess. In
the last several years, he had grieved for her, watching the castle
encompass her with its disturbed spirit. He had admired her stubbornness because he could see the valiant effort she made to fight
it. Dark circles under her eyes and her despondent steps had eventually disclosed the depth of its grip.

Now, however, he was looking into the eyes of a ray of sunshine. A wind change had blown the disturbance away. The inhabitants of the castle were so devoted to their little Princess that her
personality permeated throughout each member of the staff. If she
was depressed, every member of the staff went about their duties
as if in a grey cloud. When her face brightened, the castle seemed
bright and gay. He had felt the change immediately as he left his
office for lunch. Everyone he met was smiling and stepping lightly
about their duties.

"No wonder," he thought to himself. "The Princess gathered
all the beauty of the creation into the Great Hall just by coming
down the stairs."

It seemed a great weight lifted, and the atmosphere around the table felt like spring with a newness of purpose. The Princess was confident in the loyalty Sir Duquesse had toward her. Since she came to the castle as a lost five-year-old, he had encouraged and supported her in every way. She would always be grateful for the efforts he had fashioned to make the castle more beautiful and friendly with everything he had at his disposal. She had written many times to Uncle Francis and her mother to share all that he had done for her on the King's behalf. Like her realization of the depth of Aymée's love, she suddenly knew that here too was a devoted friend who loved her. His eyes had never reproached her, and he had ever been open about his concern for her.

Her meal, nearly forgotten in her desire to bring Sir Duquesse into her new plans, Jeanne began to share about her task for the afternoon. She included her half-developed idea for a complete solution for the poor citizens in Tours. He listened intently to every word and filed a few reactions away in his mind to consider later.

Jeanne asked his opinion of all she had said. He asked what she desired to accomplish by her trip in the afternoon. Jeanne puzzled over his question as she ate.

After a few moments, she laid her fork on her plate and said, "I am not sure that I have any expectations for this afternoon's trip, except to be among the people and try to listen to them share about their lives. M. d'Izernay will be providing a list of the King's properties in the town, and I plan to visit each and consider if it would fit the plans I am contemplating."

Sir Duquesse nodded thoughtfully and said, "You must take one step at a time. The more you talk with the people, the better picture you will have of their most urgent needs. Madame Abérnois will be a good resource to share your ideas with. Go today and do what you are led to do. We can talk when you return and see what path is before you."

Sir Duquesse pondered how to phrase his thoughts further.

"Long-term problems take even longer solutions. Do not expect just one visit to reveal all your hurdles and keep an open mind to unexpected clarifications. There are many avenues to explore to achieve your goal. Do not limit your vision to just one purpose until you feel confident you have the full picture."

Princess Jeanne appreciated his wisdom and the dramatic colors of her eyes deepened, responding to his words.

"We often jump too quickly to provide a remedy and then discover our efforts have fallen short because more wisdom was required. I believe God will guide and guard your thoughts and plans. You have such a giving heart and a loving desire toward others, Princess."

Her eyes warmed with his encouragement.

"Not everyone you meet is like you. You must hide your reactions and impulses away in your heart to consider them carefully, away from the moment of being involved in a person's life. True wisdom seeks God's guidance and waits for confirmation without surrendering to the impulses of emotion."

The dark pools of Jeanne's eyes deepened farther, and Sir Duquesse knew she was embracing the advice he offered.

"Your job is to make valid choices based on reasoning and careful thought. We all wonder why these eternal, ongoing problems that are present in every generation are not solved yet. People differ and are responsive to their gratification. If you are too transparent, there may be many who will try to manipulate you to achieve their desires.

"Keep first in your mind that you are the representative of their King. Be a faithful ambassador for King Francis and collect as much information as possible to make your plan."

Jeanne rose from the table and bending toward Sir Duquesse, she kissed his cheek and with her expressive eyes, she thanked him; then turned to complete the tasks she must attend to before leaving. He had become lost in watching her responsive eyes, and her departure jolted him to rise and bow respectfully.

Sir Duquesse sat back down, not noticing how cold the tea had become that he was drinking as he contemplated the force and change in the person who had just left him. She was undoubtedly the most intriguing girl he could ever remember seeing. A small smile played about his lips as he recalled his first view of her. He had been enchanted with her then and the difficult years of her growing had only increased his loyalty more fully to her. He had committed himself entirely to her for the five years of her presence here at the castle. He could now see the flower was beginning to blossom in maturity. The vision of her loveliness, hidden so long, is now revealed as it moves toward full bloom. He realized whoever was chosen to be worthy to pluck this flower would be the envy of every man. The future for Sir Duquesse would be entangled substantially for as long as she remained here at the castle, for he knew he could never stay a significant figure in her life. He would play his part and then release the beautiful blue bird to an unknown future.

He did not even notice the servants who cleared the table and warmed his tea. Wrapped in his thoughts, he shook his head; any woman who would come into his life someday could never equal the fullness of the heart and spirit of Jeanne.

He missed the light that had vanished as she left his side and felt sorry for himself.

"What tricks life plays on us," he thought. "I believed I was trapped in this castle with no social life. How strange that now I do not desire to be anywhere else. Like a butterfly, she has settled softly on my shoulder and has shown me her inner beauty. Now my little butterfly will leave me for other horizons. How can I endure her going?"

He rose from the table, so deep in his private thoughts that it never occurred to him that those who watched him shared, in a small way, his same feelings at her absence. Their empathetic glances followed him as he slowly made his way back to his office, blindly moving through the dimness that now enveloped the castle.

Abruptly, he chose to go instead to the Library to visit M. Bourbon. Perhaps an intellectual viewpoint on some subject would help him find his balance again. He laughed at himself that the good advice he had given her today was ironically for him as well. He wondered too if he had indeed served her well. He truly hoped so.

33. Discoveries

"Thy word is a lamp to my feet and a light to my path."

Psalm 119:105 (NASB)

Raymond and Princess Jeanne galloped down the road with the abandonment of children. It was a beautiful, though hot, day. The wind flowing against them as they rode enhanced the feelings of escape and freedom, in spite of the six castle guards galloping faithfully in their wake. After a few miles, Jeanne reined her horse in, laughing.

"What a wonderful feeling it is!" she shouted with joy. Raymond had flown by her at full speed and pulled on his reins to turn and join her. They laughed together with the happiness of the moment. As the horses walked along the road, Raymond became solemn, looking at the Princess with a serious expression.

"It has been a very long time since I have felt such joy." She nodded with an appreciation of what he said. So had it been too long for her.

They rode silently for a time, and then Raymond chuckled and turning toward her, he said, "When Fauzio and I first came for lessons at the castle, we thought you were such a brat! Little Miss Know-it-all, so much younger than us, who was a great irritation when she was always right."

They laughed together, remembering those first heated debates and Jeanne's determination to keep them on task.

"Honestly, Princess, you were very intimidating, and neither of us had ever met a little girl with such a quick mind. We almost hated you for taking lessons with us. It took many months to admit that you were smarter than we were and we would only admit that you were always right after you left the school room. How we resented what was true!"

Jeanne looked at him apologetically and said, "I missed you, Raymond. It was not quite right that Fauzio and I would fight without you. I think Fauzio only became angrier without you to back him up."

Raymond rode along, lost in his memories and thoughts. Then, without looking at Jeanne, he said, "I am at a crossroads, Princess. My future is not clear to me. I have always wanted to grow up to be a good landowner, a loving husband, and a father. Now I am torn between that dream and the awareness I have for the need to minister for Jesus among His people. I have missed studying with you and Fauzio in the Library, although what I have been learning among the chaplains has changed my heart. I cannot explain some of my feelings because there have been times of shock and disappointment at some of the practices among the brotherhood. I care deeply about the people, and so many are lost and in confusion that I feel a great need to help them. To be devoted to them by the denial of my dreams seems greater than I can give."

He looked beseechingly at Jeanne as if expecting her to give him the answers he was seeking. She did not look at him, however; she thought back to the talk she had had with Sir Duquesse at lunch.

They rode in silence again, each buried in their thoughts. Without looking at Raymond, Jeanne eventually said, "I received wise advice today when looking for help on how to proceed with this task in Tours. 'We often jump too quickly to find an answer and then discover our efforts have fallen short because more wisdom was required.' I believe God will guide and guard your thoughts and plans. You must hide your reactions and impulses away in your heart to consider them carefully, in prayer. True wisdom seeks God's guidance and waits for confirmation without surrendering to the impulses of emotion. This advice made sense to me and calmed my fears. It seems we go toward our future one step at a time and the Bible tells us that God will light our way, even though we can't see farther than the light at our feet."

Raymond received these comments silently. He was startled at Jeanne's grasp of truth. He glanced at her gratefully, continuing to ponder how well her words met his questions with wise counsel.

They soon began to encounter more people on the road. Each one looked up at them on their horses in surprise and recognition. They stopped and turned, smiling and waving. Jeanne impulsively slid from her saddle and taking the horse's reins, she walked slowly, pausing to speak to each and to ask about their day or the tasks they were on. It was much more comfortable than she had imagined as everyone was overwhelmed that their Princess would stop and speak to them as if they were her friend. The guards cantered closer, watching anxiously for any sign of disorder or danger.

Raymond dismounted too and walked along adding to the conversation any way he could. He had the amusing thought that they were sprinkling magic, golden, fairy dust along the road as they went. It was true, more than he knew, for happiness and smiles trailed along behind them, lifting the spirits of everyone they greeted. They proceeded very slowly, and at times people bunched up waiting for a turn to speak to the Princess. Finally, they had a stretch of road with no one coming near.

Raymond turned to the Princess and expressed his wonder that her presence and spoken encouragements could have such a dramatic influence on everyone they met. Jeanne laughed gaily and brushed off his remarks.

"It is such a beautiful day, and I love making new friends," she said, taking no credit. "This is a wonderful way to spend the day."

Wondering how she could initiate passing out alms to the people, she said, "I would encourage you, since you are wearing your novice's robe, to spread God's blessing among the people. We need a signal I can give you to drop a few coins in the hand of those in obvious need. What should I say to you?" Being a new experience for both of them, they thought for a while and then decided to stop and pray for guidance. There in the middle of the road, the ten-year-old girl and the thirteen-year-old boy turned toward their horses, and while petting those silky noses, Raymond asked God to guide them.

As they began walking again, Jeanne asked Raymond, "Do you think if I say, after you give a blessing, I would pray a second blessing from the Lord on them? Then you could slip a couple more coins to them. If I say 'a second and third blessing' then you can double the coins. Would that work?"

Raymond had no better idea, so he nodded in agreement. They would know right away if that would be too awkward.

Jeanne continued to work out the process, "I don't know how much trouble it will be if we meet large crowds in town. Maybe if we are always determined to stand near together, we can carry it off. What do you think?"

Raymond nodded again, feeling unsure of his wisdom in the matter. He was trying to remember if he had ever seen another priest accomplish this duty and realized he never had. Nothing that passed between him and his sponsoring priest had included any advice for this situation. He determined that they should trust God to show them how. He knew from previous attendance upon the priests and chaplains at the Chapel, he could learn much from looking deeply into the eyes of those he met. God would reveal, he decided, if he would only listen and seek God's heart.

Soon their concern for large crowds came true. They determined instinctively to always check for the presence of the other as the people pressed upon them and soon began to operate in unison. Jeanne had been reading the New Testament recently and could imagine how Jesus must have felt as the people congregated about Him, nearly pushing Him into the Sea of Galilea; so He had to find a boat to put distance between them.

Jeanne attempted to the best of her ability to talk with each person in front of her, though she soon found that before she could fully understand their needs, someone else had crowded in. She determined that they must attempt to find a stopping place to regroup and assess the number of remaining coins. She wondered if God was multiplying those coins in the purse as Jesus had blessed the bread and fishes with increase when He fed the multitude.

They were trying to move slowly in the direction of the center of town, and eventually, Jeanne saw the offices of the mayor and urged Raymond to move that way so they could enter the building. She was getting tired. Even though meeting people had energized her, the heat and the press of the crowds pushing back and forth against her had begun to take its toll. She was very thirsty and quickly excused herself and Raymond when they reached the bottom of the steps to the building. Raymond glanced at her gratefully as they climbed the steps and entered the building, barely noticing the castle guards who assumed formation at the bottom of the steps. He imagined they too were relieved to have the Princess separated from the crowds.

Surprisingly, the mayor was waiting for them inside the doors and hastily ushered them into his office. Raymond was a bit dismayed on the part of the Princess that the mayor had not seen fit to honor her majesty by meeting them before they had reached the steps. He was amused and impressed by the Princess as she extended her hand, giving the mayor an opportunity to kiss her fingers respectfully. She stood before him with her regal carriage reducing him to a mere supplicant until he showed the respect she deserved. After the mayor rose from bowing to her and kissing her hand, the Princess sweetly smiled and asked if he might have some refreshment to share with them, and something for her guards outside. Only when he had left in search of a provision to her request did she take a seat in the chair before the desk. Raymond dropped like a heavyweight into a side chair, marveling at the stamina and charm of the Princess. He felt completely drained, but her majesty was composed and serene as they waited for the mayor to return.

Jeanne was trying to determine in her mind how to approach the mayor to get him to help her find the properties M. d'Izernay had listed for her. When they left here, they must mount their horses and ride toward the properties without stopping to mingle and visit as before. Also, she wanted to be sure to find the Abérnois' home before the day flew by too quickly. She must see Antoinette and hopefully, talk with her mother. Her eagerness to complete these tasks renewed her enthusiasm, and her tired eyes again sparkled with anticipation.

Raymond, watching her from lowered eyelids as he attempted to renew his strength, continued to be amazed at the dynamic purpose that filled her and the power of her composure and loveliness. He could hardly comprehend that the girl he had grown up with was this person. His humble opinion of himself only increased his admiration for the person she had become.

"She is a born leader," he said to himself. "People will always follow her because she will capture their hearts and love. France is fortunate to have her in its royal family."

Then a shadow crossed his heart as he realized that such a rare jewel would most likely go to the highest political bidder in the devious maneuvering common among royal families. He must devote himself to prayers for her future, he realized. To lose her to some unworthy, self-centered sovereign in another country would indeed be a crime against France, and God.

The mayor returned and offered them glasses of watered wine. They carried on polite conversation, and Raymond could see Princess Jeanne diplomatically steer the discussion to the mayor's vision of how he would improve the conditions of the poor in the town. She probed like a surgeon to determine at what point his goals slipped into selfish desires for his benefit. Finally, the Princess rose from her chair. Following her lead, Raymond asked for God's blessings on the mayor, smiling as he turned to leave.

Suddenly, as though something had slipped her mind, the Princess turned to ask the mayor if he would be able to provide her with directions to other destinations on their agenda. Her inquiry appeared as though the primary purpose of their presence in Tours was to visit the mayor. Only if they had sufficient time, would they seek to find other destinations. The Princess had accomplished her purposes with such grace that they were leaving the mayor glowing over her shared interest in his goals and approval of his completion of the tasks of his official duties.

"She has caught him hook, line and sinker," Raymond thought. "Like a fish, he dangles in the wind, hoping for another opportunity to serve her. He doesn't even realize how well she knows his secret ambitions now. Poor guy, he will do anything for her."

The crowds had dispersed before they left the building and mounted their horses. Riding through the town, following the mayor's directions, they talked quietly of what Jeanne was looking to find in the buildings they were visiting. She asked Raymond to help remember the layout of each so he could help her recall them separately after they returned to the castle. Without even knowing what she was looking for, M. d'Izernay had highlighted three possibilities, and Jeanne intended to limit searching to just these three on this trip. She was increasingly aware of the limited time left to see Antoinette.

Silently praying as they wound through the crooked streets, Jeanne asked God to reveal to her if any of these buildings would fit her plans. Finally, they found the first building.

The interior smelled musty and of mice. Jeanne's nose wrinkled in disgust, and she had to remind herself that nothing was going to be suitable until it was adequately cleaned and set in order. At least the windows were intact and the stairway strong and sturdy. It was a narrow building with the stairs and a hallway side by side in the middle, with two rooms on each side branching off the hall. The second story was identical. A small enclosed yard of dirt appeared through the back door. "A possibility," Jeanne thought, "although it doesn't exactly invite me inside." She noted other details to remember and hoped she would be able to differentiate it from the others. They locked up and stepped out to mount their horses when the neighbors began to stream off their porches and gathered nearby. The mounted guards moved closer to the Princess.

Jeanne smilingly greeted each person and deftly avoided answering their questions about her interest in the building by asking them about themselves. Raymond asked God's blessing on each one, allowing the Princess to be seated on her horse. Then he too mounted up, and they rode away toward the next building. After a while, Jeanne looked at him and laughed.

"We might as well get used to it," she said. "How silly to believe we can go about our business without being seen, especially when there is such a crowd of us." They laughed together as they rode.

Although in a little better neighborhood, the second building was identical to the first, down to even the small detail of the odor of mice, with nothing to distinguish it but the surrounding buildings. Inside they giggled that in fact, they must be standing in the same building. Had they only ridden in a circle? This time, however, the buildings surrounding them did not empty and though they could discern faces in the windows, no one came to greet them. Jeanne pondered this fact as they rode away, thinking if these people would not spread their hospitality to royal visitors, she could imagine their reaction if people from the more unfortunate side of town began coming here. Jeanne dismissed this building immediately from her list, deciding that the neighborhood would sink her project before it ever started.

Directions to the third building led them across the town center to the other side. These buildings were older, though many were well-kept. Jeanne observed that the streets were not as well cared for, with numerous muddy puddles to avoid. Few of the buildings had more than one story. The fronts of the buildings sometimes revealed their bones through chipped paint and warped boards.

Then their road narrowed to a pathway meandering through some beech trees with the leaves rattling in the breeze. Grass along the side of the path was long and uncut, mixed in with tumbling wild rose bushes. Jeanne consulted her directions again to avoid getting lost. Perhaps they had made a wrong turn. Not so, she discovered, for there were no other roads to choose; so they rode on. The trees continued to march alongside the shady path until it eventually turned a corner. The guards had dropped well behind because the area appeared to be unpopulated and secluded.

They turned the corner, and the path opened out to show an old house that reminded Jeanne of a wrinkled, old man, blinking and smiling in the sun. A tall wisteria bush with spindly arms spread out over the eaves on the second floor, dripping its purple flowers like a carpet around the house. The windows appeared to wink at them in welcome, and the leaves that had gathered along the roof sloping away from the eaves looked to Jeanne like the rumpled hair of a sleepy child. She laughed out loud, turning to Raymond to say, "God loves this house! Do you think He has chosen it for us?"

Though the boards of the house had spots of chipped paint, Jeanne felt it only enhanced its comfortable, welcoming demeanor.

The windows were unbroken, although they needed a proper washing. Unattended flowers bloomed everywhere with lavender bushes of vibrant purple flowers lined up around the outside of the property, and the shaded, broad porch roof only drooped a little. Jeanne tied her horse and skipped up the stone steps. She carried the key in her pocket and impatiently looked back to see if Raymond was following her. He was standing very still, looking up toward the roof. Then he looked in her direction, and said, "At least it doesn't have mice!" He pointed to the casement window on the right side of the roof. There sat a white cat cleaning her paws in the sun. Now that they were watching her, she stretched and leaving her perch proceeded to join them on the porch.

Jeanne unlocked the door and pushed it open to the sound of hinges creaking. She stood on the threshold and looked around her with pleasure. The inside was accessible from the front to the back with a wide stairway rising from the middle of the house to the second floor. The cat caressed her skirt with its body and curled its tail around her ankle. Then it sat on her boot and began purring in a contented rumble. Jeanne's eyes followed the staircase upward to the railing that ran around the opening looking down from the second floor, giving the house a large and inviting aspect. Solid wooden floors still retained a semblance of polish and shone in the dusty sunbeams. On each side of the house, a fireplace was placed precisely in the middle of the wall. Windows all around shone with the full light of the day through their dusty panes. A hallway stretched further back revealing doors to other rooms.

Jeanne could imagine the people that would gather here, joyfully contributing their small part to meet the needs of the many. Jeanne hugged herself, believing with all her heart that God shared her vision and had chosen this happy house long ago to be ready for her.

34. New Plans

*"For I know the plans that I have for you, declares the
Lord, plans for welfare and not for calamity to give you
a future and a hope."*

Jeremiah 29:11 (NASB)

"**I**t's perfect!" Jeanne whispered. She looked excitedly at
Raymond and said, "I have found what I am looking for!"

Raymond nodded, not saying that his practical mind could only
see the needed work. "But hey," he thought, "I am not a Princess
with a host of willing workers at my command."

He was pleased that she was happy and excited about what she
saw. He willingly granted that she always seemed to see the best in
everything; even living in that gloomy castle with the knowledge
of its torture chamber still in mind, she continued to seek for good.
He was glad he was with her today. He had enjoyed being a part
of her adventure and hoped they would do it again soon. He had
been able to see what would be required of him, at least in a small
way, if he chose to follow the path of the priesthood. Deep in his
mind, however, though he refused to acknowledge it, if he could
find a woman like the Princess to love, he would choose to give up
serving humanity to serve her with all his heart.

Now that Jeanne had made her decision, she was anxious to
find Antoinette. The sun was moving quickly into the western sky,
and she knew she must head toward the castle before too long. If

they did not return promptly, it was doubtful she would be allowed to continue coming to Tours. It was critical to her that she advance this plan and was not willing to risk it by running late. She hurried Raymond outside and locked the building. The directions she had to Antoinette's home were in her saddlebags, and she searched for them in haste. Pulling them out and reading what M. Abérnois had written, she could see they were not far from her destination. As they rode along, she happily saw that the old house would be in easy walking distance for Madame Abérnois.

The sound of eight horses riding through the neighborhood brought people out of the houses, excited at their presence. Again, the Princess dismounted from her saddle and walked among them. She had forgotten to ask Raymond how many coins were left, so she delegated the blessing to him, sure he could recognize their needs. The crowd seemed to know where she was going as the way opened up and soon she could see Antoinette standing on her porch step. Jeanne waved enthusiastically, wanting to break free and run to her side. That, of course, was not the training of a Princess, so she walked on, graciously greeting everyone with a kind look and a smile just for them.

Royally, she moved gracefully through the crowd, flanked by her soldiers, until she reached Antoinette who stood immobile, shocked to her core that the Princess would seek her out. Her Dads had shared everything he could remember about the Princess since he had been working at the castle. Antoinette had asked him to repeat every detail over again, feeling she knew everything there was to know about her royal friend.

She had even imagined they had grown up together. She never expected the Princess would care as much about her, though. After all, as a Princess, she had everything she could want at her fingertips; beautiful clothes, a horse, a dog and people to do everything for her. Antoinette had even gone to school to feel like an equal. It was true her Dads was her teacher after he came home at night, so it was not like having a tutor, but Antoinette had been ready to do anything to make herself like Jeanne. Today, however, this visit was unexpected, finding her unprepared.

At least she had closed her mouth. When the Princess moved beside her and smiled, Antoinette could only stare. Jeanne had grown even more beautiful than before. Then the Princess reached out to embrace her and Antoinette was overwhelmed again, however when she looked over Jeanne's shoulder at the crowd of her neighbors clapping in happiness for her, she recovered enough to return the embrace and invite the Princess into her home. As though in a fog, Antoinette saw the Princess turn to a handsome, young man at her side. Puzzled at first, thinking she was meeting the Princess's beau, she then realized he was wearing a novice priest's robe and forced herself to listen carefully to the Princess as she introduced Raymond. Finally, she came to herself and welcomed them both to go in. Her Mumsie was standing just inside the door smiling in disbelief, nearly as incapacitated as her daughter.

The house was pleasantly cool and neat; very homey and comfortable. Jeanne was delighted to finally find her friend. She met Mumsie and happily accepted a glass of tea. For her, it was an excellent way to complete her day. She looked over at Antoinette, who was not as thin as she had been when they first met and caught her looking at Raymond.

Waiting another moment, she said, "I have waited so long to come and see you again, Antoinette. Even though the years have passed, I have always thought of you as my dear friend. Many days, I leaned on your memory as my only friend, and that helped me through the sad times. I am so happy to be here with you. You have grown up a lot. You are taller and more beautiful than ever. I remember your blue eyes and think of you often."

Antoinette gazed at the Princess as she spoke, feeling deeply the friendship offered to her. Then, as naturally as could be, they began to chatter together about the thoughts and interests of any ten-year-old girls.

Raymond shyly watched them. He was a bit envious of their shared friendship. This day with Jeanne had also been a bond of togetherness for him and he had to admit to being jealous of Jeanne's connection with Antoinette. If he were honest with himself, he would have realized that he suddenly wanted to be a friend to Antoinette like her reciprocating friendship with Jeanne.

He had tried not to stare at Antoinette. Her beauty was not as apparent as Jeanne's because she was very shy. He had to admit to himself that both were stunning in their unique way. He had dismissed his affection for Jeanne as only friendly, like a brother. Her path would go a different direction than his. To be considered her friend was honor enough.

He listened as Antoinette told Princess Jeanne about the day they had met and what had happened from then until she received the blue dress. She spoke of that miserable day with amusement, glossing over the scariest parts with humor. Everyone laughed with her, but Raymond could hear the undercurrent of fear and desperation in her voice as she shared the occurrences of that fateful night. It was in his nature to listen carefully to everyone and seek to understand the hidden emotions they secretly carried. His urge to be a protector of all poor creatures in need flared in his heart and wanting to comfort Antoinette, observed her. He noticed the curves of her delicate face and throat and the sweetness of her smile. She made him feel, well, funny, in a fuzzy sort of way.

Suddenly aware that someone had caught him staring, he glanced at Mumsie who had returned from taking glasses of tea to the soldiers and realized she had been watching him. Embarrassed, he blushed deeply, his emotions openly revealed on his face. Averting his eyes, he sought something else, anything, to distract his thoughts. He noticed a small child of two or three years old peeking out from behind a large basket with wood blocks scattered at his feet. Raymond smiled broadly and beckoned to the child to come to him. Immediately the toddler grabbed a small block of wood he had been stacking and pushed to his feet. He toddled to Raymond, holding out the piece of wood as a gift to share with this new face shining with invitation and friendship.

Delighted, Raymond centered his attention on the child. Jabbering excitedly, the child began sharing with him all that was fascinating about the wood. Raymond nodded and admired its shape and sturdiness. Completely immersed in the small world of the child he did not see the Princess rise and go to speak with Mumsie in the kitchen. Nor did he realize Antoinette had moved to sit on the floor beside him. However, the child was delighted that Antoinette had joined them and reached for her arm to pull her closer; suddenly they were in a small world of three. Antoinette bent over and kissed her little brother on the forehead with great affection, even though he was so focused on his woodblock he didn't even glance at her or pause his jabbering.

Raymond smiled at her across the curly head of the child and felt a thrill hit his chest. His heart was pounding in his ears, and he could feel the heat rising into his cheeks. Quickly looking down at the block of wood, Raymond heard Antoinette speaking in a soft voice, "This is my baby brother, Gerald. I didn't tell the Princess how close he came to dying of starvation when she saved our lives. I do not know if she could understand, but I believe you may."

Her words drew his eyes back to her face, and he looked at her with such compassion she felt he was looking into her heart. For a moment, time stood still, and Raymond instinctively pulled the child protectively closer to his chest. In that breathless instant, a bond was stamped indelibly on the souls of the two young people. A brand new world of happiness and possibilities had just opened; it was now a world of only the two of them.

Gerald did not protest at first, though he was not accustomed to being ignored. Then he threw his arms in the air and shouted out with all his strength. He broke the grip of the arms that tightly squeezed him and succeeded to bring the attention of everyone to the most important person in the room, himself.

Raymond and Antoinette laughed, relieved at the distraction, yet regretting that the spell had broken. The thrill still settled in their chests.

Princess Jeanne had been in deep conversation with Mumsie, and the outburst of baby Gerald brought their attention to the group on the floor. Jeanne suddenly realized time was passing too quickly and they must leave. Reluctantly, she turned to Mumsie and asked permission to visit again soon. Their conversation had been informative and had given the Princess many avenues to explore; however, Jeanne had not yet made clear her interest in Mumsie being a part of her plan. She quickly asked if she might leave the packets of garments they had brought if Mumsie would be willing to distribute them throughout the neighborhood. Leaning close, the Princess suggested that Antoinette might choose first what she would like for her own.

Mumsie curtsied low, graciously thanking Princess Jeanne for honoring her humble home and urged her to visit Antoinette any time she chose. She liked this young lady and could see that, though it was a strange situation, a strong bond had formed between her daughter and this royal Princess. That they would ever be able to return all the Princess had done for them as a family, she realized, was impossible. As she rose from her curtsy, her conscience sharply nudged her and she looked to heaven and silently said, "Right. It was You, God, in all Your goodness. Thank you. The Princess was willing, though, to be used by You and I will always be grateful to her for that."

Princess Jeanne embraced Antoinette and coaxing Gerald from Raymond's arms, she cooed at him and kissed his cheek. Handing Gerald to his mother, she announced they must be leaving to be back to the castle before dinner.

Mumsie glanced at Antoinette and saw that her daughter and the young man were gazing at each other again. She was disturbed at that look because of the novice robe he was wearing. As Mumsie was watching the handsome face of the young man, questions began to tumble chaotically in her mind. She recognized his look, and her insides stirred, recalling how she had felt when M. Abérnois first looked at her that way.

"No! She is only ten years old!" she protested. "He has many important decisions to make at this time in his life," she thought, watching Raymond.

She did like the young man, though, and could only imagine the turmoil he must be in about deciding his future. She adored her daughter and admitted she could not blame him. "I'll bet he never expected Antoinette to hit him this hard."

As they stepped outside, the guards began to scramble to their feet from the various shady corners around the house. Princess Jeanne directed them to bring the packets from their saddlebags and leave them with the lady of the house. Soon they were mounted and waved goodbye. Raymond's gaze lingered a moment longer on Antoinette; then he turned away; this memory would disturb his thoughts many times as the days passed.

Antoinette was still on the porch steps looking down the road as if hoping their guests would turn and come back to her. Deeply confused, Antoinette did not understand these strange, new emotions that had overcome her.

Princess Jeanne and Raymond were silent as they rode toward the road leading to the castle. Jeanne's mind focused on Antoinette and the story she had told about receiving the blue dress. Jeanne was gratified to hear how much pleasure the gift had brought. Grateful for the wise advice of both Aymée and Sir Duquesse, she could now understand more thoroughly how their counsel had helped her find a more appropriate way to help the whole family. Naturally, the family prospered with Dads working steadily at the castle, and that gave Jeanne a satisfied sense of having indeed met their needs in a lasting manner. Jeanne smiled as she thought of little Gerald, recalling how hungry he must have been that Antoinette had been forced to search for food among the trash heaps. Her thoughts turned then to the plans that were forming in her mind. Somehow, she concluded, she must find a way to keep that from happening to any child in Tours ever again.

Raymond was also in deep thought about the day, especially about Antoinette. He tried to think of something else. It was hopeless, however. He directed his thoughts to decide about his future in the priesthood, but his mind ran to pictures of his father's estate, with a woman, a baby in her arms, at the door waiting for him to return to her. Inevitably, the woman had Antoinette's face. Then he would chide himself for even letting those thoughts invade his mind, arguing that his tomorrow had already been decided.

Muddled, he was grateful when Princess Jeanne suddenly spoke to her horse and broke into a gallop at full speed. He spurred his mount to catch her, hearing the riders behind ordering their horses in pursuit. With the wind streaming through his hair, his thoughts were left behind him while he leaned into his horse's mane, urging him to catch the Princess; though by now, she was far ahead.

35. Seeking a Higher Purpose

"Lift up your eyes on high and see who has created these stars, the One who leads forth their host by number, He calls them all by name; because of the greatness of His might and the strength of His power not one of them is missing."

Isaiah 40:26 (NASB)

Jeanne rose early the next morning. She quietly slipped up the stairs to her secret room. Sir Ami sleepily followed her, curling up near the warm brazier. The stars glittered against the velvet darkness. Jeanne, standing at the window, gazed at the celestial diamonds sparkling in their beauty; she began to feel how tiny she was in a universe of such order that the stars each knew their place.

"Where do I fit?" she asked the darkness. "Do I have a specific role to fill? How can I be prepared for a life in Your universe when I am so separated and lonely?" There was no answer in the infinite darkness.

Her eyes focused on the bright morning star and she bowed her head in disappointment. Sitting on the cushions along the window, she longed intensely in her heart to have a bright star to guide her.

"Who is this girl You see, Lord? How will I follow these dreams in my head if I have no guidance from You or encouragement from those around me? Everything feels so far away."

186

She raised her eyes to a landscape shadowed and dark. The world was asleep, and the silence was deep around her. As she watched, a sliver on the eastern horizon began glowing in the night, rising higher and dancing with light; growing and advancing to wake the heavens and the earth. Floating clouds turned from light grey to pink, and then shining golden around the edges as the brilliance of the sun gained the horizon and flooded the land with its warmth.

"O Lord," Jeanne murmured, "can You make me like those clouds? Coming from dark night to grow in Your great light, pink and unsure; welcoming and enduring the power of Your fire and glory, to emerge wrapped in gold and full of light? How can You take me, so lonely and selfish, and use me to become something good for You?"

In the quiet, Jeanne sensed the immense power of the universe seeming to focus in the still shining morning star.

"Like the power of the morning star shining in the dawn, I will carry hope with me to be my guiding light and help," she whispered.

Thinking back to the joy of discovering that quaint, old house, she embraced the vision of it as a glowing beacon in the darkness of the poverty that surrounded it, so evident in the shabby dwellings of Antoinette's neighborhood. Conviction flourished in her heart to make this house a source of hope and opportunity for the poor and unfortunate of the town. She would strive to develop this 'hope house' to be a community center giving the honest people trapped in poverty an opportunity to raise themselves up, and then to turn and help others.

How should she go about getting this idea to come to life? She knew she must be very organized, wise and careful as she sought help to bring it to life. Sure that Aymée and Sir Duquesse would be eager to help, she wondered if M. d'Izernay would find a way to thwart her dream. First of all, she must go to him this morning to seek the King's approval for her to use that building in her ambassadorial efforts. Would he question her motives? Would his inquiry of the King appear negative toward her use of it? She almost felt defeated before beginning. She must be nonchalant so the steward would not see how important it was to her.

"Lord, help me in this," she prayed.

Her thoughts shifted to Sir Duquesse. Would he feel that helping her obtain workers to clean and repair the house might be outside his duties at the castle? Should she talk with M. Abérnois about finding men in the neighborhood to work on the house? Would that create other problems she could not foresee? Again, she sought God for help and guidance.

How could Raymond help her in this effort? He had been so willing to join in her adventures yesterday. She believed his heart for people made him supportive so she was sure he would want to help. Somehow, when Raymond was with her, she felt capable of making her dreams come true. A realization that he had shared her vision encouraged her in the middle of all these misgivings. Maybe she could sort her plans out by talking with him.

The day brightened, and she felt restless, anxious to begin seeking help and guidance. Jumping to her feet, she hurried to her bedroom to dress for the day ahead. The newness of the day held promise; she had goals to set to bring her dream closer to being real.

Aymée watched the Princess as she burst into the room with purpose on her face. So, something happened yesterday. The trip as ambassador to Tours had been a good idea. She continued with her morning duties, waiting for Jeanne to share her thoughts when she was ready. Jeanne fidgeted all through Aymée's attempts to brush her hair, asking impatiently that she only pull her hair away from her face and fasten it tightly at the back of her head. Anxious to be off to talk with M. d'Izernay, she decided to see how her visit with him would go before talking with Aymée about her dreams. There would be no dream if M. d'Izernay would not help her.

She was off as soon as Aymée released her hair, dashing down the stairs with Sir Ami at her heels. She slowed to walk with proper dignity as she approached the steward's office. Knowing she was about quite early in the day, she wondered if M. d'Izernay had had breakfast and his cup of tea yet. She didn't want to find him grumpy and obstinate. Before she raised her hand to knock, she determined to be sure he was ready to start his day.

M. d'Izernay opened his door at her knock, greeting the Princess with a warm smile. That nearly knocked her off her purpose as she wondered what could have prompted such cheeriness. She sat before his desk, with Sir Ami settled at her feet, waiting for him to be seated. Trying desperately to hide her anticipation and enthusiasm, Jeanne carefully formed her comments.

She took a deep breath and said, "M. d'Izernay, I realize it is very early in the morning, and I apologize for interrupting your routine. I am so appreciative for your help to further my task of an ambassador of King Francis. Yesterday, I realized that having a location in Tours to set up as a headquarters would be truly helpful. Your list of properties was an excellent way to start, and I saw each one. I have selected one of the properties as my best choice to meet with individuals where I can do the King's work in privacy. How do I go about securing this property for that purpose? Please advise me how to get the King's approval so I can begin having the building cleaned and updated."

M. d'Izernay sat across the desk with his fingertips making a tent so he could rest his chin on them. The pleasure he felt as the Princess was speaking showed on his face.

"So," he thought, "the Princess has come to me for help and advice. At last, she has realized how necessary I am to the King in my position here."

He sat up straighter in his chair and puffed up his chest like a peacock. Looking down the bridge of his nose at the Princess, he proceeded to advise her on how to advance her project. She listened carefully, agreeing to whatever he felt he should do to achieve the King's cooperation. When he finished, she asked if writing to the King herself would be helpful.

"No, no," he assured her, "I am quite able to handle all this myself. I will let you know as soon as I have received his permission."

Stifling her urge to giggle at his sense of self-importance, it occurred to her to give him the address of the property, although she was in doubt he would remember it. Then Princess Jeanne thought she should ask about avenues of getting some workmen to clean and repair the building. M. d'Izernay was feeling very benevolent; he assured her there would be no problem. He walked her to the door bowing and nodding; repeating she could depend on him to see to everything. The Princess smiled saying she would

mention to her uncle when she next saw him, how helpful M. d'Izernay had been.

"Well," she thought, as he closed his door behind her, "that
seemed to go well. At least he was agreeable and seemed happy
to help. I must write Uncle Francis myself to be sure M. d'Izernay
requests permission for the correct property."

Turning toward Sir Duquesse's office, she knelt down to pet
Sir Ami as she gathered her thoughts. Unlike the steward's office,
Sir Duquesse's door was standing open and very accessible; she
knocked on the doorjamb to alert the Chamberlain of her presence.

Sir Duquesse was delighted to see her. She could see it in his
smile. He, in turn, thought how lovely she was and was sure he
could detect a new glow of purpose in her demeanor. He shut the
door behind her to ensure privacy for their conversation and sat
beside her in one of the chairs before his desk.

"He always lifts me up and honors my royal position," she
thought. "What a contrast from M. d'Izernay."

"Princess Jeanne," he asked, "would you like a cup of tea? How
can I serve you this morning? I have been wondering how your
day went while in Tours yesterday. I hope you will share with me
what happened there."

Jeanne smiled in return, warmly feeling his genuine care and
interest. She agreed a cup of tea would be appreciated, thinking,
"It will be something to do with my hands while I am figuring out
what to say."

Sir Duquesse called for the tea. Jeanne began telling him how
wonderful it had been to ride into Tours on horseback. She said how
Raymond had been a great companion and help, and they hardly
noticed the guards that came along. Sir Duquesse poured two cups
of tea and settled back to listen to her tell about the crushing crowds
and their escape into the mayor's office.

She did not notice Sir Duquesse's sharp look when she mentioned that the mayor was waiting inside the front door when they
finally got there. He made a mental note to clarify to the mayor
his responsibility to their sovereign King or any ambassador on
the King's business. He flushed with anger that the mayor failed

to honor Princess Jeanne. It would be necessary to visit Tours this afternoon to remedy this ignorance.

Catching up with Jeanne's tale about her interview with the mayor, he was impressed to hear how astutely she analyzed where the mayor's real desires lay. He thought, "At least the old fool did not pull the wool over her eyes."

Then Jeanne hesitated and when she looked up her eyes shone with delight, and she began to tell him about her search for a building in the town to use for a headquarters for her task as an ambassador for the King. She leaned forward and began to describe the old house at the end of the beech-lined pathway. Her laughter delighted him as he watched her tell of being completely captivated by the warm welcome of the broken down old building. He could not imagine what had caused her to fall in love with this old building.

"It sounds wonderful, Princess, and I look forward to discovering it myself as soon as possible. How can I help you in this endeavor? Princess, you know I have devoted myself to serving you in the best way I can. I want to help you see your dream materialize."

"My plan is much bigger than meeting and greeting. I have been afraid that should anyone hear about it would immediately be opposed." She looked up and met his eyes.

"If I tell you, will you be patient and listen to everything before you find fault? I have my heart set on making it work, but I admit I need guidance to avoid the many pitfalls I may not be wise enough to anticipate."

She pleadingly searched his eyes, seeking affirmation that she could trust him to keep from jumping to conclusions. He prepared himself to listen carefully to what Jeanne had to share.

He had to admit that she had given this 'hope house' plan a great deal of thought. Even though he identified a few possible areas that needed clarification, he was quite impressed by her overall grasp of the difficulties of bringing it along. He could see many areas where he might assist her and wondered what kind of reception she had received from M. d'Izernay. He was eager to talk with Aymée to understand what she thought about it.

Would this be something the King would be willing to stand behind? The "almost war" with Spain had severely reduced France's available financial reserves; so it was unlikely King Francis would be generous with his resources. Surely they could enable this effort someway without asking much of the King. If they could get it in operation before the King's next visit, he might be pleased and heartily throw his weight and materials in as support.

Jeanne continued to unfold her plan in its entirety. She described how the people could come to the 'hope house' for help. Trading work for helping at the 'hope house' they could earn 'points' to buy food and clothing for their family's needs. Jeanne imagined the women, who normally sit at home, could bring their skills in knitting, quilting, or cooking and baking, and teach each other, socializing and making items to be 'sold' in the hope house to those who worked there to obtain provisions. Clothes that have been outgrown or discarded could be mended and made available to those too unfortunate to cover themselves. Understanding that the markets in the town or the farmers selling their products often dump food at the end of the day, knowing it would rot before morning, Jeanne envisioned arranging to collect that food and use it to cook healthy stews to feed those starving in the streets.

"Wouldn't it be wonderful to remove all those trash heaps on every street in the town? Men who need work could be part of a work crew to do that job. The mayor was certainly not interested in seeing them removed," Jeanne beamed at Sir Duquesse with anticipation.

Then, she admitted, "I know it will take a long time to organize and make it work, but I have every confidence that Madame Abérnois and her neighbors could put it into operation. When I talked with her yesterday, she had many ideas to add, and she did not even know I was thinking of her to start it up."

She looked at him expectantly, finally asking timidly, "What do you think?"

While Sir Duquesse was organizing his thoughts, Jeanne spoke up to say, "At least we should buy a goat for the backyard so no more babies will starve."

Sir Duquesse laughed at this and agreed that a goat would be a good beginning.

Then he looked at her seriously and said, "This is an extensive project, and you have thought it through very well from beginning to end. We must plan it in stages, learning as we go. You have a wonderful heart, Princess Jeanne, and your people are more fortunate than they know to have you looking out for them. We have to be realistic, however, and plan carefully, considering every possible mistake. Such as, if we tied a goat in the backyard now, someone could steal it easily and walk away with the babies' milk. Before bringing it to the house, we must have a strong fence built to secure the goat. You have already described the house as 'old' and a bit droopy. It will require a good going over by someone who has a keen eye for how to fix it. How would you feel if I take a look at it today when I go into Tours on another matter? Then I will have a better idea of how to evaluate with you how to proceed. Or, would you like to ride in with me and we can look at it together?"

"Oh yes," Jeanne replied, "it would be nice if Aymée could come too, and see the plan with us!" At this remark, Sir Ami immediately lifted his head off Jeanne's feet and looking eagerly at them; he "woofed" so he would not be left behind.

36. God in Us

*"For I will pour out water on the thirsty land and
streams on the dry ground; I will pour out My Spirit on
your offspring and My blessing on your descendants;
and they will spring up among the grass like poplars by
streams of water."*

Isaiah 44:3,4 (NASB)

Princess Jeanne's intense determination to bring her vision to
life resulted in often meeting with Madame Abérnois, sharing
her thoughts and seeking input and advice from a woman who
had seen the problems from personal experiences in the depths
of despair, familiar to so many in Tours. The Princess studied any
available economic and financial guides M. Bourbon could provide.
The expertise and guidelines of experts in those fields helped her
to adapt her expectations to reality. With the strength of her conviction and determination, she met obstacles head on and sought
every avenue available to diminish them. She became acquainted
with the ordinary people and their stories and then found solutions to help overcome the difficulties they faced daily. Always,
she respected their dignity, recognizing that each person she met
had suffered some impact on their lives and beliefs. Every person
had a different story, unique to their history.

Many days, Raymond accompanied her to Tours. They encouraged each other, believing that any effort to raise the brokenhearted

and dismayed from defeat to hope was a small step toward their goal. Nearly a year after the idea came to Jeanne, followed by days and hours of planning and labor, the 'hope house' began operation with faltering steps forward.

On an early October morning in 1539, shivering in the bleak light of early dawn, scruffy looking men pulled their thin shirts tightly around arms clasped to collect some warmth. Their faces showed lines of exhaustion and defeat. The grim men faced this day as they had so many days before. Without hope of change, it would be followed by more of the same. They were more occupied with the year's first, brisk, north wind and their hungry stomachs than the wait they faced for someone to pull them from the line to earn a day's wages and possibly a hot meal at midday.

Leaning against any structure they could find nearby, some dozed as they waited. Others watched the line grow to stretch down the street and around the corner. It made no difference if a man was at the first of the line or the last; employers who were looking for a day laborer needed specific skills for the required job. The sun rose beneath a cloudy sky, and it seemed the cold wind only dropped to hug the earth closer.

A group of young boys came around the corner, splitting off to go to different points along the line. Many headed directly for their fathers, first.

They held out pieces of paper, shouting, "A job! There is a job here!"

The word spread along the line more rapidly than the boys could move. Men gathered in small groups to see what the papers said; shouting questions for answers not able to be heard above the melee. Before long, every man and boy disappeared, running down the street and across the town to the beech tree lane. The crowd was like a sponge, picking up stragglers and friends along the way, swelling in size as it moved.

When they turned at the last corner of the beech tree lane, they saw the Princess standing on the porch of the house of hope. Her warm smiles radiated outward and embraced them all. Beside her on the porch were lengths of lumber, posts and fencing, tools, paint barrels, buckets and gardening implements. Madame Abérnois sat at a table on the porch to take names and list each man's skills and abilities before assigning work teams. Antoinette waited by the front door to direct them into the house after they checked in. Inside the warm house, breakfast and hot tea were waiting.

By mid-morning, anyone who happened to walk by would have seen men all over the house like ants, mending boards, replacing roof tiles, digging post holes, stretching fencing, painting, and digging weeds.

Enriched by energies and resources beyond Princess Jeanne's efforts, the house filled with enticing smells of large pots of stew and baking bread; coats and sweaters and warm clothes were stacked in rooms waiting to be handed out. Women gathered, excited at the supplies that had mysteriously appeared on shelves, pooling their energies to knit socks, hats, and gloves; to bake and quilt and mend clothes. Unemployed men found work to do completing assigned tasks like removing trash heaps from city streets, hauling barrows of gravel from hills outside the town to fill mud holes, or attending to the maintenance and repair of the hope house. Then, they moved into their neighborhoods to repair homes of widows, the elderly or sick of the neediest in the community. No longer were starving urchins and beggars rounded up for indefinite stays in the lock-up.

At the center of this hub of hope and comfort, Madame Abérnois kept a firm grasp on every aspect of activity down to the smallest detail. Like a mother hen, she clothed and fed all who came in need of help to get back on their feet again. Many of the tradesmen and merchants of the town sought out the workers at the hope house to fill their employment needs.

Jeanne's greatest satisfaction was the goats and two milk cows safely sheltered within the fenced backyard. She shared Madame Abérnois' fervor that never again would a baby die of starvation in the town of Tours.

As improvements throughout the community started to dawn on the conscious awareness of the citizens of Tours, the mayor was surprised to receive praise for the achievements that were evident everywhere. Perplexed at these laurels to his credit, he wondered what had affected their genesis. However, basking in the glory of reports being broadcast abroad of the improvements being a model of successful community development, he avoided seeking the truth behind the results. He was well aware these accomplishments were utterly devoid of his efforts and only too happy to receive the praise and acclaim.

The people in Tours felt no need to enlighten the ignorance of their mayor. Instead, their love for their Princess and loyalty to their King established a covenant of faith that remained unbroken.

The Princess worked tirelessly, inspired by the emerging changes evident as each day passed. Keeping a low profile when making visits to Tours, accompanied only by Sir Ami and a couple of palace guards, she visited the people in their homes, spreading encouragement and seeing to their small comforts.

Before the King of France came to Château de Plessis-lez-Tours in late October to hunt stag with his noble companions, word came from a number of his confidential sources about the changes evident in Tours. As the King and his party drew near to the Loire river valley, he changed his travel plans to ride through Tours instead of skirting it as he usually did. Word sent on ahead proclaimed that the King and his party were approaching the town.

The announcement of the news drew crowds from the country and every corner of town to line the roads. At the house of hope, everyone left tasks and tools to join the gathering masses. Sweet Princess Jeanne was the face of their good fortune; however, everyone suspected the King had been behind many of the resources which had mysteriously appeared. They were anxious to show their appreciation and loyalty to the King of France.

Jeanne was busy with her visits to the ill and bedridden in the town, not aware that the King's party was approaching. Mumsie sent Antoinette to find the Princess. After knocking on several doors, Antoinette finally located someone who knew where she was. She raced through the neighborhoods to the street she was looking for, just as Princess Jeanne was leaving the house. Her horse stood tethered nearby, and Sir Ami waited on the steps. Jeanne's faithful guards stood ready by her horse. Antoinette excitedly shared her news. Princess Jeanne stood silent, occupied with sorting out her thoughts. Then she invited Antoinette to climb on the horse behind her so they could go together to see the King.

The parade of horses and riders was already winding through the center of town, with King Francis in the center of his nobles and soldiers. The Princess and Antoinette could hear the roar of the crowd from many blocks away, causing Jeanne to believe they would arrive there after the King was already gone.

They had not reckoned with a mayor who used every opportunity to magnify his interests. The crowd silenced as the mayor strutted to the middle of the street to formally welcome the King of France to his town. The mayor was beginning an extended address of appreciation for the fortuitous day that brought the King's presence to Tours when Princess Jeanne, with Antoinette riding behind her, turned a nearby corner and cantered her horse up to the back of the crowd. Unnoticed at first, they watched the proceedings.

Then one of the women who regularly worked at the house of hope punched her husband and whispered loudly, "Look! It's the Princess!" Following her pointing finger, several others shouted, "Princess Jeanne!" Soon, chants of "Our Princess Jeanne! Hail Princess!" moved like a wave rippling across the multitudes, and drowned out the words of the mayor. All eyes turned to look at Jeanne, as did King Francis and every member of his party.

The King stared. At the center of the attention, the young lady dressed in a blue, well-worn riding habit with her dark hair caught up in a ribbon at the back of her head and wayward ringlets curling around her face, sat gracefully on her horse. It seemed as though all the light of the fall day had centered in her. She was looking at the faces of the crowd, smiling at them all, one by one. There was no doubting the affection she had for the people, or their love for her, although she seemed unaware of the force of their adoration. Her bright eyes found the King, and she nodded, and then slid from her saddle. After helping Antoinette down, too, she took her reins and walked toward the King.

Dropping to her knee in a deep curtsy, she paused and then rose and said, "Welcome uncle, you are looking well."

It had been nearly four years since King Francis had seen the Princess. He was seeing his beautiful sister, Marguerite, with all her grace and loveliness, only years younger with an exquisite face, fresh and pure. Whatever the King had expected, this poised, refined young lady was undeniably a surprise. He was astounded by the cheers of the people, knowing the ovation was for her. He remembered the requests that had come from Sir Duquesse and d'Izernay to "help her ambassadorship." He had granted wholesale approval and then thought nothing further of it. Smiling down at his niece, he was now sure the investment was well made. Dismounting, there in the middle of the street in Tours, he pulled his little Princess into his arms and embraced her. The crowd went wild!

Jeanne had been thinking of her work and that she might lead the King to the house of hope to show him what was occurring there; but, with such an enthusiastic crowd gathered around, it was apparent this was not a good time. Perhaps he would be willing later in the week, when he felt satisfied with the hunt, to accompany her without all this fanfare.

The King and Princess remounted their horses, and with Jeanne by his side, they rode toward the Château.

"What a jewel she is. Who could resist loving and desiring my adorable niece?" he thought. "She is ready to be Queen, and I dare not delay in beginning negotiations. It will soon be widespread knowledge that such an exquisite treasure has been hidden away here, near Tours. I must advise Sir Duquesse to be on the lookout for spies and envoys seeking just such a potential consort."

The hunt that year was spectacular, and the King left the Loire river valley quite content with the results he had observed of a well-run castle, a well-trained Princess, and a loyal town. He commended himself for having brought it all to such a success.

He had met with the steward and gotten to the bottom of the little problem on hiring the grunt in the stable. After observing the stable hand himself, he had barked at d'Izernay to have the man promoted. It had only taken a few well-placed remarks from the King of the compliments the Princess had made about d'Izernay's help, along with appropriate emphasis that the Princess was an extension of the King's royal authority. The steward was sure to align himself with the wishes of the King by viewing the Princess as his superior authority.

Jeanne had told him a little of her projects in the town, but he had been too occupied to return there and explore it further. He was satisfied by the response of the crowds in Tours that she had done an excellent job. He congratulated himself again for his decision to appoint her his ambassador.

"Excellent training!" he proclaimed, patting himself on the back.

37. Set Back

*"Then you will call upon Me and come and pray to Me,
and I will listen to you. And you will seek Me and find
Me, when you search for Me with all your heart."*

Jeremiah 29:12-13 (NASB)

T he weather deteriorated as the cold feet of winter began to tread
through the fields and forests. Jeanne threw herself into her
work in the town with a vengeance. She felt as though she was
battling against time with so many little ones and elderly folks
needing food and shelter from the cold. There were too many forgotten souls turning up on street corners.

It never occurred to Jeanne that word of the compassion and
care in Tours had spread among every village and hamlet, causing
many hopeless hearts to suffer countless ordeals to travel there. In
spite of being wrapped in her furs and wool dresses, the cold sunk
deep in her bones. Never did she consider she should sit back at the
castle by a toasty fire warming her toes. People needed her, and her
tender heart heard their calls. The winds blew colder and nudged
under doors and around windows. Sniffles turned into colds, then
pneumonia, influenza, or worse. The Princess made an effort to see
to each one, bringing hot soup and bread while smoothing covers
and bestowing the warmth of her smile on everyone. Sir Ami had
braved the elements with her, trotting faithfully by her side and quietly sitting at her knee when visiting the peoples' homes. He lifted

the spirits of all they called on, nudging arms gently and licking out-stretched fingers as a caress of encouragement.

In the beginning, Jeanne had left him behind at the Château de Plessis, much to his distress. Prowling the castle and scratching at the door, he whined and pestered until M. Abérnois was demanded to lock him in a kennel. There, the lonesome dog had wailed so miserably and barked so loudly, continuously, clawing the cage to get out until his paws were bloody and needed to be bandaged.

The next day, the Princess ordered he would accompany her from then on. There were those who criticized his mistress for spoiling him; however, M. Abérnois understood that Sir Ami was appointed guard and protector for the Princess as his life's work. Such devotion and dedication should not be denied.

Aymée scolded her for spending so much time in town and urged her to stay at the castle when the days were ugly with sleet and wind. Jeanne thanked her for her concern, reminding her that Madame Abérnois carried a much heavier load herself, and still there was further need for Jeanne's help. Raymond also had thrown himself into ministering to the townspeople, often teaming up with Antoinette to carry blankets to shut-ins and widows. The house of hope was running at full capacity, meeting the majority of needs of those who were still on their feet; however every day it was evident that the illnesses were spreading to more and more houses. Everywhere people were coughing, sneezing and shivering with chills.

It was on an unusually bitter day, as she was packing up provisions at the house of hope to take to several homes where families were stricken ill when a sudden pain in her stomach hit Jeanne and nearly doubled her over. She took a deep breath and grabbed at a nearby table for support until the pain subsided, fighting nausea. The room began spinning around her, and her hand missed the table corner. She did not feel her head hit the floor. Sir Ami leaped to her side, barking loudly. Faintly aware of Antoinette crying out, and then appearing above her, she heard a voice calling for someone to help; Raymond was beside her and then he faded away.

She was dimly aware of being lifted up on a horse with Raymond holding her tightly as they galloped along a road.

In a grey fog, she found herself wrapped tightly in the warm blankets of her bed with the pain in her stomach pushing up in her throat. She needed to find a bucket or something because it was not going to stay down. Panicky, she tried to get free of the blankets as she fought the rising tide in her throat. Aymée materialized beside her, holding a bowl and smoothing back her hair. Finished, she fell back on her pillows, her hand across her clammy brow, her shoulders and back aching deep in the muscles. As the dizziness closed in, she managed a faint smile of appreciation to Aymée, and then she slipped into darkness. It became a recurrent nightmare, the same urgent fight to consciousness to empty her stomach and then slip away into unknowing.

The castle doctor arrived and he sat with her for two days, eventually reporting there was no more help he could give; all depended on her will to live, to fight the battle on her own.

Wandering through strange dreams and nightmares, she struggled to semi-conscious awareness to realize her mother was sitting by her bed. Not strong enough to move or call out, she stared at her mother through the increasing darkness that enveloped her. She fought to see her mother again, wanting desperately to tell her how her presence at the bedside comforted her, but then a gray shadow covered her vision and turned black.

Queen Marguerite was deep in prayer for her daughter's healing and did not see her eyes open or her loving gaze before she lost consciousness again. The Queen had been at the Louvre with King Francis when Aymée sent for her after the doctor's hopeless diagnosis. Marguerite dropped every responsibility and came immediately. The messy stage of the illness had drained the Princess, leaving her dehydrated; now Jeanne lay limply, with sunken cheeks and dark circles around her closed eyelids, unconscious of any activity around her.

The news of her critical condition flew from the castle to the town carried by all who worked there. The people of Tours prayed. Antoinette and the Abérnois' prayed. Queen Marguerite prayed and sent King Henri of Navarre word, and he prayed. Sir Duquesse, M. Bourbon, and Aymée sat numbly together praying. Raymond, at the altar, agonized in prayer. Everyone in the castle made their way to the Chapel at some time and prayed. When King Francis received letters regarding her condition from Marguerite, he commanded all at the Louvre to pray.

For nearly two days Jeanne lay unmoving, seeming unreachable to those about her. Now, in the chamber of her mind, however, she lay in stillness, aware only of movements of sunshine and shadows drifting across her eyelids, hearing sounds of chimes and the singing of birds in flight like a distant melody, just out of reach. Sometimes, with the lilting music, fragrances of honeysuckle, gardenias, and lilacs engulfed her. The song would come and go, as would the sunshine and shadows, never disrupting her sense of harmony and joy. She was content to abide in the peace that surrounded her. How long she dwelt in that cocoon of serenity and tranquility, she could not determine; nothing disturbed her sense of the deep love encompassing her.

At some point, awareness of someone's presence outside her peace did distract her. Jeanne opened her eyes. Her mother was still sitting by her bed. This time Jeanne smiled and Marguerite saw her. Rising from her chair, the Queen laid her palm on Jeanne's brow, relieved to feel the fever had finally broken, and Jeanne's eyes were bright. Gently, the Queen slipped her arms around the Princess and held her close as tears overflowed and moistened her cheeks.

38. Recovery

*"Drip down, O heavens, from above, and let the clouds
pour down righteousness; let the earth open up and
salvation bear fruit, and righteousness spring up with it.
I, the Lord, have created it."*

Isaiah 45:8 (NASB)

The road to recovery was long and not without relapses. Jeanne's strength gradually renewed with a spoon of delicious broth offered each time she awakened. Marguerite faithfully attended to her every need and lovingly encouraged her to eat a little more, drink a little more and sit up a little more. Soon she could enjoy listening to Marguerite telling of the happenings around the castle, or, what she had recently heard from Uncle Francis and King Henri; even some news of activities at the house of hope in Tours.

All seemed very far away, and it was enough to nap and visit with her mother, Aymée, and her attendants Phoebe, Maddie and Chloe. Thankful for her recovery, they gathered to sing and play their instruments. Sometimes she would doze off while they were still playing. Their favorite melody was 'The Sweet Song,' and those refrains ran in and out of Jeanne's mind, whether she was awake or sleeping.

Eventually, her mother allowed her to chat for short periods with M. Bourbon, Sir Duquesse, and M. d'Izernay. She was acutely aware of their expressions of relief and delight, as though they had missed her severely, and it seemed strange to her. She had no concept of how long she had been absent or that they feared she would never return.

Downstairs, celebration at her recovery had overtaken the castle. Joy and goodwill spread among all, from the lowest worker to even M. d'Izernay. Servants competed over who could create the most festal environment. Holly and evergreens hung from every column and doorway. All sorts of Christmas decorations were displayed, and candles illuminated the rooms in anticipation of the Christ Child's birth, as well as hope that the Princess would soon descend her stairs to join them. The kitchen bustled to stock up on decorated sugar cookies, fruit cakes and sweets of every sort. Servants dusted and re-dusted, mopped and washed; they polished and buffed everything in sight until the castle shone and glistened, with light bouncing off every surface. No effort must be spared in preparation for the coming Christmas celebration and the appearance of the Princess. Even the chaplains in the Chapel were busy gathering and directing the Boys Choir as they practiced a performance just for the Princess along with the mass for Christmas.

At one point, the Bishop remarked casually to Sir Duquesse that it would be nice to host a party to celebrate the Princess' recovery. They tossed about ideas and possible plans. What had been a casual suggestion grew into a plan centered on the choir's performance and Christmas Mass, with tables of food and drink in abundance for all who attended. Invitations would be sent to the surrounding countryside with all the rooms of the castle opened to welcome them. M. d'Izernay, himself, suggested they should spare no expense, so the work began.

Sir Duquesse called M. Bourbon and Aymée for a secret meeting. They pondered and argued and scratched their heads. Finally, after tossing ideas out in disappointment and then hatching new ones, they settled on a plan and took it to M. d'Izernay for his approval. It would be costly, they knew, so they presented it with minimal expectations. It was astounding when the steward expressed his delight for the plan and suggested even more lavish ideas.

Because Queen Marguerite knew the condition of the Princess more than any other, she must be consulted to establish a date. She was told of the party preparations and asked to name a date so the invitations could go out. After some hours of deliberation and time to compose and send some messages by courier, upon receiving answers she named December 23rd as the big day.

Supplies were ordered and invitations distributed. Eventually, as more people were recruited to help, the plan of Sir Duquesse, Aymée, and M. Bourbon became evident to all. They proposed to cover the walls of the torture chamber with potted evergreen trees and crimson velvet drapes. The cages hanging from the ceilings would be encased in wire and wound with evergreen boughs, then filled with all sorts of canaries and small singing birds. Chandeliers of candles would be hung and lit for sparkling light everywhere; tons of poinsettias ordered for every spare space along the walls and floor; logs in the fireplaces would all be set aflame. Tables heavy with lustrous silver candlesticks and silver trays filled with Christmas goodies positioned around the walls. Best of all, a sizeable ornamental carriage would be brought in and decorated festively to sit in the center of the chamber so that the children and people of the town could climb in to sit and pretend they were riding like royalty.

When they finished, the vast hall showed no evidence of its former personality. It was dazzling! Crimson and green, red flowers and white sheepskin rugs, sounds of birdsong and brightly lit candles; it now turned into a lush wonderland.

Everyone on the castle grounds and in the building, no matter their work or responsibility, took a moment to come and gaze at the enchanting wonderland hall. All knew its history and hated what it had done to their Princess. They gasped and cried with delight at the incredible change wrought. Each heart wished they could be present when Princess Jeanne first saw it. Small prayers rose on wings of love that she would be strong enough to enjoy the party with them.

39. Anticipations

"Have I not commanded you? Be strong and courageous! Do not tremble or be dismayed, for the Lord your God is with you wherever you go."

Joshua 1:9 (NASB)

Princess Jeanne showed increasing progress toward recovery. Each day she had more vitality than the day before. Queen Marguerite and Aymée urged her to approach new activities slowly, fearing a relapse. They limited her at first to just sitting up awhile; then gradually helping her move about the apartment, allowing small increases at a time. The time came when the Princess began to complain of feeling restless in her familiar surroundings. Finally, she managed to walk by herself and climb the stairs to her secret room to gaze out the windows. Wrapped in covers, toasty warm from the brazier burning nearby, she read and prayed and dozed, with Sir Ami curled at her feet.

Watching the snow fall among the trees of the forest, she thought a great deal of how she spent her days during the years since coming to the Château de Plessis-lez-Tours. Memories played through her mind of her arrival and intervening years of despair; with friendships developed, educational goals achieved and ultimately, meeting Antoinette and beginning her endeavors in Tours. She challenged herself to seek what she had learned through all those experiences.

After a day of deep contemplation, she had been dozing peacefully when her mother joined her in the secret room. Her rustling movement up the stairs to sit beside the Princess awakened her. Handing Jeanne a cup of warm, spiced tea, the Queen caressed her hair and stroked her cheek before asking, "Do you think you will be strong enough to go down for a meal and to be among people in a few days? I have received word that King Francis will be arriving later in the week." She looked at her daughter with concern.

"He wants to see you and has matters to discuss with me that he feels cannot wait. It is getting close to Christmas, and I am not planning to return to Béarn until after the first of the year when I expect you will be feeling much better. I have been away a long time, and your father is anxious to know that you are doing as well as reported. Depending on the difficulty of travel in this weather, he also hopes to arrive around the time Uncle Francis will be here."

Tears slipped down Jeanne's cheeks. She searched for her handkerchief and dabbed at the corners of her eyes.

"Oh, mother," she whispered, "I am so blessed. First, you are here at my side, and now, both my father and Uncle Francis will be coming."

Jeanne's face lit up in anticipation. "I have not even realized Christmas is near. Yes, yes, I want to feel good enough to join everyone downstairs. Will you help me get strong enough? What will I wear? I must look a mess. Do I still look sick?"

Marguerite enclosed the Princess in her arms and reassured her that she looked wonderful, and Aymée would always offer her help. They would find something for her to wear and she would be beautiful.

Fatigue would soon overcome her, and she frequently had to stop to rest. She spent her days with promenades about the apartment, even a little dancing to the music Phoebe, Maddie and Chloe played and most of all lengthening times of conversation. Eventually, Jeanne was confident she would be able to attend a formal dinner with the King of France, her parents and the cherished members of her household. She determined in her heart to attend Christmas mass, knowing the Bishop du Châtel would leap at the opportunity to hold mass with King Francis in attendance.

Queen Marguerite told her the dinner and Mass would be held on December 23rd to accommodate other obligations of those who were coming from a distance. The Queen called in dressmakers who designed a dress for the occasion. Fittings, debates, decisions and more fittings filled her days.

December 23rd grew closer. The turmoil of fitting the dress finished. Marguerite and Aymée cherished the time to sit in conversation with Jeanne while listening to the quiet refrains played by her ladies-in-waiting.

The Queen confided that one of the issues King Francis needed to deliberate with her involved the circumstances surrounding Marguerite's sister-in-law who was Jeanne's godmother, Isabel d'Albret, Viscountess de Rohan. Years earlier, Isabel, Princess of Navarre and King Henri's sister, had entered into a warm attachment with René, viscount de Rohan, who had royal connections to the family of Francis, however, he possessed little wealth. King Henri's sister entreated Marguerite to help obtain permission from the King of France for their marriage. King Francis opposed the union not only for the viscount's lack of money but his unreliable habit of extravagant spending; depleting whatever meager resources were available. Isabel insisted she was resolved to accept a level of living considerably lower than her current dispensation from the King of Navarre. Convinced by Marguerite's gentle persuasion on behalf of Isabel's desires, and the King of Navarre's willingness to accept the arrangement, King Francis withdrew his opposition and the marriage proceeded.

Queen Marguerite recently received correspondence from Isabel that the viscount had thoughtlessly brought about a reverse of fortune and the Viscountess and her two children were in danger of total ruin. Marguerite was anxious about finding a provision for their future. The subject was often brought up during the hours of leisurely conversation in Jeanne's apartments.

Queen Marguerite's close companionship during the weeks of Jeanne's recovery filled a deep void in Jeanne's spirit that had been severely vacant all the years of her childhood. The union forming between mother and daughter brought Jeanne happiness and contentment she had never experienced before.

The expected arrival of the King of France and her father approached. Her mother insisted she remain in the confines of her apartment regardless that her restlessness was increasing daily. Jeanne's studies had been neglected so with lessons prepared by her tutor, Jeanne tackled her reading assignments. When she grew weary of reading, the Princess occupied herself with writing notes to Madame Abérnois for updates on the activities at the house of hope. Day by day she grew stronger and regained her natural vivacity.

40. A Special Season

"For a child will be born to us, a son will be given to us;
and the government will rest on His shoulders; and His
name will be called Wonderful Counselor, Mighty God,
Eternal Father, Prince of Peace."

Isaiah 9:6 (NASB)

On December 21st in the late afternoon, the ladies became aware of increasing clamor outside the castle. Only the arrival of the King of France and his entourage could be responsible for such an uproar. Queen Marguerite hurried downstairs to greet her brother. Jeanne was disappointed not to accompany her mother, but the decision established that she would wait until December 23rd to make her appearance. Soon, the Queen returned to report that all had arrived safely, in spite of the heavy snowstorm that had increased in intensity throughout their trip. Marguerite told her daughter that on the following day she would be absent from Jeanne's presence as King Francis needed her for counsel on pressing matters. There was no news yet on Jeanne's father who was in route from Béarn, nearly three hundred miles to the south.

The following day was very lonely, and Jeanne wandered about her apartments missing her mother. She played chess with Phoebe who was an admirable opponent at the game, but the Princess soon tired of it and sought other entertainment. Her attendants played music, and she listened and read, though without her mother's companionship it lacked the expected pleasure. Jeanne spent time watching out the windows of her secret room, hoping to catch a movement in the forests that would signal her father's arrival. Even though she had seen little of him during the last seven years, she cared a great deal for him. His appearance would be a special treat. It was well after dark that word reached Jeanne of the arrival of the King of Navarre.

The morning of December 23rd dawned bright and clear. It was cold outside, and the snow surrounding the castle seemed to stifle sound; with the castle enveloped in silence, buried in glistening diamonds of snow.

Jeanne woke in great anticipation and excitement. Her dress of white velvet and gold trim was hanging on the wardrobe. Jeanne had insisted on a simple form-fitting design for comfort, and the lines were indeed most complimentary and quite a departure from the substantial, awkward full-skirted fashion of the time. Her activities in Tours had developed her sensitivity to the contrast of meager living among the everyday people in opposition to the abundance and opulence employed among the royal and noble homes in the surrounding counties. In its simplicity, the dress enhanced Jeanne's natural beauty to a breathtaking degree. Unknown to the Princess, Queen Marguerite had ordered a long, white ermine coat with a trailing train to ensure Jeanne would be warm while attending the royal dinner, the Boys Choir performance and Christmas Mass. It was arranged that Jeanne would join the celebrations downstairs in the early afternoon. Not a whisper was heard in Jeanne's private apartments of the upcoming party that would include the populace around the castle.

Preparations were soon underway as Aymée curled and arranged Jeanne's dark, abundant hair. She was an artist at creating a comfortable but elaborate accumulation of ringlets on her head, leaving curling tendrils to frame the fresh radiance of her face; soft, thick curls fell about her shoulders accentuating her flowering maidenly beauty.

Jeanne's height was not quite five feet tall, and her petite frame seemed even smaller from the weight she had lost. Her eyes were enormous in her little face. They had always been her most attractive feature, and now their luminous glow was overpowering. Not able to establish what, in her recent illness, had brought about the change, anyone caught in the magnetic enchantment of her eyes saw an indescribable allure of peace that was almost divine. Her pale, clear complexion was even more beautiful than before and in contrast to her dark blue, astonishing eyes, it appeared translucent.

Soon after lunch, Queen Marguerite returned to gauge how Princess Jeanne was feeling and to assist with her dress. With her mother holding the cloud of white velvet over her head, the dress slid down to fit snugly around her waist. The bodice, shaped like a heart, had tiny satin buttons closing the soft dress from the cleavage to the hem. The white velvet sleeves fit tightly about her arms, with matching satin buttons from the elbow to the pointed wrists. Marguerite then held the sleeveless, ermine coat for Jeanne to slip in her arms. All in attendance of Princess Jeanne were speechless with admiration.

The Queen gently embraced the Princess and pressed her cheek against Jeanne's face, whispering,

"My daughter, you are beautiful beyond description, and I am very proud of you. I will join your father now before you come down. All those waiting for your arrival love you very much. I know this will be an exciting day for you. Please be careful to keep from getting too tired. We all want you to continue your rapid and complete recovery without suffering a relapse. Your health is our most important concern."

As Princess Jeanne waited for her attendants to arrange the train of her cape behind her, Aymée opened the heavy oak doors, allowing the rising din of voices of those awaiting her arrival to invade the quiet of her apartment. Considering how long it had been since she had been down the stairs, she was startled at the volume rising to meet her.

The Princess reached the top of the stairs and surveyed the immense crowd gazing up at her. She paused in bewilderment; the happy faces, noisy in their anticipation, were instantly silenced when, with a sudden intake of breath, they saw the Princess like a vision of an angel at the top of the staircase.

Princess Jeanne descended the stairs to an overwhelming roar of applause. At each step, she paused to look at the faces of her friends, her father, and mother, Uncle Francis, and, incredulously Antoinette with her parents and little Gerald, Raymond, Fauzio and all the familiar faces of the workers from Tours and their families. The festive decorations of the Great Hall framed the happy expressions greeting her and Princess Jeanne's heart filled with joy and happiness.

At the bottom of the stair, a way parted in front of the Princess. She stopped before her Uncle with a low curtsy and rose to his embrace. Turning then to the King and Queen of Navarre, she curtsied, embraced her mother and held the hand of her father tightly as she gazed into his familiar face with affection before he pulled her into his arms. Moving forward along the avenue she warmly greeted her cherished castle supporters, Sir Duquesse, Monsieur Bourbon and Monsieur d'Izernay; each so delighted to have her again among them, they clutched her hand, pleased to see her fresh beauty and health. As the avenue opened before her, Jeanne passed among the crowd, greeting and embracing as she went.

The crowds gathered behind her to follow in her wake as she moved along greeting those along the way opening before her, which finally ended at the hall now renovated to a wonderland. Jeanne was too busy greeting all her friends and acquaintances to realize in what direction she was moving. She was not aware when the parties of the King of France and the King and Queen of Navarre moved around the crowd to gather in the wonderland. Many others in the crowd followed suit.

When Princess Jeanne looked up to get her bearings, she was standing on the threshold of the hall that had consumed her mind for such a preponderance of time in the preceding seven years at Château Plessis. Sir Duquesse moved to one side of her and Aymée appeared on the other; each took her hand and pulled her into the hall.

The first thing she noticed was the light reflected everywhere. The Princess blinked in amazement; her gaze traveled to the cages filled with chirping birds; then to the walls covered with crimson and evergreens. The Princess gasped as she saw the huge decorated carriage with children crawling all over it. She looked about in astonishment at the hall she was standing in, staring with disbelief at the changes before her. Her escorts guided her through the applause of the multitude who had gathered to share her joy. She took her appointed seat on the festively decorated dais in the company of the King of France and the King and Queen of Navarre, who studied her anxiously for signs of fatigue. Jeanne was grateful to be seated. After greeting so many people, she began to feel a bit tired

Laughing together, Raymond and Antoinette approached, carrying plates and drinks to her, and then prepared to sit nearby in her company.

People thronged the laden tables of goodies, lost in a dilemma to decide between all the enchanting, delicious items created by the artistic talents of the Château kitchens. Many of the people of the towns and the countryside had never seen such a feast, and more than likely would overindulge before the evening was over.

Children, who typically stayed at home for evening celebrations, scampered about in awe of the grand rooms of the castle, drawn like little magnets to the wonderland hall with the carriage and food. Music filled the rooms, and whenever space allowed, merry dancing spontaneously commenced. When the Boys Choir filed into the wonderland hall, silence spread throughout the multitudes. With angelic voices, the boys sang familiar Christmas carols, followed by worship songs for the Christ Child to celebrate His birth. A hushed silence lingered reverently at the choir's conclusion; every person present meditating on the miracle they celebrated. The breathless crowd then moved into the Chapel, followed by the royal procession of the King of France, Princess Jeanne, and the Queen and King of Navarre to attend Christmas Mass.

The spirit of joy that pervaded the castle would not soon be forgotten by those who attended. Primarily, the youngsters who treasured the magical event would enthusiastically recreate their adventures and the enchantment to tell grandchildren and great-grandchildren, for such a celebration within their neighborhood would never again be repeated.

Monsieur and Madame Abérnois had wandered about the castle in a state of disbelief. M. Abérnois, with Gerald in his arms, walked his wife out to the stables so she could see where he spent his days. She was delighted at the expansive area and the beauty of the horses there. She had known for some time how much he enjoyed the work he did for he was very much at home in a stable and his greatest love had always been in working with horses. She felt like they were living in a dream since Princess Jeanne had entered their lives. As they returned to the warmth and festivities in the castle, it was even more unbelievable when they saw Antoinette, escorted by Raymond; carrying plates piled high with sumptuous, delectable morsels to join Princess Jeanne who was sitting in the company of the King of France. They watched, astonished at the cordial interchange between their daughter and King Francis. Mumsie released Gerald who made a beeline to Raymond for a hug. Exchanging amazed glances, they watched the King of France bend down and pick up Gerald to sit on his knee. They could hardly breathe when their darling son became the center of conversation between the three royals and Jeanne, Raymond and Antoinette. Not in their wildest dreams could they have imagined this occurrence when their lives were so desperate five years ago.

Raymond had concluded making a decision for his future, explaining to his father that his dream of taking over the operation of his inheritance had won over the pull he had felt to enter the Church in servanthood. Their discussion had been sincere and probing. Raymond eventually had shared his disappointments when he had witnessed errors and misdeeds occurring within the brotherhood. Raymond's studies at the castle had disclosed the compromises of truth lost in a hierarchy's ruthless grab for power and wealth. The in-depth discussion had also revealed his father's leanings toward the ideas of reform now being so persecuted in the country.

Raymond had returned to his father's manor to learn the operation of a prosperous estate. He continued to support Princess Jeanne in her work in Tours. Raymond was happy. The stress he had felt, but ignored, to devote his life to the priesthood had lifted once he made his decision. He had always loved working on the estate and devoted himself enthusiastically to taking over the operation from his father. Also, his time in Tours had provided an increased opportunity to expand his friendship with Antoinette.

They were well suited. When the couple grew closer, Antoinette shared with Raymond that her father revealed he was descended from a noble family. Born in Picquigney in Normandy, his family was slaughtered during an invasion and the estate overtaken as booty by attackers. M. Abérnois, who was just a baby, had been smuggled away from danger to the estate of a distant friend near Châteaubriand. He had grown up working in his landlord's stables, fearing the invaders who had killed his family would discover his identity and seek his death. The estate of his landlord had suffered declining fortune when illness and poor judgment turned aside the once lucrative profits to suffer unfortunate failure. M. Abérnois had moved south, seeking employment with the estates along the Loire river valley. Hired by a large estate near the village of Mosnes, the faithful completion of his duties had seen him promoted to the position of the horse trainer. He knew his employer was a hard, ill-tempered fellow living with only his gratifications in view. M. Abérnois took care of his responsibilities and maintained as much of a distance from his employer as possible, so he was reluctant to make it known that he had met a beautiful girl who lived in Nevers and worked in the village bakery. He lost his heart and married her after finding a rental home not far from the estate. Life and love flourished. Before long they were joined by a baby daughter whom they considered the most beautiful child ever created.

Not long after Antoinette began to crawl around the house, M. Abérnois was brought home by his fellow workers, near death with his left arm ripped from his shoulder. Mumsie desperately applied what little emergency care she knew, knowing that his life was dangling in the balance. As if from a distance, she only heard a portion of what the men told her about the accident.

While tethered to a horse he was training, M. Abérnois was putting the horse through his training procedures. The owner of the estate and stables stopped to watch and became irritated that the horse was stubborn and unresponsive. He raised the whip he carried over his head and brought it down on the face of the mustang, the tip-end striking it in the eyes. The horse went berserk, running and bucking in every direction around the corral, eventually breaking through the fence and galloping in pain and terror at top speed over the rocky terrain. M. Abérnois was still firmly attached by the rope wrapped around his upper arm. When the rope finally broke, and the horse disappeared over the horizon, the estate owner walked to where M. Abérnois lay, broken and bleeding, to shout in anger that after witnessing such a pitiful demonstration of training horses, he was fired and if ever caught around the estate again, he would be shot.

The doctor arrived at the house and did his best to save the injured arm and patch up the broken ribs, gashes, and cuts around M. Abérnois' head.

Word spread through Mosnes. Neighbors and friends brought food in sympathy for their misfortune. It was not long before the person knocking at their door was the landlord of their house. Not able to work meant having no way to pay the rent. Bound with bandages and in excruciating pain, M. Abérnois loaded what little they could handle, and they made their way together, walking down the road toward Tours.

They spent several nights camping on the ground at a distance from the road in fear of being robbed of their small provisions, reluctant to light a fire that might attract attention to their presence. Sometimes they stayed longer at their camp, delayed by a raging fever that plagued M. Abérnois.

After nearly two weeks, they reached Tours. Not knowing anyone in the town, they found their way to the poor street where the widow Croix lived. Filled with compassion, she had invited them to stay with her until they could find somewhere to shelter.

Shortly after their arrival in Tours, Mumsie gave birth to a tiny little boy who struggled to stay alive. The impact of the recent disasters had taken their toll, and Mumsie's milk was never enough to feed the baby. In the two years following the death of her baby boy, desperate to find a way to feed her husband and child, Mumsie took in laundry, hauling water and lugging heavy baskets back and forth to the affluent houses across town. Mumsie's grief deepened as two more babies were born, to sicken and die for lack of nutrition.

Antoinette straggled along beside her mother through every circumstance, never aware of the prosperous home she had occupied in her past. She loved her Mumsie and Dads and rejoiced with Mumsie at every small improvement in Dads' health. Ignoring the continuing pain, he forced himself to search for work; meeting closed doors at every effort.

There was no explanation, except the hand of a loving God, to account for the events that brought them here tonight, watching their daughter receive favor from royalty.

Mumsie had not mentioned to M. Abérnois her observations when first meeting Raymond. He would have laughingly teased her for being a hopeless romantic. They watched together as the tender interchanges between Antoinette and Raymond became more than a little obvious. M. Abérnois looked inquiringly at Mumsie, seeking confirmation of what he was seeing. She nodded, with a tiny smile of satisfaction that her suspicions had been correct. Raymond had been around the house of hope many times in the last year or more, working together with Antoinette. His manners were impeccable, and his show of respect for Antoinette and her parents was commendable.

M. Abérnois began watching him with a different point of view. Raymond's position as the heir of a noble estate holder was a positive aspect of anyone's account. Whether Raymond's family would accept the daughter of a stable groom as a desirable prospect for their son would be another matter. For the first time in his memory, he regretted not bringing documentation of his birth with him. It would have been an instant death sentence if ever discovered when he was smuggled away under dark of night, so his rescuers had never even considered bringing it with him. Now, at least twenty-five years later, there was no hope of resurrecting the proof of his noble parents.

He whispered to himself, "I am so sorry Antoinette, for you are so deserving of such a well-placed, good-hearted man." Mumsie did not hear his whisper since she was engrossed in watching her beautiful daughter delight in her fantasy world.

41. Gentle Interlude

"Turn to me and be gracious to me, for I am lonely and afflicted. The troubles of my heart are enlarged; bring me out of my distresses."

Psalm 25:16-17 (NASB)

The glow Jeanne felt in the days following the party continued to warm her heart for many days. She replayed the memories over and over, like the well-worn pages of a favorite book. The sparkling lights and festive beauty of the wonderland hall filled her imagination, and the wonder of it stayed with her. When she walked down the aisle of the Chapel with her hand on the arm of the King of France as the King and Queen of Navarre followed, she filled with thankfulness to her God who had made the moment possible. There was such beauty in the celebrations of the birth of the Christ Child that her heart was overflowing with delight. She had weathered the demands of that day and the evening's merriments well and continued to feel stronger each day. Able to participate in all the activities enjoyed by her uncle and parents, the Princess treasured every moment and passed the days in blissful happiness.

The day of Jeanne's twelfth birthday was bittersweet. A small, intimate celebration with her mother, father, and Uncle Francis, wiped away all the bitter disappointments that had plagued her since her arrival at Château de Plessis. Tomorrow, however, the joy of being reunited would end as the King had pressing business waiting, and so did the King and Queen of Navarre; they would again move out of her daily life circle.

When the time came to bid them farewell, Jeanne's heart broke. She wanted more than anything to be allowed to continue under the care and supervision of her parents. Nothing here at the castle could fill the hole left in her heart as she watched them disappear into the snowy forest. Turning back to the castle, she felt buried under a crushing weight of loneliness.

Wandering through the castle aimlessly, she watched as the festive decorations were being taken down to store away. Even though the cages were still full of singing birds and potted evergreen trees continued to cover the torture implements along the walls, the hall without the wonderland felt desolate and empty. The evil, torturous methods did not weigh heavy on her thoughts; it was the lonely emptiness that consumed her. She was not motivated by a pressing need to return to the house of hope in Tours; she knew the benefits would continue, driven by the hearts of all those special people who labored there. She achieved her educational goals as defined by M. Bourbon; her Uncle Francis had been robustly appreciative of the financial position of the castle under the watchfulness of M. d'Izernay and Sir Duquesse. Aymée, appointed as her mentor and governess, was now a cherished friend. The coming year stretched out before her with little anticipation.

Jeanne occupied her time writing thoughtful letters to her mother, reliving the moments in her company and sharing her memories of the happy Christmas party. Days passed, and Aymée was again disturbed to often find the Princess in her secret room, in tears of overwhelming loneliness.

As she moved about the castle meeting her daily obligations, her manner toward all about her continued to be warm and loving; however everyone was aware of what her red, puffy eyes revealed. She read books at M. Bourbon's recommendations, then, would lay them aside in boredom. Her enthusiasm for playing chess disappeared. Raymond and Fauzio were no longer available to discuss or argue since both had returned to their noble estates; Raymond to work his inheritance and Fauzio to soon begin his duties as a page at King Francis' castle in Amboise. Sir Duquesse would request that she walk with him about the grounds of the manor in spite of the weather conditions, to take advantage of fresh air and exercise. She agreed to accompany him as she had no other purpose to employ as an excuse.

Dreary weeks of January gave way to the weary entrance of the first days of February. It was a cloudy, depressing day, warming only enough to melt the top layers of the snow and then freeze again, leaving a thin layer of ice covering everything outside.

A strange carriage came slipping and sliding down the road and nearly crashed into the entry to the castle. It was piled precariously high with baggage and trunks and followed by even more laden carts. The frazzled, exhausted, coachman climbed from his perch and slid over to the doorway, knocking to announce their arrival. The message was delivered to the Library where Sir Duquesse, M. d'Izernay, and Aymée were together with Princess Jeanne. Sir Duquesse opened the message and read it aloud to everyone. It was from Queen Marguerite who relayed that she had arranged for her sister-in-law, Princess Isabel d'Albret, Viscountess of Rohan, to take residence at Château de Plessis with her two children.[xi] These arrangements had been urgently made when orders of eviction arrived for the Viscountess due to the depth of debts incurred by the Viscount.

Immediately Sir Duquesse, d'Izernay, and Aymée moved into action to assist the viscountess in disembarking from the cold carriage to move into guest apartments available in the enormous castle.

Staff lounging about in the nether regions of the castle jumped to action with the need to light fireplaces in cold rooms, obtain fresh bedding and draw baths; while in the kitchens cold ovens were awakened while bread and pastries were set to rise. Life began to flow briskly through lethargic castle veins.

Princess Jeanne stood sympathetically near the castle entrance to greet and welcome her aunt, although they never before had met. She was curious about the Viscountess after being told so much about her circumstances by her mother. Isabel was in such a disheveled state and so profoundly embarrassed at her circumstances, she was barely courteous; even quite curt, when introducing herself and her children. Princess Jeanne murmured her welcome and condolences, aware of the resemblance of her aunt to her father. King Henri's chiseled facial features were handsome and regal, displaying the strength of mind and purpose. Viscountess Isabel had similar characteristics that seemed highlighted by sunken eye sockets and a broad brow, wrinkled and frowning.

Jeanne greeted her cousin, Françoise, with delight to find she was only two years older than the Princess. Françoise must have taken after her father, with his dark hair and long slender nose. The contrast of her pale, smooth skin against her black hair and dark eyes was quite becoming. Françoise's younger brother, Neil, who was six, was a handsome, young boy who clung to his mother, looking fearfully about the castle. The Viscountess entered, attended by the six ladies of her court, among them the Sénéchale de Grammont, and her daughter, Catherine d'Aster. [xii] Catherine, a few years older than Jeanne, greeted her with a warm and friendly manner. The Princess liked her immediately.

For the first time in weeks, Jeanne was excited at the prospect of dinner and spent additional time with her choice of dress and attention to her appearance. She had requested the First Butler to see that her cousin Françoise and Catherine d'Aster were seated on each side of her. Her royal tables were lively and entertaining. An enjoyable acquaintance began to develop into a close friendship among the three maidens.

The personalities of each of the young ladies were entirely different, and any onlookers watching their fellowship could not determine if their differences kept them from more profound devotion to each other or if perhaps it was because of their differences they were able to enjoy such close fellowship.

The lovely Françoise was demure, timid and dependent. She shrank from conflict and yielded to those with stronger opinions rather than defend her view. Catherine, a child of a noble and illustrious family, was known for her superior abilities and beauty. A year older than Françoise, she carried herself in confidence of her womanly attractions and her thoughts were often on the efforts being made to attain a commendable attachment. Referring often of Princess Jeanne's attractions regarding an early marriage, the maidens passed many hours in contemplations of the possibilities of their futures. Without a doubt, Jeanne, having heard her father's discussions regarding the approaches of Charles V to espouse the Princess to his son Philip as consort to the future King of Spain, was well aware of her many prospects.

M. Bourbon was delighted to have oversight as the girls met with him to broaden their educations further. Their discussions were both wide-ranging and profound with ideas and opinions that grew from their divergent histories and studies. Jeanne's vigorous and vivacious views occasionally resulted in a lack of courtesy toward gentle Françoise, who she chastised for her weak, vacillating energy wherever Jeanne felt the truth should be adamantly supported and upheld.

The coming months for Jeanne passed in the contented enjoyment of her new found friends. When the time came for Catherine d'Aster to return to Gascony with her mother, Jeanne sorely missed her. She had much admired the social graces and vitality of conversation in her company. Not too long after, word came from the Queen of Navarre of completed arrangements for other accommodations for the Viscountess and her court; young Neil was to be a page in the house of the Dauphin, eldest son of the King of France; Françoise was adopted as her own by Queen Marguerite. She would be resident at the courts of Nérac and Pau, educated by Marguerite's gentle guidance and in the company of the many young damsels of her court.

Faced again with the utter loneliness of the castle, Jeanne wrote passionate letters to her uncle, urging, pleading, and demanding him to allow her to return to the care of her parents or at the very least, to bring her to the courts of Fontainebleau. More than ever, her friends in the castle closely watched her desperate wanderings, estranged from them in a state of despondent gloom and grief.

She sought for strength to endure by reading the Psalms, seeking to borrow from David his confidence in the faithfulness of his Lord.

"But know that the Lord hath set apart him that is godly for himself; the Lord will hear when I call unto him." [Psalm 4:3 KJV].

"Depart from me, all ye workers of iniquity; for the Lord hath heard the voice of my weeping. The Lord hath heard my supplication; the Lord will receive my prayer. [Psalm 6:8-9 KJV].

"Oh give thanks to the LORD, for He is good, For His lovingkindness is everlasting. Let the redeemed of the LORD say so, whom He has redeemed from the hand of the adversary." [Psalm 107:1-2 KJV].

She remembered the spiritual teachings of her childhood and believed God was sovereign over her life, but could not accept her present conditions as a lesson preparing for her future.

She recalled the sense of peace she had experienced in the garden and sought desperately to recapture it. She sat in silence in her secret room. She hoped for peace to settle on her anxious spirit while peering deeply into fires burning in fireplaces. She waited, sitting in anticipation in the dark Chapel. She could not find the peace she was sure was there. Waiting on God to relieve her loneliness and depression became unbearable, and she was soon sure He had moved too far from her to care about her misery.

Pacing the floors in confusion, she wondered why she had been allowed friends to enjoy; then lost them so quickly. She cried out to God in anger; demanding if He cared, as the Scriptures said, He would change the heart of the King of France to grant her pleading requests.

She was not angry that Françoise was blessed to be her mother's constant companion; instead, she felt deeply hurt that her uncle denied her the same opportunity to join their warm company. She called out to God in her loneliness, begging for Him to hear her prayers. "Lord, help me! Satan has filled the garden of my heart with despair!"

42. Ominous Proceedings

*"But seeing the wind, he became afraid, and beginning
to sink, he cried out, saying, 'Lord save me.'"*

Matthew 14:30 (NASB)

Though she received no reply to her petitions to the King of
France, the persistence of Princess Jeanne began to be an embarrassment to King Francis. Unknown to Jeanne, the King was suffering pressure from many of his contacts regarding the interest of
Charles V in espousing his son Philip to Jeanne. The threat of the
enemy who was ever attempting to disrupt and destroy the sovereign reign of King Francis by fomenting trouble and plotting
schemes to split off and devour regions along his southern borders
was a perpetual thorn in the side of the King of France. Any hint
of a possible plot or sortie by his enemy sent King Francis into a
fit of anger.

The constant barrage of Jeanne's pleadings awakened old suspicions as to the intent of Henri of Navarre and fanned to a raging
flame fear of a secret arrangement. King Francis became even more
convinced of his need to counteract any possible contacts made
by the Emperor of Spain toward the King of Navarre who Francis
suspected might be open to such an agreement. It would be an
outstanding match for Princess Jeanne's future, as no other opportunity could begin to afford a more powerful and revered position
throughout Europe than consort to the King of Spain.

What King Francis knew, and what he did not believe would occur to Henri II of Navarre, was that the Emperor's expensive and humiliating failure to invade France would be forgotten by the acquisition of such rich and productive provinces as Jeanne's southern heritage. King Francis was also well acquainted with the betrayal of the Emperor whose deceitful history demonstrated he was more than capable of entering into a betrothal agreement only to betray its promises as soon as he had the lucrative inheritance under his control. Francis knew he must oppose the possibility of any such agreement vehemently.

It happened that in May of that year, already burdened with the constant pleadings of his niece, Francis acknowledged to himself her continued seclusion at Château de Plessis could not long be maintained. He was troubled about returning her to the care of her parents which would undoubtedly motivate the Emperor to powerfully persuade the King of Navarre to agree to an understanding of Jeanne's marriage.

To allow her at court in Fontainebleau would cause chaos of petitions by hopeful suitors; Francis was also well aware that Jeanne at court without her mother's supervision would be an untenable position to place her in at her age. He resolved to search for an alternative creditable or commendable spouse of his selection. An announcement of the affiancing of Jeanne d'Albret, Princess of Navarre, would frustrate any secret understanding between Spain and Henri II of Navarre. This matter had occupied the King's mind and discussions for many weeks.

It was on an especially lovely day, replete with the fragrance of spring flowers that the Duke of Cleves and Juliers journeyed to France seeking assistance from the King of France.[xiii] The Duke of Cleves found himself in a contest over his succession of the duchy of Guelders.

The contention for Guelderland had become a complicated disruption that occupied all of Germany. Three claimants to the duchy of Guelders were, first, the Duke of Cleves and Juliers, grandson of Ulric, last Duke of Guelders who had died without male heir. Secondly, Duke of Lorraine, nephew of the deceased Ulric; and thirdly, Charles V, Emperor of the Holy Roman Empire and King of Spain, who demanded the duchy belonged to the crown as there was no male heir, and, also, that the territory was of the House of Hapsburg. The Emperor based his claim for possession resulting from disinheritance of a former Duke who bequeathed his dominions to the Emperor's great-grandfather, Duke of Burgundy. The Emperor refused to accept the petitions of the two princes; pronouncing them as a void in view that both traced their descent through female members of the family.

Emperor Charles V, who lived for the expansion of his occupied territories, had justified in his mind the legality of royal escheatment of the disputed region of Guelderland. Faced with the Emperor's threats of accumulating military forces stationed along the borders of Guelders, the Duke of Cleves had set what defenses he was able. It was apparent that the Emperor's superior numbers would be most challenging to overcome. In an effort of last resort, the Duke of Cleves had journeyed to France and the court of Amboise where Francis was in residence at that time. The Duke was well aware that his petition of assistance to the King of France was likely to be dismissed out of hand if he was even allowed an audience.

The welcome the Duke of Cleves received from King Francis exceeded his highest expectations. He received promises of both money and men for his battle, as Francis was heartily supportive of any conflict against the Emperor.

Moreover, the King unexpectedly offered to bestow on the Duke of Cleves, the hand of his beautiful niece, Jeanne d'Albret, heiress of Béarn, in marriage. The King was most satisfied to be exonerated of the burden of dispensing with the problem of Jeanne's future. In one brilliant stroke of diplomacy, the King denied any plans of the Emperor of acquiring the southern provinces of France. Also, he had dealt a powerful thrust to cause Charles V alarm, for the Duke of Cleves was known for his affiliations as a Lutheran. [xiv] The Duke was reputed to be a chief upholder of the reform doctrines in Germany, which would provide King Francis with a connection with the German Lutherans who were always in revolt against the imperial scepter of Emperor Charles V.

The Duke of Cleves was twenty-four years old, handsome and possessed of accomplishments that distinguished him as a superior soldier and leader. An expert horseman, he presented an admirable display of the latest fashions and richly engrained saddle and rein, along with the wit to discuss literature with the vain professors at the court of France. His overdone, effusive admiration of the beautiful art collection of King Francis was borderline fawning. The revenues of Cleves were ample to maintain its sovereign; the position of the Duke, in Germany, was one of power and dignity. He was a man's man, and King Francis found him likable.

He had to admit that the Duke's fawning solicitude was a bit tiresome, but disregarding that, the King strutted about his castle proud that he had arranged a future for his niece and struck a fatal blow to the heart of the Emperor's grasping efforts. That was the best part, in Francis's opinion; even though he had to acknowledge secretly to himself that Jeanne's incredible heritage and beauty deserved a dispensation as consort to a much higher level of royalty.

Impressed with his exceptional completion of her development to such an ultimate and desirable pinnacle, Francis congratulated himself and thought satisfactorily that now the Duke of Cleves would forever be indebted to the King of France.

The King of France had only one stipulation attached to the betrothal, which being, Princess Jeanne would be permitted to remain, the first three years of her marriage, in France under the guardianship of her mother.

King Francis sent a letter to the King and Queen of Navarre relating the details of the agreed betrothal of Jeanne. King Henri II was livid with anger. Several aspects of the agreement threatened the future and safety of Béarn. Previously, the King's effort to dissuade Henri from entertaining approaches by the Emperor had included a promise to wed Princess Jeanne to King Francis' second son, Henry, Duke of Orleans.[xv] That promise had been blatantly broken when the Duke of Orleans married Catherine de Medici. King Henri also feared that espousing the heiress of Béarn with a Duke already embroiled in conflict with the Emperor would most certainly threaten the d'Albret domains on the southern borders of France by exposing them to the first assaults resulting from the anger of Charles V at the announcement of the alliance.

Queen Marguerite, in submission to her brother, only attempted to appease her husband's anger. She was pleased to learn of the Lutheran leanings of the Duke of Cleves and refused to join her husband in outrage at the royal decree. For her, the orders of her brother took precedence over every opposition. King Henri's anger further quelled when word sent by Francis threatened military occupation of Béarn in the event of resistance. Henri's vehement objections on behalf of Béarn remained ignored. The feelings of Jeanne received no consideration in the least. Her future was used to further the political advancements of the King of France.

One beautiful day, accompanied by his noble companions, a hunt initiated at the command of King Francis took place along the river Loire. Attended by a few of his favorite men, the King separated himself from the larger party and eventually ended up near the gates of the Château de Plessis. The sound of many hoof beats had alerted the workers in the stables and stock pens on the peripheral edges of the castle grounds. A servant boy was sent immediately to notify the castle of the impending arrival of these esteemed guests. Shortly, the party's horses galloped up and were reined in, stomping and snorting, to gather in front of the entrance to the castle. Stable boys dashed to the group to collect and lead the horses to the stables when the men dismounted. The King, alone, descended from his horse, walking abruptly to the entrance with evident purpose. No one followed.

His arrival was announced, and Jeanne summoned to his presence. Excited that Uncle Francis had come to visit her, Jeanne flew down the stairs and into his arms with delight. The interruption of her loneliness had arrived at a splendid time for, though the warm weather had been inviting, the aspect of her aloneness removed any enjoyment for individual outdoor activities.

She danced in circles of pleasure around him until he commanded her to sit down and listen. Jeanne was a bit taken aback by his brusque tone. He loomed above her, refusing to take a seat. From many corners of the Great Room, sensing that this might be momentous, unnoticed ears slipped into hidden places to overhear what would be said. Both M. d'Izernay and Sir Duquesse moved near to their open office doors, seeming to study their notes as they stood to listen. M. Bourbon crept silently from the Library and snuck into a corner close to the conversation. Aymée had followed Jeanne to the Great Room and as quietly and unobtrusively as she could, moved behind a nearby pillar.

When King Francis announced to Princess Jeanne the agreement of her betrothal, she sat in stunned silence.[xvi] All castle activity stopped suddenly, shocked into complete stillness.

Jeanne could not breathe. Her muscles would not move on command. Her mind sought for any rebuttal that would find traction for argument. Her tears rushed to her defense to drown the hurt, but shock intervened to sting her eyes. Jeanne's heart shouted against this ultimate betrayal. Hurt delayed the anger, but only for a short while. Overpowering surprise and indignation overcame the Princess, and she burst into a flood of tears.

The King continued to issue orders, his voice rising in volume and authority. She was to prepare to leave immediately, as promptly as possible, to join her mother in Alençon. He stood uncomfortably waiting for her to regain her self-possession.

Finally, she pleaded passionately and resolutely; crying out, "I humbly beseech you, Uncle, that I will not be compelled to marry M. d'Cleves!"

Surprised his decree met with resistance, King Francis, who could never brook opposition to his will, turned coldly from the weeping child, repeated his orders for her immediate departure from Plessis, and then left.

An ill wind bearing the disturbing news blew through the castle like a wilderness cyclone. Soon, it was streaming out the gates and down the road to shake the town of Tours. The shock and fear that followed the news devastated all in its wake. Hearts cried in unison at the impending loss of their treasured Princess; followed by anger that hit like an aftershock. Mass anger at the betrayal of their little darling rumbled back along the road, howling toward the castle: What could their esteemed King be thinking? He had torn their precious darling from the loving arms of France and flung her into the cold clutches of a German stranger!

When Raymond heard the news, he cried out in protest and dropped to his knees overcome with guilt at his selfishness. So preoccupied with his dreams of a home with Antoinette, he had forgotten to pray for the future of the Princess. Suddenly conscious of his vulnerability in the capricious hand of fate, he desperately prayed for divine intercession against this ignorant proclamation by the ultimate power of the land.

Antoinette and Mumsie heard the news before M. Abérnois came home that evening. The house of hope mourned as all effort had come to a screeching halt. These people, who loved their Princess for the hope and promise she had initiated in their lives, gathered in gloomy groups pondering the possibility of an unpredictable future. Antoinette, Mumsie, and Dads gathered for dinner but had no appetite. They stared around the table at each other, seeking some sort of reassurance that life would continue without further upset.

All the small individual rumblings joined together and grew into a second aftershock, rolling in a resounding thunder across the region; what would become of the Château de Plessis lez Tours? What would happen to their economy? Their jobs? Their purpose?

People pondered the disconsolate fate of the Princess, only to wrench their thoughts away to face the fear of where their futures might lay.

Back at the castle, the process of preparing for this anguishing separation began slowly. It seemed impossible to determine how to plan appropriately for the coming journey, as no firm itinerary appeared. Decisions of what to take and to send later to Nérac loomed. The path beyond meeting the Queen of Navarre at Alençon remained veiled in uncertainty.

The Princess was no longer alone in her sorrow. The tears of the castle flowed freely. Red eyes and runny noses were evident everywhere. Aymée would accompany the Princess to meet her mother, so she attempted to comfort Phoebe, Maddie, and Chloe, as they moved through a fog about their uncertain future. It seemed apparent that the positions here were at an end; there was always the hope they would be sent for later to join the Princess; however, there was little enthusiasm to follow her to Germany.

Jeanne wandered through the Library, selecting and discarding books, caressing the figures on the chessboard, contemplating the memories gathered in that room of learning and growing. Whenever she met Sir Duquesse, M. Bourbon or M. d'Izernay, she clutched them in desperation, not wanting to let them go from her embrace. For men who had been trained to withhold their emotions in public, they overlooked the tears of the Princess that soaked their suit coats and mingled their tears with the beautiful hair spread across their chests. All manner of excuses urged those in the kitchen to suddenly retrieve something from the Great Room, where one by one, they touched and hugged their precious girl. Their lives had been consumed and dedicated to serving her for seven years. Such devotion must not be dismissed lightly.

Jeanne insisted that her favorite mount be prepared in the stable to travel with her. Sir Ami hugged tightly to her side wherever she wandered, fearing that what he sensed amiss in the atmosphere of the castle would tear him away from her; she had to stop frequently to pet him and promise that he would also go with her. Rising to her feet in fresh tears, she wanted to take everyone with her, to pack up the entire castle and move it along behind her.

Aymée and all who helped complete the task of preparing the Princess for her trip did the best they could, and eventually, the effort was completed. Aymée stood in Jeanne's bedroom counting off on her fingers all that might be needed. Just in case it would fill an unexpected demand, she had folded and packaged the beautiful white dress Jeanne wore at the Christmas party. She stood caressing the soft velvet, recalling the ethereal beauty of the Princess as she descended the stairs that day.

Aymée had served the King of France faithfully all the days of her life. She admitted to times of irritation and disappointment at his choices during the years, mostly caused from her allegiance to Queen Marguerite. At this moment, she was bitterly disappointed in both the King, for his selfish dismissal of the heart of her Princess, and with Marguerite, for submitting to his decision without defending her daughter's interests. It was the first time she could remember that she was embarrassed and disappointed by the royals she had devoted her life to serving.

Without further delay, the Princess dressed in her traveling suit and saw her necessities loaded on several wagons with her horse tethered to the back of the carriage. The time had come. The entire household gathered outside of the entrance to the castle and in eerie silence, blew kisses to the precious child who had been their lives; knowing that her forthcoming marriage would more than likely not be a happy one. Aymée preceded the Princess into the coach and waited for her to complete her farewells. Aymée also was leaving a portion of her heart with so many in the castle and could not stem the flow of tears down her cheeks. Sir Ami would not suffer to enter the carriage before the Princess. Instead, he attached himself to her left boot like a wood tick, only entering the carriage in step with her.

The crowd wanted to trade places with him, and a twitter of jealous laughter moved across the air. The Princess paused on the step to turn and wave, tearfully repeating her thank you's again and again. Then the doors shut and only the small face of the Princess could be seen peering out the window as the coach and wagons crawled reluctantly up the road and disappeared among the trees of the forest.

Princess Jeanne of Navarre was leaving Château de Plessis lez Tours with more than she had come with; she had gathered to her heart so many friends in those years, and she would leave with enumerable memories to last throughout her life. Why then, she wondered, when she was going with so much was it so incredibly painful?

She had harbored desperate loneliness all these years, refusing to acknowledge the blessings surrounding her. She had desired the lively fellowship of companions her age; she had longingly wanted to be attached to her mother and father's household; she passionately loved France, and she had been cultivated and prepared to assume a role of Queen. As her past disappeared behind her, all these desires now were met by order of the King of France, she admitted, at least for the next three years. It was what was coming after which so wholly betrayed her now.

While the carriage moved along the roads, this time the Princess did not hide in the corner of the coach; she employed every tool she had acquired during her years at Château Plessis to formulate an argument against what the King had decreed.

43. What Now?

"Examine me, O Lord, and try me; test my mind and my heart. For Thy lovingkindness is before my eyes, and I have walked in Thy truth."

Psalm 26:2-3 (NASB)

Standing bereft in the Great Hall of Plessis, Sir Duquesse stared about him at the vast emptiness of the enormous castle. The light had gone out. Numb with loneliness, he could not comprehend how she had survived and overcome her own abandonment and devastating betrayal. Yet she lived. With a strength he could not fathom, she fought so hard to defeat her despair. Now, she was gone and her strength and light went with her; to face even greater battles, alone.

The heavy spirit of the unhappy castle closed in about him. Desperately, he looked about for something else that could occupy his mind. Abruptly he realized: there was nothing here for him to do! He had accomplished the task assigned him and had no ties to the Château de Plessis. He walked determinedly to his quarters and threw a few items into a satchel. Shouldering his satchel, he strode from his room and went toward the stables. He saddled his horse without a word to any of the stable hands, mounted, and galloped toward Alençon.

Duquesse stopped in Paris for food and rested his horse. He sat in the alehouse near his inn. The ride had been intense and invigorating. He lounged on a bench near the window and considered his options. How would he explain his abrupt departure to King Francis?

There had been no instruction left following the king's announcement to Jeanne and his prompt going. He remembered the shocked silence that followed the King's exit. Everyone at the castle had stood stock still. Only Aymée had the presence of mind to hold Jeanne in her arms and lead her upstairs. Perhaps he should use this occasion to seek an audience with the King to ask for his commands for the dispersal of the staff at the Château. He pondered that thought for a few moments and then signaled the manager of the alehouse.

The old man chuckled and said, "Yes, the King is at Fontainebleau. I hear he is to introduce that little firecracker of a Princess to her new groom to be." Sir Duquesse went cold at the old man's disrespect.

She was here! He would not have to ride on to Alençon to find her! Leaving his mug half full on the table, he rushed out the door. He bathed and changed his clothes and called for his horse to be saddled.

As he mounted, he asked himself, "What am I doing? What do I think I can do?"

He was halfway to Fontainebleau before the answer came to him. He desperately wanted to see how she was, and then to stay near her to be supportive in any way he could. Perhaps she would be encouraged by the face of someone she knew loved her.

He was glad he had spent many hours at Fontainebleau with the King discussing plans for Château Plessis because he knew the castle well and did not have to ask directions to the Grand Hall of the court. The room teemed with the usual handsome courtiers and beautiful ladies that followed the King like sycophants and leeches, currying for the King's favor and to be nearest him. They were vicious gossip mongers, and he had never been comfortable in their presence.

Sir Duquesse looked rapidly around the large room for any evidence that Jeanne was among them. She was not there. He skirted the crowds, not stopping to greet anyone.

Eventually, he located the Duke of Cleves basking in the adoration of a gaggle of women. Slipping behind one of the large potted plants, he watched, hidden behind the leaves. He had heard nothing of this man before the King's command to Jeanne that he would be her husband. Listening carefully, he admitted the Duke was surprisingly attractive. He had a muscular physique and athletic body, gleaming blonde hair and brilliant blue eyes. No doubt the qualities of his face were well appreciated by the people of his kingdom, as he bore the distinctive attributes of the Germanic race.

The women about him were swooning for his attention. He appeared to be quite proficient in the social banter of the court. Sir Duquesse judged him to be a few years younger than himself.

44. Introductions

*"Thus says the Lord to you, 'Do not fear or be dismayed
because of this great multitude, for the battle is not
yours but God's."*

2 Chronicles 20:15b (NASB)

King Francis had sent a courier to meet Jeanne's carriage with
orders that the Princess should stop in Paris before proceeding
to Alençon and her mother; he wanted Princess Jeanne to come to
Fontainebleau to meet the bridegroom he had chosen for her.

A murmur moved through the crowd, and all heads turned,
as if on a swivel, to the far door of the Grand Hall. The maiden
who stood there was so incredibly lovely the other women in the
room appeared jaded and gaudy. The crowd divided to open a
path between her and the King. She moved with her customary
grace and poise along the way opening before her. Princess Jeanne
floated with her head held high, and her deep blue eyes focused on
her Uncle with determined defiance. The crowds watched her proceed across the room, incredulously realizing, though it was astonishing, her beauty exceeded that of her famous mother. Dressed in
her white dress and ermine cape, with Sir Ami moving regally by
her side, she walked gracefully toward the King of France.

Whispers and gasps of appreciation traveled around the enormous room. Comments ricocheted among the crowd, not only
of Jeanne's fresh, maidenly glow but also shock at her apparent

disdain of the opportunity that lay before her. She acknowledged the King's introduction of the Duke with a haughty, dismissive nod.

The fact that she found him repugnant was intolerably evident to the King as she turned away immediately after the introduction to move to the other side of the room. Presenting her back to the homage of so brilliant a cavalier as Duke William de Cleve, she dismissed his presence by walking away. Her demeaning removal from her prospective bridegroom's company incurred the King's severe displeasure. Clacking tongues repeated the rumor that someone had even seen the bride-elect curl her lip in disdain.

The Princess had several acquaintances that she had come to know while visiting Fontainebleau with her mother years earlier and they flocked to her side to get close to the center of attention and hear what she had to say. The Princess carried on her conversations with skill and ability seldom seen by so young and accomplished a maiden. Without revealing a hint of her thoughts regarding the Duke, or even a tiny morsel of gossip-worthy words to be repeated, she observed the actions of the Duke without looking in his direction. Her developed sense of honesty and genuine truthfulness was disgusted at the servility of deportment of her chosen bridegroom whenever he was in the presence of the King or the all-powerful Constable de Montmorency, chief of the army, grand master of the court and the King's favorite adviser. Aymée, who had remained nearby, pulled the Princess aside to scold her for the cold dismissal of her soon-to-be husband that would undoubtedly influence his future appreciation of her as his wife.

Princess Jeanne hissed to Aymée dismissively, "Why would I, who have had invitations from royal princes, humble myself to receive a mere foreign Duke?"

Sir Duquesse battled with a multitude of emotions. He was delighted to see the fire in her eyes in defiance of her uncle's command. He was overwhelmed at her graceful beauty again. He saw the appreciation and pride of the King of France at her approach. He watched for any sign of reaction from the Duke and became incensed at his casually superior acknowledgment of the King's offering.

He could not move from his hiding place as the cameo of introductions unfolded. His training in self-discipline saved him from
shouting approval as Princess Jeanne turned her back on the Duke
with disdain and walked away. He rejoiced as she elegantly relo-
cated to the far corner of the Grand Hall to engage in conversation
there. Glancing back to the Duke for his reaction at her dismissal,
Sir Duquesse was astounded to watch him shrug his shoulders and
return to the worship of the women nearby. He looked again at the
King who stood rooted to the floor, shaking with livid fury.

Sir Duquesse could not take his eyes from the animated conversation carried on by the Princess as she moved through her acquaintances. Watching, he began to recognize small occurrences that
betrayed her tension. He instantly knew that she had summoned the
courage to meet this ordeal head on, defiantly drawing a line in the
sand that she would not cross. She had shouldered this confrontation alone, without support from any direction. He knew instantly
he was needed, for nothing else than to prop her up as she formed
a battle plan; she needed his unrelenting support.

King Francis seethed with displeasure at the open stubbornness demonstrated by the Princess and her display of rejection of
his choice. He had severely underestimated the dawning intellect
and strength of character now evident in his young charge. Poor
Aymée received the brunt of the King's anger, expressing himself
with emphatic severity. He commanded her, on arrival at Alençon,
to repeat his words to Queen Marguerite and to make it understandable that she must induce the Princess into submission to his will.
The ongoing jealous suspicion further inflamed his anger that the
King of Navarre had been exerting his influence on Jeanne to upset
the course of the King's decree.

The Princess returned to her apartments to change into traveling clothes again. She was exhausted, and the coming disapproval would be painful to endure. Aymée arrived, frowning and
scolding with every fiber of her being. Jeanne guessed that the heat
and intensity of Aymée's anger resulted from her fear of the rage
of King Francis.

Aymée had already received a significant portion of his anger
because she had failed to impress on this child the fear, respect

and full submittal to the wishes of the King. There was no defense for Aymée in pointing out the repeated and continual practice of the King to spoil and pamper his niece. He had been the one to succumb to Jeanne's strong will, and forthright insistence on what she viewed was true and right. The King had been as entranced as everyone by Jeanne's vivacious personality and singular intensity to defend her values. All true; however as the governess, she had been tasked to train the Princess in propriety and admitted she had failed miserably in the area of royal respect and submission to the King of all France, who tolerated no opposition to his commands.

Knowing that in Alençon, Queen Marguerite would soon straighten out her daughter with every method at her Majesty's disposal, Aymée knew she must do what she could to persuade the Princess to consent to her coming marriage. She spent what time she had left alone with the Princess to cajole, plead and demand that Jeanne admit the errors of her stand, threatening the inevitable destruction of all relationships of her family with the King of France if she continued in obstinate refusal to his will.

At the end of Aymée's tirade of disapproval, Jeanne fled the room, telling Aymée she must find a quiet place to think. Composing herself with the dignity and poise required to appear to anyone watching that she was entirely in control of her emotions, she moved purposely toward the library of the castle. When she entered, she thankfully was alone.

Sir Duquesse had lingered where he could see the door of her bedroom. He followed at a distance and saw her enter the castle library. It was a good choice, and he moved quickly to a more private entrance to the library so he could join her without being seen by others.

Princess Jeanne stood before a window looking out at the fabulous gardens of Fontainebleau before her. She instantly sensed someone's presence nearby and turned with composed anger at the interruption. Upon seeing the familiar and caring face of Sir Duquesse, her poise crumbled, and she moved into his arms to bury her face against his chest. It was like finding shelter in the storm; her tears dried up in an instant to know someone understood and still loved her. Sir Duquesse gently removed her from his embrace and led her to a near couch. Sitting her down firmly, he merely said, "How can I help you?"

Her pent-up thoughts and emotions released and she poured out her view of her situation. Listening, Sir Duquesse nodded in agreement and understanding. After some time, when she relayed to him she would be leaving for Alençon within the hour, he urged her to compose herself and to conform to the travel plans without complaint. He would follow after and spend the travel time contemplating possible plans to further her position. It was evident that she could not avoid the impending nuptials and that there was no opportunity to escape the inevitable.

He encouraged her to maintain her courage and to resolve to endure the coming ceremonies with her customary grace and poise. Whatever she must face, he would at least be present to support her. He reminded her that after the marriage ceremony she would be in the custody of her mother and father for the next three years. They would then pursue every avenue possible to save her from her fate that waited in Germany. The Princess objected vehemently at first, and then realizing that he was right in his assessment, she bowed her head in disappointment and resignation. Rising from the couch, Princess Jeanne replaced her distraught demeanor with the determined royal aspect resident in her conscious mind. She left the room in total control, buoyed by the support of her friend.

Returning to her apartment, Princess Jeanne dismissed Aymée from her presence; then she paced the floor in the solitude of her room. She was just a child in her twelfth year and was appalled at the forces arrayed against her. The quietness of the room deepened her isolation, and Jeanne realized there would be no way to stop her impending doom. Never, in her short life, had she heard of another woman who fought against an arranged marriage having ever been successful at averting the inevitable. Her thoughts ran back to the moment of hearing of Louis XI and his bride of nine. She did not know which had appalled her more, the terrible future Charlotte had faced or the horrible torture chamber of Louis XI. Facing the same appalling future herself, the walls of the room closed in on her. Desperately, she thought, "At least I can make a record of my protest, not that it will make a difference."

She had pondered the impact her resistance would have on her parents and the probable loss of her uncle's love. She acknowledged the severity of the threats against her and considered the foreign stranger that endangered her future. At so young an age, thoughts of marriage had barely crossed her mind until recently brought up during her friendship with Catherine d'Aster. The discussions the girls had shared had cultivated her knowledge and expectations of possible worthy matches; those being much superior to marriage to an unknown Duke from a small kingdom in faraway Germany.

Aymée was astounded at the regal cooperation of the Princess as they settled inside the carriage for the trip to Alençon. She studied her, trying to analyze the unusual change that had come over her. She was obedient and agreeable to every suggestion and request, responding with respectful accommodation, but Aymée sensed subdued defiance below the surface. The trip was completed in near silence as the Princess stared at the passing landscape. She would meekly respond to any attempt at conversation with polite discourse, as was her duty, but then returned to her thoughtful solitude immediately.

45. Discipline

"O Lord, the God of our fathers, art Thou not God in the heavens? And art Thou not ruler over all the kingdoms of the nations? Power and might are in Thy hand so that no one can stand against Thee."

2 Chronicles 20:6 (NASB)

At Alençon, Marguerite received the report from Aymée with great concern. Queen Marguerite entered her chamber nearly breathless at the shame and hurt that she had just endured from her brother's message. He was furious and spoke all sorts of unthinkable threats against the future of Navarre, her husband and her relationship with her beloved brother if she failed to bring about the proper submission and compliance of her daughter. She had sensed that he saw this rebellious pose as a threat to the authority and absolute power of his sovereign reign. If his twelve-year-old niece could refuse his commands without repercussion, so could anyone.

She was appalled to hear of the encounter between King Francis and Jeanne when her daughter had received his decree with such impudence, daring to question the order of the King and arguing for him to change his royal mind. Marguerite's apprehension increased by her knowledge of the King's suspicions toward her husband and knew she must make an effort to reassure Francis of King Henri's loyalty, and also to apologize for her daughter's behavior. She must eliminate this dilemma and repair the damage that was occurring between her and her brother. Francis had been the focus of her life since his birth, and she had reinforced and supported him in every way possible; she had poured her life and talents into him, sacrificing her happiness many times. Now, that connection and devotion were threatened to dissolve with the obstinate repudiation of the Princess. She must conquer this disobedience and mend the tear in the fabric of her brother's love.

The Queen took a deep breath and squared her shoulders to prepare for battle. At that moment she was betrayed by the memories of her humble submission to marriage at age seventeen to the ill-tempered Duke of Alençon. Then, unbidden, the memories tumbled through her mind of the unbearable years that followed, only ending by the Duke's death. She knew this was her weakness. No one, except Aymée, had perceived the misery she had endured, never questioning the authority and disregard of those exercising their power over her young vulnerability during those years. She could not justify Jeanne's stubborn refusal to submit, but she had to admire her determination. Taking a deep breath, she entered her daughter's room.

Jeanne was changing from her traveling clothes, and Aymée was unpacking the trunks. The Queen immediately began to question her daughter severely about her blatant disobedience toward the King. The Queen declared her disappointment and admonishment of the behavior displayed before her future husband. She demanded that Jeanne cease her rebellious attitude and apologize to the King in submission to his commands. Jeanne's vigorous rejection of her demands left the Queen floundering in confusion of what could be further said to persuade her.

Looking defiantly at her mother, Jeanne declared with haughty rejection, "I merely took the liberty of speaking frankly to the King, as I have been in the habit of saying to him all that I think or wish. How can you possibly consider that I would willingly give up France or the treasure of my inheritance of Béarn to espouse a Duke?"[xvii]

Flabbergasted, Queen Marguerite declared, "If you continue to repel the requests of the King of France and the advice of your parents, I will surely have you whipped into submission. You will prepare for the ceremony of your betrothal. We will then proceed to Châtellerault for your nuptials before the court of France."

Returning to her room, the Queen slumped into the nearest chair, wondering how she could have ever let that ludicrous remark slip from her mouth that she would have her beautiful daughter whipped. She was shaking from the encounter and buried her head in her hands, wondering how circumstances had come to such peril and what would she have to endure before it was over.

In Jeanne's room, Aymée had fled at the entrance of the Queen. Her divided loyalties were causing excruciating pain, and she could not bear to witness the encounter between Queen and Princess without being forced to take a side. It would be unbearable to decide between her cherished friend who must discipline the precious child Aymée loved with all her heart.

The Princess stood stiffly in shocked despair as she watched her beloved mother turn her back and leave the room in anger. Aymée had withdrawn, leaving Jeanne alone. Her mind was a blank, black void. Eventually, she remembered the comfort she had received after talking with Sir Duquesse and she pondered what he had said.

After some time, she sat at the desk and began to compose and write a curious protest in her own hand. She had inherited the gifts that her parents were famous for, coupled with her own superior intellect and intense educational process, so she wrote:

"I, Jeanne de Navarre, persisting in the protestations I have already made, do hereby again affirm and protest, by these present, that the marriage which it is desired to contract between the Duke of Cleves and myself, is against my will; that I have never consented to it, nor will consent; and that all I may say and do hereafter, by which it may be attempted to prove that I have given my consent, will be forcibly extorted against my wish and desire from my dread of the King, of the King my father, and of the Queen my mother, who has threatened to have me whipped by the baillive of Caen, my governess. By command of the Queen, my mother, my said governess has also several times declared, that if I do not all in regard to this marriage, which the King wishes, and if I did not give my consent, I should be punished so severely, as to occasion my death; and that by refusing, I might be the cause of the total ruin and destruction of my father, my mother, and of their house; the which has inspired me with such fear and dread, even to the cause of the ruin of my said father and mother, that I know not to whom to have recourse, excepting to God, seeing that my father and my mother abandon me, who both well know what I have said to them – that never can I love the Duke of Cleves, and that I will not have him. Therefore, I protest beforehand, if it happens that I am affianced, or married to the said Duke of Cleves in any way or manner, it will be against my heart, and in defiance of my will; and that he shall never become my husband, nor will I ever hold and regard him as such, and that any marriage shall be reputed null and void in testimony of which, I appeal to God, and yourselves, as witnesses of this my declaration that you are about to sign with me, admonishing each of you to remember the compulsion, violence, and constraint employed against me, upon the matter of this said marriage.

(Signed) «Jeanne de Navarre,»
«J. d'Arros,»
«Frances d'Navarro,»
«Arnauld Duquesse.» »[xvii]

Princess Jeanne requested to be served her meals in her apartments, and with courteous insistence, she asked to be left alone until the time came for her to appear for the ceremony. It seemed strange to feel so alienated from Aymée who had been her dearest support for so many years; yet, now she seemed to oppose the Princess in every regard.

The servants of the castle remarked one unusual event. The Princess was the recipient of a note from an unknown friend, which she promptly responded to with an answer. Sometime later, she made a solitary excursion to the library of the castle. She returned to her rooms after about an hour. Her actions, when reported to the Queen, were dismissed, knowing her daughter's love for reading.

46. Desperate Measures

"O our God, will Thou not judge them? For we are powerless before this great multitude who are coming against us; nor do we know what to do, but our eyes are on Thee."

2 Chronicles 20:12 (NASB)

The Duke of Cleves arrived at Alençon to prepare for and to complete the ceremony of betrothal and resided in another wing of the castle.

The following day, the Princess appeared at her appointed place, attired in her white dress and ermine cape, and completed her necessary responses. She did not notice the Duke's attempts to show his disregard for her person or the vows of the ceremonies. She did not look his way or glance at him at any moment of the vows. The elaborate, magnificent chapel of Alençon echoed the hollowed responses of the couple, leaving no doubt in the mind of the bishop of Seéz, who officiated, of the emptiness of their commitment.

At the completion of the ceremony, Princess Jeanne returned directly to her rooms, requesting that she be left to herself again until their departure. She had been aware of the one friendly face partially hidden behind a column in the back of the chapel. The knowledge of his presence had strengthened her.

The Duke, who soon grew weary of the disdain of his bride-to-be, had attached himself to the Queen of Navarre, whose beauty and enticements so attracted him that he was able to ignore the rebuffs of her daughter.

It was again reported to the Queen the activity of the Princess when she returned to the library late in the evening. Marguerite was comforted knowing her daughter had so resigned herself to the events of the day that she was able to find entertainment among the books of the library.

The support and conversations with Sir Duquesse those two times had enabled the Princess to retain her composure during the ordeal, and then to organize her thoughts to build a defense against her forced nuptials. She had written and signed a document defining her resistance against the marriage, and had furthered her objection by writing a second missal in support of her earlier argument. Sir Duquesse had enabled the documents to be duly witnessed and signed by two other members of the household of the Princess pressed into service on the trip to Alençon.

The second document had been composed in the afternoon after the betrothal ceremony and was signed that evening by the same members of her household. It read as follows:

"I, Jeanne de Navarre, in the presence of you, who love the truth, signed the protestation which I previously presented, and who perceive that I am compelled and obliged by the Queen my mother, and by my governess, to submit to the marriage demanded by the Duke of Cleves between himself and me; and that it is intended, against my will, to proceed to the solemnities of a marriage between us; I take you all to witness that I persevere in the protest I made before you, on the day of the pretended betrothal between myself and the said Duke of Cleves, and in all and every protestation that I may at any time have made by word of mouth, or under my hand; moreover, I declare that the said solemnity of marriage, and every other thing ordained relative to it, is done against my will, and that all shall hereafter be regarded as null and void, as having been done, and consented to by me, under violence and restraint; in testimony of which I call you all to witness, requesting you to sign the present, with myself, in the hope that by God's help it will one day avail me."

(Signed) «Jeanne de Navarre,»
«J. d'Arros,»
«Frances d'Navarro,»
«Arnauld Duquesse.» [xix]

47. Inevitable Occurrences

"For it is He who delivers you from the snare of the
trapper, and from the deadly pestilence."

Psalm 91:3 (NASB)

Jeanne received a very cordial and affectionate welcome by her uncle upon her arrival at Châtellerault. Word had been sent ahead relating her cooperation in Alençon. The slightest hint of her objection was just brushed aside by the King as childish and unreasonable. Much effort in the way of preparation was in progress and the most sumptuous arrangements completed.

Princess Jeanne escaped to her rooms, crushed and disillusioned at the prospects before her. She was comforted to know that Sir Duquesse had made his way to Châtellerault and would be among the throngs of the King's court. The crushing realization that even the presence of a dear friend would not lift the weight of facing the ordeal before her, she woodenly acknowledged that what would happen after tomorrow was unknown and could very well contain her greatest dread. Her future lay in shadowed suspense, portending ominous year upon year of lonely exile that would ultimately kill her.

She spent the remainder of the day distraught on her bed, shedding hopeless tears of self-pity. Late in the day, there was a knock on her door. She scrubbed at her face in a ridiculous effort to hide the effects of her tears and meekly called out "Enter."

The door opened to reveal a team of seamstresses bearing her wedding dress. She examined it with the same dread that she viewed the upcoming nuptials. She would be attired in a gown of gold cloth, heavily beset with jewels. Her coronet of very rich gems to encircle her brow was appropriate for the eminent wife of a Duke; the border of her mantle trimmed with ermine. She endured the ordeal of the fitting, and at the departure of the seamstresses, she dissolved again in tears.

The following morning, in spite of her exhaustion from such an emotional night, Jeanne prepared for the ceremony with determination and again assumed regal defiance toward what she must endure. The strength of her character had won the battle during the previous night, and she now refused to wilt under the challenges she faced. She may not be able to stop the circumstances speeding forward with her in tow, but she would express her objection at every possible opportunity.

Jeanne permitted all assistance to dress her and arrange her hair, though her solemn endurance was apparent. The weight of the jewels that adorned the gold cloth of her dress was incredible. [xx] She found it difficult to move about and had to muster an astonishing amount of energy to walk. She enlisted the assistance of the ladies of her chamber to support its weight, moving with her to her appointed station as the approaching bride. She appealed to anyone near to please provide a chair for her support as she waited.

The doors of the Grand Hall were opened to reveal an extravagant display of every influential member of the state, surrounded by a never-before-seen excess of decorations, floral arrangements, and candelabras. This copious, extreme display far exceeded even the splendid coronation of the Emperor Charles V. Huge throngs of nobles, courtiers, and ladies crowding into every available space filled the enormous hall to bursting. Thousands of eyes were turned to her, charged with curiosity. She felt the intensity of their waiting judgment like a solid force. This ceremony would provide meat for gossip and discussion for many years.

Princess Jeanne closed her eyes, seeking the strength to face her fate with dignity. When she opened them, her uncle, the King of France, was making his way down the long aisle toward her and presented himself to accompany the bride down the aisle to the altar. Jeanne, determined to carry her case to the last moment, struggled to rise, finally collapsing weakly back into the chair, entreating her uncle that the weight of the jewels and gold dress were too heavy for her to move forward.

The King, annoyed, glanced up at the sea of eyes of the brilliant multitude that surrounded them, watching every move and reaction; he called for Constable de Montmorency to assist him. He then commanded the mighty Constable to pick the Princess up in his arms and to carry her to the altar. In deep humiliation, the Constable fulfilled the command of his King amid an increasing volume of murmurs of shock. Along with the shock and appalled comments about the Princess, rumors sped in hushed tones that Montmorency, being the choice of the King for this degradation of the dignity of his position, had somehow lost favor and would, most likely, soon be dismissed from service to the King.

After plopping the Princess unceremoniously at the altar, Constable de Montmorency retreated to the outside hallway to regather his dignity and contemplate his embarrassment. The ceremony proceeded, and the nuptials completed in front of hundreds of gawking witnesses. It was July 15, 1540, and Princess Jeanne was twelve years old.[xxi]

A magnificent banquet and ball followed the nuptials. Princess Jeanne was expressly ordered by the King to appear. As the ball ended, she was formally directed by the Duke of Cleves to return to the guardianship of the Queen of Navarre and her governess, "until such time as the Duchess should have attained suitable years to fulfill the conjugal engagements she had contracted."

The following eight days were full of brilliant pageants, festivities, and tournaments in celebration of the marriage. As the honored bride, Jeanne was again forced to attend.

She did the best she could to avoid and ignore the Duke, who chose every opportunity to fawn over her and press his suit as her consort in an attempt to save his pride and reputation, making constant efforts to escort her and attend to her perceived needs. She was disgusted at his persistence in light of her obvious disapproval of his company and his person. Eventually, the excitement for the tournaments and knightly displays claimed his attention and the Princess was relieved from his constant presence.

At the end of eight days, the Duke of Cleves returned to his home to renew his fight with Emperor Charles V, encouraged by the promise of King Francis that he would personally march a troop of royal soldiers into Germany under his command; or perhaps, he would send the Dauphin of France, in his place.

48. Safe Haven

*"Many are the afflictions of the righteous; but the Lord
delivers him out of them all."*

Psalm 34:19 (NASB)

Jeanne, Duchess of Cleves and Juliers, was happy to see the
Duke return to his own country. She was anxious to join her
parents and to return to her home kingdom. Impatiently, Jeanne
also wanted to put as much distance as possible between her and
King Francis. She found it difficult to be civil when in the King's
presence because the resentment she felt against what he had forced
on her was almost as profound as the hurt she felt for his betrayal
of her womanhood.

Jeanne had some consolation provided by a joyous reunion
with Sir Ami who was kenneled in some far-distant corner of
Fontainebleau. Sir Ami had refused to eat, curling up near the
edge of the kennel, overcome with despair that he might never see
his Princess again. Unknown to Jeanne, the Duke had displayed
intense dislike for Sir Ami who shared the aversion of the Princess
for this stranger. The Duke had proclaimed that the dog would not
accompany his consort to Germany on that day in the future.

Finally, the King and Queen of Navarre and Duchess of Cleves
departed and returned to Nérac. Jeanne was very eager to watch the
passing countryside since she had no recollection of the landscapes
of her travels when she was five, on her way to Château Plessis.

Sometimes she would leave her mother in the coach to ride her horse beside her father, with Sir Ami running joyously alongside. Renewing her companionship with her father provided treasured moments while riding in the crisp fall air.

Before Christmas, the King and Queen of Navarre, accompanied by the Duchess of Cleves, took up residence at their elegant castle of Pau. For the following three years, Duchess Jeanne spent hours of contentment in the society of her mother and the company of her cousin Francoise and the various damsels of the Queen's court.

Sir Ami's happiness deepened as Jeanne settled into contentment. His reunion with his Princess after that lengthy and excruciating separation at Fontainebleau portrayed the bond and loyalty of his heart for her. She was never out of his sight. Her nearness was so paramount to him, even when she merely crossed to the other side of the room he uncurled his long legs and rose to follow, sinking nearby to watch her movements alertly. His supreme pleasure of promenading with his mistress through the luxurious hallways and great rooms of Pau could be exceeded only by brisk runs beside her horse or meandering walks through the gardens to sniff all the delicious smells.

As soon as possible, with her mother's permission, Jeanne sent for her ladies-in-waiting, Phoebe, Maddie and Chloe to join her from Château Plessis. She also wrote a letter to Antoinette requesting, if her parents would agree, that she join her at Pau and begin training to be the Princess's lady-in-waiting. She missed her friend and treasured her genuine affection.

Antoinette was surprised and overwhelmed by the invitation of the Princess. Discussing the opportunity with Mumsie and Dads, Antoinette admitted she had no idea what was involved if she accepted Jeanne's invitation. With the help and guidance of her parents, she learned that she would be a constant companion to Jeanne, and Princess Jeanne would assume her living expenses, clothes, education, and travel. From that position, she gained a level equal to the noble ladies of the court, eligible as an appropriate prospect for marriage into an aristocratic family. It would be an opportunity to be much desired. Mumsie hugged Antoinette and spoke earnestly about the honor extended by her friend. She assured Antoinette that though her family would deeply miss her, they would be so happy for her. They would only desire her happiness to be without guilt. At age thirteen, Antoinette would soon be of marriageable age, and such an opportunity would further her ability to consider a nobleman within her choices.

When Antoinette found the courage to share Jeanne's request with Raymond, she was astonished by his reaction. They walked together along the path of beech trees, stopping when they found the privacy of a wooded spot off the road. Raymond looked deeply into Antoinette's blue eyes as she spoke of Jeanne's invitation. When he had declared with enthusiasm his support for her going, he had seen confusion cloud her eyes.

She had given her heart to Raymond when she first met him and felt their deep friendship had revealed his own like thoughts toward her. His delight that Jeanne had asked Antoinette to join her at Pau had stunned her. With confusion, she studied his face, trying to understand how he could be so pleased that her departure would take her a considerable distance away from him.

Gently, he stroked her cheek and said, "Antoinette, for years I have held you dearest to my heart, hoping that someday I may hold you in my arms as my wife. Since the first day I met you, I have lived my life for you, planning and working to prepare a suitable home to bring you to after our wedding. You have been my dream, though I have known there would be those in my life who would not consider your position in life worthy of my choice. I have ignored those voices, refusing to let them diminish my dreams of happiness with you. The time has not been right for me to declare my love for you and reveal my affection openly. I do that now, with all my heart, because I could not bear to let you part from me not knowing how much I love you. I ask you now to be my wife on that future day when you return to me for our wedding. Until that time, your position at the court of Princess Jeanne will eliminate any protests against my hopes."

The uncertainty in Antoinette's eyes softened into a shimmer of joy. She heard what she had secretly longed for and in spite of being separated from her soulmate, she could see hope for a lifetime with him.

"Do you see, my love, what a great benefit it will be for you to be at Pau to be prepared to become my wife? Only, I must be sure that your heart is betrothed to me while you are gone."

With that, Raymond gathered her into his arms and kissed her properly, expressing the love and longing he had bottled up for so long. Antoinette was so astonished at the outpouring of his love that her thoughts were whirling. When his lips met hers, she felt that she was falling down a well, lost in a dizzy ecstasy of joy.

Antoinette felt lifted by the whirlwind of his declaration and swept along in a blur of anticipation as she packed and traveled to join Jeanne. The coming months overflowed with disbelief and astonishments at the sumptuous delights befitting a member of Jeanne's household.

Antoinette would never conceive how Jeanne's friendship had even come about, or how her dear friend who possessed so much could need her, and so she returned her love in trust and loyalty to the Princess. She excelled in her position since her tasks were expressions of love that required no conscious exertion on her part. She only needed to share her devotion as she always had, without any thought that to do so required any effort.

Admittedly, within her own life, she acquired refinements from her gracious surroundings and associations. She participated for hours under the gentle and eloquent instruction of the Queen of Navarre along with the other young ladies of the court. She unconsciously assumed the mannerisms and bearing of a royal lady, confidently moving through her society with poise and gracefulness. Jeanne's friendship and appreciation of her devotion had advanced Antoinette's self-confidence and dignity. The hours of study and discussion stimulated her intellectual abilities. She grew accustomed to participating in social interactions and learned the art of encouraging conversation. Much to Antoinette's surprise and Jeanne's delight, she became much sought after during the elegant dinner parties and social fetes held occasionally in the ballrooms and gardens of Pau.

No longer suffering immediate threats to her security and happiness, Jeanne's temperament softened, and her education expanded further through association with the reformed teachers and refugees in Béarn. Her natural tendency to probe to the origin of any presented fact and find proof of its truth was not discouraged. Discussions with the gentle Gérard Roussel on theology and doctrines of reform were received and put to the test of her inquiring mind. Her search to discern the truth of every tenant was endorsed until her curiosity was satisfied. The only circumstance that cast a hint of distaste to these opinions was the professed Lutheran tenets embraced by the Duke of Cleves; any connecting bond with the Duke continued to be repugnant to the Princess.

The relationship between Jeanne and Antoinette grew closer as they discussed and pondered the ideas of the reform advocates and how they differed from the upbringing they had experienced when the Catholic Church dominated all citizens of France and Europe, spreading even to the hills of Jerusalem to expand Christianity as portrayed by the doctrines of men. Through deep searching and debate, the simplicity of the Gospel embedded in the hearts of both women. Each agreed that something was missing in the tradition, formality and absolute power of the bloated Church which was fighting with such fervor the unvarnished truth of the Word of God.

Antoinette often wrote to Raymond to share the ideas and conclusions of their discussions in hope to seek his agreement. Their relationship grew with great strides as they revealed their thoughts and feelings in communications that explored their intimate growing beliefs. Separation in distance provided a fertile garden for the growth of understanding and intimacy of their minds.

Jeanne teased Antoinette continually about the handsome young suitors that buzzed around her radiance seeking to win her affections. Antoinette was complimented, but her heart was devoted to her man in Tours.

49. Abandoned Again

"For I am convinced that neither death, nor life, nor angels, nor principalities, nor things present, nor things to come, nor powers, nor height, nor depth, nor any other created thing, shall be able to separate us from the love of God, which is in Christ Jesus our Lord."

Romans 8:38-39 (NASB)

Unknown to the Duchess residing contentedly in the south of France, her spouse, the Duke, was in dire circumstances. In August 1543, Emperor Charles V entered into the duchy of Cleves, with an army of 40,000 infantry and 8,000 horses.[xxii] The King of France was at that time employed in reconstructing fortifications of the castle of Landrecy on a stupendous scale. Somehow, the King had forgotten that the Duke had mounted his defenses against the Emperor based on the promises of the King of France to send troops and money. Facing certain destruction, the Duke of Cleves sent courier after courier to implore the urgent aid of the French army. The Duke's messengers returned with vague promises of future assistance. Principal towns of the Duchy were conquered or slaughtered before the oncoming arms of the irate Emperor. Within days the conquest of the duchy of Cleves was complete.

In a panic, the Duke sought support and advice from his few statesmen still available. Almost beside himself at the uncertainty of his position, his courage abandoned him. On the unfortunate counsel of his advisers, he determined to prostrate himself before the Emperor to beg for leniency. He would make peace with the Emperor regardless of any inflicted cost of personal humiliation.

The Duke of Cleves, uninformed of the exertions made in his favor by King Francis, proceeded to entreat the Emperor for audience, which was granted with the Emperor the day following. On arrival, he received access into the royal tent on the field of battle where the Emperor sat on a chair of state with his crown and scepter. The Duke threw himself at the feet of the Emperor and begged for clemency of pardon and grace. Among the stipulations attached to the treaty he signed was: first, he must return his public faith, and also the religion of the Duchy, to the Catholic Church; and secondly, he must renounce his alliance with the King of France.

After signing the treaty with the Emperor, the Duke sent a messenger to the King of France canceling all ties of alliance with France. The Duke demanded that his consort, the Princess Jeanne de Navarre, be brought immediately to Aix-la-Chapelle, as the time of her guardianship under her royal mother now was completed.

The King of France, meanwhile, had begun to make plans to come to the aid of the Duke. He concluded that the most effective protection for the Duke would be to conduct Jeanne to Aix, where their marriage would be consummated. Not aware of the recent defeats and humiliations of the Duke at the hand of the Emperor, he ordered his Cardinal Du Bellay to Béarn to immediately conduct his niece to Luxembourg where the King was stationed, and he would escort her from there to Aix.

The nightmare Jeanne had feared most came upon her; the occurrence she feared and had ignored as remote had materialized. With tears, she protested she would die if compelled to obey her uncle's summons. She implored her father to save her from exile and a destiny she shuddered to contemplate. Resolutely she closed her ears to any remonstrance or exhortation of Queen Marguerite who again attempted to impress upon her daughter the necessity of submission to the will of the King.

All the Princess's pleadings were to no avail, and she was obliged to depart. Accompanied by the King of Navarre, she set forth for her new home. The bitterly angry farewell of her mother left them both grievously hurt. In direct rebellion against her consort, the Duke, Jeanne insisted that Sir Ami accompany her so she might have at least one warm companion that would be devoted to her.

The dread of her future and the harsh conditions of her travel had drained all the resources of her usual vivacious energy. Her despair and abandonment by those who should have loved her more had sucked from her the will to live. It was like she was five years old again, weeping unending tears of desolation in the corner of her coach. Sir Ami huddled as close to her side as possible, trembling in sympathy. The nearer she traveled to the French frontier, the more she was depleted and overwhelmed by gloomy depression. Jeanne and her father, nearing Luxembourg, had arrived at the city of Soissons. She remained there one night to gain strength.

Jeanne lay sleepless in her bed staring at the ceiling, gripped in fear. Her pitiful life had finally come to this unthinkable place. She tried to find courage in the lives of other Princesses who had endured a similar fate but found only more despair. She questioned if love even existed, convinced that she had never seen it displayed for her.

She cried out, "God, are you even there or have you forgotten me? Where is Your love?"

She threw off her covers and paced the cold floor in her bare feet. Sir Ami walked beside her, stopping when she did to sit, gazing forlornly up at her. So disconsolate was she, she could not imagine living to endure tomorrow, and cast about looking for a way to end her life. Defeated, she threw herself on her bed, weeping.

Her sobs had finally calmed, and she had returned to the stupor of resignation when a sharp knock sounded on the door, and her father called, "Jeanne, Jeanne, you must wake up!"

Pulling her covers up to her chin, she weakly called for him to come in, overcome with terror that the Duke had come to fetch her himself. It was the middle of the night. Her fear was upon her, and she had nowhere to run from it.

Her father burst through the door waving urgent dispatches from King Francis. He handed the King's message to her, smiling broadly, and announced the abject surrender of the Duke of Cleves to the Emperor. Jeanne looked at him, confused; not knowing if that meant she was now a prisoner of the Emperor or if the Duke was thrown in prison and she now had no home or sustenance in Cleves.

The King of Navarre shouted in answer, "No, No. Because of the Duke's surrender to the Emperor, King Francis has consequently determined to procure the dissolution of the Duke's marriage with you. The King has directed that you should return and take up residence with Queen Eleanor at Fontainebleau until he decides on what measures to pursue under the circumstances.[xxiii] We will leave within the hour. Can you be ready? Are you able to travel?"

Jeanne flew into her father's arms, breaking out in new tears of relief. "Oh father, can it be true? Am I truly saved? I can leave in minutes if we are to go to Fontainebleau! God has heard my pleas and has brought about my escape! Oh, you have no idea how happy I am now. Do I dare to believe? Do I dare to live?"

Sharing her joy, Sir Ami bounced in circles around her and her father barking noisily.

Queen Marguerite who received a message with the new developments was appalled at the total reversal of the cowardly Duke of Cleves. Particularly incensed at the Duke's concessions to the emperor regarding his faith, she immediately returned correspondence to King Francis declaring, "Monseigneur, I would rather see my daughter in her grave, than know her to be in the power of a man who has deceived you, and inflicted so foul a blot on his honor."[xxiv]

Now that it suited the King to untie the knot he had so forcefully insisted that the Princess form with the disgraced Duke, it was granted that her aversion might now have a reasonable foundation. He demanded that she produce some documentation of her protests and objections to the alliance. Trembling with the hope of her release from the nuptials performed, she provided the documents she had written and had witnessed on the days before her betrothal and marriage vows. Confident that the documents would be relevant to the case, the King ordered his French minister to seek, in application to the Holy See, for a bull, annulling the marriage.

The plea placed in the record for annulment stated, ". . . for the violence done to the inclination of the Princess throughout the affair."

The Duke of Cleves, who would not be expected to express disappointment at losing his ungracious bride, received word of the plea to the Pope and dispatched an envoy to Rome to state his agreement to be released. His unseemly eagerness to recover his matrimonial liberty came as a blessing.

Jeanne returned, with her entire household, to the castle of Plessis-lez-Tours, at the suggestion of the King, to establish a distance from her kindred to imply she was beyond their influence, to further satisfy the Holy See.

Sir Duquesse had returned to Château Plessis after the wedding ceremony. Before leaving, he had renewed some old acquaintances at Fontainebleau. He intended to keep abreast of any news regarding Jeanne's affairs.

He had been satisfied that for three years, she would be safe and happy in Pau with her royal parents. Since King Francis had allowed the dispensation of the staff at the castle to slip his mind, Sir Duquesse had gathered all who had served so faithfully for the Princess to report again for service. He would keep the castle in excellent care and maintenance until the day when the Princess determined to dispose of it. He had seen the documents of the King bequeathing the castle to Jeanne when she had first arrived at age five, although only in name until she reached legal age. The Princess never knew that the Château-de-Plessis-lez-Tours was a portion of her dowry. It was the hope of Sir Duquesse when she discovered she was the Château's owner; she would consider it a familiar haven to return to in time of need.

When the news of the occurrences taking place near Aix arrived, the castle shifted into high gear in preparation for their Princess to return.

As Princess Jeanne walked at last into the Great Room of the Château de Plessis, her staff welcomed her like a long-lost daughter. She looked about in satisfaction at the familiar surroundings, the memories of her departure still fresh in her mind. The great fear that had come upon her and then so precipitously been wiped away by a divine power was always a wonder and a miracle to Jeanne. She felt she had peered into the depths of Hell, then had been drawn back by such a mighty love, she would forever be grateful.

Her faith was, at that moment, invested only in the Almighty God who held her in the palm of His hand; not on the human beings He had created, who previously failed her. She could not count on the King of France, her royal parents in Navarre, or any man she might love and marry in the future, but only on God alone.

Jesus had died for her, to save her, and she knew deep in her soul that since He had done that, He would guide and direct her future steps according to His great love and purpose, to complete her joy and hope. Jeanne wondered in the dark of night, gazing at the stars beyond her windows, why were her prayers answered? Remembering all those other Princesses down through the centuries who had suffered as much or more as their lives were ordered and directed by others more powerful than themselves, she found it was impossible to express her thankfulness in words. Wondering if God had created her 'for just a time as this,' like Queen Esther in the Bible, how would she be called to serve Him, she wondered?

50. Love as It Should Be

"Things which eye has not seen and ear has not heard,
and which have not entered the heart of man, all that
God has prepared for those who love Him."

1 Corinthians 2:9 (NASB)

A few weeks after the return to the castle, the Princess and Antoinette were sitting in Jeanne's secret room talking of all the events they had been through together. Antoinette reached over and enclosed Jeanne's hand in her own and spoke in a low voice.

"Princess, you know I love you dearly, and I have so much to be grateful for because of you. You came into my life from such a different and faraway world and poured blessings out on my family and me ever since. I would desire to serve you faithfully all the days of my life, in any way I can."

Jeanne embraced her sweet, faithful friend at this declaration.

"It is because those are my deepest feelings for you that I find myself with a dilemma. One of the most wonderful blessings I have received from our friendship has been when you brought Raymond with you to my house. Our friendship has grown, and now, Raymond has asked me to be his wife. I know it is proper for Raymond, first, to request permission from my father. However, I asked him to let me ask for your permission first. You brought him to me, and I lost my heart to him that first day. He says he has felt the same about me. Not only did you introduce us, but you have also made it possible, by asking me to be your lady-in-waiting, for his noble family to accept me as a socially acceptable candidate to marry their son. They are most agreeable with our planned betrothal and marriage. Can you forgive me for leaving your service to marry Raymond?"

The pain of losing Antoinette from the daily circle of her life hit Jeanne very hard, as she had always known her friend's devotion was pure and honest, never expecting to receive anything in return for her love. It was going to be a painful separation; however Jeanne could only want the love of her two best companions to blossom and come to fruit.

"Of course, Antoinette," she cried, "I only wish for you both the very best in love and life. You know how I will miss you for you mean so much to me. Now, you must follow your heart and happiness, and we will plan your wedding together, with Mumsie. How happy I am for you!" Clapping her hands in delight, she hugged Antoinette tightly.

The wedding was quite beautiful. Held in the Chapel of the castle and decorated with white ribbons and white roses on each of the pews and candelabras filling the altar, it reflected the innocence of the sweet couple. The Bishop du Châtel officiated, and the pews filled to overflowing with the townspeople from the house of hope, castle staff and the friends and relations of both families. Antoinette was beautiful, dressed in a gorgeous gown created and designed by the bride, Jeanne, and Mumsie and sewn by the seamstresses of the castle. With her blue eyes sparkling with happiness, Antoinette was escorted by her Dads, walking to the altar carrying a single white rose. Her beauty and purity shone like such a bright light; it seemed to blind Raymond as he watched her approach him.

Their tender vows were so meaningful and expressed so lovingly that everyone, except the bride and groom, was sniffing and dabbing at their eyes. When the Bishop presented Monsieur and Madame Raymond DuPuy, the entire audience jumped to their feet with applause. Princess Jeanne was overflowing with happiness for the sweet couple. Ironically, the contrast between her recent wedding and this one was painfully obvious. It was difficult to rebury the resentment she felt of the occurrences of that wedding; there were no memories of tender first-time love.

51. Free to Live

"If you love me, you will keep my commandments."

John 14:15 (NASB)

Princess Jeanne, Duchess of Cleves, had been reunited with King Francis and was again in the King's favor. He had chosen her to be godmother to his grand-daughter Elisabeth who was born to Dauphin Henry II and Catherine de Medici; the godfather was King Henry VIII of England.

"How ironic," Jeanne thought, "that King Francis appointed me as godmother to the child of Henry II when he broke his promise to betroth me as Henry's future wife."

King Francis's sudden reversal of that promise to achieve his political ambitions and obtain control of the city of Milan by marrying his dauphin Henry to Catherine de Medici exposed the preeminence of political maneuvers over moral commitment in the character of the King of France.

On Easter, in the spring of 1545, Jeanne presented her fourth petition for the annulment of her marriage. Bishop Châtel held mass, with attendance by the prime minister of King Francis, the ambassador of the Emperor, the bishop of Angoulême, and Cardinal de Tournon, representative of Pope Paul. At the conclusion of the mass, Princess Jeanne went to the front of the Chapel and repeated her protest declarations with great dignity and self-possession. Swearing on a book held by the Cardinal de Tournon, she verified as accurate all she had declared and signed. Then, Cardinal de Tournon carried, by hand, Jeanne's plea to Pope Paul in Rome for his approval.

The bull of announcement of the annulment of Jeanne's marriage vows delayed due to the vacillations of Pope Paul IV. Jeanne was finally released from the odious alliance later in the year of 1545. [xxv]

For Jeanne, the disposal of the hated specter of that ill-conceived marriage was like an enormous weight lifted off her shoulders. For the next two years, Jeanne settled contentedly into her home, and her surroundings no longer appeared to her like a cage, but the castle Plessis was a familiar retreat. Her serenity and joy prospered; she was happy with cultivating the life that pulsed around the heart of Château de Plessis. The company of her friends at the castle, her ladies-in-waiting, and newlyweds Raymond and Antoinette were sufficient to occupy her social needs, although, on occasion, she would visit her Uncle Francis at the court at Fontainebleau where she was well received. The eligible status of Princess Jeanne d'Albret of Navarre was much discussed, with her presence attracting possible suitors who circled her like bees to a hive.

On a cold, blustery day in the spring of 1547, a royal courier knocked on the door of the castle and demanded entrance. He then requested a private interview with the Princess. Alone in the Library, the courier relayed the news that King Francis had died on March 31, 1547. He handed Jeanne a letter from her mother and excused himself to complete his sad errands about the countryside.

Queen Marguerite had written from her sister's convent in Tusson, in Angoumois, where she received notice of her brother's death.[xxvi] She relayed the additional information that Henri, King of Navarre was sojourning in Mont de Marsan. The Princess immediately made arrangements to join her father in Mont de Marsan and together they went through the period of mourning for a month, together.

In their conversations, King Henri conveyed to Jeanne the dramatic changes in the court of recently crowned King Henry II after the death of Francis I. Politically and socially, the personality of the new King and his circle of influential cabinet changed dramatically.

The prominent powers behind the throne and reign of Henry II resided with his mistress, Diane de Poiters; the princes of the house of Lorraine d'Guise; and the Queen, Catherine de Medici. Constable de Montmorency, who had been dismissed from the cabinet of Francis I and exiled in disgrace, was recalled to the court of Henry II and invested in unlimited powers by his sovereign.

The few opportunities Princess Jeanne spent at the court of Francis I, including her appointment as godmother to Elisabeth, daughter of the Duke of Orleans and Catherine de Medici, were impacted by her strange relationship with Catherine.

Married at age fourteen to the Duke d'Orleans, Catherine was not known for her beauty.[xxvii] Her boy-husband did not love her and privately demeaned her ancestry, her inability to produce an heir, and her plain looks. Henry reserved his adoration for the widow, Diane de Poiters, twenty-four years older than he. Queen Catherine surmounted these disappointments by assuming a facade of smiling serenity and composed resolve; however, simmering beneath her false cordiality was a calculating and vengeful spirit. When the Dauphin Francis sickened and died in 1536, dark rumors spread that poison may have been the cause, and the most likely person to benefit could be Catherine de Medici. Regardless of the truth of the rumor or its falseness, the Duke d'Orleans now inherited the crown on the death of Francis I in 1547.

Catherine's early childhood was in itself a tragic start. She had been orphaned at birth and raised as a ward of her uncle, Pope Clement III, who provided for her comfort but neglected any influence on her moral growth. She had inherited the superior intellect of her Medici ancestors and the art of deceit from her aunt Clarice with whom she spent most of her upbringing. Able to discern the most intimate resentments of a person, she had learned to probe for weak points to employ her weapons of jealousies and hatred among the powerful. When her husband filed to divorce her, with dexterity she wielded her secret warfare of lies and deceit and the judge dismissed the plea. When her neglectful husband wore the crown as King of France, she had born Elisabeth and a young dauphin to succeed him to the throne. Her position was secure.

The encounters between Catherine de Medici and Princess Jeanne were rife with undercurrents. Devotion to truth and honesty became so deeply embedded in Jeanne that her very presence threatened the deceitful life and maneuverings of Catherine. Catherine was aware that her position of wife and future Queen of France had first been appointed for Jeanne d'Albret by King Francis before he broke his promise to the King of Navarre.

The natural beauty and gracious purity of mind and conscience of the Princess caused Catherine to hate her. Covering her intense dislike, Queen Catherine's smooth manner and pretense of a companionable demeanor raised an antipathy in Jeanne, who was aware of the Queen's dislike but did not care to understand its source. Opposed in interests, in principles, and in sympathies, whenever the two royal ladies were together, there was underlying controversy.

Princess Jeanne spent as little time as was considered acceptable at the court of Henry II. The gossip circulating of her recent marriage and annulment was uncomfortably rampant, and her presence seemed to stimulate its popularity. Because of reports of the Queen of Navarre's declining health, Princess Jeanne joined her mother in Béarn. With her absence, the courtiers of the court conferred about possible competition for the hand of the Princess of Navarre.

BOOK 2. THE SWORD AND FIRE

"You will never know if you have faith until your faith
is exercised."

Charles H. Spurgeon

1. Immortality Threatened

*"You are of your father the devil, and you want to do
the desires of your father. He was a murderer from
the beginning, and does not stand in the truth, because
there is no truth in him. Whenever he speaks a lie he
speaks from his own nature; for he is a liar and the
father of lies."*

John 8:44 (NASB)

When released from her ties to the Duke d'Cleves, Jeanne's only desire was to begin her life anew with dreams to hope for, truths to discover and to love others with the same love that God loved her. Nevertheless, she had not endured fiery tribulations to prepare for a peaceful life of contentment.

She did not realize her past experiences had developed in her such a tensile strength. Also, she was not aware that Satan's formidable opposition had focused its evil on this small, irritating warrior for truth. Just the fact that Jeanne had survived the ordeals of her childhood without malice or bitterness drew its hateful attention.

If Jeanne had conceived the massive forces aligning against her, she would have quailed and trembled, seeking somewhere to hide! Oblivious of the strength of this hostility, she sought only the truth of the words of her Holy God.

The beastly evil had settled over the inhabitants of Rome through many centuries before and feasted on the selected morsels of men's souls. Many seekers at that time turned to the churches for Holy guidance and truth and had tasted the choice bread of the gospel and drank from the everlasting fountain of living water. Many tragically then turned toward the lures of power and the intoxication of licentious enticements. At first, bending to small compromises and partaking of 'little sins,' they finally surrendered utterly to grow fat and comfortable on the ways of the world, enjoying the riches of Babylon which lay at their feet.

Innocent souls were not aware that the shadow covering them had begun to form or even when it grew increasingly darker. The web of a shared acceptance of society's norms wrapped them tighter and blinded their eyes to the trap that encircled them. The religious leaders of the time closed their ears to the warnings of righteous men. The absolute truths of God's Word became irritants, and the Church viewed these critics as undoubtedly too foolish or ignorant to perceive the vast benefits within their reach.

Strengthening itself with men's souls, fat with willing carnal gluttony, the evil shadow moved from Rome to feed on other substantial fertile areas of unsuspecting victims. Ravenous, the Mother Church continued to feast on the multitudes of misguided souls led by spiritual leaders to break the third commandment and become idol worshipers, until the darkening shadows grew to cover the populated world.

Satan, the "father of lies," controlled this evil influence, employing great deceits to camouflage the danger. By subtly falsifying and twisting the words of truth just enough to draw unsuspecting seekers into its trap of damnation of immortal souls, it grew massive.

The Reformation had torn and divided countries into religious factions. Europe was suffering an earthquake of dissension as the forces of the embedded Catholic religion battled mightily to keep hold of the governments and wealth under their control throughout the land.

The popes themselves were chiefly responsible for the disrepute which they and their clergy had fallen into throughout Europe. Implementation of the shameless traffic of indulgences disguised a kind-of tax which ostensibly was payment for penance of sins committed in this life. Priests acting as intercessors for penitents and their relatives claimed the right to forgive previous sins. Promises of eternal life in return defrauded the ordinary people of hard-earned income sacrificed on the altar for loved ones but instead were secretly applied toward defraying the licentious pleasures of the Vatican. The pontiffs descended from spiritual things to murder, dissolution, fraud, and deception, though they sought to shield their crimes under the mantle of imaginary infallibility.

The principles of right divinely implanted in every bosom rebelled against The Church's efforts to persuade them that the terrible power of binding and loosing sins, or the power of eternal salvation or damnation, could rest with the Pope as the absolute privilege of Christ's vicar upon earth. The deeds of blood and debauchery overflowing from the Vatican to curés and priests throughout Europe tainted any belief of parishioners in the façade of meek and Christian deportment which ought to characterize the father of Christendom. Shameless courtesans and ribald priests met in the antechambers of the papal palace. The marble halls of the Vatican were often stained with blood, shed in midnight brawls, or secret assassinations in which the supreme pontiff was more than suspected of having planned. Those illusions upon which the vast and mysterious edifice of Roman Catholicism subsisted, now exposed, imperiled its foundations with destruction.

For fifteen hundred years, leaders of the church had grown accustomed to luxurious living and unlimited dominance in the hearts of ordinary men and kings. Corruptions of power and deceit as the means to gratifying their sensual pleasures of authority and license became acceptable. The Church at the commencement of the sixteenth century had sunk to the very depths of infamy.[xxviii] Threatened at the height of their power by the ideas of reform against these abundant abuses was intolerable.

The fight to defeat reform was entered with evil, vicious determination to annihilate the opposition. Faith and truth no longer existed in the world; moral principle had fallen without a foundation of authentic religion. Frightful selfishness and skepticism ruled everywhere; and men, with no loftier restraint on their consciences than that imposed by the frivolous codes of knightly honor, lived in mutual distrust, hatred, and dissimulation. The basest nature born into every heart of humankind broke the bounds of decency and reveled in unlimited licentiousness as Europe descended into chaos under the banner of religious fervor.

Jeanne walked in the light and trusted in the salvation of her soul through her savior Jesus Christ. She had no idea that the glow of her spirit emanating through her faith was threatening the dark aspects of Satan's evil force engulfing society and revealing the gaps in its doctrine and theology. It could not bear opposition! The battle was on!

Malevolence gathered its forces to surround and conquer; plotting vicious traps to beckon to the natural appetites of the lust of the flesh, the lust of the eyes and the pride of life with age-old weapons of hatred, deceit, and revenge. Who can stand against it? Who can be a watchman on the wall?

Only one who has been anointed by the Holy One. Just the one who will station themselves to stand and see the salvation of the Lord on their behalf; the one who will put their trust in the Lord their God.

"Who will stand up for me against evildoers? Who will take his stand for me against those who do wickedness? They band themselves together against the life of the righteous and condemn the innocent." (Psalm 94:16, 21 (NASB).

As Jeanne embraced truth and submitted her life to the hands of her faithful Savior, she became a God-appointed symbol to the world, standing against the falsifying of His word of truth in the 16th century. Who would have guessed that such a small figure of a woman in an enormous world would stand among the leaders of that century's fight against evil? Certainly Jeanne did not.

"For our struggle is not against flesh and blood, but against the rulers, against the powers, against the world forces of this darkness, against the spiritual forces of wickedness in the heavenly places." (Ephesians 6:12 (NASB).

Jeanne certainly never thought herself a warrior; her goal was to be a faithful caretaker of a husband, children and the kingdom of her inheritance. It was God who was preparing her for battle.

2. Interruption

"For God has not given us a spirit of timidity, but of power and love and discipline."

2 Timothy 1:7 (NASB)

Jeanne was involved in her most favorite pastime. She sat in Queen Marguerite's apartment at Pau, listening to the music being played by the combined ladies-in-waiting of both women, in pleasant conversation with her mother and Francois de Rohan regarding the books they were reading. This time was a most peaceful interlude in the life of Jeanne de Navarre. The unpleasant episode of the entrance and exit of the Duke of Cleves in the lives of the d'Albret family was over and behind them. Hard feelings had been forgiven, and the family bond strengthened. Marguerite and her daughter had moved into a close friendship and relaxed devotion toward each other. They welcomed sweet Francoise as a part of their intimate circle. Their shared interests provided delightful intellectual discussion and pleasant entertainment.

On this new May morning in 1548, the sun was shining through the windows high in the castle wall, casting a golden glow across the chamber. Jeanne was basking in the serene, happy company of the Queen, comfortable in the security of her life at age twenty. To feel so free and loved was entirely new in her life. The ladies were quite intent on their current conversation regarding the Catholic Church's worship of the Virgin Mary; an issue that had occupied many hours of Queen Marguerite's study and discussions with the leaders of the reform movement. They had been searching together through the scriptures and Marguerite's many resources for any verification to pinpoint the validity of that doctrine

A knock sounded at the door. Phoebe answered the door and brought the message to Princess Jeanne. Prince Philip of Spain was in the library of the castle waiting to call on the Princess. The ladies had heard several months earlier that soon after Jeanne's false marriage to the Duke of Cleves; the Emperor had arranged a marriage for Prince Philip with the daughter of the King of Portugal. A year after the wedding, Philip's Portuguese consort had died giving birth to a prince.

Now, Prince Philip renewed his efforts to win the hand of Princess Jeanne. His desire to have Jeanne as his consort was driven, not only by her beauty but also by his father, Emperor Charles V, who was pushing to bring all of Navarre and Béarn under the crown of Spain.[xxix] Philip also acted on the many reports he heard of Jeanne's superior intellectual abilities.

The Princess entered the library to find Prince Philip standing at the windows, admiring the beautiful gardens of Pau. Queen Marguerite had dedicated much of her life planning and cultivating the exquisite, inviting paths through colorful beds of flowers and shrubs.

The Prince bowed low at the entrance of Princess Jeanne and gallantly kissed her hand, holding it warmly in his own a bit longer than needed. He held her gaze with his own dark eyes to emphasize his newly aroused appreciation of her beauty. He thought himself a gallant man to be coveted and desired; his attention should honor any woman. It had never entered his thought that the Princess could have no interest in his possible courtship. His offer of marriage would give Princess Jeanne the opportunity to reign with him in the most potent and significant court in all of Europe. To refuse his proposal would be mad.

Without a hint of discourtesy, she pulled her hand from his grasp, nodded respectfully in return and moved to be seated in a nearby wing-back chair. It was all she could do to keep from shuddering at his touch. His presence was repugnant to her as it brought to her mind every betrayal of Philip's father, Emperor Charles V, toward her mother and uncle.

Jeanne expressed her sympathy to the Prince for the loss of his consort. She was well aware of the Prince's motive of this call, having no interest to encourage his suit. With extraordinary skill, she steered the conversation away from intimacy and countered every effort he made to move into speaking of his intentions. Tea service was brought and served, and after a little time, the Prince, who would soon be the most powerful regent in Europe, found himself escorted to the front door of the castle of Pau.

As he rode away, he pondered how considerately the Princess had engaged in light conversation and deftly dismissed him from her presence. As he assessed the various desirable qualities of the woman he had just left, the Prince realized that she was perhaps, the most genuine and honest lady throughout all of Europe he ever met. There was no falseness anywhere in her person, and regrettably, he was convinced, whoever could win her heart would also gain her complete devotion. Her dismissal delivered politely and firmly; plain and straightforward; she desired no further pursuit from the Prince of Spain. He rode away chagrined at her refusal. He pondered with increasing admiration, the intellectual discernment and diplomatic talents of the Princess of Navarre. Disappointed, nursing his wounded ego, he made a note to never be found opposite her in a critical negotiation.

3. Courtship

Thou art my hiding place; Thou dost preserve me
from trouble; Thou dost surround me with songs of
deliverance. 'I will instruct you and teach you in the
way which you should go; I will counsel you with My
eye upon you.'"

Psalm 32:7-8 (NASB)

Word traveled quickly to Fontainebleau of Prince Philip's approach toward the Princess of Navarre. King Henry II immediately sent word to Pau commanding Princess Jeanne's presence at court. The suspicions of the deceased King Francis I had been passed on to King Henry II about King Henri of Navarre's willingness to agree with the Spanish emperor. As current King of France, Henry preferred Princess Jeanne to choose a suitor from the court of France.

Obeying the command of the King, Princess Jeanne d'Albret, and her household appeared at court. She disdained the fashionable adornments of feathers and shiny baubles currently in fashion after the habits of Queen Catherine de Medici; instead, she displayed her natural beauty, enhanced only by the purity of her serene countenance, her animated pleasant conversation and agreeable, regal demeanor.

For Princess Jeanne, truth was a living force and indwelling reality of the fiber of her being. Much as light radiating from her inner being, Jeanne walked in integrity, holiness, faithfulness, and simplicity. That bedrock of truth and honesty at her core could not abide the smoothly dishonest attentions of those she discerned as coarse and deceitful. Princess Jeanne never imagined her appearance would cause such a hum of discussion among the vain courtiers and ladies. She was the center of an ever-growing knot of suitors vying for her attention. She soon discouraged those of fawning, false character by frank and open conversation and sharp retorts. Many of her admirers soon dropped away, uncomfortable in her unwavering demand for honesty.

Two of the most renowned cavaliers of the court and the King's favorites were Antoine de Bourbon, Duke de Vendôme and Françoise de Lorraine, Duke de Guise.

The Duke de Vendôme was the son of Queen Marguerite's sister-in-law, sister of Marguerite's first husband, Charles of Alençon. Queen Marguerite and Françoise, the Duchess de Vendôme,[xxx] had maintained an intimate and lasting friendship during the years after the death of Charles. Not only was Antoine unusually handsome, of princely demeanor and highly popular at court for his captivating personality, but his attention to Jeanne appeared mixed with a casual display of indifference toward her return attentiveness.

His talents as a soldier achieved a considerable reputation. He was, by inheritance, a prince of the blood, of the House of Bourbon and next in line to the throne of France should anything happen to the sons or grandson of King Francis I, King Henry II, his dauphin, Francis II, or his younger brother, Charles, Duke d'Anjou. Antoine d'Vendôme had a noble presence and carried himself with grace. He was admired and copied at court for his tastes in fashion and most popular with the fair damsels who coveted to be his partner, as he was a most proficient dancer. The Duke d'Vendôme lived in the center of a merry crowd in search of gay pursuits; well thought of and much sought after by all the beautiful courtesans at the French court.

Henry II, while favoring both men, preferred François de Lorraine, Duke d'Aumale, Duke de Guise,[xxxi] the chief rival of Antoine, Duke de Vendôme, for Jeanne's hand. The character of the Duke de Guise was opposite of the Duke d'Vendôme. François had sterling qualities that were deficient in Antoine d'Vendôme. He was loved by the populace of Paris, freely distributing his enormous wealth; was preeminent in intellect, as well as acclaimed in military prowess, and an avid proponent and supporter of the arts. A staunch devoted Catholic, he was charming, of good humor and affable. Not only did he present himself as a notable rival for the hand of the Princess of Navarre, but King Henry also pressed the suit of the Duke d'Guise to Jeanne as his majesty's preferred choice.

Soon, the rivalry between the Duke de Vendôme and the Duke d'Guise became the focus of every activity of the court of Henry II. Each nuance of Princess Jeanne and her two suitors was watched, analyzed and discussed by every courtier and courtesan; their conjecture of the outcome was their major entertainment.

Under their jealous, watchful eyes, the Duke d'Vendôme would gallantly make his way toward Princess Jeanne, elaborately doffing his feathered hat, bowing low in silent admiration of her beauty. He would take her hand, kiss it lingeringly, and tuck it snugly under his arm. Subsequently, he would guide her in a slow promenade about the Grand Hall, passing conspicuously before the crowd; with their foreheads pressed together, he engaged Jeanne in quiet murmurings of conversation punctuated by occasional laughter, often stopping to gaze devotedly into her eyes. He would swing her into his arms and dance about the hall in graceful, accomplished steps. The onlookers would 'ooh' and 'ahh' as they swept about the room. Anyone who attempted to cut in on the couple would be left standing alone as they twirled away. Antoine de Vendôme would not relinquish his claim on the Princess to anyone. Jeanne was flustered at his approach, complimented by his admiration and enjoyed his pleasant company. Her heart would skip a beat when he claimed her arm, and she would feel a warm rush when he took her into his arms to dance.

François presented himself with formality and grandeur when appearing at her side. He wore his wealth and noble respectability with exquisite propriety, bestowing his attention on only those who he judged as worthy of such distinction. To everyone who observed, they were a perfect match of royal majesty. There was power in every look, word or move made by the Duke d'Guise and all who came in contact with the man knew instinctively that his forceful personality was able to control kingdoms and influence kings. He had an affable manner and would wander about the Great Hall with Jeanne's hand on his arm, discoursing about the latest works of Leonardo de Vinci or other patrons of the arts. He was highly intelligent and enjoyed matching wits with Jeanne on a multitude of subjects. He wooed her on a more cerebral level, bringing all his remarkable accomplishments modestly forward to lay at her feet as his gift to her. Jeanne enjoyed his company and noble bearing; however, there was no thrill at seeing him or disappointment when he left her company. She found herself subtly looking about for the presence of Antoine de Vendôme.

4. A Choice

"Let love be without hypocrisy. Abhor what is evil; cling to what is good."

Romans 12:9 (NASB)

The self-possessed dignity of the Duke d'Guise tended to offend the pride of Jeanne d'Albret, and she impetuously declared her dislike of the King's offer to select him as her consort. The King then shifted his approval to the Duke d'Vendôme and sent word to the King and Queen of Navarre of his endorsement of that match. [xxxii] Jeanne made clear to her parents her preference for Antoine d'Vendôme and her emerging warm affection for him.

Previous experience had offered little to prepare the Princess for affairs of the heart. Now free of the miserable attachment to the Duke d'Cleves and at age twenty, able to select her chosen husband without the interference of any who might try to decide for her, she followed her heart. Perhaps it was the vivacious personality and attention of the most desired catch, coupled with the fluctuations of his passions toward Jeanne that caused her to miss or ignore the underlying, capricious faults of Antoine's character. Perhaps, too, the subtle pressure of King Henry to make a choice soon caused her to bow to his coercion and decide before a lengthy acquaintance could allow greater insight into his fundamental values. It became increasingly apparent to all observers that Princess Jeanne had committed to a tender attachment toward Antoine.

Surprisingly, the King of Navarre had developed a suspicion of the frivolous pursuits, extravagant living and dissipated habits of the Duke d'Vendôme, which he believed would result in great unhappiness in the future of the Princess. Before the announcement of the affianced couple, the King of Navarre exacted a promise from his future son-in-law to give up the degenerate practices of his life before Henri would bestow on him the hand of his daughter.[xxxiii]

The marriage contract between Jeanne d'Albret and Antoine d'Bourbon, Duke de Vendôme, was signed October 20, 1548, at Moulins, in the presence of the King and Queen of Navarre, King Henry II and Queen Catherine de Medici of France, duchess d'Vendôme, and Cardinal de Bourbon, Antoine's brother.[xxxiv]

Jeanne floated on a cloud of emotional excitement as she and her ladies prepared for the wedding ceremony taking place the following day. She giggled and laughed like any bride-to-be while packing items for her wedding night. Her ladies could tell the Princess was obviously naïve and nervous about the coming "first night of her marriage" so they urged Queen Marguerite to talk with the Princess, while they withdrew to give the Queen and her daughter more privacy. After, when Queen Marguerite returned to her apartment, Jeanne sat alone with her thoughts. Butterflies had taken over her stomach, and her imagination increased with the warmth that suffused her entire body.

She could not help but remember her innocent fear when traveling to meet the Duke of Cleves at age fifteen. Overcome with the aversion she felt at his presence; she could not imagine how she could endure such an offense against her person. She was sure she would not have survived. Then her thoughts settled on the coming night with Antoine. She thought about how she longed for him to hold her in his arms. How much she wanted to know every intimate detail about his body and how she wanted him to know hers; to have his baby; to make one person out of the coming together of two. She crawled into her bed, holding thoughts of warm anticipation in her heart.

In his rooms, Antoine was frantically pacing his floor in wretched anxiety. The Duke was miserably assaulted with doubts as to the validity of the annulment of the former marriage of Jeanne to the Duke of Cleves.

"What if the documents presented to dissolve that marriage were false?" he shouted. "I cannot marry this woman if the consummation of the nuptials happened before the annulment."

He had no thoughts of his bride-to-be. Thinking only of himself, Antoine was in a sudden panic of cold feet. King Henry, who was visiting the intended groom, was shocked to learn Antoine refused to proceed with the marriage ceremony to be held the next day before the entire court at Moulins. In a frenzy of jealous fury and bitter lamentations, he announced his intention to depart Moulins and return to his castle at Châtellerault. He was consumed with vacillating alarm and indecision; ready to bolt at any second; he very nearly poured unmerited disgrace on Princess Jeanne.[xxxv]

It was only by the royal command of King Henry II that the Duke was persuaded to postpone his departure to meet with the King and Queen of Navarre, Aymée de Silly, and Queen Marguerite's leading lady-in-waiting, on the morning of the wedding. These highly esteemed witnesses solemnly reassured Antoine that consummation had never occurred. Finally, by the word of Queen Marguerite, whom Antoine highly held in deep respect he found satisfaction. The Princess had not spent any time with the Duke unless forced to appear in the presence of the Queen.

Not knowing the full story behind this unfortunate delay, Princess Jeanne sat waiting, beset by bitter memories of that regrettable disruption of her young dreams and aspirations. Was the tragedy of that calamity to hound her all the days of her life? How, having fought so desperately against that heart-wrenching wrong, could she be held in contempt and judgment forever? Was that 'sword of Damocles' going to hang over her head all the days of her life? Helpless to defend herself against the fears of her chosen husband, she sat in her bridal attire and awaited his decision.

As the time for the wedding came and passed, the multitude of courtiers gathered as witnesses began to whisper and rustle with a restless impatience. As more time passed, impatience moved into outright suspicion and conjecture. More delay in the ceremony stimulated the imaginations of the gathered guests to engage in fancies of suspenseful inventiveness while impatiently waiting to see what would happen next. Gossip about the bride's former annulled marriage and previous alliances of the groom that had dissolved years ago spread rapidly through the crowd. Only after the bridal procession and splendid royal pageantry appeared were the wild speculations abandoned. The wedding proceeded without further delay.

As Jeanne walked down the aisle toward Antoine, she searched his face for any hint of indecision. He watched her coming toward him with such a display of love and desire in his smile, her heart fluttered, and happiness flooded over her. She was satisfied that she could find no pretense in his face.

After a week of marriage festivities, balls, tournaments, and banquets, the newlyweds departed to their castle at La Fére, in Picardy where Antoine was governor of the province. After a brief sojourn there, they proceeded to Pau to appear before the citizens of Béarn, Jeanne's subjects upon her eventual succession as heiress to the throne of Navarre. The new duchess d'Vendôme wanted only to settle into a comfortable and long anticipated role of wife and mother.

Antoine witnessed the deep devotion and affection of the people of Béarn for Princess Jeanne; also, he observed their firm commitment to their beloved Queen Marguerite and her support for the religious reform led by the refugees she had embraced and sheltered. Many of the citizens of that small kingdom shared her faith. In his mind, Antoine could see a future benefit of displaying his support for measures of reform.

Soon, he was acknowledged and included by those devoted citizens, one with Princess Jeanne as approved successors to Henri and Marguerite of Navarre.[xxxvi] Emperor Charles V of Spain heard of Jeanne of Navarre's acknowledgment by the populace of Béarn and immediately proclaimed to annex the kingdom of Navarre to the Spanish crown formally. Then the Emperor declared his son, Prince Philip, as King of Navarre. This action was enabled by the Emperor's claim to Navarre as his right by the complete surrender of the Duke of Cleves while he was married to the Princess; ignoring, intentionally, the fact of the annulment of that marriage. Upon receipt of that news, Henri II, King of Navarre, vigorously prepared defenses and raised military arms in preparation to fight this claim on his kingdom.

Queen Marguerite had accompanied King Henri to the castle of Odos in Bigorre to assist her husband in arranging defenses against the Emperor.[xxxvii] The war prepared by Henri was on the point of breaking out when the King's attention and planning were suddenly interrupted at the illness and death of Queen Marguerite, December 21st, 1548.[xxxviii]

Marguerite and Henri had enjoyed a sustaining and devoted union, seldom seen in royal circles. Even the competing devotion of Marguerite to her brother, Francis, did not break the intimate dependence they had for each other. The loss of his beloved consort and joint ruler of nearly twenty-two years genuinely devastated King Henri; after his Queen's death, King Henri made only feeble efforts to resist the hostile attempts of the Emperor.

Marguerite's death was a great calamity for Jeanne. Her life's battle to be near her mother to soak up her wisdom and demeanor of grace had ended. King Henri and Jeanne mourned their loss together. No one beyond their common bond could understand the profound loss that had left an unfathomable emptiness in their hearts. The Princess regretted the lost opportunities for her coming children who now would not know the beautiful, gentle spirit of their renowned grandmother. Consumed with her deep sorrow, Princess Jeanne watched her father begin to fail, limiting his kingly efforts to the nearby areas of Béarn.

The gentle guidance and firm hand of the gracious Marguerite was, unfortunately, the singular influence that held the capricious Antoine in check. He had admired and respected the Queen of Navarre all the years of his upbringing during her friendship with his mother. It was because of this admiration for the Queen that he desired to please her. The Duke de Vendôme was attached to his young wife and was proud of how highly esteemed others held her, but now without the restraining hand of Marguerite, he began to slide into his former dissipated lifestyle of royal feasting and raucous companions.

While Antoine seldom was committed to more than the enjoyment of the moment, Jeanne was wholly devoted to maintaining her vows of marriage as with every other obligation, in the earnestness of purpose and diligence. The Duchess was noble-minded, unselfish and determined to act from principle, regardless of what level of self-denial she might endure.

The Duke's lifestyle embraced luxury, gaiety, passion, and compromise of conscience. In spite of his vacillating moral values, Duchess Jeanne tenderly loved her husband. Her response to his disappointing behavior was to adopt for herself an increasingly dignified reserve. A shadow covered the beautiful eyes, and fresh innocence of the young Princess of Navarre which betrayed her failed efforts to curb the thoughtless and unmanageable activities of her husband. A crease between Jeanne's eyebrows, accompanied by a trace of caution in her eyes became a permanent feature as if Jeanne felt that she could prevent any impending humiliation or embarrassment on the strength of her own prim, dignified appearance. So in love with her husband, she struggled with the realization his commitments were compromised so easily for his pleasure of the moment.

Jeanne sought to share with Antoine every honor and adoration of her position of future sovereign, hoping to increase his sense of importance at her side. She strove to encourage and support him with all the love in her heart for him, hoping his heart would answer. It soon became apparent that his decisions depended on whatever motives attracted him that would satisfy his gratification.

Although Antoine enjoyed his time spent in riotous living, he was also pleased to romance his wife at every opportunity. Both experienced intimacy with a closeness that was very satisfactory for the duchess. However, after having been a wife for two years, she worried that she had not yet been able to bring the hope of an heir to the houses of Vendôme and Albret. Her father, King Henri, adamantly expressed his disappointment, declaring to Jeanne the similar sentiment of the citizens of Béarn on the subject. Her father's impatient questions as to what could be the cause weighed heavily on the young Duchess, creating an extensive sense of failure.

Finally, two months of apprehension mixed with anticipation had passed without the appearance of her monthly blood-flow, and Jeanne welcomed other signs of bodily changes in the hope that, at last, she would be a mother. One morning, instead of jumping from her bed to begin the tasks of the day, she sat on the side of the bed trying to control her touchy stomach. When Jeanne sank back down beside Antoine hoping the queasy feeling would pass, he opened his eyes and looked at her with questions in his eyes. A little smile played around her lips, and she said, "Good morning my love! Would you like to be a father?" His eyes widened, and he gently gathered her into his arms and snuggled his face into her neck, kissing her gently.

With unbounded joy, the news circulated that the Duchess of Vendôme would be retiring to the castle of Coucy to await the birth of her first child. Soon after the announcement of her pregnancy, the bold whispers disappeared that her barrenness was a judgment from God for her release from her covenant to the Duke d'Cleves. Again, the specter of that unfortunate episode in her life had raised its ugly head.

5. Joy and Misguided Trust

"These things I have spoken to you, that in Me you may have peace. In the world you have tribulation, but take courage; I have overcome the world."

John 16:33 (NASB)

On the 20th day of September 1550, Duchess Jeanne held her infant prince in her arms. He was named Henry, Duke de Beaumont.[xxxix] Her first childbirth was long and difficult, and she was slowly recovering her health and energy.

Each day passed with increasing awareness of the claims of her husband for her constant companionship, her royal obligations, and anxieties for her household responsibilities. Jeanne admitted the ordeal of birth had drained her of her usual vigor and independence. Hearing the cries of her tiny son, she agonized that she was physically unable to respond to the calls of motherhood. Remembering her mother, with demands of being a Queen, and pressed by the requests to be a devoted counselor to the King of France, Jeanne began to understand the difficult decisions made when placing her care in Aymée's capable oversight. Jeanne now found herself faced with a similarly difficult decision. Desiring the same loving care and environment for her son, Jeanne sent word to Aymée asking that her precious friend and nursemaid would become responsible for the new prince's care.

Since the time Jeanne had returned to Plessis as the mistress of her castle, Aymée had retired to her own home. She had accepted an offer of marriage and was now abiding at her husband's castle at Orleans. She was not young when Jeanne had first been given to her care, however, twenty years later, she was an infirm, elderly woman. During the intervening years, old age had finally taken a toll on the health of Aymée, depleting her energy and stiffening her joints. Unfortunately, her circulation had become so impeded that she was very sensitive to every cold draft through the castle at Orleans.

Consequently, Aymée kept her apartments at an extremely high temperature at all hours. It was into this uncirculated inferno that she brought her helpless charge, keeping him tightly wrapped and continually bound in blankets. Unwittingly, Duchess Jeanne surrendered her precious heir to the woman who so lovingly brought security into the Princess's young life, not aware that her old nurse now refused to allow the prince any access to fresh air or outdoor activities. Confined to the heated environment of an infirm old nurse, the prince gradually wasted away, weakening daily.

As Jeanne's slow recovery began to show positive gains, the duchess became aware of rumors that circulated while she had been confined to her apartments, fighting to rejoin the world. Antoine had taken advantage of the freedom from her oversight by returning to the entertainment, companions, and debauchery of his former life before their marriage. The months of closeness they had shared while waiting for the arrival of little Henry had been heavenly. Then the excitement Antoine had demonstrated on being a father had only lasted a month or so. Growing bored with the attention being focused on the baby, in addition to Jeanne's inability to accompany him to find other amusement, the Duke d'Vendôme sought former avenues of entertainment. Jeanne had sensed his discontent, grieving his decreasing appearances to be with her or the baby.

When the Duke de Vendôme received orders to join the royal forces in Picardy to defend the borders against invasion, Jeanne shouldered matters at home in his absence. As she grew stronger, she missed her husband's presence, rarely hearing from Antoine when he was in military camp. Though she faithfully sent letters to Antoine, he never responded with messages of his own, waiting until granted leave to rejoin her in person.

Jeanne began correspondence with friends who may have heard a word of the battle or her husband's activities. Always upright in her behavior and relationships, Jeanne found it humiliating to seek others to be informed about news of her husband. She descended into a familiar sense of rejection, fighting against old perceived wounds of unworthiness that her husband could find other women preferable to her love. The obsession that his casual loyalty to their marriage was a reflection on everything about her became the focus of her thoughts.

Word alerting her to her son's condition finally reached Jeanne at her castle at Gaillon in Normandy, where, already in her second pregnancy she had retired to be close to the location of the royal troops and Antoine. Jeanne immediately rushed to Aymée's castle in Orleans to see for herself. She was so shocked by her son's appearance that after sharply reprimanding Aymée, Jeanne took her son with her. The little prince was too weakened to survive. He died just short of two years old.[xl]

6. An Heir to Present

"Be of sober spirit, be on the alert. Your adversary, the devil, prowls about like a roaring lion, seeking someone to devour."

1 Peter 5:8 (NASB)

Jeanne's second child, another son to become the heir of Navarre, was born in August 1552; the baby received the title, Count de Marle.[xli] Overwhelmed with grief over the death of her first little prince, Jeanne was devastated with the guilt of her neglect and ignorance of the state of his care. Her emotional frailty, compounded by insecurity about Antoine's activities and the rigors of a second birth, resulted in a deep depression that plagued her days. Her thoughts filled with misgivings that God was punishing her for the annulment of her marriage to the Duke d'Cleves.

That unusual character trait displayed throughout her life to face the truth of her circumstances honestly prompted her to take responsibility for her failure of oversight. Strengthened by her determination, she ignored her weakened state and insisted on superintending her infant's care herself. Each day, she demanded her attendants care for the infant in her presence, watching over every aspect of his feeding, bathing, and dressing. Jeanne soon had a healthy, robust baby to proudly present to her father and her future subjects at Béarn.

Soon after subduing the hostilities that called the Duke de Vendôme to join the royal forces in Picardy, the Duke, his consort, and their new prince journeyed toward Pau for the Christmas festivals. King Henri, so impatient to hold his heir to the kingdom of Navarre, met them at Mont de Marsan. With great pride he cradled the infant and chose every opportunity to present him to the citizens of Béarn, being such a proud and happy grandfather.

So pleased that his grandson was a healthy heir to his kingdom, King Henri arranged a hunting party in the lands around Mont de Marsan in celebration. The King insisted the Duke and Duchess of Vendôme join the company of hunters.

It was a beautiful day outdoors to enjoy such an outing, and Jeanne looked forward to the fellowship of her husband and father. Jeanne delayed the hunting party because she wanted to ensure that the four-month-old baby was well fed and contentedly asleep before leaving him with the nurse that had been engaged by her father to watch the prince during her absence. He was so warm and cuddly in her arms that she lingered over him, kissing and rocking the infant prince before leaving.

The beautiful fall weather could not be enjoyed thoroughly in the dark castle rooms, so the nurse took her charge to sit in an open window of the castle to breathe the fresh air. Before long, a young gentleman of King Henri's chamber happened to be walking by. He was interested in initiating a romantic attachment with the young nursemaid and was delighted to see her at the window. The prince was sleeping placidly in the arms of his nurse, and the gentleman asked to view him more closely; then he asked to hold him. The nurse consented and handed him out the window to the young man.

Before long, the two young people, passing the baby back and forth, were eventually teasing each other by pretending to hand the child over, but instead, snatching him back. It was a careless pastime of two individuals unconscious of its possible hazards.

Suddenly, the young maid mistakenly thought the baby was in the grasp of the young man when he was not. The sleeping child fell from her hands to the marble steps below the window that led to a basement entrance. The baby's rib had broken in the fall. The two young people desperately sought to stifle the infant's agonized cries, and he eventually fell into an exhausted sleep. The pair agreed to conceal the accident when the hunting party returned.

In the days following, the constant crying of the child was not explainable. Jeanne was frantic at the endless wailing of her child and sought all help available to determine why he screamed with terror whenever he was touched. Nearly out of her mind with fear, she continuously tried to tenderly comfort and relieve his suffering screams, but with no success. His death after four days revealed the cause of his shrieks. Although the guilty parties received justice, Jeanne was inconsolable.[xlii]

The grief of Henri, King of Navarre, was excessive and unreasonable; blaming Jeanne for his loss. Henri insisted his daughter was responsible due to the neglect of her maternal duties, calling her 'inhuman.' He threatened to obliterate her from her inheritance by marrying a second time and fathering a male heir himself.

Beside the deep hurts he inflicted on his daughter, this threat had teeth, Jeanne discovered. King Henri had taken a mistress who had been his comfort since the death of Marguerite. In time she had given birth to an illegitimate son and recently had been pressing the King to acknowledge him as the heir to the throne of Navarre. In Jeanne's great grief and weakness, this declaration consequently caused her to solemnly promise that if she ever had another child, she would place its care under her father's management.

Upset and disappointed at Henri's bitter, unjust and unmerited blame toward her, the Duke and Duchess departed Mont de Marsan, refusing to accompany the King of Navarre to Pau. They turned instead to the beautiful estate of La Fleche in Anjou that had been the sumptuous palace of Antoine's mother, Françoise de Alençon. The grief at the loss of their second precious son joined Jeanne and Antoine in a common bond of grief and mourning.

When word arrived that the military battles against invasion at Picardy had increased, Antoine again left to join and strengthened the troops on the border defenses before the efforts there deteriorated. Jeanne spent her days remembering the lives of each of her babies, assessing her faults in their care and honestly facing the causes of their deaths and her part in them.

She spent hours seeking forgiveness from God and searching for a way to forgive herself and those other individuals who had played a part in her babies' deaths. Jeanne's process of forgiving was arduous and agonizing. Her abundant tears flowed with no lament to God stifled. It was a desolate and cleansing process only achieved in her complete seclusion. The solitude of the lush gardens of La Fleche offered peace and renewal for Jeanne in the absence of the Duke.

For Antoine, the distraction of the battle and his pursuits in the army camp alleviated his griefs, and he was only too happy to find other occupation. On occasion, he would leave the military field to return for brief interludes with his consort at La Fleche. Jeanne's tender affection for Antoine and her peaceful abode at La Fleche healed the profound physical and emotional hurts of the Duchess de Vendôme. Missing her husband's presence and after accomplishing her soul searching, Jeanne renewed her correspondence to ascertain his pursuits and pastimes at camp.

In the spring of 1553, Jeanne found herself again expecting a child. After sending a courier to notify her father of the news, Jeanne determined that summer to join her husband at the camp of Picardy. Devoted to him, Jeanne was his constant companion. Her brilliant mind assisted the Duke with astute observations of plans and ramifications for necessary military decisions. Her support and encouragements to the troops in Picardy lifted their spirits. Jeanne enjoyed being near Antoine. She was a woman in love and saw only the good in him. Being nearby, involved in all his activities was for her, a demonstration of her love and devotion. Antoine's response was disappointing; Jeanne brushed it off, attributing his abruptness to his many responsibilities. After a time, Jeanne was forced to acknowledge that her husband's deficiencies of leadership stemmed from his vacillating judgment.

One day after extensive surveillance of the troops that required tramping through mountainous terrain, Antoine's company, accompanied by the Duchess, returned to their camp in late afternoon. The entire group had been joking and laughing together. As they entered their tent, the Duke playfully picked up a long-barreled musket and pointed it at Jeanne, believing it unloaded. He struck a flame and pulled the trigger. The troops who accompanied them were shocked when, with an explosion, the musket discharged. Horrified, they believed the duchess fatally shot. Jeanne believed it herself until it became evident that she had no wound. The bullet had fallen to the floor as Antoine raised the musket and pulled the trigger. She stood before everyone agitated and quite pregnant, but unharmed. Only strong nerves had saved her to endure such a fright which could have initiated a miscarriage of the child in any normal expectant mother.[xliii]

Jeanne returned to her private tent to recover her composure. She was aghast at the near disaster her husband had indulged in for his random pleasure. The fear of the possibilities of that careless action brought into vivid focus the realization this upsetting episode was only too characteristic of the thoughtlessness of her husband, confirming Jeanne's disappointing assessment of Antoine's deficiency in judgment.

After some days, Jeanne chose to remove herself from the discomforts of camp life and took up residence nearby in the royal palace of Compiègne until the birth of her baby. Occupied with thoughts of her husband's weakness of character and philandering, she was interrupted by the arrival of some guests requesting an audience with her. Rising to greet a delegation of officials of Béarn, she received reassurance all was well with her father. The group encouraged her to travel immediately to Pau to place herself under the care of the King of Navarre, for the safety of the coming birth of the heir of Navarre.[xliv] Jeanne faced a dilemma since she had reached the ninth month of her pregnancy; however, persuasion by the intense interest of the distinguished officials representing her Béarnois citizens toward their future monarch changed her mind. She had desired to be near Antoine for the birth of their child, but as the future Queen of Navarre, she again realized her subjects must take precedence over her desires. Sending word to Antoine, Jeanne left immediately. Although she had attended to every detail for her comfort, the journey was painful and lengthy, lasting nearly eighteen days in a bouncing litter, drawn by mules.

Arriving at Pau safely, she was grateful the Lord had allowed her to reach Pau before going into labor. She was warmly welcomed by her father, who immediately installed her in Marguerite's luxurious apartments in the castle of Pau. In the early morning hours of December 13th, 1553, Jeanne gave birth to her third son. [xlv] Henri waited nearby to receive the infant in his arms to present him to the gathered officials of the Béarnois citizens. Named Henry III de Navarre, a strong peasant woman took the future King of Navarre to raise with her children.

Jeanne's anxiety over the health and safety of her young son increased when shortly after placing the prince with a nurse, the principality experienced an epidemic of an illness signified by a low fever. The nurse became ill, and the child moved to another for his care. A second nurse also fell sick of the same disease. Six more successive nurses were assigned and subsequently also became ill. The prince finally was placed in the care of the wife of a poor laborer who resided in a cottage on the banks of the river Gave. The cottage bordered on the park surrounding the castle of Pau, a location that enabled the Duchess to frequently and privately visit her son.

In February of the following year, Jeanne had healed and regained her strength enough to reside near Baran and again follow her husband. Word reached her there in May 1555, that her father, who was setting up troops for an invasion of Spanish Navarre, had died, stricken ill with the epidemic that continued to plague areas of his kingdom.[xlvi] She was genuinely devastated at the loss of her father, whom she had renewed a close relationship with since the birth of Henry III. Jeanne's only consolation at this traumatic loss was her knowledge that at least the King had held and enjoyed his grandson and heir.

Although her attendants now called her Queen of Navarre, she was deeply grieved over the loss of her father and was uncomfortable acknowledging the mantle of royalty that fell on her shoulders. She longed for her father's comforting authority and her mother's wise counsel. The welfare of her subjects now lay squarely on her.

Queen Jeanne dispatched a courier to Antoine requesting his urgent appearance at Baran and commanded that his troops address him appropriately as King of Navarre. The title of king flattered the vanity of Antoine, and he could only think of the power and prestige he would now obtain as ruler. He immediately left the field of battle and joined his Queen at the château of Baran.

7. King and Queen

"The thief comes only to steal, and kill, and destroy;
I came that they might have life and might have it
abundantly."

John 10:10 (NASB)

After Antoine's hasty trip to join Jeanne at Baran, they rode by horseback to present themselves to the nobles of Béarn. On occasion, the new King of Navarre would throw his head back and laugh heartily, rejoicing in his new position. He loved the idea of being king.

Jeanne would look over at his exultation, offended that he could so openly revel in his new position while she was deeply mourning the death of her father and the weight of responsibility she now carried. She had hoped he would fortify her and share in her loss. She longed for his strengthening companionship; it was disappointing to realize he was living in his little world of selfish ambitions and could only appreciate his new empowerment.

At Jeanne and Antoine's arrival in Pau, they received warm greetings from the barons and nobles of Béarn who deeply grieved for their lost King. Their expression of being grateful to Jeanne for coming quickly, as well as their apparent loyalty and allegiance for their new Queen, was heartwarming. Jeanne was comforted by their shared sympathy and grief for Henri of Navarre. Antoine stood awkwardly by, not acknowledged as a fellow mourner.

Before the end of the meeting, Queen Jeanne made clear her desire that she and Antoine be recognized as co-sovereigns of every aspect of their reign. She had sensed Antoine's offense at being reduced to a position of only being her consort. Perhaps, she thought, he would live up to his title of King and assume the acquired responsibilities of governing a kingdom wisely.

Sitting in the office in the castle, everything she touched reminded her of her father. Perusing the documents and papers on his desk that must be read and attended to, she began to realize the difficulties facing her as the new ruler of such a disputed and coveted kingdom. The letters she had to go through unfolded considerable disparagement between the strong Huguenots that had gathered under her mother's gracious policies of providing refuge and the subjects in the southern provinces that adhered to the traditional Catholic faith of France. Keeping her kingdom united as one would be difficult and would require delicate diplomacy to avoid civil war.

The Queen of Navarre was impressed to discover that her parents had managed the resources of her kingdom wisely to establish its financial position firmly. Well aware of the desire of both the King of Spain and the King of France to expand their own country's ownership over her lucrative, prosperous kingdom, the Queen knew she must keep its independence secure. Remembering her desire to include Antoine in the responsibilities of their royalty, she rang to inquire where her consort might be and to request that he join her to be briefed on the matters she had just discovered.

When her attendant returned, he told her the King was at present touring the vaults of the castle to inventory the vast treasures stored there. Jeanne's stomach sank as she realized the cherished keepsakes of her heritage now were threatened by Antoine's grasping desire for wealth and luxury. The Queen buried her head in her hands in disappointment and sorrow, recognizing her King had no interest in the affairs of governing, only his insatiable desires for his pleasure. She then rose and proceeded to join him in the vaults.

Jeanne found Antoine in the jewel-chamber, busily making a record of the precious treasures stored there: cups of agate and crystal studded with gems, sacred jeweled vessels, jeweled salt cellars, ewers of silver gilt, vases of rock crystal, and mirrors set in frames adorned with diamonds; splendid rings, and charms. A more unusual article on the list was the celebrated tortoise-shell upon which carried Prince Henry at his baptism. There was a great variety of decorative pieces of gold plate for the adornment of the banqueting board. And an exquisite statue of a young maiden of gold represented riding upon a horse of mother-of-pearl, standing upon a platform of gold, enriched with ten rubies, six turquoises, and three beautiful pearls. Another item of rock crystal, set in gold, enriched with three rubies, three emeralds, four pearls, and by a large sapphire, set transparently, the whole suspended from a small gold chain.

The King and Queen of Navarre had already appreciated the works in the Art Gallery of the castle of Pau of fifty large portraits of eminent personages; sixty small portraits; twelve medallion portraits, and fifteen landscapes; also, twenty-five wax medallion pictures of kings and princes, arranged together in a glass case.[xlvii]

With difficulty, Jeanne tried to impress on Antoine the history and personal value of each of the pieces on his list, emphasizing that nothing treasured in the vaults could be removed without the decision of Jeanne alone. Disturbed by the greedy glint in her consort's eye, Jeanne returned to her office and wrote a memorandum establishing her son as sole heir to the contents of the vault upon her death.

At court in France, King Henry II now regretted his support of the marriage of the Princess of Navarre to the Duke de Vendôme. He realized the reality of the fertile lands and commonwealth and power of the King and Queen of Navarre. There were many enemies of Antoine de Vendôme at the court of France where the Duke of Guise had been busy insinuating to the King of France and his council that the monarchs of Navarre were too weak to reign. D'Guise implied the King of France should seize the excessive wealth of the heritages of Navarre and Vendôme. The King and his council plotted to maneuver Queen Jeanne into a position of relinquishing her control over her kingdom.

Now that the Duke de Vendôme was officially King, a move was made to take advantage of his moral weaknesses and exploit his royal authority over the Queen. The King of France, especially, knew of Antoine's egotistical, excessive love of pleasures. He determined to persuade Antoine to make concessions that would weaken the Queen of Navarre's claims on her kingdom. Sure that an offer to increase Antoine's holdings could persuade his vanity to agree to trade his consort's heritage for his gain. The King of France believed that Antoine could be motivated to relinquish the wealthy kingdoms of Spanish Navarre and Béarn by ceding to France in exchange for lands closer to the duchy of Vendôme. Not long after Antoine and Jeanne arrived in Pau, a summons from the King of France came ordering the King of Navarre to appear at court at St. Germain immediately, alone.

Antoine was flushed with the sudden prestige and honor now due him as King of Navarre. He was delighted to receive the summons of the King of France. His imaginations of the honors now due him when presented to the King of France were the only focus of his thoughts.

Jeanne was uneasy about Antoine's visit to St. Germain because she was genuinely unsure of the stability of his character and convinced of his ignorance of political maneuverings. It was evident to her that the King had summoned him to stroke his vanity of now being King of Navarre while separating him from Jeanne's advice.

In vain, she tried to warn the new King of the dangers he would be encountering; he ignored her petitions and left as quickly as possible. Jeanne's gifted intellect and years of playing chess facilitated her uncanny ability to anticipate political moves with strategic efforts of her own. Jeanne was now also very much aware of the undependable nature of her husband who could risk the future of the kingdom of Navarre.

When Antoine arrived at St. Germain in obedience to the royal command, the King of France offered his proposal along with ostentatious royal favor and distinctions to flatter the new King of Navarre of his recent ascent to royal rank. King Henry II also relayed his disapproval of the level of heresy so rampant in the kingdom of Béarn, enlisting Antoine's cooperation to place the rebellious domain under the control of France. King Henry II had confidence in his knowledge of Vendôme's tendency to affect loyalty to whatever faith would benefit him the most at the time. King Henry II was suspicious that Antoine was, at heart, in favor of the Catholic Church and preferred for all of France to return to that particular faith. King Henry II turned out to be right.

Antoine listened attentively to all the presentations and promises of the King of France, contemplating the favorable considerations toward his gain. Proud of being the King of Navarre, to his credit, Antoine's regard for his courageous and politically astute consort caused him to request an interval of reflection before answering. After the short time allotted for consideration, he acknowledged he had no power to dispose of the crown of Navarre without consulting the Queen.

The King was displeased at this response, yet the necessity to obtain the permission of the Queen must be done. The King grudgingly granted authorization for Antoine to confer with Jeanne, insisting he promise that Jeanne would immediately return with him to continue the conversation of the cessation of their principality. The King also ordered that should he or the Queen attempt to return to Béarn before returning to the court, they would be forcibly retained.

Queen Jeanne traveled to Coucy and sent word to Antoine of her presence there. While waiting at Coucy, the Queen paced the floor, imagining all possible scenarios that might be occurring at St. Germain. She pondered the appropriate defensive moves she might put in motion to revoke any agreements Antoine might make with the King of France.

Hearing all that Antoine reported to her, especially the plans of Henry II to despoil her of the territories of her father, Jeanne was incredulous. Queen Jeanne was appalled to learn they were threatened with military force to keep them as prisoners of France. Jeanne, filled with contempt and indignant determination, believed that this effort could be turned to the confusion of her enemies.

Queen Jeanne isolated herself to ponder the plot initiated against her splendid heritage. The disappointing convictions she now had of her sovereign consort's inability to understand complicated political maneuvers cemented her determination to shoulder the responsibilities of governing her kingdom alone.

Without revealing her thoughts or actions to anyone, Jeanne contacted a loyal baron, Bernard d'Arros, one of the twelve barons of Béarn. Meeting confidentially with him, she revealed the scheme of Henry II's council and her plans to defeat the plot. D'Arros enthusiastically agreed with his Queen's planned countermove. The baron was still in command of the levies King Henri had been collecting to raise troops, at the time of his death. Jeanne renewed the warrant enabling d'Arros to continue as military commander-in-chief of the principality and ordered him to deny any request for access to the levies, except by her order.

King Henry II had appointed, under his pay, bishop of Mende to be his chancellor of Navarre and ordered this bishop to foster agreement among the leaders of Queen Jeanne's principalities to accept the transfer to the rule of France. The bishop, who happened to be the illegitimate son of Cardinal Duprat, was just as corrupt and ignoble as his father. The promise of wealthy payment was sufficient to turn his loyalties from Navarre to France. Jeanne had long been suspicious of the bishop's intrigues and now advised d'Arros to observe him. As expected, the bishop approached d'Arros because he held the power of the levies, to recruit his support for approval of the proposed transfer. D'Arros pretended to agree to the bishop's plot until he was able to get a list of all the other conspirators who the bishop had enlisted.

Jeanne, Queen of Navarre, proceeded to present herself beside the King of Navarre to the King of France at St. Germain. With determined serenity and submission, Jeanne carefully answered Henry II's request.

"Your Majesty, may I remind you of the structure of the government of Béarn. If each of the states of the principality is in favor of the exchange, I, as Queen, would have no opposition to your proposal. However, because of the loyalty of the states to their sovereign, I would need to meet personally with each to absolve them of their oath of allegiance."

This declaration put the King of France in an awkward position. He was aware of the truth of her statements and realized that once he granted permission for her to go to Pau, he could no longer forcibly keep the Queen and King as prisoners to compel them to yield to his proposal. Grudgingly, he granted the royal couple leave to go to Pau. Convinced the proposal would be acceptable because of the advance work already accomplished by the bishop of Mende, King Henry II demanded that the five commissioners he had empowered to receive the oaths of allegiance to the crown of France in the transfer of the states of the principality accompany them.

Jeanne and Antoine left for Pau immediately. While in route, Jeanne sent word to have Prince Henry brought by his nurse in Moissens to Pau, as well as a message to d'Arros of their impending arrival in Pau. The Baron called together the leaders of the states of Navarre to complete his Queen's plan and informed them of the plot of the Crown of France to steal the kingdom of Navarre from its rightful sovereign and revealed the part of the Bishop of Mende's role. Upon learning of the part of the bishop of Mende in the plot, the people burned his house and chased him to the borders of the kingdom.

Arriving at Pau and safely inside the dominions of her kingdom, Jeanne sent word to Henry II that the states of her principality had found the aspect of transfer of allegiance to the crown of France so repugnant that she was unable to rally their support. The commissioners of King Henry II were so dismayed at the upheaval around them; they requested an escort to the border to ensure their safety.

Jeanne was satisfied that she had averted the futile grab by King Henry II of France to bring the kingdom of Navarre under the rule of his crown. Antoine begrudgingly admitted that his consort and Queen had outmaneuvered King Henry's attempts to undermine their sovereign rule. Silently, he harbored resentments against her for so brilliantly deciphering the real motives behind his summons to court. Antoine could now see how foolishly he had walked into the King's trap. The new King of Navarre admitted that she had realized what he had not seen. In Antoine's embarrassment, seeds of bitterness sprouted in his heart and resentment began to grow.

Jeanne turned her attention to planning their coronation. Jeanne loved her kingdom heritage and its people. The citizens of Béarn enthusiastically applauded their Queen with devoted allegiance that she had stood her ground against the powerful moves of the King of France to annex their kingdom. Jeanne was satisfied that resolution of the matter was accomplished and held no animosity against Antoine for his part. It was her sincere desire to share her sovereignty with her consort, and she planned the coronation for them both to pledge their allegiance as joint sovereigns.

Jeanne and Antoine took the oath of allegiance to maintain the ancient laws, charters and the privileges of their subjects; to maintain their territory intact, and to administer impartial justice to all. Afterward, Princess Jeanne and Duke de Vendôme were formally proclaimed joint sovereigns as King and Queen of the kingdoms of Navarre and Béarn.

At the time of her coronation as Queen of Navarre in August 1555, the little Princess of Navarre had been married, gained an annulment, married again; mourned the death of her uncle, her mother, her father and two children; had birthed the heir to the throne of Navarre; and quelled a treasonous attempt to remove her as Queen of Navarre. She was 27 years old.

8. Broken Faith

*"How have you fallen from heaven, O star of the
morning, son of the dawn! You have been cut down to
the earth, you who have weakened the nations! But
you said in your heart, 'I will ascend to heaven; I will
raise my throne above the stars of God, and I will sit
on the mount of assembly in the recesses of the north. I
will ascend above the heights of the clouds; I will make
myself like the Most High.'"*

Isaiah 14:12-14 (NASB)

Queen Jeanne became increasingly aware of the difficult decisions facing her regarding the division of religious adherents of
her kingdom. The Queen continued to attend the Catholic Church
of her upbringing. Her husband basked in the adoration of the
many believers of the reform movement when they realized he was
sympathetic to their cause. Responding to that acclaim, Antoine
flaunted his approval of the most fanatic leaders and brought them
under his protection and patronage, blindly pursuing the policy that
had gained such applause when he first came to Pau.

Occupied by her attention on the care of her child and orderly
upkeep of the royal castle, Queen Jeanne received correspondence
from the powerful Cardinal d'Armagnac, archbishop of Toulouse,
relating the Pope's disapproval of the rampant heresy reported from
Béarn. Jeanne was faced with the impact of her husband's displays

to gain approval of his subjects. As a child, she was only too aware that a papal interdiction had removed the province of Upper Navarre from the control of Marguerite and Henri II, then sovereigns of Navarre, for the heresy perceived of Queen Marguerite by her protection of the refugees of the reform movement. It was the unscrupulous actions of the Cardinal d'Armagnac that had initiated the papal intercession against Henri and Marguerite d'Albret, in spite of the protection they received from the King of France. Jeanne, always sensitive to the discernment of political attitudes within France and her domains, became aware of the intense disapproval of the Pope and her own noble Roman Catholic subjects at the unpredictable behavior of Antoine regarding his demonstrations of faith.

Jeanne was alarmed at the position in which her consort had placed her kingdom. She viewed the intense disapproval of the papacy as extremely dangerous in its effort to re-establish the power of the Romish religion. The papal dominance was threatened, and like any wounded animal cornered and facing extinction, those powerful principals would take decisive action to maintain their supremacy. The recent desires of King Henry II to avail himself of her kingdom along with a possible relationship to the Cardinal d'Armagnac's censure of Antoine prompted Jeanne to order intervening bills to subvert the threats insinuated against her consort. Her first edict demanded that within Bearn all ecclesiastics must rely on permissions of their parish priest. Her second edict ordered all who desired to preach in public must obtain a license from the bishop of Lescar.

Antoine stormed into Queen Jeanne's office in the castle of Pau with a vivid display of his anger; he thundered that she had effectually cut off his abilities to declare special permissions for the sermons and public worship set up by Protestant ministers that advertised and emphasized his affiliations with the reformers.

The Queen looked at her consort with surprise as he bellowed his enraged remonstrance, "What have you done? How can you perceive to issue edicts without consulting me? You have acted independently without my approval!"

The Queen quietly stood up and declared, "You may choose to put your heritage at risk by outrageous displays of heresy, but I do not and will not allow you to fritter away what has belonged to my family for generations!"

Angered that her edicts would reflect poorly on him when his favorite reform adherents realized the loss of his protection, he soon was compelled to acknowledge the wisdom of her decisions to take swift actions. He received a letter from King Henry, on receipt of notice from the Holy Father insisting that measures be taken to discipline Antoine's reckless behavior of flaunting his favor toward the reform believers in Bearn. King Henry II and his council threatened to send armed troops under the direction of the Duke d'Guise to quell any heresy and to take possession of the principality of Béarn and its surrounding countries if the heresy within its borders did not diminish.[xlviii] Antoine was embarrassed that his consort had recognized the risk before he had. The King of Navarre rudely betrayed his irritation by his attitude toward his Queen.

On receipt of the ominous threat and reports of other royal troops moving toward their borders, the Queen ordered additional edicts prohibiting all public assemblies for public worship. When Jeanne heard of the King of France summoning Antoine to appear before him in person, she saw it as an unexpected opportunity to visit the court of France at Amiens to seek favor for her son Prince Henry III, the King's nephew. She determined they should leave immediately.

When the King and Queen of Navarre appeared before the King of France, many of the complaints Henry II leveled at Antoine had already been diplomatically resolved, and it was evident that the King had been receiving duplicitous reports phrased to shed the worst possible light against the King of Navarre. His discussions with the King revealed to Antoine how his behavior on so many fronts had been twisted and misrepresented in such a way that nearly caused the sovereigns of Navarre to be bereft of their kingdom. Antoine was deeply jarred to realize that he had skated so near impending disaster that, without the proactive efforts of his consort, everything would have been lost.

Just as their meeting was concluding, the young prince of Navarre became impatient with the long wait he had endured behind the doors leading to the King's chamber. He escaped the Court Doorman and impetuously burst through the doors, running to climb into his father's lap. Such a handsome and merry child, he immediately charmed the King of France, who held him on his knee to converse with him. Delighted with Prince Henry III of Navarre, the King asked him if he would like to marry the King's youngest daughter, Marguerite de Valois, who was four years old. [xlix] Such an alliance would be an honor that essentially gave the prince virtual adoption into the royal family, with its attending privileges and a place in the line of succession to the throne of France. No written alliance regarding the marriage of the two children at some future date materialized at that time however the King's word was unbreakable when spoken in front of witnesses. No discussion followed that included the Queen of France's agreement, thereby leaving the alliance somewhat open-ended until acknowledged by Catherine d'Medici.

While in attendance at the royal court, Queen Jeanne became increasingly aware of the dangerous power employed by the family of Guise. François d'Guise and his brother, the Cardinal Lorraine, dominated the King's Council and assumed positions of power insisting nothing in all of France could happen without their approval.

Jeanne was dismayed at how King Henry II willingly agreed to allow the d'Guise family to act in his stead and to control the councils of the King of France wholly. She could soon see that they had maneuvered to entwine themselves by marrying as many members of their family to the royal offspring as could be accomplished, moving to dominate and eventually move onto the throne of France politically.

There was deep and obvious jealousy buried in all the machinations of the d'Guise against the King and Queen of Navarre. The Duke, François de Guise, harbored a burning resentment that Jeanne had preferred the Duke of Vendôme over himself; and added to that bitterness was the decades-old hatred for the house of Bourbon who, by right of birth, placed the princes of the blood next in line for the royal crown of France. The Bourbon's renowned heritage put them above the d'Guise family in royal rank. Unfortunately, Antoine's weak and vacillating character lessened the power and authority of the house of Bourbon, while the superior intellect, energy and political adroitness of the house of Guise far outweighed the ineptitude of the house of Bourbon.

The determination of the family d'Guise to embroil France in a war with Italy over the dominion of Naples occupied the deliberations of the council of France. Eventually, the fiery proclamations of the Cardinal de Lorraine persuaded the King's council to send an army into Italy.

Antoine stormed into his apartment, stewing and shouting over the decision of the council to invade Italy. His ego was insulted that he had not received a military command in the expedition. The weight and leadership of the Duke de Guise in controlling the council's decisions was pointedly dictated to avoid any office of prestige or respect for King Antoine by excluding him from any military position. His consort looked at her husband with sympathy, knowing that he had no idea of his ineptness to understand the complicated vagaries of military command; even more pitiful was his incapability to perceive how he was being belittled and ridiculed to further the power grab of the d'Guise brothers.

Jeanne needed to return to Pau, as she was nearing her eighth month of another pregnancy. Turning to Antoine as he paused in his rantings to catch his breath, Queen Jeanne spoke quietly and persuasively, urging King Antoine to view this opportunity as fortunate as it would enable the royal couple to return to their realm to attend to matters of sovereignty required of them in Béarn. Appealing to his royal duty and to the pomp and splendor that was rightfully his as King of Navarre, Jeanne watched Antoine turn to look at her as if he just now realized she was indeed very pregnant and travel of any kind would soon be impossible.

Jeanne felt it an opportune time to leave the court as she constantly entertained a small fear that at some unsuspecting moment, a reason would be manufactured to confine her little family to the dungeons now daily filling with suspected heretics.

With Antoine's agreement, the Queen of Navarre asked for an audience with King Henry to request leave to travel to Pau for the delivery of her baby. King Henry granted her request; then given their discussion of the betrothal of the two children asked that she leave her son for education at the court of France with Madame Marguerite, the King's daughter. Jeanne declined his offer, surprised when the King did not insist. Since this was the only mention of that future alliance other than the initial remarks made by King Henry, Jeanne presumed that Queen Catherine discouraged the request as she most likely had her own plans for her daughter's marriage.

Grateful to return to Pau, it was not long after the brutal journey that Queen Jeanne gave birth to her fourth child. A precious, gentle little girl, she was named Madelaine, after her forbearer who had governed the kingdom of Navarre before King Louis XI of France was crowned. Whether the long, arduous trip from the court of Amiens to Pau was the suspected cause, the infant Princess survived for only a fortnight.[1]

Again, Jeanne mourned the death of another baby. She sank into a deep depression with thoughts that accused her of somehow being responsible that three of her children had not survived. Jeanne's despair, fed by thoughts that somehow the annulment of her marriage to the Duke d'Cleves was a sin that now demanded punishment on the lives of her babies, weighed darkly on her mind.

Even Antoine's efforts to relieve her sense of guilt could not assuage her deep sorrow. Jeanne had become too aware of her consort's abilities of deception and now placed no faith in his reassurances. Her depression deepened with her sense of loneliness, knowing she could no longer depend on Antoine's faithfulness.

A sad atmosphere of isolation permeated the relationships within the castle of Pau. Jeanne concentrated on the education and development of Prince Henry, spending as much time with him as her duties would allow. King Antoine occupied himself in various unknown pursuits that took him away from the castle. The encounters between the King and Queen felt awkward and stilted to Jeanne.

Antoine, for his part, had no idea that his relationship with the Queen had changed and was blind to any cause of his for the Queen's distance. Jeanne struggled to discard her disappointments in her husband and the loss of the close marital relationship she had always desired. She became painfully aware that their relationship was based primarily on the consistent satisfaction of Antoine's desires. Jeanne turned increasingly to study of the scriptures in her efforts to understand forgiveness.

9. Opposition Simmers

*"Abide in Me, and I in you. As the branch cannot bear
fruit of itself, unless it abides in the vine, so neither can
you, unless you abide in Me."*

John 15:4 (NASB)

The royal couple was so isolated in their kingdom, dwelling on the divided loyalties of their marriage, and they were unaware of a most dangerous secret plot developing between the family of d'Guise and the newly crowned King of Spain, Philip, who both harbored a common hatred for the sovereigns of Navarre for similar reasons. These enemies were alarmed and enraged by any form of heresy in Europe, so staunch were they in defending the purest form of Catholicism. They diligently pursued every avenue to discover and stamp out every heretical thought or idea on the continent.

The fluctuations of faith and support of reformers by Antoine marked him for their specific efforts to gain his arrest and persecution. Adding fuel to their fire of hate were the resentments held against Antoine for having been born a prince of the blood, and the almost fanatical bitterness that Jeanne had repulsed the courtship of both Philip of Spain and François d'Guise, choosing Antoine d'Vendôme instead.

With no knowledge of the bonds of revenge forming against them, the King and Queen of Navarre declined to be in attendance at the marriage of Claude, second daughter of King Henry II, and the Duke d'Lorraine, of the house of Guise. Jeanne respectfully excused herself because she was in the ninth month of her fifth pregnancy. Antoine also declined, choosing to be in attendance for the birth. The loss of three previous children weighed heavily on the couple.

The infant Princess was born on February 7, 1559, and was named Catherine. Jeanne was intent on her recovery from this, her most difficult delivery, as her health became significantly depleted. At first, little Catherine was sickly, and Jeanne had put all else out of her mind but tending to her child.

While Jeanne was focused inward, concerned with a full recovery and on caring for her family, she was unaware of the surge of persecutions of heresy taking place throughout Europe. The coalition of forces of the d'Guises and King Philip of Spain had revived the Edict of Chateaubriand. This edict ordered all courts to detect and punish all heretics. It placed severe restrictions on Protestants, including the loss of one-third of their property to be granted to the informers who brought their heresy to the attention of the courts. This offered a convenient opportunity for deceitful individuals or ecclesiastics to claim as their own large, wealthy estates, by only being willing to bear false witness. Church leaders pronounced that it was forbidden to discuss religious topics at work, in the fields or over meals. Ironically, priests and curés were discoursing copiously against any ideas of reform and openly made efforts to force conversion on Protestants to return to the Catholic faith to avoid persecutions.

Catholic leaders viewed Huguenots as a threat to the social and political order, arguing that not only must they be exterminated, they also had to be humiliated, dishonored, and shamed as the inhuman beasts they were perceived to be. Catholics threatened increased charges of heresy and treason against reformers throughout France.

The intensities of the hatred of Christian against Christian among those who had lived side by side for centuries as countrymen were appalling. Attacks on Catholic priests and prominent laymen were the result of Huguenot rage in Nimes. Neither side was free from bloodthirsty guilt. The tragedy of these evils demonstrated the willingness of neighbors to allow sectarian beliefs to break down the barriers of civilization, community and accepted morality.[li]

King Henry II issued his Château de Compéigne ordering that the death penalty applied for all convictions of heresy. Persecutions began afresh; inquisition chambers multiplied and arrests of five members of the Parliament of Paris on the odious charge of heresy spread terror throughout France. Thankfully, having retired to Pau, the King and Queen of Navarre left Paris before these severe measures were in place.

Jeanne maintained an ongoing correspondence with her dear friends Antoinette and Raymond DuPuy. Her thoughts flew to them when she heard of the intensity of persecutions in Paris, knowing it must inevitably have spread throughout the surrounding countryside. The DuPuy's estate, located outside of Tours, seemed too close to Paris. The discussions Jeanne and Antoinette had shared while together convinced the Queen her friends must be under intense pressure if their allegiances were known publically.

Not long after the news of mounting persecutions, convictions, and executions throughout France had reached the royals at Pau, a word also arrived that soon King Philip II of Spain and Elisabeth, the first daughter of King Henry II and Catherine de Medici, and goddaughter to Jeanne de Navarre, were to be wed. Henry II had signed a treaty with the Holy Roman Empire in April 1559. The Peace of Cateau-Cambrésis ended the 65-year-long, exhaustive Italian wars and was sealed with the betrothal of Elisabeth to King Philip of Spain to sweeten the agreement. She would be King Philip's third wife.

Jeanne grieved in her heart for the young bride-to-be, influenced by her personal feelings of antipathy for the vengeful, thirst for power of King Philip's character. The marriage of thirteen-year-old Elisabeth proceeded by proxy until she reached the age to complete her conjugal duties.

Then the shocking news arrived that King Henry, participating in the celebrations after the wedding, was jousting in the lists against Constable de Montmorency. An accident had occurred, and

Montmorency's lance struck his majesty the King in the eye and penetrated his brain. Eleven days later King Henry II of France died, leaving the kingdom in the hands of his son, Francis II, age 15, and his consort, Mary Stuart age 17, niece of the Duke d'Guise, who had married Francis II the year before.[li]

10. Sinister Influences

"Unless the Lord builds the house, they labor in vain who build it; unless the Lord guards the city, the watchman keeps awake in vain."

Psalm 127:1 (NASB)

With the death of Henry II, the family of Guise moved firmly into a position of undeniable power. The only hope to avoid such overwhelming control by the d'Guise faction in France would be to balance the weight of authority with the House of Bourbon. Constable Montmorency sent word by courier to Nérac, where Antoine and Jeanne were in residence, that Antoine must proceed immediately to the court of France to balance the power against the family of Guise. The decision of young King Francis II, at age sixteen, to choose as his leading counselor, Antoine, King of Navarre, must be obtained to achieve that balance. These unexpected events plunged the royal court into apparent confusion and political turmoil.

Jeanne recognized a prime opportunity for Antoine to achieve recognition and preference by the new King. Urging him to act immediately and leave at once to join King Francis II and the Regent Mother at court, Jeanne was bewildered at her consort's indecision. Antoine, for unknown reasons, hesitated to commit to going to court. Seeming not to hear or consider her advice, Antoine ignored her reasoning. He dithered, seeking information from others rather than his consort.

When the princes of the blood expressed their objections to the Guise family taking their historical positions of honor, they appealed to the young King who settled the disagreement by declaring, "by the consent and counsel of the Queen, my mother, I have chosen my uncles, the Duke de Guise and the Cardinal de Lorraine, to govern my realm."[lii]

Still, Antoine vacillated for more than a month, uncertain that he should make the trip to Paris. When he was implored by his younger brother, prince de Condé and the most respected Huguenot leaders to make haste and begin his journey, Antoine only agreed to set forth if they joined him at Vendôme to serve as bodyguards. Bishop de Mende had advised him that if any harm came to the members of the d'Guise, it was the intention of King Philip of Spain to invade and occupy Bayonne or Navarreins. Queen Jeanne took these threats very seriously as she knew only too well the depth of Philip's intent to oppose any elevation of Antoine in the French government, especially should he assume supreme direction of the military resources of the realm.

Finally, Antoine made his departure. After he left, Jeanne summoned the baron d'Arros to Nérac and committed the care of her children to him while she toured her principalities and commanded reinforcement to the garrisons, double stores of provisions and military ammunition, especially for the fortresses of Bayonne and Navarreins.[liii]

Arriving in Vendôme, Antoine was enthusiastically welcomed and hailed by his subjects. He also received word that the Guise had attempted to obtain a royal mandate against Antoine being allowed to enter Paris, but fortunately, Catherine de Medici blocked the order. The King's mother was beginning to fear the growing power of the d'Guise family.

When he grew near to Paris, he received notice that the court had moved to St. Germain and vacated Paris. Intending to settle into his usual quarters at Fontainebleau and wait for the return of the King and his entourage, he sent his Chamberlain on ahead to make preparations. To Antoine's shock and dismay, the Chamberlain returned to report that the Duke and duchess d'Guise now occupied his regular apartments and the suite of the Queen of Navarre.

By the time Antoine was just outside of Paris, the King had returned to the palace at the Louvre instead of Fontainebleau. When the Duke d'Guise received word Antoine would soon arrive, he persuaded his young King to leave the castle to go hunting. Antoine arrived at the Louvre to find there was not one of the royal household available to greet him; with no preparations made for his arrival and further orders left by d'Guise directed all his baggage and that of his party be scattered about the courtyard, blocking every entrance or pathway. He was again informed, as at Fontainebleau, that the Duke and Duchess of d'Guise now occupied his accommodations at the Louvre.

Antoine's indecisive mind could not grasp and settle on an appropriate response or solution. He stood perplexed, wholly defeated and not knowing what to do in the face of such a profound insult. He considered returning to Nérac immediately but could find no one to act on his order to reload the baggage.

While standing perplexed amid his belongings, a servant was sent to convey him to the quarters of the Queen Mother, Catherine de Medici who had been informed of his coming by the Cardinal de Lorraine. When Antoine entered her quarters, neither the Queen Mother nor the Cardinal, acknowledged his presence.[liv] Not knowing what else to do, the King of Navarre went through the usual motions of obeisance. When he had finished and stood silently waiting, Catherine, who was sitting at her tapestry, coldly greeted him, and then resumed her conversation with the Cardinal who was standing at her right. Antoine was so completely confused and daunted by such a cold, insolent reception, in panic, he impulsively embraced the Cardinal, to the shock and chagrin of those who had accompanied him. He then stood stupidly aside, waiting.

Just then word came that King Francis II had returned from hunting, so Antoine rushed to greet the young King in the courtyard still crowded and strewn with his baggage. Francis dismounted from his horse, turned to the King of Navarre, and saluted him with stern reserve. So appalled and confused was Antoine, while the Duke d'Guise, beside the King, held himself rigidly aloof, the

King of Navarre again embarrassed himself and all others present who sneered at his cloyingly subservient manner toward the Duke d'Guise. Many of Antoine's followers and supporters deserted him at that moment, either returning to Paris or joining the stronger side of the d'Guise.

11. Pressure

"He went a little beyond them, and fell on His face and prayed, saying, 'My Father, if it is possible, let this cup pass from Me; yet not as I will, but as Thou wilt.'"

Matthew 26:39 (NASB)

Francis II had not yet had his official coronation. It was not long after the embarrassment in Paris that Antoine received a summons to be in attendance at the coronation ceremony in Reims on September 18, 1559.[lv] Catholic forces had been busy planning traps to eradicate all Huguenots in France. All the princes of the blood received a summons initiated in an effort to plot their assassination; the conspiracy was intended to include Queen Jeanne. After hearing from her consort regarding his treatment in Paris Jeanne suspected evil intent in the actions of their enemies. Jeanne declined to leave her domains of Nérac to be present.

After the coronation of the King of France, Antoine wrote Jeanne that his majesty was sending the three Bourbon princes on errands to three different far-reaching locations in France. Antoine was appointed to accompany Elisabeth of Valois, the fourteen-year-old Queen of Spain, to the Spanish border to be met by King Philip's noblemen. He would then return to Béarn. The separate destinations appointed to each of the princes of the blood raised misgivings in the heart of the Queen of Navarre. She spent long hours poring over Antoine's letters trying to decipher the intents of her enemies but could find no logical purpose for the assignments except to separate the princes from their families and to increase their fatigue from travel to be lulled into a sense of security.

Remaining in Nérac, Queen Jeanne received disturbing reports of the inquisition courts that were arresting and executing supporters of the reform movement. People were being hanged, burned and disemboweled at an unprecedented rate while estates and properties were taken over by ecclesiastics, priests, and informers.

A message delivered from Antoinette DuPuy revealed Raymond's estate had sold, so the DuPuy's could move to other properties in Upper Languedoc of the province of Champagne to occupy vacated properties inherited from distant relatives. In confidence, Antoinette admitted this decision had been reached from fear of exposure of their beliefs and were fleeing to a calmer region of France where persecutions were not so rampant. She asked Jeanne to destroy her correspondence to protect the future of her children, Sara and Jean Charles. This ending request impressed on Jeanne the seriousness of their predicament. As she burned the letter, Jeanne stood peering into the flames wondering if the tribulations of her life and loved ones would ever end.

The Cardinal d'Armagnac, appointed as inquisitor-general over the duchy of Albret and Béarn, appeared unannounced, in Navarre. He had been given the order to strike fear into the heart of the Queen of Navarre with the power he had been endowed with. His first move caused the minister M. Barran to be arrested and thrown into prison. Jeanne responded immediately by issuing a warrant which designated the Cardinal's act as unauthorized and illegal, releasing the minister directly. She then demanded the Cardinal to appear before her and admonished him to respect the ancient ecclesiastical codes of Béarn.

The Queen successfully rebuffed the Cardinal's efforts to terrify and intimidate the protected reformers in Béarn, while throughout France executions, trials and condemnations rampaged with pitiless severity to exterminate heresy. Not only heretics were targeted, but any who dared to oppose the orders of the princes of Guise were also doomed. Unrest and tumult spread throughout the country.

A counter-conspiracy rose within the populace to forcibly remove the Catholic princes of Lorraine from the councils
of the King and to take the young sovereign King into custody.
Multitudes massacred in Paris and Amboise by Huguenot factions
brought instant reprisal. Some of the conspirators implicated Prince
de Condé and King Francis II questioned and then released him.
Condé sought refuge in Nérac.

The family d'Guise, incensed at this bold move against the
Catholics, plotted to eliminate the princes of the blood by any effort
possible, carefully planning a conspiracy meant to trap the Bourbon
brothers in Paris and then execute them. Francis II was persuaded
by his counselors and Queen Mary to write Antoine, ordering him,
forcefully if necessary, to bring his brother, Prince de Condé, to
court in Orleans for trial for the Huguenots' revengeful massacre
of Catholics in Amboise.[lvi]

Jeanne recalled the illogical dispersion of the princes to far
corners of France and suspected appallingly sinister implications
of this second effort to cause the princes of the blood to again
be gathered in one place. She forcefully expressed her opposition against her husband going to Orleans, unless accompanied
by an armed force, powerful enough to overwhelm and awe their
enemies. In agreement with Jeanne's forebodings, many of their
Huguenot nobles and allies offered their services.

Antoine dismissed Jeanne's wise counsel again, persisting in
plans to go to Orleans at once, and denied the need of a large escort
as unnecessary. Antoine assumed a façade of valor and insisted
his duty required him to heed the summons of King Francis, stubbornly refusing to acknowledge the pleading advice of his wife or
the information provided by worthy spies.

Even as he journeyed, he continued to receive warnings and
information confirming this appearance before the King of France
would be fatal for him, d'Condé, and Bishop d'Bourbon. Upon
arriving at Poiters, Antoine found himself barred from entering.
Confused, the King of Navarre returned to Lusignan to await letters of advice from Catherine de Medici.

When royal troops appeared on the borders of Béarn with
orders to invade and conquer Béarn and arrest Queen Jeanne if she

refused orders to turn over five Huguenot ministers who had found refuge in her country, Queen Jeanne and her children retired to the strong fortress of Navarreins, refused to turn over the Huguenots, and waited.

After two suspenseful weeks, information arrived that King Francis II with Cardinal de Lorraine and the Duke d'Guise rode into Orleans at the head of 8,000 troops, and ordered all noble persons to attend court the following day, no excuses accepted, regardless of age or illness.[lvii]

In Orleans, when citizens gathered in attendance in response to the King's command, further orders came that all arms be collected and every heretic exposed for arrest. Warrants issued for the arrest of hundreds of nobles in attendance included even the bailiff of Orleans and Aymée d'Orleans, Queen Jeanne's old governess, who were taken into custody. This shocking move struck fear in all of Orleans, as well as in Navarreins and throughout Béarn.

12. At Knifepoint

*"If the world hates you, you know that it has hated Me
before it hated you. If you were of the world, the world
would love its own; but because you are not of the world,
but I chose you out of the world, therefore the world
hates you."*

John 15:18,19 (NASB)

When Antoine and his brothers arrived in Orleans, they were
received publicly by King Francis II who was in attendance at
the tribunal held by the Cardinal de Lorraine. Armed royal guards
surrounded the platform on which the throne stood. It was an ominous and foreboding welcome.

After greeting the King, the King of Navarre and the Prince
d'Condé were escorted by armed guards to their quarters. Soon
after, there was a knock at their door. Looking fearfully at each
other, Prince Condé urged King Antoine to take up his sword in
case their visitor meant to do them harm. A courier held out an
envelope. He waited outside after the door closed in his face. The
message was an invitation to visit with Catherine d'Medici at her
apartments, and the courier would escort them.

Relieved that there were no armed guards to be seen, they set
out with the courier. Catherine d'Medici graciously received the
two princes and carried on a trivial conversation for some time,
appearing to be intent on information about the activities of Queen

Jeanne. Catherine desired that Antoine insist his consort join him at Orleans. Upon leaving that meeting, the Prince d'Conde was surrounded by royal guards, arrested and imprisoned for his participation in the conspiracy at Amboise. No doubt, except for the protection of Catherine de Medici, Antoine would most likely have shared his brother's prison cell.

Antoine committed himself to conferences and meetings with contacts to arrange freedom for his brother, exhausting all avenues available to him, as well as any suggested by his consort. On November 25, 1559, d'Condé was tried, found guilty and sentenced to death by beheading.[lviii] Within this time of Antoine's desperate efforts to free his brother, Francis II, in a conversation with his mother, Catherine d'Medici, exposed the conspiracy devised by the Guise brothers to kill the King of Navarre. Francis II planned to arrange a meeting with Antoine on some pretense and then provoke the King of Navarre into an argument that would end with Francis plunging his dagger into Antoine. The Cardinal de Lorraine, Duke d'Guise, and Marshal de St. André, who alone would also be in attendance, would finish the killing in 'defense of the King of France'.[lix]

The regent Queen was horrified to hear the terrible sin her young son was being pressured to commit by the Guise brothers. Incensed at the manipulation of her innocent and naïve young son to participate in such an atrocious, despicable deed, the regent Queen summoned the King of Navarre to meet with her. Cautious and aware of the terrible power wielded by the family of d'Guise, the Queen Mother did not expose the entire plot; however, she did warn Antoine not to allow any confrontation with the King of France when summoned to his presence.

Without being fully aware of the extent of the danger he was in, Antoine met with Francis II. In typical fashion, he submitted in acquiescence to every charge brought against him for the condition of the kingdom, as well as any provoking thought presented by Francis. Such conciliatory behavior was fittingly the manner of his normal vacillating personality, and the King could find no opportunity to become outraged enough to complete his part in the plot.

Strangely, not long after this failed assassination attempt on Antoine's life was reported to Queen Jeanne by Catherine de Medici, the young King of France became ill with a mysterious infection that baffled the physicians in attendance on the King. Every effort of the day was made to defeat the unknown disease with no success. The young King languished and grew weaker.

Queen Jeanne maintained the safety of her family by continuing to reside in the fortress of Navarreins. Upon rising from her bed, she sought her Lord, reciting from her Bible, Psalm 18:1-3, "I love Thee, O Lord, my strength, the Lord is my rock and my fortress and my deliverer, my God, my rock in whom I take refuge; my shield and the horn of my salvation, my stronghold. I call upon the Lord, who is worthy to be praised, and I am saved from my enemies. (NASB)"

Turning to the tasks of her day, she loved her children and saw to the needs of her kingdom with a clear mind, steadfast courage and a light heart.

Her deep trials and afflictions brought an urgent need to seek God. Daily she sought the protection of her Lord Jesus Christ and believed in His faithfulness and love. She treasured thoughts of the nearness of her Lord Jesus Christ in the midst of her trials, knowing that when the black clouds are thickest, His light shines brightest.

13. Brief Mercy, Hidden plots

"Contend, O Lord, with those who contend with me;
Fight against those who fight against me. Take hold of
buckler and shield, and rise up for my help."

Psalm 35:1,2 (NASB)

The family of d'Guise, terrified of the possible transfer of power in an uncertain future with Francis II near death, pressed hard to complete the demise of d'Condé and petitioned the Regent Queen to order the arrest of Antoine. Without making any commitments, the Queen Regent of France summoned Antoine for another private meeting where she offered to give him the elevated position of lieutenant-general of the military forces of France so that her next son, ten-year-old Charles IX, would be crowned the King of France. If he did not renounce his position of next in line as the leading prince of the blood, he would forfeit his own life and that of his brother, d'Condé. Antoine, relinquished his right to the crown of France to save his life.

On December 5th, only six weeks after having been crowned King, Francis II died.[lxx] His funeral procession became a somber representation of those many French citizens sacrificed during his short reign. It was the power grabbing policies of the adherents of the Catholic Church who should bear the blame, though those leaders hid behind claims their actions defended the name of truth and righteousness.

Catherine d'Medici and Antoine of Navarre were jointly now the caretakers of the future of France. As promised, d'Condé's release from prison took place. The widowed Queen, Mary Stuart, who had supported her brothers d'Guise in all of their schemes, retired, as did each of her brothers, to their lands and properties.

Antoine, overwhelmed by his new position in the court, sent word to his consort, Queen Jeanne, to join him at St. Germain to help him by her counsel. After arranging for the proper disposition of Béarn's governing, Jeanne, with Prince Henry and her daughter, Madame Catherine, traveled to Nérac to wait for further information from the court at St. Germain. It was evident to Jeanne on reading his letter that Antoine was incapable of working out the strategies and plans of such a preeminent position of directing France's military forces. She was only too familiar with the King of Navarre's vacillating moods. He could want her advice one day and then reject and resent her the next.

Nor could Jeanne forget the changeableness and deceitfulness of any activities of the present court where great caution was required. She had suspicions that the positive overtures by Catherine d'Medici were only to persuade her to leave the safety of her fortified country. Jeanne was well aware that Antoine's security during the recent tumultuous upheaval of power had been due, in large part, because of her strong fortification of her kingdom in the south. She also intended to keep young Prince Henry, and her daughter Catherine, safe.

When experienced in person, the task of trying to weigh the real attitude of the French court was always a complicated and changing kaleidoscope of political interpretations, fractured, devious and vengeful. Jeanne tackled this puzzle with only the skewed perspectives of her correspondents to study. She received another most friendly, familiar and fawning letter from Catherine d'Medici pressing Jeanne to immediately proceed to court to discuss the prospect of betrothing little four-year-old, Madame Catherine, to Henry d'Anjou, Catherine's youngest son. Catherine closed her letter, insisting that Queen Jeanne "cannot have a more affectionate and sincere relative than herself." This phrase raised Jeanne's suspicions even further.

14. Critical Declarations

"Thou have loved righteousness and hated lawlessness;
therefore God, thy God, hath anointed thee with the oil
of gladness above your companions."

Hebrews 1:9 (NASB)

The continuing news of the atrocious persecutions and killings of Protestants throughout France had occupied much of Jeanne's study and correspondence. She personally concluded that the efforts of the Catholic Church to fight against the ideas of the Protestant reformers were based more on the religious hierarchy's decision to maintain its grasp on the wealth and power of the church, as well as its political influence in the governing of the country, than to further the love of Jesus Christ. Her intensive reading, study, and searching through many theological debates had convinced her some accepted and practiced beliefs, rites, and ceremonies that had long been above question were based on only doctrines of men. With the benefit of the many refugees who had sought freedom within the borders of her country, she had partaken in in-depth discussions with learned men who had spent their lives to find the truth of the matter.

In her notes within her studies, Jeanne wrote, "There is One who cares for me. His eye is on me, and He holds me in His mighty hand. He knows my every difficulty and His omnipotent hand will bring me help.

The darkest cloud will pour rains of mercy. After the deepest, black night, morning will dawn. He will bind my wounds and heal my broken heart.

He loves me as much in times of trouble as in days of happiness. He calls me in love and fills me with the love of Jesus Christ. To honor my Christ, I want to love others as He has loved me. Help me, Lord, to see you in every person. Show me how to love You by loving those You bring into my life."

Jeanne believed to the bottom of her heart that a personal right to pursue worship without fear of persecution or discrimination was inherently the right of every individual. Realizing that she could not forego her deepest beliefs of truth to accommodate the demands of the Roman Church in areas of idol worship and payments for mercies based on falsity, she concluded she could no longer sit on the fence. If she condemned lack of truth in others, she must demand honesty in her own life. That an outward, public alignment with the Protestants would precipitate a dramatic force against her was apparent. The powerful forces of the Catholic court of France and the Papacy would be rallied to dispute her, only intensifying the opposition already inaugurated against her. The one comforting confidence was that her consort, Antoine, agreed with her reformed point of view, as did many of the citizens of her kingdom.

In agreement with the advice of her council, Queen Jeanne determined to make public her allegiance and support of the reformed religion; she did so by publicly taking Holy Communion by the reformed ritual at the cathedral at Pau. Upon returning to her apartments, Queen Jeanne spent the afternoon in solitude, contemplating and praying for guidance as to how she was to proceed from there.

Queen Marguerite of Navarre had provided Jeanne with the writings of her favorite reform advocates, including manuscripts of Lefevre's sermons preached before the scholars at the Sorbonne. He fearlessly proclaimed the futility of works without faith; declared only Jesus Christ as the one mediator between God and man; and boldly denounced the idolatry of those who offered prayers to the Virgin and the Saints. Jeanne returned to reading these writings to find strength in the face of opposition.

15. To Be or Not to Be a Huguenot?

"Say to my soul, 'I am your salvation.' Let those be
ashamed and dishonored who seek my life; let those be
turned back and humiliated who devise evil against me."

Psalm 35:3b-4 (NASB)

N ow that the King of Navarre and Catherine d'Medici shared
equally the power of governing France, all went smoothly until
the return of the Guises to court. Catherine d'Medici recognized the
number and influence of the Huguenots in the kingdom and shifted
her policy to welcome them to court. Ministers of the reformed
faith were permitted to preach in the Grand Hall of the palace.
Antoine wrote to Jeanne, urging her to bring the children and join
him as the reform movement is equally welcome at court.

Knowing of Antoine's willingness to believe whatever he heard
if it was agreeable to him, Jeanne again waited to see if the truth
validated what he said. She soon heard of the conflicts of differing
faiths reported, and brawls taking place in the palace halls.

When the Cardinal de Lorraine and Duke d'Guise returned
to court, they were aghast that the reformation was becoming so
widely accepted. They immediately corresponded with the Spanish
crown and Papal Nuncio who promptly reported the license of religious practices occurring at Fontainebleau. Soon a strong alliance
was formed between the King of Spain, the Papal hierarchy, and the

brothers de Guise. In one accord, this triumvirate of an agreement was a dominant force intent on eliminating the heresy of reform.

The ambassador of Spain and Papal Nuncio received direction urging that dissention be sowed between the King of Navarre and Catherine d'Medici. Not only did the plan seek to destroy Antoine's relationship with Catherine d'Medici, but it also ordered that everything possible is done to destroy the Queen of Navarre by undermining her marriage to Antoine.

Public arguments were instigated with Antoine by the Duke d'Guise. Antoine was easily maneuvered into disputes when left to his petty jealousies and emotional tempers without the wisdom and counsel of his consort. Others viewed him as a petulant child demanding his way. Deeply disappointed in the unstable vacillations of the King of Navarre, many of the Protestant leaders and nobles withdrew their support and returned to their homes.

Later correspondence from Catherine d'Medici further confided to Jeanne the knowledge that Antoine was secretly meeting with the Spanish ambassador to reclaim the kingdom of Navarre by exchanging Jeanne's heritage of Béarn for the island of Sardinia. This information astonished the Queen of Navarre at the base betrayal of Antoine to his vows of the sovereignty of Béarn.

Catherine urged Jeanne to come immediately to control the irresponsible actions of Antoine. Catherine herself felt endangered by the undependable undertakings of the King of Navarre, notorious for waffling and wavering during any negotiation or secret political meeting regarding the kingdom of France. Not only did Catherine report Antoine's danger to France, but she also called into question the faithfulness of Jeanne's spouse to their marriage vows, reporting that Antoine's attention to Catherine's maid of honor, the beautiful Mademoiselle de Rouet, was becoming a matter of public comment and criticism.

Jeanne received this latest information of Antoine's activities and betrayal of her trust with immense sadness. She recognized his continuing submission to the evil allure of wanton pleasure and immoral self-indulgence. His chronic lack of character had placed her and her children in a dangerous position.

Knowing she would receive no comfort in confronting him, she concluded her only avenue would be to risk the danger of going to Paris and attempt to counteract his actions with defensive measures of her own. Her heart was broken to see how far Antoine had drifted from her but the hurt was more profound that he could pile betrayal on top of rejection by attempting to wrench from her the most precious heritage of her children. She could not imagine a more deadly weapon to use against her. This sword had cleaved to the very soul of her identity. Even the faith she had shared with the heart of her heart must surely be in danger if he had so utterly turned toward evil. Now, however, she could take no time to grieve. She must go immediately to Paris to protect herself and her children.

The religious divide of France, embroiled with the opposing political interests at court, was so intense the future of the survival of France became suspect. Catherine de Medici intended to unite the kingdom by taking a neutral stance toward both faiths and allowing immense equal access. The deeply engrained animosities defeated her intentions with hatred simmering at the depths of the divided beliefs.

Cardinal de Lorraine had arranged a conference to be held in Paris to bring together the leaders of the opposing religious views to debate the tenets of each faith. The Cardinal believed himself able to discourage any further appeal of the reformed faith as he considered himself a most excellent and accomplished orator. When Queen Jeanne made public her plans to travel to Paris accompanied by her children, the Cardinal de Lorraine and other Spanish factions dreaded her arrival. If Queen Jeanne arrived in time to join the debate, her foundation of truth, intellect, and ability to penetrate deceitfulness might reveal their evil designs. They commenced the conference before her arrival in St. Germain. The great debate, professed to unite the broken country, rapidly deteriorated into political harangues, personal arguments, and vicious name calling. When neither side emerged victoriously, the d'Guise and Spanish Catholic leaders returned to plotting to gain control over their ancient enemies, the princes of the blood and the reform forces aligned against them. In particular, they opposed the unintentional, famous symbol of the Reformation, Jeanne d'Albret, Queen of Navarre.

Their intent now was to further separate Jeanne and her consort by persuading Antoine to recant his loyalty to the reformed religious doctrine and join with the Duke de Guise, the throne of Spain and the Pope to champion the right of the Roman Church to triumph and prevail. In a secret meeting arranged for Antoine to meet with the Papal Nuncio, Ste. Croix and the Spanish ambassador, Chantonnay, both suggested that the King of Navarre's marriage to his consort with her treasonous and obstinately heretical beliefs was poisonous to his political advancement. The Papal Nuncio then assured Antoine that the Pope was eagerly waiting to annul his marriage on the grounds of a false annulment of Jeanne's marriage to the Duke of Cleves. This action would enable Antoine to wed the widowed Queen, Mary Stuart, which, they suggested, would allow the political cooperation needed to assure the family of Guise to join in proceeding to depose the Queen Mother and make Antoine de Bourbon alone regent to the young King of France.

In response to these evil counsels, Antoine only asked, "If I do agree with this plan, how can I retain Béarn when I reign as King in Navarre only by the right of Queen Jeanne?"

With a quick and easy answer, the Papal Nuncio assured him that the Pope would deprive the Princess of her lands because of her crime of heresy and would confer the domains of Béarn on Antoine alone. The King of Navarre, in his usual indecision of mind, asked for permission to ponder for a period the advice he received.

The proposal to retract his allegiance to the reform movement was not difficult for Antoine as he had only adopted that allegiance as an avenue to enjoy the gratuitous benefit of the esteem of the citizens of Béarn. In contrast, Jeanne based her beliefs on principle, after much biblical study and research, and would not sway from what she perceived as truth.

Before Jeanne arrived at court, Antoine had publically established his faithlessness toward his spouse by engaging in an apparent and scandalous relationship with the beautiful lady of Catherine de Medici's court, Mademoiselle de Rouet. The young lady the Queen Mother had warned Queen Jeanne about, when in fact, it was by her order that this young beauty was assigned to pursue and entangle the susceptible Antoine to supply Catherine a weapon to use against him in her intrigues. The result of this affair was the birth of a son, named Charles de Bourbon, [ix] a few weeks before Jeanne's arrival at the French court.

Instigated by the evil powers that sought to create animosity between the King of Navarre and his consort, Antoine publicly displayed extreme coldness against his spouse when she arrived. Mademoiselle de Rouet disrespectfully flaunted her illicit affair and child in Jeanne's presence, insulting the Queen of Navarre by loudly declaring her a heretic with a sour disposition; of sedate gravity, incapable of levity. The flighty mistress engaged in exaggerated gaiety and liveliness when Jeanne was in her presence to amplify what a dull and gloomy person Antoine's old wife appeared.

Jeanne soon assessed her surroundings and perceived the evil forces aligned against her. She found herself in a desperate fight for her very survival and everything she loved and treasured. Her exceptional intelligence and education had prepared Jeanne to assess political intrigue and respond with extraordinary command, presenting a strong and frigid demeanor to hide her anxieties. She was an expert at perceiving the motives of those around her but had not maintained the softer qualities evident in her mother, Queen Marguerite, which had endeared so many. Her childhood vivaciousness had faded over the years among the distresses and disappointments that had plagued her. What had been a precocious loveliness in her maidenly appearance had hardened into a protective shell of detachment that many considered unapproachable, excepting her most trusted companions. Those who knew her saw her as serene and stately, with a fresh complexion, dark hair and large, expressive eyes of deep melancholy. Of Jeanne's most significant losses, she missed most deeply the loyalty of her friendships with Antoinette de DuPuy and Sir Arnauld Duquesse. Her ladies-in-waiting had remained faithful although two who had followed her from Chateau de Plessis, Phoebe and Chloe had accepted offers of marriage and now were ensconced in their own homes with families.

At the time she had maintained her household at the Chateau de Plessis before her annulment from the false marriage to the Duke de Cleve, Sir Duquesse and Jeanne's lady, Chloe, had formed an attachment which resulted in marital bliss shortly before Jeanne had moved to Pau to be with her mother. She had been delighted to see their happiness as Sir Duquesse became the lord over the Chateau de Plessis in her absence. Only Maddie remained devotedly at her side in her present difficulties.

Jeanne seldom expressed disapproval toward anyone, choosing instead to maintain an uncompromising indifference toward any person deserving her reproach, adopting an aloofness that distanced her from that party. When she was severely outraged, her sharp, incisive rejoinder fell with considerable weight on the ear of the offender. Antoine was no match for his consort.

To distance himself from her nuptial bond, he chastised her for her demonstration of loyalty to the reform cause; forbidding her from attending the sermons of reformed ministers. These preachers spoke openly at court by permission of Catherine de Medici, who then issued a confusing counter-command that all ladies of the court must attend Mass.

One day, as Jeanne was stepping into her carriage to attend a Protestant sermon, Antoine walked up to her, took her hand, dismissed the carriage and led her back to her apartments. He then forbade her to attend any protestant teaching or gathering and demanded she attend Mass instead. He insisted that she outwardly conform to all things associated with the Roman Catholic Church.

Jeanne coldly replied, "It is not my purpose to barter my immortal soul for territorial aggrandizement, and will not be present at mass or any ceremony attached to the Romish Church."[lxi]

Her pointed remark revealed to Antoine her awareness of his efforts to barter away the kingdom of Béarn for his benefit.

16. Prey in a Snare

"At my stumbling they rejoiced, and gathered themselves together; the smiters whom I did not know gathered together against me, they slandered me without ceasing. Like godless jesters at a feast, they gnashed at me with their teeth. Lord, how long wilt Thou look on? Rescue my soul from their ravages, my only life from the lions."

Psalm 35:15, 16 (NASB).

Antoine's enemies had persuaded, at every possible moment, he rid himself of his attachment to his antagonistic consort to smooth the way for divorce and resulting transfer of power, wealth and property. Queen Jeanne had already heard enough during their previous arguments to have discerned the faithlessness of Antoine's purposes. Her ability to immediately identify wrong demonstrated, and respond with deadly accuracy to the heart of the matter, confused and irritated Antoine who found himself unable to justify his actions or words in response. In uncontrollable aggravation, he had revealed the enormity of the evil plot against her and her heritage and even threatened to deprive her of her children. Unless she proceeded in strict obedience to his commands to attend ceremonies of the Catholic Church, he would bring charges of divorce against her.

Jeanne stood stoically silent before Antoine, enveloped by a rush of deeply embedded memories: a five-year-old child weeping desperately in a cold carriage, and an anguished, terrified twelve-year-old traveling to a foreign land and future, betrayed by those she loved more than any others. Like an enormous, deep chasm opening suddenly at her feet, Jeanne's past and future merged into a black pit of betrayal that would plunge her into sorrow too deep for recovery. Abruptly she felt bereft of any of the traits that had assembled and upheld her strength of character and prevailing spirit. Tears began to overcome her.

Jeanne, looking at the angry face of her husband, realized that this threatening, contemptible coward before her, intent on the foul wrong of destroying her family, had boasted of his intention to despoil her and her children of the inheritance of her ancestors. Indignation replaced her tears. With scorn, she regained her composure.

In scathing eloquence, she remarked on the dishonorable and treasonable liaison he had entertained with the treacherous Papal Nuncio and Spanish ambassador; she warned him that the purpose of the advice he had been listening to was his degradation in order to elevate the house of Guise, his hereditary enemies, to supreme power over the realm.

"Monseigneur, it is for the purpose to overthrow you that they seek to embroil you in opposition with Condé, Admiral Coligny, and his party. It is not my purpose to abandon my dominions to my foes; I know how to hold, with the aid of my true subjects, the royal heritage conferred upon me by God."

Jeanne paused to gather her emotions before addressing his infamous threat of divorce.

"Although my fate does not move you Monseigneur, at least have mercy upon your two children. Do you not know that this repudiation of their mother, while consummating her ruin, will also destroy them?! That they will be branded as bastards?! They, your children! The fruit of a holy union recognized by men, upon which God bestowed his benediction, and the legitimacy of which is now only questioned by our mutual enemies!"[lxii]

Under the blind delusions of passion and gratuitous selfishness, Antoine had never contemplated the obvious facts now brought before him by his consort. He was unable to disprove the assertions she flung at him and turning on his heel, fled from her presence.

17. Alone Against the Tide.

"Do not fret because of evildoers, be not envious toward wrongdoers. For they will wither quickly like the grass, and fade like the green herb."

Psalm 37: 1, 2 (NASB)

Alone, after the exit of her husband, Jeanne dissolved in the stifled emotions she could no longer hold at bay. Her years of marriage had been a support and haven to her in the midst of the painful losses of her parents and three children. Regardless of her husband's inconsistencies and debauched habits, she cared deeply for him. She had aligned her devotion toward him with her natural choice of purpose and commitment. Jeanne was inherently merciful, rarely harboring grudges or resentments against anyone who wronged her. Her spirit was free from the heavy weight of hatred and bitterness. Too proud to complain, she had witnessed with indignant silence her consort's attention to Mademoiselle de Rouet and had endured his slights and wrongs toward her.

She recognized his inability to understand the maneuvers exercised against him, well aware of his weaknesses. She mourned his alienation. The fear for the future of her children rendered her helpless to trust her emotions under the scrutiny of the court, so she kept to her chambers in solitude for many days.

She demanded her consort give her permission to return, with her children, to Béarn. As typical for Antoine, he reported to the court gathered with the Queen Mother that he had 'commanded' the Queen of Navarre to return to her homeland.

For no reason that she expressed to others, Jeanne delayed her departure. Antoine had ceased his threats to wed Mary Stuart and eventually, growing impatient, he confronted the Spanish Cardinal directly to determine if the Pope was ready to bestow the lands of Navarre as well as Béarn on him upon the resolution of certain conditions. The Cardinal hesitated, stating that it might take some time to eliminate the opposition of the pontifical council.

Disappointed at this response and still hearing in his mind the accusations of his consort's insights, Antoine allowed Jeanne's departure from St. Germain. He insisted, however, that the Prince of Navarre must stay with him. Jeanne grieved that the mind of her son might be contaminated by association with the depraved court, causing her great regret. Jeanne and her daughter, Catherine, moved to Paris before planning to depart for Béarn.

Without knowledge of the intense hatred against her by the triumvirate of Spanish, French and Papal political forces, she lived in relative solitude, concentrating on the education of her daughter and correspondence with the Prince of Navarre. Letters from her friends who aligned with the Protestants continued to warn her of her personal peril by remaining in the kingdom of France and urged her to depart as soon as possible to her land. She bore tremendous stress over the need to leave for her safety and that of her daughter, against her reluctance to leave her son in the hands of his father.

Antoine was flattered when the junta that had formed against his consort called him the leader of their conspiracy. When they confided to him fabricated information supposedly discovered by unknown sources, his irritation against Jeanne increased dramatically. The discussions turned to drastic contemplations against the Queen of Navarre who was named the sole impediment to their goals and those evil promises that so entangled the King of Navarre. He was not the least troubled at the suggested vicious, bloody undertakings to accomplish her death. Antoine did not object.

Not only had this conspiracy planned for the death of the Queen of Navarre, but they also blatantly discussed the treasonous dispatch of the Queen Mother. The object of these plots was to raise the d'Guise family to a pinnacle of undisputable power, to demolish the movement of reform against the Catholic Church, to exterminate all humanity associated with that movement from France and to depose the Queen Mother as regent for the young King, Charles. Having dispensed with Catherine de Medici's power, her death and that of young Charles would be merely a matter of unfortunate occurrences, paving the way for the total control of France by placing Duke d'Guise on the throne. Not perceiving that these lustrous plans had not included him, Antoine aligned himself on the side of the d'Guise and betrayed not only his consort, but he also abandoned his heritage as a prince of the blood and turned his back on his brothers. He became impatient to be rid of Jeanne and irritated at the lack of action against her.

It had been a grave error to allow the Queen of Navarre to move away from the court, where she could have quickly been arrested, to live in Paris. It was also a mistake to have held their council meetings in St. Germain without allowing Catherine de Medici to attend. Of course, they could not have discussed their evil plans so openly with the Queen Mother in attendance. Deep in their conspiratorial discussions, they had not accounted for the suspicious mistrust so embedded in the defensive make-up of the Queen Mother, who for her own intelligence and protection, had a tube installed among the heavy tapestries hanging from the ceilings of the council room. She was able to listen in the room above to all the discussions.[lxiii] It was from this source that Queen Jeanne received an urgent warning to depart Paris immediately.

18. Hounds of Hell

*"Their works are works of iniquity, and an act of
violence is in their hands. Their feet run to evil and
they hasten to shed innocent blood; their thoughts are
thoughts of iniquity; devastation and destruction are in
their highways."*

Isaiah 59:6b,7 (NASB)

Having already received permission from Antoine to depart
for Béarn, Jeanne arranged the last visit to her son, Prince of
Navarre, who was much attached to her. It was a difficult meeting
for both of them. Prince Henry clung to his mother, sobbing in desperate fear that he might never see her again. Her only thought was
to implore him to be strong and brave and to never, ever agree to
profess faith in the Catholic Church. When Jeanne left Paris, she
left a part of her very self with Prince Henry.

The separation of Jeanne and her son was a demonstration of the
horrible splitting of families and friends within France as the War
of the Religions spread malignantly through the country bringing
death and destruction on an ever-widening scale. Families massacred, towns demolished, beliefs devastated, and fear was on every
face. The Catholic factions released the terror of the inquisition
on all who opposed their demands to belong to the Papal Church.

Regardless of the wrongs she had endured from Antoine,
Jeanne still had loved him and though her heart had finally turned

wholeheartedly away from him, she had left a broken remnant of the young maiden in the springtime of her love and marriage behind with Antoine d'Vendôme, in whom she had seen what he might have been.

Jeanne, now realizing she was in mortal danger, and there would be no reconciliation with Antoine, made urgent preparations to travel to Vendôme on her way to Béarn. Leaving Prince Henry and understanding the current threat of imminent death caused such stress it brought on the symptoms and discomforts of the severe illness she had suffered when age eleven. Traveling was nearly impossible, so she made plans to move in small increments and layover at selected towns for several days to regain her health. As she reached Vendôme, she received word that forces had been dispatched in pursuit of her to bring about her immediate arrest.

Along with this information, also word came of Huguenot forces that were being sent to her in Vendôme to protect her further travel. Jeanne was most appreciative to receive from Condé his regrets for the treatment she had received from his brother, Antoine, and that 400 men would arrive to invade the town, allowing her time to rest and renew her strength.

Not only was the town invaded, but the vicious mercenaries of that number also pillaged and destroyed the Catholic relics and buildings, sometimes brutally murdering any who stood in their way. When they left a couple of days later, the Protestants of Vendôme counted themselves fortunate and blessed to have been overlooked by the brutal scavengers. Princess Jeanne, in solitude with little Catherine, rested undisturbed within the safety of her husband's ancestral castle.

Upon leaving Vendôme, Jeanne was accompanied by a small force of Huguenot nobles as she proceeded to Châtellerault. When Antoine of Navarre and his conspiracy of the Catholic triumvirate learned that Jeanne had left Vendôme without arrest, he was outraged.

On the road to Duras, little Catherine was happy to travel with her mother for the time they spent together was filled with merry songs and little games to divert her from the tedious monotony in the confines of the carriage. On their arrival at Duras, Madame

Catherine delightedly joined the company of the children in the home of M. d'Duras, cheerfully romping and running about the estate as her mother rested. The Queen of Navarre welcomed the hospitality gladly offered her as stress had increased her indisposition and she was feeling very ill. She was received with great magnificence by M. de Duras, a renowned Huguenot Leader.

During the days she rested there, Queen Jeanne read reports dispatched to her of the terrible occurrences of persecution of Huguenots in the surrounding lands. She listened with great sympathy to the grim reports, especially the most numerous incidents at the hand of an especially brutal and ferocious marauder named Montluc who was an admiral for the King of France.

In his anger at Jeanne having been able to depart from Vendôme, Antoine had personally sent word to Montluc to pursue and intercept her passage before she could enter Béarn. Montluc, a bloodthirsty warrior, received with pleasure the charge of tracking and arresting her, envisioning using the most unimaginable, beastly methods.

Leaving Duras with the small company of Huguenots as an escort, she arrived in Caumont feeling extremely ill. Forced to take to her bed, she was roused by an urgent warning that Montluc had reached Duras in pursuit of her and was speedily coming to Caumont to take her prisoner. Terrified to realize that she and her daughter were in such imminent danger, she sent an urgent request to the barons d'Arros and d'Audaux of Béarn to meet her on the banks of the Garonne with force mighty enough to protect her into Béarn.

At dawn, Jeanne commanded her daughter who was in a deep sleep at that early hour, to be brought to her immediately; then she rose from her sick bed and seating her daughter in the saddle in front of her, she fled Caumont and galloped at the greatest speed toward Béarn. The trumpets of Montluc sounded in the night as they caught sight of her, and the waiting forces brought by the barons surrounded their sovereign to escort her into the safety of her principality.

Catherine had clung to her mother in desperate fear, not understanding what was happening. She could sense her mother's tension as they flew through the darkness. When the friendly forces of

Navarre joined them, Catherine could feel her mother's body relax and traveling at a more moderate speed, soon fell asleep with her head cradled against her mother. Jeanne held her daughter tightly as she rode, contemplating the terrible risk they had avoided and considering her husband's total disregard for the safety and well-being of his daughter.

Crushing awareness filled her of the total severing of the ties that had bound them. At age thirty-three, Queen Jeanne bitterly resolved that she would never again be caught in the web of romance for it had only deprived her of her ability to think for herself, or to make necessary decisions for the governing of her heritage and the protection of those she loved. Antoine's neglect had poisoned her life; curtailed her power as a sovereign Princess; her fine and noble spirit, so inclined toward good in its aspirations, had been wounded and her womanly impulses deadened.

As soon as they reached Pau, the Queen of Navarre dispatched orders to send 6,000 hardened and experienced soldiers to assist prince Condé who had seized Orleans before Jeanne left Paris and was now raising a large force to occupy French lands and drive out the Catholic forces. The additional troops Jeanne provided now allowed d'Condé to meet their opposition with an army as large as the forces of the King. When Antoine heard what Queen Jeanne had done, he was livid with anger.

Within three months, the Huguenots had successfully moved into possession of twenty-nine towns, representing a significant portion of France freed from the clutches of the Inquisition.

These achievements did not last long. The power of the Catholic triumvirate ordered Catherine de Medici and young King Charles IX to return to Paris from St. Germain. The Queen Mother complied as she feared the combined power of the Guise family with Antoine de Bourbon. These leaders placed their forces strategically against the Huguenot armies and efficiently executed their plans to reclaim those areas the Huguenots had freed. Civil War desolated all the provinces of France. Montluc and other marauding bands continued their grisly rampages throughout the country.

The Queen of Navarre toured the borders of her small kingdom and reinforced all her fortresses with additional troops, supplies, ammunition, and food. Word reached Antoine at Paris of her preparations, causing him to watch amazed and astounded at the effectiveness of her sovereign moves to protect her people. Her proficiency to govern and defend her kingdom aggravated his anger. After finishing these efforts satisfactorily, Jeanne returned to Pau and the routine matters of ruling her kingdom.

One morning, her secretary brought the dispatches of the day, among which she found a letter from Queen Mother Catherine de Medici, requesting Queen Jeanne's cooperation to speak with the leader of the Huguenots, d'Condé, to encourage him to participate in negotiations for submission to stop the battles and restore the country. Catherine felt at this time she no longer needed to hide her inherent dislike for Jeanne and instead chose to use scorn and intimidation to drive her point home. Jeanne, who had always been aware of the deceit and lies so often employed by the Queen Mother, held no regard for her proposals or offers and disregarded her tactics of intimidation with contempt.

Jeanne had another, more profound reason to despise the request of the Queen Mother since her arrival at Pau. She had received word that at the actual time she was fleeing for her life and the safety of her daughter, Prince Henry had come down with a virulent form of smallpox.[lxiv] The young Prince had called loudly for his mother, who after getting word of his condition, implored the Queen Mother and Antoine to send her son to her at Pau. His life, it was reported, was in imminent danger.

Her urgent entreaties were silently ignored. She then learned Prince Henry was in the constant care of the Mademoiselle de Rouet and would not be allowed to travel to her. Desperate, Jeanne begged that he at least be transferred away from St. Germain into the care of her longtime dear friend, Madame Rénée, Duchess of Ferrara, who was also the mother-in-law of the Duke d'Guise. To this, finally, did her husband and the Queen Mother agree; they never considered allowing such a precious hostage as the Prince to slip from their hands.

The letter from the Queen Mother requesting her help to persuade d'Condé did not find Jeanne in an agreeable frame of mind. Her reply was abrupt, though cordial, with reminders to the Queen

Mother of her promises made to Jeanne that remained unfulfilled. Further, Jeanne advised, since the position of the Queen Mother and the King continued as captives of Antoine and the triumvirate, Jeanne had no influence with d'Condé.

19. Death is Personal

*"Those who are tall in stature will be cut down, and
those who are lofty will be abased."*

Isaiah 10:33b (NASB)

The summer heat had passed, and Jeanne was sitting in the beautiful gardens of Pau after a long promenade with Madame Catherine through the grounds of the castle. Occupied with the promise of other pastimes, Catherine had gone with her nursemaid, and Jeanne remained in quiet contemplations as to what she wanted to do to establish further peace in the principalities of her kingdom. After an hour or so of considerations, Jeanne assembled her council and released letters patent by her order that public celebrations of divine worship within Béarn were permitted as long as they followed the Protestant ritual. This order prohibited any worship of the Catholic faith throughout her kingdom.

The triumvirate and a very agitated Antoine had issued in June 1562, a proclamation charging all Huguenots who aligned with d'Condé with high treason and were subject to the penalties to be inflicted by the law of the realm. As a result of this proclamation, the royal armies had opened a military campaign against Condé and had captured Poiters on August 1, 1562,[lxv] and on the 29th of that month, the town of Bourges surrendered. The army then laid siege to Rouen. The port town fought valiantly and refused to surrender. Finally, on the 26th day of October, an assault was mounted that ended in the surrender of the brave Huguenot forces who fought there.

In the midst of the battle, Antoine, who was in joint command with the d'Guise brothers, was overseeing the fight, and while standing in a trench, was struck by a bullet which penetrated his left shoulder.[lxvi] Physicians were called, and Antoine transferred to his tent for their care. The doctors reassured him his life was not in danger, although he must be quiet and tranquil to allow the wound to heal around the bullet.

Antoine heeded the advice of the doctors for several days, however in his boredom, he welcomed to his tent Mademoiselle de Rouet and other noble companions that had followed in the train of the Queen Mother as she inspected the troops and watched the events of the battle. With Mademoiselle de Rouet beside him in his bed, unending gaiety, music, dancing, and performances of young boys participating in sports events or young girls dancing, created much excitement for the injured King of Navarre.

When a courier brought word to Antoine of the surrender of Rouen, he insisted on making a triumphal entrance into the city through the breach of the wall.[lxvii] He commanded that his litter be carried, surrounded by his victorious troops, into the city and then back to his tent. Before he had gone far, he fainted, and his bearers carried him back. His inflamed wound worsened from such exertion, and a burning fever and delirium consumed him. Mademoiselle de Rouet never left his side, and the same scenes of ribald license within his chamber continued in spite of his declining condition. After several days, the Bishop of Mende was summoned to advise him that his life would soon be ending. Antoine received the news with resignation. Physicians banned the noisy crowds from his tent, and he was urged to make his will, which he did, leaving his vast wealth to Prince Henry.

Unfortunately, this unhappy prince of the blood, of the House of Bourbon, always perceived his errors when it was too late to amend them. He had professed the Romish faith, and then later, for the fifth time in his life he changed his belief, returning to the Lutheran tenets of faith. He spent his next days grieving over the many wrongs he had committed toward his consort and even voiced regret that she had not made an effort to visit him.

His brother, Cardinal de Bourbon arrived and arranged that Antoine be taken by boat on the river Seine from Rouen to St. Maur. On the trip, he suffered great pain and was overcome with delirium and convulsions on arrival at St. Maur though all possible was done to relieve his discomfort. Not long after, he died. It was November 14, 1562, and Antoine de Bourbon, Duke de Vendôme and King of Navarre, was forty-four years old.[lxviii] Several weeks after his demise, the King of Navarre was buried at the Cathedral of St. George in Vendôme. His funeral was attended only by his brother, Cardinal de Bourbon, and few mourned his passing while the country continued in battle and his brother, d'Condé was again taken prisoner by the Duke de Guise.

20. Laments, Traps and Accusations

"For 'whoever will call upon the name of the Lord will be saved.'"

Romans 10:13/Joel 2:32 (NASB)

Jeanne mourned her loss deeply, retiring to her castle in Orthez for her mourning period. Alone in her solitude, Jeanne mourned only for the Antoine of her first love, choosing to forget the wrongs received at his hand during the latter years of their marriage. True to her inherent trait of mercy, Jeanne corresponded with an old friend and arranged for Antoine's illegitimate son, Charles de Bourbon, a future in the church. He eventually became Archbishop of Rouen.

Upon emerging from her mourning, the first thing Jeanne did was to bestow her cousin, Neil, Viscount of Rohan, lieutenant-general of Béarn during her son Prince Henry's minority. Jeanne was widowed when thirty-four-years old.

In early 1563, with d'Condé in captivity, the Catholic forces succeeded in overcoming every town lost to the Huguenots, except for Orleans which held out, stubbornly refusing to surrender. In February, Duke d'Guise laid siege to Orleans and while in command there, was assassinated by a Huguenot.

With the powerful Duke de Bourbon and Duke de Guise in their graves, Catherine de Medici found herself in her most powerful position yet, unencumbered by interferences from those two powerful families.

Preposterously, three months after becoming a widow, Jeanne received an ambassador from the King of Spain who was directed to explore the possibility of betrothing the Queen of Navarre, not to the King himself, but to his son. Philip had coveted the domains of Jeanne's kingdom since before his father, the Emperor Charles V, had died. He was only too aware of the contempt Jeanne had for him for the persecutions she had endured for so many years, but still blinded by the power of his reign, the King of Spain could not conceive that she would ignore his offer to be the Queen of Spain when his son succeeded to the throne.

Although flabbergasted at the arrogance of her long-time enemy, Jeanne listened carefully to the proposal and feigned a willingness to pursue further discussions of the matter, stipulating, however, only under complete secrecy. She was determined to learn the real motives behind the offer. Interestingly, the ambassador began to make the same promises that had been presented to persuade Antoine regarding the island of Sardinia. Then the ambassador had returned to Spain and reported her positive response in his account to the King.

Jeanne, in Pau, called her council and commanded several orders to be carried out immediately throughout her lands. First, she proclaimed an edict that disallowed all worship of the Romish church within the domains under her sovereignty, establishing the consecration of Jeanne's sovereign realm as Reformed. Further, she ordered all properties, churches, chapels, houses, title deeds, buildings, hospitals and lands of bishops, canons, abbés, deans, archdeacons, deacons, priors, curés, monks, nuns and priests, lay or ecclesiastical, owned by the Pope or by the Catholic Church be seized and transferred to the ownership of the government of Béarn.

She ordered the seizure of crucifixes, idols, images, relics, shrines, religious figures, artwork and all vessels used at the celebration of mass. She further caused the high altar removed and the holy wafers burned. After the ordered cleansing at the Cathedral in Lescar, the Queen participated in the first Protestant service performed there.

Aware of the deficiency of ministers available to officiate in the seized cathedrals she had provided as churches for her Protestant subjects, she wrote to Geneva requesting a noted minister named Raymond Merlin, and twenty other preachers to administer the word of God to her people. She pronounced that only the Holy Word be preached as being most surely grounded on the doctrine and written word of the prophets and apostles.

When approached again by the ambassador of the King of Spain who arrived intending to threaten the 'unfortunate widow' with the loss of that promising proposition to be the future Queen of Spain, he threatened to withdraw the proposal if she refused to reverse her commandments of banning the Catholic faith from being observed in her countries. The ambassador also took the opportunity to severely reproach Jeanne for her heresy and lack of remorse, and to urge her to repent and return to the faith of her ancestors. Jeanne abruptly interrupted and asked the Spanish ambassador whether being of the religion she was, she could be allowed to marry a Spanish prince of the Romish faith?

He replied, "If you, madame, were sensible of the offense which you have committed in the sight of God, I should have great hope of the fortunate issue of this negotiation; but as you experience no remorse, I cannot anticipate a happy result."

Her contempt for the ambassador and his unscrupulous King now fell in words of power as, with flashing eyes, she leveled her most intense outrage at their deceitful maneuvers. Stating that although she desired the favor and friendship of the Catholic King, nevertheless, she was not as defenseless as he presumed: She commanded the allegiance of 1500 gentlemen of valor, all professing the Reformed Faith; besides 30,000 soldiers, who would die to accomplish her will; and all the warriors who fought in France during the last civil war had placed their swords at her disposal.

Then, with extreme contempt, she asked if it was the intent of the Pope and the King of Spain to conveniently appease her with the same delusive hopes relative to the realm of Sardinia they had offered Antoine? She rained on the poor ambassador incisive and revealing objections to his King's continued and vicious interference in her sovereignty, as among princes it was the rule not to interfere in the internal government of each other's territories. She, therefore, requested his Catholic Majesty to remember this fact and to refrain from interfering, or from promoting disaffection in the countries over which she ruled as sovereign.[lxiv]

The ambassador left her presence and hurried home to Spain to report the occurrences of this conversation to his King, Philip II, who in turn, fired off his affronted response regarding Jeanne's heretical position to the Pope.

Pope Pius IV, inflamed by the insidious representations of King Philip, turned his wrath against the Queen of Navarre, directing the Cardinal d'Armagnac to take remedial actions in Béarn immediately. The Cardinal wrote a severe reproach to Louis d'Albret, bishop of Lescar, for allowing the destructive occurrences in his cathedral; and then turned his castigation on the Queen and her subjects.

The Cardinal's letter admonished the Queen with insolent insinuations that he felt great and just regret to learn of the destruction in Lescar of the images, the altars, the jewels, ornaments, and silver, and priests denied from celebrating accustomed services. He deplored that this outrage was committed in the Queen's presence and under her commandment. He was aghast that she must be under the immoral persuasion of her evil council who surely impelled her to plant a new religion in her countries of Béarn and Lower Navarre. The Cardinal feared that her actions would deprive her people of the religion of their ancestors and cause great rebellion against her sovereignty. Then he reminded her of the disapproval of her country's surrounding sovereigns of Spain, France, and the Pope who would most certainly invade and lay claim to her kingdom in their affront at this new religion. The Cardinal then conceded that the Queen would most likely rather be poor than not to serve God.

However, he was sure she was in danger of losing the heritages which her royal ancestors had preserved, fearing she might deprive her son of his succession to her crown and that her children would share the dishonor and disappointment she had inflicted on her subjects.[lxx]

Like her mother, Jeanne was a gifted writer, and with her superior intellect and discerning abilities, she was not intimidated; promptly sitting down to pen her reply.

"TO THE CARDINAL D'ARMAGNAC.

Having knowledge from my earliest years of the manner in which you devoted yourself to render service to the deceased King and Queen, my father and mother, your present strange delusions shall not prevent me from acknowledging and lauding such fidelity; nor also, from owning that you have, until lately, continued such towards her who has inherited their worldly substance. I could, nevertheless, have desired that this good and faithful friendship on your part, should not have been lessened, or rather crossed by that which I scarcely know, whether to term religion or superstition: nevertheless, I thank you for the warnings which you have given me, taking them as I do with reservation, as inconsistent, like the mingling of Heaven with the clay of earth. As to the first point upon which you comment—the reformation in religion which I have commenced at Pau, and at Lescar—I am very earnestly resolved, by the grace of God, to continue such reformation throughout my sovereignty of Béarn. I have learned to do so from my Bible, (which I read more than the works of your doctors,) in the book of the Chronicles of the Kings of Israel, from whence I take king Joash for my pattern, in order that I may not be reproached, as were some of the kings of Israel, that, professing myself a servant of God, I yet destroyed not the high places consecrated to idols. As for the ruin which you state that my evil counsellors prepare for me, I am not yet so forsaken by God and my friends, as not to have still some worthy persons near me—persons, who not only wear the semblance of religion, but practice its precepts: or, such as the head is, so are the members. Neither have I undertaken, as you assert, to plant a new religion, but only to build up again the ruins of our ancient faith, in which design I feel certain of a fortunate issue.

I clearly perceive, mon cousin, that you have been deceived, both in the matter of the answer of the States, and also upon the condition of my subjects generally. The said states have tendered me obedience in religious matters. My subjects, ecclesiastical, noble, and plebeian, have, without one single exception, offered me obedience, and continue daily to pay me the same deference, which you will own, differs materially from your assertion of their menaced rebellion. I do nothing by compulsion: I condemn no one to death, or to imprisonment, which penalties are nerves and sinews of a system of terror. I know the kings my neighbours perfectly: the one hates the religion which I profess: I also abhor his faith. Yet despite this, I feel assured that we shall not cease to live in amity. Nevertheless, I have not taken so little heed of my affairs, nor am I so destitute of relations, allies and friends but that my remedy is promptly at hand if he decided otherwise. My other neighbor is he who sustains my strength, and who is the root of my race, from whence the greatest honour I have is to be an offshoot. This my neighbor abhors not the reformed faith, as you say; but permits its exercise around his person, by the nobles and princes, amongst whom it is my son's happiness to be included; and finally, throughout his kingdom.

You have invented a response for me which I approve, when you assert that I would rather be poor than cease to serve God. Nevertheless, I do not perceive that I am endangering any worldly interest; but, on the contrary, instead of lessening my son's heritage, I augment it, and increase his greatness and honour, by means which every true Christian ought to seek. If the spirit of God did not lead me to this conclusion, my common sense would teach me the lesson by an infinity of examples; but more especially, by that of the king, my deceased husband, whose history is known to you from beginning to end, and whom you beguiled by the promise of all those fine crowns which were to be his, if he fought against true religion and his conscience—a fact his death-bed confession testifies; also, the words which he addressed to the Queen, protesting that, if he recovered, he would cause the ministers to preach everywhere throughout France, the doctrines of the reformation. Behold the true fruits of the gospel, which divine mercy perfects in due season! Behold how the Eternal Father cares for those in favour of whom his clemency has been invoked.

I blush for you, and feel shame, when you falsely state that so many atrocities have been perpetrated by those of our religion. Pull the mote from your own eye, then shall you see clearly to cast out the beam in your neighbour's eye! Purge the earth first from the blood of so many just men shed by you and yours; take in witness of which the facts that you are well aware I know, of the origin of the first seditions, when patiently, and by the permission of the king and Queen, our ministers, according to the edict of January, preached the word of God, when, by the evil counsel of M. le Légat, of the Cardinal de Tournon, and of yourself, all this subsequent trouble was concocted; you, aiding your designs by imposing on the easy good nature of the late king, my husband. When I assert this, I do not mean to palliate the evil that had been done under the guise of true religion, to the very great regret of her faithful ministers, and of all worthy persons. I, for one, am most earnest in demanding retribution against those, who thus pollute the true faith, from which pestilential persons, by the grace of God, Béarn shall be exempt, as it has been to the present time, from this and other ills.

I perceive by the description that you adventure upon, that you do not know our ministers; or, at least, that you have not profited greatly by their converse; otherwise, you would know that they preach the necessity of obedience to their temporal rulers, patience, and humility, according to the pattern set them by their great examples, the martyrs and apostles. You state that you do not wish to enter into controversy with us upon a doctrine which I assert is so true, that you cannot prove its falsity. Herein I agree with you; not because I doubt the sufficiency of our faith, but that I fear I should reap too little profit from the holy desire which possesses me to show you, out of charity and love, the true path to our Sion. You are pleased to assure me that the number of our people is small. I, on the contrary, inform you that our faithful increase daily. As to what you remark respecting the books of the ancient fathers of the church, I hear them constantly quoted by our ministers, and approve them. Nevertheless, I own that I am not learned as I ought to be in this matter; but neither do I believe that you are more competent than myself, having observed that you have always applied yourself more to the study of politics, than to that of divinity. When you state that we have left the true faith to follow the religion of apostates, look to yourself first—you, who have unworthily rejected the holy food with which the late Queen, my mother, fed you, before the honours of Rome darkened the eyes of your understanding. We unite in opinion, as you state, on the necessity of studying the

Holy Scriptures; but we care not to look beyond. We do not deny that therein are things hard to be understood; but we know that the errors which thereon ensued in the early church, inflicted but a slight wound in comparison to the cancer which now devours your ecclesiastical theory. I agree in all your comments on the Prince of Darkness; and own, that you and yours afford admiral examples of the evil nature which you censure.

As to the difficulty in interpreting the true meaning of the words, "this is my body," Saint Augustine in his treatise against Adamantius, has amply vindicated that matter (as I have learned more by the teaching of our ministers than by study of books), when he says that Jesus Christ made no scruple to name the body when he gave its symbol. I think that our ministers have more profoundly studied this passage than you, and yours; else you would not fall into the error of asserting that Jesus Christ said before the communion, "Henceforth, I speak no more in parables," when it is manifest by the 13th chapter of St. John, that he uttered those words after the conclusion of His Holy Supper. Turn to the 22nd chapter of St. Luke's Gospel, and learn for the future to comprehend a passage before you quote it: an error of the kind, nevertheless, would be excusable in a woman, such as myself; but, certainly, mon cousin, to see an old Cardinal like yourself so ignorant, kindles shame.

You desire to learn in what degree I put confidence in the books of your learned doctors in theology: I reply, in the measure that they take Holy Scripture for their guide and model. I find that the works of Calvin, Béze, and others, are founded on the word of God. You say, that you wish to refer our ministers to the decision of a general council—a thing which they themselves desire, provided that efficient security of person is guaranteed; they, in demanding this, having before their eyes the examples of John Huss and Jerôme of Prague. I know not where you have learned that there are so many diversities of sects amongst our ministers; though, at the Colloque de Poissy, I became very sensible of your own divisions in doctrine and practice. We have one God, one faith, one law; and the Holy Ghost has promised to be with His Church to the end of time, to bless, and to maintain this faith.

I thank God that I know, without the aid of your teaching, how to serve and please God, the king my sovereign lord, and all other princes, my allies and confederates; all of whom I appreciate better than you can do. I, also, know how to bring up my son, so that, hereafter, he may be great and revered; and to maintain myself in communion with that church, without the pale of which there is no salvation. You request me not to think it strange, or to take in bad part, what you have written. Strange, I do not deem your words, considering of what order you are; but, as to taking them in bad part, that I do as much as is possible in this world. You excuse yourself, and allege your authority over these countries, as the Pope's legat: I receive here no legate, at the price which it has cost France; I acknowledge over me in Béarn only God—to whom I shall render account of the people He has committed to my care. As in no point have I deviated from the faith of God's Holy Catholic church, nor quitted his fold, I bid you to keep your tears to deplore your own errors; to the which, out of charity, I will add my own, putting up, at the same time, the most fervent prayer ever left my lips, that you may be restored to the true fold, and become a faithful shepherd, instead of a hireling. As respects my present enterprises, if you cannot convince me of evil by stronger argument, cease, I pray you, to importune me. I pity, from my heart, your worldly wisdom, which, with the apostle, I deem foolishness before God. He will not disappoint my hopes in Himself; He is not a liar, like men; and He will never desert those who place their trust in His providence, Your doubts, mon cousin, may well make you fear; while my steadfast faith gives me assurance. I must entreat that you will use other language, when next you would have me believe that you address me, impelled, as you affirm, by motives of respect, and by the duty which you say that you owe me; and, likewise, I desire that your useless letter may be the last of its kind.

I have seen that malignant, pernicious, and most seditious letter, which you have thought it expedient to write to mon cousin de Lescar, who is about to answer you. Suffice it for me to inform you that, I perceive that you are determined to bring upon this little country of Béarn, that deluge of misfortune in which you have recently attempted to drown France. You envy our happy condition; the which being bestowed by our great God and master, He will maintain for us, despite your malicious conspiracies. I pray Him to pardon your crime; though do I even tremble at the prayer, lest it should be replied to me as to Samuel weeping and interceding for Saul.

From her who knows not how to subscribe herself; being fearful of signing herself your friend, and who even doubts her relationship to you; but whom, in the day of your penitent repentance, you will find,

Your good cousin,
Jeanne"^{lxxi}

When Jeanne presented to her council the letter she received from Cardinal d'Armagnac and a copy of her letter in reply, they applauded their Queen and proclaimed that God had guided her hand. Hundreds of copies of the charges of the Cardinal d'Armagnac and her letter of response were printed and spread throughout the citizens of her domain who received it with enthusiasm and great acclimations of the courage of their Queen.

The exasperated Cardinal immediately sent his own copies of the two documents to the Pope in Rome and his papal council, with his comments requesting her arrest, "so that in the midst of the turmoil she created, she shall be plunged into an abyss dark as the most dismal of any sepulchers." Cardinal d'Armagnac truly desired the literal fulfillment of his comments, so incensed was he about her rebellion. It was, however, not the will of God that his desire be granted.

21. The Weight of Revenge

*"Therefore, justice is far from us, and righteousness
does not overtake us; we hope for light, but behold,
darkness; for brightness, but we walk in gloom."*

Isaiah 59:9 (NASB)

The halls of the offices of the Pope resounded with calls for
excommunication and inquisition of the Queen of Navarre,
while the provinces of France continued in turmoil and discontent.
The Queen Regent, Catherine d'Medici, and Prince Condé had
signed a treaty after the deaths of the King of Navarre and Duke
d'Guise which favored the Huguenots by edict ordering the nul-
lification of censures and penalties against heresy. The treaty was
accepted, under protest, by the French Parliament. Neither side
was content as throughout the country Catholics searched out and
imprisoned or slaughtered perceived heretics, refusing to accept the
edict of pacification. In retaliation, Huguenots pursued and murdered Catholics with uncontrollable lawless ravages.

In the disunion evident in the court of France, Catherine
d'Medici continued to employ her usual plots and intrigues. To
subdue Prince Condé to a more subservient and agreeable position of power, she again applied the evil trap which had ensnared
his brother, Antoine. Her weapon of choice was the beautiful and
beguiling Mademoiselle de Limeuil. Condé, in the midst of pleasure and dissipation, forgot to demand the fulfillment of stipulations

Catherine d'Medici chose to evade. Most importantly, the agreement that he should be appointed lieutenant-general of the French army was ignored.

The supreme pontiff was so incensed at the defiance of the Queen of Navarre that he, with the Holy Office of the Inquisition, were focused toward bringing charges of heresy against her and seven eminent French prelates. In October 1563, the Pope published his famous Monitory against Jeanne d'Albret. This document stated the Queen must appear before the Holy Tribunal of the Inquisition on charges of heresy. If she disregarded the citation and failed to appear, she was to be "declared convicted of heresy, excommunicated and accursed, her kingdoms, principalities, sovereignties, lordships, and domains, being given to the first despoiler; or to those on whom his holiness, or his successors, may please to bestow on them." This Bull was confirmed and sealed on the 28th day of September 1563.[lxxii]

The extreme proceedings of the Pope found little support. Enough awareness had permeated society to recognize there was little evidence that such ecclesiastical seizure of property brought beneficial results to religion. At the Council of Trent, the eminent prelates unanimously recommended the Pope withdraw his bull.

The sovereigns of several European countries, especially Catherine de Medici of France as regent for her son, King Charles IX, wrote in utter rejection that the presumption of the papal court might lawfully depose princes. The negative responses were indicative of the decline in the prestige of decrees of ecclesiastical discipline and papal prerogatives. The Pope was intent not to reverse his charges against Jeanne d'Albret; however, the negative pressures forced him, after much angry discussion, to issue a second formal decree to virtually consider the Bull against Jeanne to be of non-effect as concerning her arrest and penalties.

The relief from the evil intents to destroy Jeanne d'Albret through excommunication was not the end of her peril. The King of Spain and Pope Pius were not willing to give up their assault, driven by their animosities against her. They now turned to bring about the annulment of Jeanne's marriage to Antoine d'Vendôme and declaring it void and her children illegitimate, thus to deprive them of succession to their rightful heritage.

Here again, Europe rose in defense against this powerful encroachment by the pope to invade and change such an intimate and personal matter without distinction or warrant. Still, Catherine de Medici was most adamant in her disapproval; notifying the pontiff that any move of this sort against the Queen of Navarre would cause a breach between the Papal and French councils to necessitate bringing the vast armies of Charles IX of France to her defense. Sympathy for Queen Jeanne did not motivate the Queen Regent. Catherine was too well acquainted with the complicated succession prerequisites of France. She knew that to declare King Antoine's son was illegitimate would place the Cardinal de Bourbon first prince of the blood and the rightful successor to the throne of France.

A priest, Cardinal de Bourbon, was incapable of bequeathing his rights to succession to his issue; therefore, the succession would devolve on the Prince de Condé and his children. Such a claim by Condé, the acknowledged leader of the Huguenot faction, would settle an immense accession of power on the supporters of the Huguenots. The subsequent letter sent by Charles IX to the Pope discouraged further discussions by the pontifical council, and the matter was set aside for the time.

22. Deadly Chess

*"Through many tribulations we must enter the
kingdom of God."*

Acts 14:22b (NASB)

J eanne d'Albret, Queen of Navarre, looking back on her life
may have seen only calamity and persecution. Current sorrow,
opposition, rebellion, and domestic misery had darkened so much
of her life that the gloomy days of Plessis-lez-Tours appeared in
her memory as a light-hearted period. The beautiful, gracious and
enchanting woman had exchanged the soft and winning pursuits
of her sex for the sword of the warrior and the pen of a statesman,
by necessity. It is a wonder that the pressures of misfortune did not
turn her into a bitter tyrant intent on retribution.

Barely had the year of 1563 turned the page to another birthday
for her when the provinces of Lower Navarre, along with the par-
liaments of Bordeaux and Toulouse issued a decree pronouncing
Jeanne's sovereign rights over Béarn invalid. They claimed that the
provinces under her rule were subject to the controlling power of
the King of France and therefore she could not establish a new religion or civil code without the consent of her sovereign King. These
decrees among her southern provinces were from the evil persua-
sions and influences of the French general Montluc in the area.

Queen Jeanne faced this move to block her sovereign powers
by going directly to the libraries of Béarn where, in the vaults in

the basement, she found the dusty volumes of the ancient codes of government for Béarn, Navarre and the southern provinces. After extensive research to understand the old codes that had protected the royal leaders of the kingdom safely for so many years, she found the answers to her questions and the course of action that lay ahead of her. She must procure the explicit recognition of her independent sovereignty over Béarn from Charles IX and must leave immediately to journey to the court of France.

Intent to procure that recognition of her independent rule, Jeanne again assessed the difficulties facing her and plotted her moves and countermoves as though playing a game of chess.

Beset with misgivings of who she should nominate to govern the principalities during her absence, she turned to the brother of her childhood friend, Catherine d'Aster. The Count de Grammont was one of the leading nobles of Béarn. United by their shared affection for Catherine d'Aster, during all the years of Jeanne's sovereignty as Queen of Navarre, he faithfully supported and served her. He was also respected and well-liked by the Béarnois. Count de Grammont agreed to attend to the needs of governing Béarn and its principalities.

Leaving immediately, the Queen of Navarre thought to demonstrate her independent sovereignty by appointing a large party to accompany her. Her entourage included illustrious nobles of her country, an ample display of force with large troops as an escort, five strong jurists able to argue the intimacies of the precepts of Béarn, and a representation of the reformation clergy of eight celebrated Protestant ministers. It was Jeanne's purpose to present her royal power and abilities as sovereign of Béarn; not to give the appearance of defiance and offense against the stance of the Catholic throne of France.

Jeanne left Nérac soon after her birthday in 1564 to seek a document of independent sovereignty from the King of France, so she would not be required to ask approval by the King of France for every move or decision. She arrived in Paris the first of March and was satisfied when her jurists ably argued her case for independence before the Parliament of Paris and were granted approval.

Only the requirement of the King's signature of approval was needed to accomplish her goal.

Catherine de Medici, not aware of the Queen of Navarre's intentions to appear at court, had persuaded King Charles IX, to progress throughout his kingdom to view and assess the villages, cities, provinces, and fortresses under his royal charge. The Queen Regent and Charles IX traveling through the regions were expected to stop next in Mâcon, so Jeanne met them there. She arrived in the city to a resounding ovation by the citizens who had embraced reformed teachings and in overwhelming numbers had joined the Protestant cause.

Jeanne attended the services in the Protestant church newly built in Mâcon and invited anyone who would like to hear the sermons of the ministers who traveled with her, to join her where she was residing when they preached.

The day after the arrival of the court in Mâcon, the Queen Regent sent word to the Queen of Navarre that the King was offended by her Lutheran ministers being allowed to preach in the presence of the Roman Catholic court. Denied from holding any other gathering of her religion in public or even, in her private quarters, Jeanne was quite incensed at this order. However, her political understanding of the intrigues of powers caused her to staunch her anger to alleviate the negative influences that could undo all she had previously accomplished toward her intended goal.

Most of all, when Jeanne learned that her beloved son, Prince Henry, was traveling with the court and was also in Mâcon, the joy of receiving that word eliminated continued thoughts of anger. Her jubilant reunion with her son overcame all weight of the burdens facing her regarding the government of her kingdom. Prince Henry was as elated to embrace his mother as she was to hold him in her arms.

During this reunion she could see that Prince Henry was growing in courtly graces and was reassured by him that he still invested faith in the reform religious precepts she had passed on to him, however, he was compelled by Catherine de Medici to attend mass with his companions, the brothers of the King. Queen Catherine also discouraged learning in a prince and Jeanne could

see a glaring deficiency in her son, being more inclined to entertainments, games of chance and gallant frolics, than in reading and
study, so typical of regular residents at court. Jeanne's awareness of
her ten-year-old son's lack of learning prompted her to make efforts
to urge the Queen Mother to allow Prince Henry to be placed again
under her care. Catherine responded coldly, ridiculing Jeanne's
prudish fears while refusing to take seriously her disapproval of
the antics, profane oaths and indecent songs always on the lips of
the King and his brothers.

When the court announced its intention to depart for Lyons the
day following the celebration of mass, Jeanne also prepared for her
departure to seek an audience with the King there. Then an order
came from the royal court that, with no exception, all citizens of
Mâcon were to join in a procession through the streets in pomp and
solemnity, to the cathedral St. Vincent for mass, carrying lighted
torches as an expiatory offering for the prevalence of heresy among
the city's inhabitants. The Huguenots of the town sought Jeanne's
intervention on their behalf for exclusion from this order. Her pleas
met with firm resistance. Departing for Lyons, the King and his
court left the Protestant citizens of Mâcon profoundly offended
and alienated.

Jeanne progressed to Lyons herself, fearing that the events in
Mâcon had caused prejudice against her suit. The King, however,
granted her request to establish her independent sovereignty of
Béarn, much to her surprise and relief.

News of the death of the Princess d'Condé, consort of the
Prince d' Condé, severely oppressed any celebration of confirmation of independent sovereignty. Soon after receiving the unhappy
news, Queen Jeanne left Lyons to go to Vendôme.

When last she had been in Vendôme while on the first leg of her
journey to Paris, Jeanne had received her dear cousin, Françoise
de Rohan whom she had not seen since Françoise left Pau after
Queen Marguerite's death to take her place at the French court
in the train of Catherine de Medici, among her maids of honor.
Françoise had grown into a beautiful, gentle woman. While among
the brilliant, attractive women of the court, Françoise was singled
out by the Duke de Nemours who applied toward her every talent

he had in romance and warm homage of attachment. The Duke was considered the most captivating cavalier of the court; wealthy, handsome and brave. Both Mademoiselle d'Rohan and the Duke de Nemours had royal heritage, and it appeared to be an auspicious match. Eventually, the couple exchanged rings of betrothal.

At the tournaments celebrating the coronation of King Henry II, the Duke de Nemours had worn the colors of the beautiful duchess d'Guise and had publicly made a show of his appreciation of her whenever they had occasion to meet. Though the demonstrations of the Duke de Nemours of his inclination to a preference for the duchess d'Guise continued, the Duke plied his power of persuasion over the lovely, compliant Françoise. Her impending motherhood soon became apparent. The affairs and lax morality so prevalent at the court of France resulted in the acceptance of the condition of the beautiful Mademoiselle d'Rohan, and persistent pressure was applied toward Duke de Nemours to at least bestow on her the legality of his name. François had the papers of betrothal as evidence of his profession of commitment toward her and their future marriage. All appeared to progress to the celebration of their nuptials.

Unfortunately, when the Duke d'Guise was assassinated, the enticing Anne d'Este, Duchess of Guise, became eligible to remarry. The Duke de Nemours, when faced with the beguiling allure of the now-free Duchess d'Guise compared with the insipid beauty and childlike gentleness of the unfortunate Françoise, chose not to honor his commitments to Françoise or her child. When that mistreated maiden appealed her suit to a higher power in Rome, the hierarchy considered the weight of her preference for being a Huguenot plus being aligned to the house of Albret, raised in the manner of Marguerite de Navarre. The Duke de Nemours opposed the suit, backed by the powerful influence of the Catholic family d'Guise. The court of Rome denied her suit and declared her child illegitimate; the Duke de Nemours was awarded dispensation to marry the widow of the Duke d'Guise. Françoise sought refuge in Navarre and spent the remainder of her life in sorrow and obscurity.[lxxiii]

Jeanne returned to Pau with her questioned right of sovereignty settled by the ruling obtained in Lyons. In her absence unrest and turmoil had threatened the provinces as Montluc spread rebellion and discontent. The Count de Grammont had taken appropriate measures to put down the treasonous forces in the Lower countries, and when Jeanne returned, her diplomatic efforts and sovereign right began to calm those upsets.

In spite of continuing to take measures against upheaval in the lower provinces, Lower Navarre had risen again in revolt, agitated by the urging of the ecclesiastics upset by the edicts that denied them from practicing their ceremonies. Jeanne's suspicions grew when, on closer inspection, she noted the uprisings appeared to be planned in a coordinated order, each insurrection closer to Pau. She also received news of Spanish forces gathering on the other side of the Pyrenees, led by King Philip of Spain. Jeanne received explanation by courier that the purpose of the troops of the Spanish monarch had arrived in Tarragona to expel the last of the Moors from his domains.[lxxiv]

As the Queen pondered these pieces of news, a notice came of the presence of a courier from the French ambassador who asked for urgent admission to meet with her.

23. The Divide Deepens

"There shall no man be able to stand before you; the Lord your God shall lay the dread of you and the fear of you on all the land on which you set foot, as He has spoken to you."

Deuteronomy 11:25 (NASB)

The courier from the French ambassador laid before the Queen a plot so unbelievable, a plan so evil and vicious in design that it staggered Jeanne in horrified astonishment.

The King of Spain, Pope Pius IV, Cardinal de Lorraine, Cardinal de Armagnac, the former Chamberlain to King Antoine, marshal d'Montluc, and unfortunately, the Cardinal d'Bourbon, had joined forces and planned in careful detail a plot to seize Queen Jeanne and her daughter from their castle of Pau. They would then be transported to the nearest location of the court of Spanish Inquisition in Madrid. Prince Henry was already under the custody of the King of France. The initial forces had arrived and now hid among the citizens in Pau. The courier urged the Queen to immediately leave Pau and flee to the protection of the King of France.

Jeanne dismissed the courier and pondered the information she received. The message told her that the exposure of the plot had hinged on an unexplainable, unexpected turn of events.

An unknown disgruntled subject of Béarn named Diamanche, who harbored hatred for the anti-Catholic edicts ordered by Queen

Jeanne, was included in the discussions among the originators of the evil plan. His insignificant part was to notify the King of Spain when Montluc had infiltrated the areas around Pau and was in place. On his journey to inform King Philip for that purpose, he was stricken ill and delayed to find shelter in a small village in the Pyrenees where his condition worsened, so that all about him believed he was dying.

A young and devoted valet of Queen Elisabeth, Jeanne's affectionate goddaughter, whose job was delivering messages between the Spanish king and his wife, was unoccupied at the time, so he was sent to determine the condition of the ill man. The valet was not privy to the plans of the terrible plot; moreover, he was staunchly loyal to his royal mistress. While attending Diamanche, who was delirious with a high fever, the valet listened to vague rantings of the sick man about the inevitable results of a plot against the Queen of Navarre. With little effort and probing questions, the valet eventually heard enough to cause him great alarm.

Surprisingly, Diamanche rallied and began to recover. By then, the valet had carried the disturbing information to his mistress, Queen Elisabeth. Elisabeth had great affection for her godmother and in shock and fear for her wellbeing, alerted the ambassador to France, Everard Saint Suplice, to warn the Queen of Navarre immediately.[lxxv]

Jeanne, alone in her chamber after receiving such a dire warning, dropped to her knees and sought the wisdom of her great God. She did not ask for help for herself; she begged to be able to sufficiently protect her children and the people of her royal responsibilities. Jeanne was appalled that so many of the most influential forces in Europe had directed their hatred toward her for so many years, and had ultimately united to plot and carry out this evil move to strip her, a legitimate, equivalent sovereign, of her royal treasures, her beloved children and her own life.

As she meditated on the promises of God's love and salvation so evident in the scriptures she studied daily, she prayed that God would do as He had said in His Word. She asked to be gathered under the shelter of His wings like a mother hen gathers her chicks. She thanked Him that He held her in the palm of His hand.

She reminded God of His promise in Isaiah 41:10-13, (NASB) *"Fear not, for I am with thee, do not anxiously look about you, for I am your God. I will strengthen you, surely I will help you, surely I will uphold you with My righteous right hand. Behold, all those who are angered against you will be shamed and dishonored; those who contend with you will be as nothing and will perish. You will seek those who quarrel with you, but will not find them, those who war with you will be as nothing, and non-existent. For I am the Lord your God, who upholds your right hand, who says to you, do not fear, I will help you."*

In Isaiah 42:6, (NASB) *"I am the Lord, I have called you in righteousness, I will also hold you by the hand and watch over you, and I will appoint you as a covenant to the people, as a light to the nations."*

In Isaiah 43:1b-3a, (NASB) *"Do not fear, for I have redeemed you; I have called you by name; you are Mine! When you pass through the waters, I will be with you; and through the rivers, they will not overflow you. When you walk through the fire, you will not be scorched, nor will the flame burn you, for I am the Lord your God, The Holy One of Israel, your Savior."*

And in Romans 8:31(NASB): *"What do we say then to these things? If God is for us, who is against us?"*

Jeanne prayed in faith that God, having been faithful through all the troubled years past, would not now abandon her in this current peril. The Queen rose from her knees strengthened in her spirit and fired off a series of orders to commence defenses, restock, and strengthen the fortresses of her kingdom. Then she quietly moved her daughter and Maddie with her to her strongest fortress of Navarreins and waited, stocked with ample supplies for a long and arduous siege.

The Queen of Navarre, safe behind the walls of her fortress, wrote to Catherine de Medici denouncing the cruel and treacherous plot. She claimed that King Philip had aimed a lethal blow at all sovereign heads in Europe by threatening her, a sovereign Queen. She demanded punishment for all who had joined the conspiracy.

Catherine de Medici responded that she was 'amazed at the revelation of the abhorrent plot'; however, no investigation or punishment was allowed to proceed. She gave no reason for her refusal to hold those high powered conspirators accountable, and Diamanche went unpunished in spite of the Queen of Navarre's continued inquiries and demands. Finally, the Queen Mother sent a resolute message to end the discussion: the Protestants had planned similar plots against their kings, and Queen Jeanne and her family were unharmed; therefore she considered the matter ended.

During the weeks of confinement at Navarreins, Queen Jeanne again devoted herself to search and study the ancient codes of her kingdom. She made significant changes and rewrote many of the codes which no longer were effective or beneficial to the citizens of her provinces, especially the southern portions of the kingdom. She presented the new codes to each of the provinces for approval. Those former provinces so plagued with discontent over their sovereign received the changes with applause, recognizing her care and attention to their interests.

24. God's Oversight Continues

"And you shall know the truth, and the truth shall make you free."

John 8:32 (NASB)

J eanne had no sooner left the safety of her fortress of Navarreins, returning to her residence at Pau to celebrate Christmas, than she received correspondence that the Queen Mother and King Charles IX would resume their progress about the kingdom of France, inspecting each of their defensive forces, weather permitting.

In January of 1565, winter set in with brutal force. All the rivers of France froze for several weeks, and the roads were blocked with snow, making travel and communication nearly impossible. While touring, the King and his party became stranded for ten days at Carcassone when six feet of snow fell, delaying their journey. The Queen Mother had planned this long excursion with an excuse, which she acknowledged publically, to reunite with her daughter, Queen Elisabeth, King Philip's consort, at Bayonne, located inside the territories of the Queen of Navarre.

When the traveling party of the court of France finally reached Bayonne in July under the veil of a mother's visit to her daughter, it concealed a more ominous hidden intent to plan a final solution to the all-absorbing pestilential, political dilemma of the 16th century—the suppression of heresy. Initially requested by Pope Pius IV, King Philip arranged the meeting.

Queen Elisabeth was unaware of the underlying evil purposes of the visit arranged by her husband and her mother. Determined to ensure that no whispered information would indicate the existence of clandestine meetings, Catherine de Medici organized these secret conferences to be held in attached quarters of her daughter's apartments in the dead of night while the young Queen was sleeping. Those who attended came through a secret passage from the Queen Mother's compartments to the outer chamber of the young Queen.

The Queen of Navarre had been forced to take to her bed as the stresses of so many attempts on her sovereign prerogatives had again raised the symptoms of her persistent illness. Her physical energies depleted, Jeanne's active and inquiring mind worked overtime searching for what might be the purpose of such festivities held in one of her cities. Her curiosity grew more intense when it became evident, as Queen of the territory of the festivities, Jeanne had not received an invitation to attend. The puzzling question of why she had not been invited by her goddaughter and friend, Queen Elisabeth if only to embrace her or to honor the common decency of one sovereign to another, seemed strange.

King Philip arranged extravagant daily activities of jousts, parades, balls, fêtes and pompous pageants to honor his consort and her mother, Queen Catherine, and to distract those who were with the French King from knowing the actual purpose of the selected few who arrived by specific invitation. The courtiers and damsels of the French court believed the entertainments were for their pleasure.

King Charles included Prince Henry of Navarre in his entourage. Catherine de Medici had intended that her son, the King, be surrounded by the best and brightest counselors. At twelve-years-old, the Prince had developed a keen, wise and upright character, an inheritance from his mother. The Queen Mother saw only the pleasure-seeking evidence in the developing young man and insisted that he be included in the royal party because he was the brightest and wisest representative for the Béarnois.

Although the Prince did not know of the secret midnight meetings, he was born with his mother's discernment, and while participating in the daily fêtes in the Queen Mother's chambers, he positioned himself where he was able to overhear Catherine's secret conversations in that public place. When he heard a remark made to Queen Catherine by the Duke de Alba, Bishop of Pampeluna, minister and favorite counselor of Spain's King Philip, his persistence brought reward. He sent word to Queen Jeanne that he had overheard the Duke d'Alba remark 'the only way to tranquilize the nation and subdue the disaffection of the princes was to obliterate all adherents of heresy, with no exception of royal blood, by a massacre in the manner of the Sicilian Vespers.'[lxxvi] That name was well known to signify a cruel slaughter that began at the sound of evening vesper bells on Sicily in 1482. D'Alba continued, insisting that it should be the intention of the King to exact from every noble of France the pledge of a profession of faith, exposing any to death that refused to adopt the doctrine of the Roman Church.

Jeanne received this information from her most trusted informant with little need for contemplation; she now understood the fabricated façade being held in Bayonne. Without delay, Jeanne immediately sent word to the Duke d'Condé, to the Admiral de Coligny, to Cardinal Châtillon and all the leaders of the Huguenots. Fortunately, these eminent Huguenots heeded these warnings in equal haste and each, in turn, took measures to move their families away from their current accommodations to secure a haven in a safe fortress. It was only by hours that the targeted individuals escaped the evil plots on their lives.

When the royal cavalcade left Bayonne and proceeded on its journey of inspection it soon arrived at the ancestral castle of the Queen of Navarre, at Nérac. Jeanne received the French court with all manner of magnificent pomp and splendor that she had been witness to in the courts of the King of France, Francis I, and her royal parents of Navarre. Though the perfidious meetings so recently held in Bayonne were fresh in the minds of Queen Jeanne and those of her guests, no evidence appeared in the gracious demeanors and conversations of any of the parties.

When the entertainments and ceremonies were concluding, Jeanne indicated she would be accompanying King Charles and his regent mother, in the company of Prince Henry, as the traveling court moved on to Paris. When the travelers reached Moulins, word reached Jeanne of difficulties arising in her southern regions, and she was pressed to deal with them. Requesting a leave of the King to proceed to Vendôme to tend to her government, she also asked the King that Prince Henry might join her to meet his ancestral subjects in that great city of his father. Jeanne left immediately to go to Vendôme with Prince Henry.

Catherine de Medici was incensed when she learned of the King's granted permission as she had never planned for Prince Henry to escape from her control; however the young King Charles had not been included in that confidence.

When another uprising of revolt rose against Jeanne's sovereignty, the Queen of Navarre found she was forced to proceed immediately to Pau to attend to the matters of governing these unsettled displays. Once back inside the borders of Béarn, with her son safely beside her, Jeanne wrote to King Charles that emergencies of government had forced her return to Béarn and she now determined to keep her son under her care. Catherine was infuriated that Jeanne had cleverly out-maneuvered the Queen Mother's grip on such a valuable hostage.

The apparent persistent hatred harbored by the leaders of the Catholic faith had neither diminished nor disappeared. The Huguenots throughout France and Navarre were again subject to the wrath of Catholic forces who harvested from the countryside the innocent victims condemned to the threshing floor of the dreaded Inquisition.

The continuing battle between those who believed in truth as presented in the Bible and those who chose to adhere to practices and false precepts arranged by men for their gain and control devastated France.

The plots against the Huguenots in general, and against Queen Jeanne and her children mainly, continued. At the core of each of these attacks were determined intentions of Pope Pius, King Philip, and the Cardinal de Lorraine, sworn to eliminate Queen Jeanne from the face of the earth. By methods only known to the Holy God who reads hearts and knows the intentions of every mind, continuing plot after evil plot was exposed and revealed in time to enable the appointed victims to escape the traps set against them.

During these trying days, Catherine de Medici demanded, wheedled and insisted that the Prince of Béarn return to her at court. Jeanne ignored these letters from the Queen Mother, determined never to release her son to the animosities of a Catholic power again.

The forces of the Reform Cause had chosen d'Condé as the military leader and with his leadership, and the unifying of the many troops throughout France, a strong push was made that again freed many cities from fear of the Inquisition trials. Retaliations against the ecclesiastics and priests that had imposed their demands on poor farmers and merchants and turned them over to the prisons on heresy charges fell soon on the backs of those unfortunate clergies in vengeful attacks. The armies of Charles IV were then sent to punish the citizens for their acts of revenge, and the Catholics rose in hatred to repay the despicable heretics.

More and more citizens of France were exploring the tenets of each faith, and multitudes turned their backs on the conviction that had sustained their ancestors, to follow a belief in a personal relationship with a savior that had given His own life for them. The truth shining through the scriptures that were now translated and printed for each person to read and ponder provided evidence for their own eyes, the reality of the faith they chose to believe.

In answer to the spread of heresy, the King's forces, formed to defeat the new faith, increased their efforts to demolish the contemptible virus. A great divide splintered across France with bloody massacres and vile butcheries in a second bloody war of religions.

Queen Jeanne, who God had gifted with an excellent command of oratory, met with the forces led by Condé and encouraged those who followed him to support the new faith.

"You who are firmly built up in the faith must now set an example of fortitude and resignation; to refuse to bow your knees to Baal. The blessed hour is at hand, when those who are of Israel must risk the loss of their worldly goods, to build temples wherein God may be adored in spirit and truth, with bodily worship, and with the homage of the heart, not where abominable idols are now enthroned in front of a mighty and jealous God."[lxxvii]

25. A Great Pardon

"For I know whom I have believed and I am convinced
that He is able to guard what I have entrusted to Him
until that day."

2 Timothy 1:12b (NASB)

Two years passed after Queen Jeanne removed Prince Henry from the clutches of Catherine de Medici to within the boundaries of her kingdom. Jeanne considered this accomplishment one of the most miraculous of her thirty-five years of life. At last her most precious treasures were free of the evil entanglements and its immoral influences of the French court.

During this time, the Queen of Navarre had joined Prince d'Condé at the gatherings of his troops to encourage their bravery and praise their efforts. Prince Henry had captured the hearts of the Huguenots, and they had bowed in homage to him as their future king. Jeanne supervised his further education, providing a preceptor for both her children. Under Jeanne's diligent supervision, Prince Henry added wisdom and knowledge to his brilliant mind, military acumen and skills by training, and courteous, gentlemanly graces. The progress of her children warmed the heart of their mother and brought her great joy. Their presence near her was her greatest delight.

A year later in July 1567, the time came for her to concede to the most difficult emotional battle up to that point, Jeanne d'Albret, mother and Queen released her son to take his place at Condé's side as joint commander of the Huguenot armies. Prince Henry rode away to do battle in front of men dedicated to being used by God and to fight for their Queen, the God of their faith and for the two men who led them.

Jeanne's heart and mind had always been with the brave men who fought and gave their lives for the faith they believed. Now, she obsessed with the reports of actions of the troops. She studied maps and analyzed the moves taking place on her chessboard of France. More than once she thought back to the life-changing game of chess she had played with M. Bourbon in the Library of Chateau de Plessis for the salvation of her kingdom of Navarre. As she had concentrated every fiber of her being, her mind, her wisdom, her insights, to win that board game so many years ago, she now applied even more diligently all the gifts at her disposal with even greater energy.

Along with the struggles to advise and direct the leaders of the troops, it happened that the clergy in Lower Navarre and Foix rebelled and formed a league to end the life of their sovereign Queen and her son and kill all the Protestants living in the principality of Navarre. They vowed to re-establish the dominance of the Roman Faith. The nine clergymen signed their names in blood, so determined were they to see their plans fulfilled. When Jeanne's presence was requested to hear the testimony of one of the conspirators who had turned traitor and brought news of the plot, it was the first she heard of the rebellion. When Jeanne listened to their plans, she immediately commanded troops to bring the cities of Lescar and Oléron under submission. The league of conspirators had already set their policies and initiated actions, and before the soldiers could reach the town of Oléron, had massacred hundreds of the Protestant townspeople. The culprits were pursued by the troops, arrested, tried and sentenced to death.

The basis of the rebellion by the clergy was their disagreement with the recent proclamation issued by Queen Jeanne. Jeanne called the heads of each of her principalities to a council in Pau. She also requested that Prince Henry return from the battlefield to attend. On the first day of the council gathering, when the Queen addressed the chamber, she outlined the condition of the country, revealed her plans to bring about a united kingdom, established her intention to enforce the edict under objection, presented Prince Henry, and ended by announcing a royal act of grace.

Rather than seek vengeance for those who had led the rebellion and to those who had sought her life and carried out the despicable murders in Oléron, Queen Jeanne granted a full and complete pardon.[lxxviii] This royal pardon was heartily protested by many of the leaders of the principalities as the town of Oléron still filled with wailing and bloodshed as a result of such unlawful violence.

The day after the gathering of the council, a delegation of citizens of Foix and Lower Navarre requested an audience and protested again the hated edict that suppressed the Roman Catholic religion as the dominant faith. She assured the committee she determined to enforce the decree to suppress the Catholic faith, as "she was willing to tolerate its profession, but denied its ascendancy," and dismissed them.

Unfortunately, peace and goodwill were not among the results of the Queen's efforts to follow the example of the unmerited grace of her God.

26. Battle Weary

*"Therefore, since we have this ministry, as we received
mercy we do not lose heart, but we have renounced
the things hidden because of shame, not walking in
craftiness or adulterating the word of God, but by the
manifestation of truth commending ourselves to every
man's conscience in the sight of God."*

2 Corinthians 4:1-2 (NASB)

Maddie, Queen Jeanne's faithful lady-in-waiting, had persevered
at Jeanne's side through all the travels, banquets, balls, escapes,
perils and dangers. She had devotedly attended to packing and
unpacking, to repairing and mending thousands of dresses and to
caring for her Queen in sickness and in health. Love impelled her
never to falter. She was devoted to her mistress and served without
complaint, though her age had crept up on her in spite of her dedicated service. Nevertheless, her aching joints and diminishing
energy eventually began to gain the upper hand even though she
enlisted younger ladies to help her with her tasks. Maddie had to
acknowledge the twenty-five extra years of her age over that of her
mistress was a significant matter. She was tired.

Not only had her age caused consternation, but she also lived
with an overwhelming burden of grief. The love of her mistress for
the people in the principalities of Navarre had become her love. She
grieved as she accompanied her Lady through the provinces and

witnessed the terrible aftermath of massacres and bloody rebellions. Her eyes could not forget the orphaned children, the broken bodies, the gracious women torn to pieces and flung like garbage on the heaps of corpses. Her mind reeled at the evil that had stripped the countryside of every vestige of dignity, had invaded homes, had torn at the fiber of families, and had instigated such lawlessness it reduced men to beasts.

Maddie accompanied her mistress everywhere, inwardly in awe of the Queen's ability to observe and rise above the grief and shock to inspire and encourage the survivors who wandered in a nightmare of loss and broken dreams. The Queen always reassured her people to stand firm in their faith and not be comforted by the promises of peace offered in exchange for the damnation of their mortal souls. Maddie had listened to her Queen's speeches and private musings enough to know in the deepest core of her own heart that this despicable war battled for the souls of men. Such horrible persecution against ordinary men, because they seek to serve the true God rejecting the rituals designed by men to supplant the power and grace of the one Christ, was unthinkable. Precise observation of the real truth in the mind of the old maid could not fathom the depth of evil in the hearts of the clergy struck blind and deaf to the calls of God.

Her tender mercies, as she nursed her majesty through the increasing bouts of illness, were not for the Queen only; her caring touch was her only weapon against the overwhelming disarray of the world around her. She observed her lady closely, knowing the increasing stress of leadership along with the accumulation of scenes of devastation about the Queen would soon trigger another relapse of her old sickness.

Maddie heard the rumors spread by other servants employed in service to the Queen, whispering how their majesty the Queen must surely be losing her grip on sanity as she sat for long periods seemingly unconscious of the world around her, staring into space until aroused by a direct question. Maddie understood because she had seen the same scenes that must be replaying in the Queen's mind. Maddie spoke no rebuke because she knew all the others could not comprehend what they had not seen. She had seen and continually prayed that God would shepherd the mind of her mistress and strengthen her to continue to fight in His service.

The war was not going well. After many battles and deaths, the Catholics eventually captured and killed the great Prince d'Condé. Prince Henry and Condé's son then joined the Admiral Coligny to unite with his troops. The death of the brave Condé was a significant loss for the Queen for she had loved him like a brother. He had displayed in his life all the attributes deficient in his brother, Antoine.

The anguish of Queen Jeanne increased as the Protestants began to run out of funds. Jeanne wrote to Queen Elizabeth of England and sought her help. Jeanne offered the valued diamond and ruby jewels long held in the vaults of her Navarre ancestors to the Queen of England, also a Protestant. Queen Elizabeth responded and agreed to send troops and supplies in return. Sympathetic to the Protestant cause which had resulted in such devastation in France and Navarre by both sides, Elizabeth promised to treasure the items in her care until Queen Jeanne could reclaim them at a time in the future.

27. Who Can Stand?

"For momentary, light affliction is producing for us an
eternal weight of glory far beyond all comparison."

2 Corinthians 4:17 (NASB)

A t the death of Condé, the Catholic rebels in the southern provinces of the kingdom of Navarre again turned against their
Queen and provided inroads for the Spanish troops along the
Pyrenees Mountains to move in and overtake the southern states
of Foix and Lower Navarre. The cleansing efforts of the Spanish
forces soon had diminished or forced into hiding any Protestant
believers. From there the Spanish troops proceeded to move north
and aligned with the marauders of Montluc until they had gained
control of all the fortresses inside Béarn. Slaughter was rampant,
and many people escaped with only their lives, fleeing to secret
hideouts unknown even to friends and relatives. Jeanne, who had
joined the Huguenot leaders in La Rochelle, watched in dismay as
her kingdom crumbled.

Queen Jeanne gathered to her the viscounts that had been
leading the battles against the Catholics and had been failing so
miserably at their task, to discover where their problems lay. It
became evident that the bickering and back-biting among these
leaders had destroyed their effectiveness in the war. Jeanne called
on the Constable de Montmorency who had recently returned from
exile in England after fleeing when he had killed Henry II on the

field of tournaments held for the wedding celebration of Henry II's daughter Elisabeth to King Philip of Spain. Montmorency had been so humiliated by his part in the unfortunate accident he had felt unable to show his face in his native France. The Wars of Religion that raged in France prompted him to return. Before Antoine d'Vendôme had surrendered his allegiance to the Romish Church, Constable de Montmorency had been an encourager for Antoine to assume his rightful place of power as the first prince of the blood. He had returned to France to try to convince Antoine of his obligation to live up to the history of his renowned ancestors and was present at the siege of Rouen where Antoine died. The Constable de Montmorency possessed the most brilliant military mind of that time but the burden of guilt that plagued him from the time of the accident would not release him.

Queen Jeanne called the Constable in front of the viscounts at her command and appointed him lieutenant-general of all the forces of her kingdom. The reluctant warrior bowed before the will of his sovereign as she bestowed on him unlimited authority. Jeanne called on the Constable as a tried and trusty combatant, the last resort to free her subjects and to relieve their sufferings from the terror of the opposing forces. The edicts she had published had been abolished, and the reformed believers in her towns barred from worship. Her heart committed to sacrifice everything she possessed to right the wrongs of sacks and pillages against her people.

Constable de Montmorency rose to meet her faith in him and with his loyal army, swept through the southern provinces, banished the captains and commands, then moved north with such speed, his troops met only one battle of resistance. Reports received by Jeanne indicated great confusion in the Catholic forces. The leaders seemed to be accepting conflicting orders, strangely retreating from skirmishes instead of advancing. Confidential spies blamed the confusing laws on Catherine de Medici's involvement in the plans of the war of the Catholics, by detaining one captain and ordering another to hold steady or move forward, as she endeavored to maintain the balance of power between the Catholic forces to ensure her power over both. Queen Jeanne dismissed these conjectures of her spies. She was convinced that the hand of God was in control of the battle, not the minuscule, feeble attempts of Catherine de Medici to keep her grasp on the scepter of France.

As d'Montmorency marched north through the provinces of Navarre, the nobles and ordinary folk crawled from their hiding places and joined the army, swelling to an enormous number. Conquering besieged cities and freeing towns from bloody persecutions along the way, Montmorency marched across the provinces nearly unchallenged and posted the flag of d'Albret on the castle of Béarn. In fourteen days he had reclaimed Queen Jeanne's domains, conquered the occupied city of Orthez, routed the royal armies, took their leading general prisoner, and arrested the rebellious barons who had plagued the southern provinces of Navarre for twenty years, finally planting the flag of the Queen on the ramparts of Pau on August 23, 1569. He faithfully followed the orders of the Queen; his stern, commanding fervor for terrible justice directed toward all who had treacherously acted in rebellion against their Queen. Jeanne's last words to the constable after she gave him unlimited power had been, "Go, valiant Montmorency, go and free Béarn! Smite the traitors and those guilty nobles whom no past clemency has been able to subdue." [lxxix]

Montmorency determined the course of swift justice and summarily executed the barons. Barons who had conspired with the royal troops in other states of Navarre, upon receiving news of the justice meted out by Montmorency in the Queen's stead, fled to the mountains and disappeared within the boundaries of Italy and France.

Montmorency accomplished all that the Queen of Navarre requested and on her orders, proceeded with his army to wait at Condom to join with the forces of Admiral Coligny and jointly bring the strength of their troops on Languedoc.

28 Queen and Warrior

*"Let love be without hypocrisy. Abhor what is evil; cling
to what is good."*

Romans 12:9 (NASB)

In October 1569, Coligny had laid siege of Poiters against the
Duke d'Guise, son of the deceased François d'Guise. Duke
d'Anjou, a twisted, vengeful man and younger brother of Charles
IX joined with the young Duke d'Guise in defense of Poiters.
Between the two brave royal admirals, the battle was fierce and
deadly against the siege of Coligny. The fight only lasted two hours,
with the defeat of the courageous Huguenots bloody and brief. In
the midst of the melee, Coligny met a general commanding the
German mercenaries in the royal army who shot him in the face.
Coligny recovered his balance in the saddle and disregarding his
massive injury, shot his assailant dead on the spot. The Huguenots
rallied their troops around Coligny and retreated rapidly to regather
forces at a nearby town, turning their backs on the savage slaughter
commenced by the German mercenaries against all left on the field
of battle.

The Huguenots carried their renowned general by litter to safety
and left him alone in a tent, injured and untended, as they sat about
their fires and discussed the failure of the battle. Nursing their emotions, they laid blame at the feet of the unfortunate Coligny who

could neither defend himself nor even speak in answer to their accusations.

Word had traveled quickly to the Queen who was still in residence at La Rochelle. Her response was to take to her horse immediately and disregarding her safety, speed to the encampment to offer her support and encouragement to the defeated troops. When she arrived to find the grievously wounded Coligny abandoned, unattended and isolated by his officers, the Queen was indignantly appalled to see this renowned fighter treated with such disrespect. She was overcome with fury and publically expressed her opinion of the selfish ingratitude of the officers.[lxxx]

The admiral saw the Queen enter the opening of his tent and believed an angel came from heaven for his rescue. Tears moistened the cheeks of the stern warrior as he clasped the royal hand stretched so compassionately towards him. The admiral was deserted by his officers and the nobles, who showed no pity for his deplorable condition, and by all his friends. Only one woman, who displayed none of the frailties in common with her fair sex, heroically advanced to the camp to encourage and comfort the afflicted, and to re-establish order in the affairs of the defeated troops.[lxxxi]

Immediately after her arrival and care of the admiral, Jeanne called a council of all the confederated princes of the Huguenot army. She issued several resolutions of war, inspired the troops, proclaimed the excellence of the injured Coligny, sent emissaries to surrounding countries to seek help, restocked supplies from her purse, and raised the disheartened soldiers to their former level of prestige and pride. She appointed her son and the Duke d'Condé as joint commanders of the army. They had previously fought with the Admiral Coligny to learn his wisdom of battle, but he had only allowed them to observe from afar. By her command, Jeanne placed her only son in harm's way for the sake of her country. Lastly, the Queen assumed the responsibility of defending La Rochelle and sent the remaining army to meet up with Montmorency's troops to winter and recoup, ordering that January of 1570 should open with a campaign invading Languedoc, orders which her officers adopted with renewed purpose.

A message sent by one of the captains after the armies' safe arrival to join with Montmorency, reported, "Our escape was owing to the imprudence of the Catholics. They despised our prowess; but like a ball of snow they allowed us to roll along the ground while gradually our dimensions augmented until we had grown into a mass, the size of a house."

The movement of the Huguenot armies which dismissed the Catholic forces stemmed from a fierce struggle of jealousy in the house of Catherine de Medici. King Charles resented the fame of his younger brother, Duke d'Anjou whose prominence of military skills garnered credit for the victories. Charles felt the fetters that held him tightly under the direction and decisions of his mother and could only push against her dominance by countermanding the orders she issued to his troops.[lxxxii] Upon hearing this bit of information from her spies, Jeanne thanked God over and over for His constant overwatch, "For God is not a God of confusion, but of peace."

Without a doubt, the confusion and delayed retaliation could not last long. Although the Huguenot troops passed through the land with a limited sacrifice of lives of the inhabitants, the hate of the Catholic forces had been fanned to such a fever pitch of revenge by the royals of France and the family of d'Guise that their armies left a swath of slaughter and bloody retribution in their wake.

Princess Catherine attended her mother when she moved from castle to castle in her efforts to continue upholding the freedoms of the kingdoms of Navarre. Princess Catherine, then in her twelfth year of age, had inherited her mother's rare mind and demure demeanor, reciprocating with her every fiber the love and devotion of her dear mother. They had an unusual relationship of intimacy and respect.

Within the castle of La Rochelle love and affection reigned. Without, the territories adjacent to La Rochelle were ravaged by combat between the rivals. The Huguenot leader commanding the reformed forces was the valiant La Noue who led a victorious battle against the Catholics at a small village of St. Gemme. La Noue was wounded by a ball that fractured his arm, and he was forced to retreat to La Rochelle to seek medical aid. The castle doctors did their best but were unable to save his arm, as gangrene had set in and La Noue was faced with amputation or soon death. His friends and doctors implored the brave warrior to proceed immediately to have the arm removed as every second he waited endangered his life and soon it would be too late. La Noue insisted that it would be no life without two arms and he preferred death. One of his friends, so grieved by his refusal while his peril mounted, sought out the Queen for her interference.

The Queen soon stood at his bedside, gently requesting him to yield to the requests of his friends; otherwise, the cause of the Huguenots would be diminished, and his wisdom and example lost. She urged him to continue to provide his brave example to his fellow soldiers and to endure every opportunity offered to prolong that inspiration. The Queen reminded La Noue of his duty to his country and his faith, to persevere in life so that he, on the inevitable event of his death, might be secure in having fulfilled his duty to the last.

La Noue, so vanquished by the words and emotions of concern by the Queen, relented and agreed to have the arm removed. The Queen immediately called the doctors and remained at the bedside to tenderly remove the bloodied bandages from over the wound. She then held his arm secure while the doctors proceeded to sever the arm, speaking in quiet undertones words of comfort and encouragement. During La Noue's convalescence, the Queen continued her friendly care; she sought out a famous machinist, who fabricated an iron arm, most ingeniously contrived so that La Noue was enabled to guide his horse. Throughout the remainder of his life, La Noue served his Queen with dedication and devotion. Whenever speaking of the removal of his arm, he would become awash with emotions at the Queen's sympathy and care for him at that time.[lxxxiii]

29. Evil Veiled

*"There will be tribulation and distress for every soul of
man who does evil . . ."*

Romans 2:9 (NASB)

The successes of the Huguenot armies under the command of
Montmorency had soon moved to within a league of Paris
after their path of successive victories. It became evident to King
Charles IX and Catherine de Medici that treaty must be sought to
avoid total conquest. Between mother and son, animosity and distrust boiled and prohibited any common agreement on their designs.

King Charles sent generous offers of peace to Queen Jeanne. He
offered conditions most agreeable to the future of the Huguenots.
Catherine, entirely of a different mind, agreed to conduct the negotiations, while behind the scenes, in her usual duplicitous maneuvers, she fostered plans and conspirators of a like mind to dupe
the Huguenots into a vulnerable position and then slaughter them
all at one time.

Jeanne stood gazing out a window in the highest garret of
La Rochelle. Her mind was so focused on the difficulties of her
kingdom she didn't register the incredible landscape bathed in the
golden light of the setting sun. Longing to return to the familiar
surroundings of her ancestral castle in Pau, the Queen was weary;
every muscle in her body hurt from the jarring swiftness of galloping horseback through countryside and villages of a war-torn,

devastated land. How genuinely she wanted to see this immoral war end. The latest correspondence from King Charles IX encouraged the Queen of Navarre to reciprocate and enter into negotiations immediately to accept his offers, for the good of the people and the much-desired peace in the land. She sighed because her whole being longed to find hope in these recent offers of peace, then shook her head and turned from the window.

The articles presented for treaty permitted the Huguenots to celebrate their worship publicly in two towns in every province throughout the realm. Every individual was declared to be at liberty to profess the Reformed Faith, without dread of persecution. The Huguenots were to be admitted equal rights with their Roman Catholic fellow-subjects to partake in the benefit of all public institutions. They were likewise declared eligible to fill every post in the state. The King proposed to publish a general amnesty for all past offenses and to announce the Queen of Navarre, her son, and the prince of Condé his loyal and faithful subjects. All protestant estates confiscated were to be restored. The King, moreover, permitted his Protestant subjects of the south to appeal from the judgment of the parliament of Toulouse, hitherto irrevocable, to his majesty's Masters of Request.

Finally, the King consented to permit the Huguenots to retain possession of the towns of La Rochelle, Cognac, Charite, and Montauban, as conquests achieved by their arms. A condition stipulated that the princes of Navarre and Condé, with forty of the Huguenot chieftains, bound themselves to "restore these towns to the crown of France, two years after the faithful execution of this edict of pacification." She believed all to be empty promises.

Too long Jeanne had watched the duplicitous promises of the Queen Mother and her sons evaporate like a wisp in the wind. Nothing was beyond the selfish methods of these monarchs to maintain their iron grip on power and wealth and eradicate any opposition with deadly devices. The barons of Béarn and Queen Jeanne's counselors, blinded by these offers of peace, could see no reason to debate these conditions and they put increasing pressure on their mistress to agree and put an end to the devastation of war.

Jeanne could find no reason to dispute their orders except for the pervading cloud of distrust that darkened any hope in her that these offers of peace were anything but a front to achieve a darker motive. History and perception were powerful forces that had continually supported Jeanne's decision-making prowess, and she persisted in doubt and hesitation. Eventually, to establish his good will, King Charles sent his offer of conditions to his parliament and obtained their approval. The requirements were submitted to Jeanne at La Rochelle for her signature of the agreement.

Admiral Coligny and the Huguenot army were in no condition to further the combat, desiring the comforts of home and bed. The barons, having read of the restoration of all confiscated estates, were ecstatic and impatient to return to their normal lives. Jeanne, in her wisdom, could not understand why the conditions that had been offered and indignantly rejected only three months ago were now agreed to promptly without protest. Catherine de Medici was renowned for her patient processes of revenge against those she hated, and Jeanne wondered, "Can the Queen who never pardons, pardon me?" Convinced that this peace was clothed in black to conceal a coming calamity of vastly darker destruction, Jeanne hesitated.

The pressure from the barons was unmerciful for their Queen to agree and sign the agreement offered. As a body, they could only see a future of peace and prosperity for their families, and soon a malevolent spirit spread within the council threatening disappointment at the stubbornness of their Queen. Since the Queen stood alone in her objections, she agreed to the peace on the 26th day of August 1570.[lxxxiv] The celebrations of her people were limited to the peals of bells, resounding guns fired on the ramparts of La Rochelle and cheers for King Charles, Queen Jeanne, and Prince Henry. Then the populace went back to the monotony of their lives.

Jeanne kept her troops active even though she allowed them to return to their home provinces, in case she should need them at a moment's notice. No cordiality or trust appeared in spite of the proclamation of peace. As the weeks went on, King Charles neglected to activate the clauses of the edict of pacification, plus word reached La Rochelle that the King of Spain had sent to

Charles a force of 3,000 horse and 6,000-foot soldiers, "in case he might need them."

Most threatening to Jeanne was the warmly solicitous notes she received almost daily from Catherine de Medici requesting her to proceed to court, accompanied by her son. At first, the Queen Mother professed an urgent need for the Queen and Prince of Navarre to attend the upcoming marriage of King Charles and Elizabeth, daughter of the emperor Maximilian II. Jeanne suspected that the Queen Mother was intent on her presence at court to take her captive. This belief increased as the requests grew more demanding and insistent.

King Charles and the court were so enraged that the Queen and Prince would not remove from the safety of La Rochelle that a courier was sent to inquire of Queen Jeanne why she so tenaciously declined to attend to the court. The courier presented the question and received a politic answer of the needs of the governing of her provinces that prohibited her from being absent from her kingdom. A subsequent offer arrived of the King and Queen Mother's desire to negotiate the marriage of the King's sister, Margaret de Valois to Prince Henry of Navarre, as a final and absolute reunion of France's opposing factions. Jeanne declined, remarking that she would not be persuaded to leave her kingdom until receiving a document that would lay out the conditions of the contract of marriage, considering the two parties were of differing faiths, for her to consider.

Jeanne was uncomfortably astonished at the perseverance of King Charles as he continued to adamantly demand her presence at the court in St. Germain to resume negotiations on the marriage contract, especially after he had sent an additional courier with suggested points of condition for her to consider. Again, Jeanne refused to depart from La Rochelle, more suspicious than ever of the unlikely overtures of the King. Another courier was dispatched, reassuring the Queen of Navarre that measures had been taken to obtain the dispensation of the Pope for Margaret to marry a non-Catholic and to allow the marriage of such close kin as two cousins. This offer, Charles insisted, contained evidence enough of his good intentions to enable Jeanne to proceed immediately to court to finalize the contract.

At the beginning of the year 1572, Queen Jeanne ventured to return to her castle at Pau, leaving the safety of La Rochelle to meet with the barons of Navarre. The barons vigorously voiced their desire to settle into a peaceful existence within their vast estates and to enjoy their families. Throughout Navarre and all of France, the leaders of the Huguenots became insistent for their Queen to proceed to the court of King Charles to negotiate the marriage contract which they could only see as a benefit to them. They believed the assurances of Catherine de Medici who had busily been making secret innuendoes that the Queen of Navarre delayed granting peace for her subjects by refusing the negotiations to insist on something more advantageous to her benefit. Catherine had undertaken careful measures to spread these odious rumors among the various provinces of Jeanne's sovereignty. She represented the behavior of Jeanne as a Princess of reckless ambition, ready to sacrifice the welfare of the realm to her resentments. These rumors slithered among Jeanne's subjects proclaiming falsehood as truth and eventually erupted causing angry accusations by the barons demanding Jeanne to negotiate a marriage of convenience to further peace with France by this alliance.

Another courier was dispatched from King Charles to Queen Jeanne, with a supposed final plea to achieve peace by completing negotiations at his court. Pressured from every side, Jeanne called together her state council. She hoped that these counselors would finally oppose the match so unrelentingly desired by the King and his mother. The august advisors assembled in Jeanne's presence had believed the promises of the royals of France and convinced by the ugly rumors, implored Jeanne to proceed immediately to St. Germain. Jeanne received their advice silently, then bowed her head and relented to the will of her council.[lxxxv]

Jeanne wrote to King Charles to tell him of her plans to make her appearance at his court. She then announced to her council that she was appointing Prince Henry her lieutenant-general in her absence and ordered that he continue to abide in Béarn until her return. The council responded with angry displeasure. Jeanne firmly withstood their representations and asserted her sovereign right to act as she pleased in the matter. She repeated that her son would not leave Béarn until she demanded his presence after the completion of the negotiations, and ordered that he would always be in the protection of 500 of her most trusted and most reliable troops. Jeanne knew too well the sort of people she was contending with and was resolute in her decision. Soon after, she left her ancestral home of Pau.

When Jeanne crossed the border of Béarn, a deep-felt depression weighed heavily on her spirit. Maddie, who sat across from her in the carriage observed a change in her demeanor, especially in her face. It seemed to droop and age, taking on a grayish cast. She watched her mistress closely, concerned that the stress of the past two years and the task that lay before her had brought on another attack of her chronic malady.

The Queen sat motionlessly, her eyes fixed on a distant spot, breathing evenly. It was a familiar aspect when the Queen was playing back the recent scenes of war and devastation. Within the quiet of her mind, Jeanne was acknowledging a fearful presentiment that her road was bearing her toward a dreaded end. Now, at forty-four years of age, she felt too tired to tackle further battles and could only summon courage and strength through prayer.

Images of Prince Henry filled her mind. He had changed a great deal since they had reunited in Bayonne. Jeanne shut her eyes and pictured him on that day when they had embraced with such love. They had traveled everywhere together as she introduced him to the principalities of his heritage. The citizens of her kingdom loved him, cheering the heir to the throne of Navarre with devotion and admiration. How proud she was to watch him interact among the barons with respect and humble command. He was naturally born to lead, and all who met him freely offered their loyalty and support. He had developed into a fine young man, chivalrous, courteous, astute, so very handsome, and admirable in his pursuits in the face of battle. Prince Henry, raised under the iron fist of Catherine de Medici had cherished the warnings of his Protestant mother and had maintained the true faith in his heart and spirit, though he had been forced for years to attend mass while at court.

Jeanne gazed out the window of the carriage, and her heart swelled in thanksgiving to her Lord Jesus Christ for blessing Henry with a discerning mind. Even being separated from her counsel and direction, he had seen through the smoke of deception and incense that clung to the presence of Catherine de Medici. Although the Queen Mother had indulged him in pursuits of pleasure, licentious living and games of chance in hopes of reducing the young prince to a manipulative pawn in her hands, Henry had maintained his upright conscience and devotion to his mother.

Jeanne contemplated the task before her and even more convinced in her exhaustion that the battle that lay ahead would be the toughest and most dangerous yet. She must endure this weary travel. What she could accomplish in these negotiations would decide the future of Navarre and all of France.

Jeanne looked at Maddie sitting across from her. She, too, was worn out. Her faithful maid had fallen asleep. Her mouth had dropped open, and she snored loudly. Jeanne looked away, unwilling to be disrespectful even though she had stared with eyes of love. They had grown old together, sharing one life. Jeanne treasured this loyal and trustworthy companion and made a mental note to arrange specific provision for her dear Maddie to retire in comfort and security when her service came to an end.

Jeanne's quick mind chided her at that thought. Who could say there would be any comfort and security left in France or Navarre in the future? Again, the profound disturbance of an evil presentiment engulfed her. She hoped that their evening stop would provide some rest for them both. Enduring the task of upholding a fragile, crystal hope for the future was exhausting.

When Queen Jeanne and her party arrived in Tours about the third week of January 1572, a message was received from the Queen Mother to remain there. The court was residing at Blois, and under careful questioning, the messenger revealed that a papal representative had arrived to persuade King Charles to betroth his sister to a Portuguese prince rather than the son of an excommunicated heretic. The courier also expressed that the Queen Mother, Princess Margaret, the widowed Princess d'Condé with her future daughter-in-law, Marie d'Cleves, would be visiting the following day. Jeanne had considered abiding at the Château de Plessis, but her trial was upon her, and she dismissed that idea, not wishing to inconvenience her coming visitors or her long-time friends at the Château.

Jeanne welcomed her distinguished guests the following morning and met for the first time the beautiful and bright Princess Margaret. Memories flooded her mind of the moment in the past when Margaret's father King Henry II had first encountered Prince Henry, at the age of five years, during a tense meeting with King Antoine and Queen Jeanne. It was at that meeting that the King became unexpectedly entranced by Prince Henry and he impulsively offered him the hand of his four-year-old daughter, Margaret. Jeanne was delighted with the demure grace and sharp wit of the Princess although she perceived the apparent pressure of her mother and her brother on the Princess to only say what she was told. In a letter to her son that evening she reported the loveliness of the Princess who had been induced to share her appreciation of the merits of the young Prince Henry.

Behind the façade of Princess Margaret's obedience and manners toward Jeanne lay a bitter resentment and a grieving broken heart. Margaret was as adept as her mother at duplicity; however, her assumed compliance covered the hate and fear of the two forcible controllers of her destiny. During the awful years of battle in France, after the death of François d'Guise, Margaret had been engaged in a secret romantic attachment with the young d'Guise who became the present Duke in his father's place. Margaret had lost her heart completely and under clandestine arrangements, had given everything of her body and soul to the young Duke. Her dreams filled with visions of a future marriage of devoted shared affection. When Margaret's brother, Duke d'Anjou, learned of her secret love affair, he was incensed with rage and vowed to murder her lover. Another of Charles' favorites warned that Anjou had confided in his brother his anger against the Duke d'Guise and without direct measures to end the tryst, Anjou would see the young Duke murdered. Frantic, the Duke d'Guise sought his mother's advice, who had also heard ominous rumors. By the following day, the young Duke d'Guise had betrothed and espoused the Princess de Porcien, who dearly desired the attachment and whom he had courted to hide his real passion for Princess Margaret. At that broken time in her life, Margaret hated her mother and her brothers for denying her happiness with the only love of her heart.

Among the privacy of her ladies, Margaret sneered at the mention of the Prince of Bearn, proclaiming "that she would never resign herself willingly to the loss of the Duke de Guise, to whom she had given her affections and her faith; neither would she, of her own free will, accept for a husband the Duke's greatest enemy."

Jeanne sought every opportunity to speak with Margaret alone, to discern for herself the genuine feelings of the prospective bride. Margaret was, however, never given a chance to converse in private, without the presence of Queen Catherine, and was soon whisked away by her attendants to the privacy of her apartments where Jeanne could not approach her.

After the beginning of social interactions and the departure of Margaret from the company, Queen Catherine, and Queen Jeanne, in all their pomp and magnificence, sat down to begin the marriage negotiations.

"Like two old buzzards eyeing each other across a fresh corpse," Jeanne thought, as the two stared at each other in preparation for battle.

The first few days were frustrating and defeated as absolutely no progress occurred while the matriarchs traded remarks in their effort to root out the real designs of the other. Finally, Queen Catherine thrust the first sword, insisting that the marriage would take place in Paris on the steps of Notre Dame Cathedral, as had all royal weddings of France been held there by tradition. Then the Queen Mother insisted that the royal couple would reside after the ceremony at the court of France. Along with that, Queen Catherine demanded that a chapel with all its attachments requisite to celebrate mass, be provided in any castle the newlyweds would inhabit throughout the kingdom of Navarre and Béarn so the Princess could continue in the worship of her Roman Catholic faith. Then, with the intention to draw first blood, the Queen Mother declared that the Prince should abstain from attending the worship of his Protestant faith while at court.

Jeanne maintained her calm and voiced her extreme disapproval at those conditions, responding with sure resolve that she would have the ceremony performed by proxy, standing in the prince's place herself; after the ceremony, Jeanne would accompany the new bride to Pau to join her husband. To this, Catherine ended the discussions after making explicit her firm denial of acceptance. It was questionable who had accomplished the deepest thrust as the indignant mothers left the charged field of battle.

Incensed at the subterfuge used to bring her to the court to propose such demands, Jeanne rejected the negotiation altogether. It was only her persistent desire to save the souls of France from the damnation of idol worship that kept her from returning to Pau. Besides, she had not yet spoken with the King whose own previous messages had begged her to come to court to negotiate directly with him. Jeanne decided to wait for an audience with King Charles. In a few days, she received a summons from the King to join him at Blois.

Once settled at Blois and greeted with great enthusiasm by the King, the negotiations began again. To Jeanne's intense disappointment, Catherine again led the discussions, as the King was absent due to "other pressing matters of state." The only visible change in the negotiations was the appearance of the hall they met in and the friendly and accepting demeanor of the Queen Mother as she listened patiently to Jeanne's expressions of her views. Then, laughing gaily, Catherine would ridicule whatever statement was made by Queen Jeanne and would twist the meaning of what she had just said to repeat it as the opposite of the original intent. Away from the negotiations, Jeanne would hear an incorrect interpretation from someone not participating in the discussion, casting false impressions to make Jeanne look a fool. This game went on for hours and days until Jeanne ran out of tolerance and left the negotiations.

Catherine believed that she had taunted, ridiculed and succeeded in humiliating the Queen of Navarre, although Jeanne maintained her demeanor of perfect self-control and dignity. Her composure incensed Catherine.

Jeanne commented on the differences between the demands made by Catherine to the promises that had been made previously when the King and his mother offered so much to get her to visit the court. Catherine insisted that such efforts had never occurred and rudely laid the blame for the stalled negotiations on Jeanne's selfish desires and refusal to order the prince to join her at Blois. The repeated emotional mandates of the Queen Mother to have the Prince join his mother at court magnified familiar suspicions in Jeanne's mind of Catherine's evil intentions toward them both.

It was true, although no evidence had been placed in Jeanne's hands to confirm it. Both Charles and his mother had been currently active in planning a massacre of the Queen, the prince and all the Huguenot leaders who would accompany them when all had been gathered in one place to complete the annihilation of the Huguenot faction for good. It was not the devotion of these two for the good of their ancestral faith against reform, but their insistence on eliminating the competition that could deprive them of their sumptuous, luxurious wealth and power.

Away from her meetings with Jeanne, Queen Catherine spent her time visiting with individuals from Navarre who had accompanied their Queen to court. She misrepresented Jeanne's comments and spread divisive remarks that Jeanne only kept the Prince hostage in Béarn to prevent him from agreeing with the King's offers, to benefit herself with personal riches. When Jeanne challenged Catherine with the untruthful statements reported, the Queen laughed derisively and insisted that Jeanne had fabricated such reports in her mind.

Suddenly, Catherine refused to continue the negotiations when Jeanne declined to summon her son or to submit in agreement with the celebrations of mass. Instead, she insisted that Jeanne summon three of her ministers to join her in Boise to meet with three Catholic priests to continue negotiations without the presence of the Queens.

Jeanne wrote Prince Henry, "I am in travail, and in such extremity of suffering, that had I not foreseen all that has happened I must have succumbed beneath the torment. I observe, however, that they aim to obtain your presence here; therefore, mon fils, look well to yourself, for if the King undertakes to accomplish this, as it is said he will do, I am greatly troubled for the result."

Jeanne's forebodings weighed heavily on her declining strength, as she could see no hope of the efforts she engaged in being accomplished. The ancient war of evil to defeat good was being played out over the small, bent figure of the Queen of Navarre who burned with an inner fire to vanquish the foes of the true faith of worship without the trappings of ceremonies and idol worship.

She completed her devotions and prayers and rose daily believing her God undergirded her weaknesses with His ultimate authority and power. She would continue in battle until God chose to remove her.

The negotiations continued in the hands of the ministers with lengthy discussions regarding the resolution of the differences in worship until the end of March, with no success.

Jeanne notified King Charles of her plan to return to Pau since the negotiations had descended into a hopeless morass and the hope of any accomplishment in such confusion and trifling insinuations as presented by the interference of Queen Catherine had become impossible. King Charles, suddenly exasperated by the amount of time spent dickering over details, pronounced his order giving sovereign agreement to all of Queen Jeanne's conditions on only one concession that the Prince of Béarn appeared in person for the ceremony rather than by proxy of his mother.

Catherine preserved a gloomy and sinister silence at this announcement. Solicitations poured upon Jeanne from all quarters to meet Charles in his liberal desire to satisfy his subjects and to restore peace to his realm. Jeanne's forebodings had increased with her receipt of the King's capitulation and the stresses she had endured ultimately sucked away any energy or resistance left.

She felt abandoned by every Huguenot leader, counselor and noble gathered at court to support her. Only her gallant son stood steadfast in agreement with her. To the others, the sole request of the King, after dismissing all other stipulations, that Henry should proceed in person to the wedding in Paris, appeared reasonable.[lxxxvi]

Defeated by her advisers, Jeanne consented to the marriage agreement, though not a single notation regarding the public worship of the royal couple appeared in it. King Charles was incredibly generous in drawing up the financial arrangements and poured abundant sums of monies and properties on the couple through Princess Margaret's dowry. He determined that nothing should interfere with the completion of his sister's marriage. He wrote to the Cardinal d'Lorraine to request a papal dispensation for the cousins to marry. Instead, he received the pontiff's refusal to issue the requisite dispensation, however not on the grounds of near kinship, but of Prince Henry's heretical roots. Charles chose to ignore his holiness and commanded the marriage should go forward.

30. Double Dealing

*"Behold, I have refined you, but not as silver; I have
tested you in the furnace of affliction."*

Isaiah 48:10 (NASB)

Exhausted and unsettled, Jeanne returned to her apartments at
Blois seeking rest. Princess Catherine, Jeanne's precious companion and daughter had joined Jeanne at Blois, along with her preceptress. During the long days of negotiations, Princess Catherine
had remained in Jeanne's apartments attending to her studies.
Her seclusion from the life of the court was expressly ordered
by her mother who wanted no contact by her daughter with the
licentious, promiscuous social gatherings of jaded damsels and
rude, coarse courtiers evident throughout the castle. Jeanne found
great comfort in the company of her chaste and beautiful twelve-
year-old daughter.

Not long after Jeanne had finished her part in the negotiations
and sought the privacy of her apartments to rest and renew her
spirit, Princess Catherine became ill with deep congestion in her
head and chest. For several days her symptoms increased, and
Jeanne frantically sought assurance of her survival. The doctors
of the castle attended the child for three days, using the accepted
method of blood-letting to remove the evil spirits of her illness.

When they reported no sign of improvement, they left Princess
Catherine to the prayers and care of her mother. Jeanne prevailed

in both categories and nursed her daughter lovingly with the same methods she had experienced at her mother's hands at the Château de Plessis. The Princess responded and soon was well on her way to recovery.[lxxxvii]

During this anxious time, Jeanne persevered alone by her daughter's side and ignored her weariness and declining health. She attended to her daughter's convalescence, taking on herself the entire burden of Catherine's care. A message was delivered to Jeanne as she sat at the bedside of her daughter. The letter reported receipt of a dispensation of approval from the most holy pontiff and that all objections were successfully overcome for the marriage to proceed. Jeanne was distracted by pondering the method of procurement of this approval since she was well acquainted with the hatred professed toward her by the Vatican. Jeanne excused herself from time with Princess Catherine and returned to discussions. She met with her Protestant ministers and advisers to determine the details of the ceremony that might endanger her son's immortal soul and their rulings on vows taken by the prince in the presence of the priests officiating at the ceremony and mass. Upon determining the answers to her questions, she wrote her decision to follow the instructions of her ministers to the letter. The King received her notice with irritation and waved away any attention to it, determined to discuss the matters face to face with Prince Henry on his arrival at court.

The mother of the prospective groom then moved her household to Paris to reside at the Hôtel d'Condé until the wedding. Jeanne arrived in Paris in late May. The wedding would occur on August 18, 1572. Jeanne, accompanied by her attendants and Princess Catherine, toured the boutiques and shops of Paris where Jeanne purchased jewels for her future daughter-in-law, gloves and ribbons for Princess Catherine, and small accessories for her son. She seemed to her faithful attendants to be swept up with anticipation for the festivities surrounding the upcoming nuptial celebrations and in the arrival of her son. She spared no generous inspiration or impulse in these vigorous shopping trips, buying lavish, expensive gifts for her children, her friends, and her castles.

Jeanne either was unaware or chose to ignore the many vicious remarks made by her enemies in Paris. The Queen of Navarre received criticism for her prim and starkly plain choice of dress, and her unwillingness to participate in court gossip and slander. She refused to engage in superfluous social interactions or casual flirtations so necessary to the flaunting immoral gatherings among the elite courtiers. French society had sunk to the level of gutter trash at this dark time of history when abandonment of moral values reflected the lack of leadership of both religious and secular guidance. The city of Paris mourned that Margaret of Valois would join in marriage to the disgusting son of such a prude.

31. Triumph

"And this is eternal life, that they may know Thee, the only true God, and Jesus Christ whom Thou has sent."

John 17:3 (NASB)

On the evening of June 4, Jeanne returned from an especially gay adventure among the small shops of Paris and retired to her bedroom; declining formal dining on the excuse she had no appetite. Her son had not arrived yet in Paris, and she confided to Maddie her desire to be rested when he appeared. After a couple of hours of restless tossing and turning, she called Maddie and complained of severe pain in her chest and arms, requesting additional pillows to support her back that she might breathe easier. Maddie began a vigil through the night as the pain increased to an unbearable level and Jeanne was desperate to get her breath. By morning, the seizure had passed, but Jeanne's breathing became severely impaired. The doctors of the King were summoned but could provide no suggestions of relief.

Jeanne recognized that recovery from this malady was not likely and called to her side those who she conferred with to arrange her Will and the future of her daughter, not forgetting provisions for the faithful Maddie. Those in attendance on Jeanne could see the intense pain she endured without complaint. Among the Huguenots gathered in Paris, great grief and sorrow overwhelmed them, so much had she inspired and served them in her royal capacity and strength of faith on behalf of their cause.

On occasion someone would insist on seeing her, interrupting her peaceful vigil to inquire about a small detail of the royal nuptials soon to take place. Jeanne's wrinkled brow revealed her irritation, and she declined to answer. Her attention focused on the joy of her future; her worldly affairs submitted to the hand of God.

Maddie alerted Jeanne's favorite protestant ministers, who had come to Paris to advise the Queen on details of Prince Henry's upcoming marriage ceremonies, of the rapid decline of the Queen so evident to her attendants. When they arrived at her bedside, Jeanne requested that they read from the Bible in the Book of John, chapters 14 through 21. Comforted by the words read, Jeanne lay quietly, her eyes closed, laboring to breathe. She was attentive to the promises written of her Christ, smiling at favorite passages and occasionally raising her finger to request a specific verse to be repeated.

Listening for the heavenly bells and breathing fragrances of gardenia and honeysuckle, she waited for Christ to take her hand. On June 9, 1572, sometime between 8:00 and 9:00 in the morning, the heroic and valiant spirit of Jeanne d'Albret soared in victory to the arms of her Savior.[lxxxiii]

Epilogue

"And He said to Cain, 'What have you done?
The voice of your brother's blood is crying
to Me from the ground. And now you are
cursed from the ground, which has opened its
mouth to receive your brother's blood from
your hand.'"

Genesis 4:10,11 (NASB)

Princess Catherine, so devoted and affectionate of her mother, was inconsolable. She was alone in the foreign city of Paris and mourned with only her preceptress. Prince Henry received the news of his mother's death while traveling with the 800 nobles and troops toward Paris. He halted his progress at Poiters when he received the news of his esteemed mother's death. After a week of intense grief, he became violently ill and delayed from moving on.

The King of France had ordered, upon receiving news of the death of the Queen of Navarre that the Queen would be interred at the mausoleum of the princes of Bourbon at the cathedral of Vendôme beside her husband, Antoine, King of Navarre. King Charles ignored Queen Jeanne's request for burial at a place she had chosen near Pau.

Jeanne lay in state in Paris on the lower floor of the Hôtel d'Condé where the Protestants of the city filed by to pay their respects. Margaret of Valois visited there, accompanied by companions that had despised the Queen of Navarre and her Protestant faith, who showed no respect, only mocking ridicule. Margaret was aghast at the dark curtains, lack of candles, no symbols, no priests and no chants. She was appalled at the somber plainness of the Protestant surroundings. Catherine d'Medici refused to acknowledge the life or death of her lifelong enemy. After that period of visitation, Jeanne's body, in her formal, sovereign, regal robes, was placed in a leaden coffin filled with lime and transported to Vendôme for burial.

Prince Henry recovered gradually from his illness, although he was beset with anger and resentment when remembering the treatment his mother had received while expending her energies with such fortitude to arrange his marriage. He planned to meet the funeral procession in Vendôme to attend her services; however, his illnesses had delayed his journey so long that he arrived after his mother's burial in the vault beside his father. While in Vendôme, he mourned with and comforted Princess Catherine, was informed of the contents in his mother's will and assumed the trappings of his rightful position as the new King of Navarre.

On July 9, 1572, an impressive cavalcade of gallant mounted nobles dressed in mourning accompanied King Henry of Navarre through the gates of Paris, followed by an impressive array of all the eminent Protestants nobles of Béarn, Navarre, and France.

Had Queen Jeanne been alive for consultation, she never would have allowed such an extensive display of the leaders of the reformed religion together in one place. Her constant advice to her son and advisers had always been to avoid such a gathering of the most formidable leaders of the Huguenots. Out of respect and admiration for their Queen, the devotion of these great leaders of that time unwittingly ignored her wise counsel.

The nuptial ceremony of Margaret de Valois and the King of Navarre occurred on the steps of Notre Dame on August 18, 1572. During the vows, the officiating Cardinal de Bourbon asked Margaret if she would accept the King of Navarre as her husband; she made no reply. After several pregnant moments of silence, King Charles stepped forward and pushed her head down; that nod served as agreement and the ceremony completed.

Three days later, Admiral Coligny was assassinated by a Catholic refugee from Poland. Rumor insisted it was at the command of Catherine d'Medici and Henry, Duke d'Anjou because they were afraid of the strength and prowess of the eminent Protestant cavaliers residing in their city. The King of Navarre, along with one hundred mounted soldiers, confronted King Charles at the Louvre, demanding an explanation and punishment. Catherine d'Medici, so adept at stirring her son to blind rage, fanned his emotions and belittled his abilities until on Sunday eve of St. Bartholomew's Day he commanded that his royal army massacre all Protestants in Paris. Two thousand Protestant men, women, and children died that day on the streets of Paris. In the following weeks, the violence and bloody killing spread throughout France. Though no record could possibly gather all the numbers accurately, an estimate reported at least seventy thousand citizens murdered or escaped across the northern borders.

The King of Navarre and his bride, along with the Prince d'Condé, were virtually held captives at the Louvre, unable to lead or influence the Protestant forces. A report stated that most of the Protestant victims offered little resistance.

The country of France faced an uncertain future locked in the powerful grasp of the Church, secured by shedding the blood of all dissenters. Almighty God was denied His rightful place in the hearts of the people who bowed under the deceptive sham of their licentious leaders to steal, kill and destroy their immortal souls.

The vicious persecutions depleted France of its brightest and bravest citizens who fled France to seek shelter in other countries. Those who could not escape faced certain death. Some of the best of these believers of the true gospel found their way to the New World to build a strong foundation of the true faith in that developing land.

Last Word

Revelation 18:1-5; 8; 20-24; 19:1-2 (NASB)

18 *¹"After these things I saw another angel coming down from heaven, having great authority, and the earth was illumined with his glory. ²And he cried out with a might voice, saying, "Fallen, fallen is Babylon the great! And she has become a dwelling place of demons and a prison of every unclean spirit, ...*

³For all the nations have drunk of the wine of the passion of her immorality, and the kings of the earth have committed acts of immorality with her, and the merchants of the earth have become rich by the wealth of her sensuality." ⁴And I heard another voice from heaven, saying, "Come out of her, my people that you may not participate in her sins and that you may not receive of her plagues; ⁵ for her sins have piled up as high as heaven, and God has remembered her iniquities." . . .

⁸"For this reason in one day her plagues will come, pestilence and not mourning and famine, and she will be burned up with fire; for the Lord who judges her is strong." . . .

²⁰"Rejoice over her, O heaven, and you saints and apostles and prophets, because God has pronounced judgment for you against her." ²¹And a strong angel took up a stone like a great millstone and threw it into the sea, saying, "Thus will Babylon, the great city, be thrown down with violence, and will not be found any longer. ²²And the sound of harpists and musicians and flute-players and trumpeters will not be heard in you any longer; ²³and the light of a lamp will not shine in you any longer; and the voice of the bridegroom and bride will not be heard in you any longer; for your merchants were the great men of the earth, because all the nations were deceived by your sorcery. ²⁴*And in her was found the blood of prophets and of saints and of all who have been slain on the earth.*

19 ¹*After these things I heard, as it were, a loud voice of a great multitude in heaven, saying, Hallelujah! Salvation and glory and power belong to our God;* ²*because His* **JUDGMENTS ARE TRUE AND RIGHTEOUS***; for He has judged the great harlot who was corrupting the earth with her immorality, and He has* **AVENGED THE BLOOD OF HIS BOND- SERVANTS** *on her."*

Castles of France inhabited by Jeanne d'Albret in her lifetime

Castles are listed in order of appearance in the book.

Fontainebleau

Pau

Château de Plessis

Alencon

Châtellerault

Soissons

La Fère (in Picardy)

Coucy

Gaillon (in Normandy)

Mont de Masan

La Fleche (in Anjou)

Compiégne

Baran

Orthez

St. Germain

Louvre

La Rochelle

Blois

End Notes

Book 1.

i.   Margaret Walker Freer, *The Life of Jeanne d'Albret, Queen of Navarre, Vol. I,* London: Hurst and Blackett, Publishers, 13, Great Marlborough Street. London1855. p.2.

ii.   Ibid, p.21.

iii. Kendall, Paul Murray. *Louis XI: The Universal Spider,* (New York: W.W. Norton & Company Inc., 1971),

iv. Margaret Walker Freer, *The Life of Jeanne d'Albret, Queen of Navarre, Vol. I,* London: Hurst and Blackett, Publishers, 13, Great Marlborough Street. London1855. p. 3,4.

v.   Ibid, p. 15.

vi. Ibid,

vii. Ibid, p. 16.

viii. https://en.wikipedia.org/wiki/Table_manners; How To Behave Samuel R Wells. New York: Fowler &Wells Co., Publishers, 753 Broadway. 1887; http://spotidoc.com/doc/214150/how-to-behave; HISTROY–BELLE ÉPOQUE on board COMPAGNIE GÉNÉRALE .... http://www.earlofcruise.com/2017/08/histroy-belle-epoque-on-board-compagnie_29.html

ix. Margaret Walker Freer, *The Life of Marguerite d'Angoulême, Queen of Navarre, Duchesse d'Alencon and De Berry. Vol. 2,* Cleveland: Burrows Brothers Company, Publishers — 1894, Elliott Stock, London p.148.

x.   https://en.wikipedia.org/wiki/Martin_Luther

xi. Margaret Walker Freer, *The Life of Jeanne d'Albret, Queen of Navarre, Vol. I,* London: Hurst and Blackett, Publishers, 13, Great Marlborough Street. London1855. p.16.

xii. Ibid. p. 17.

xiii. Ibid. p. 19.

xiv. Ibid. p. 24.

xv. Ibid. p. 25.

xvi. Ibid. p.14.

xvii. Ibid. p. 30.

xviii. Papiers d'Etat du cardinal Granvelle publiés d'aprés les MSS. De Besançon, par Charles Weiss, III., docum. 30.

xix. Papiers d'Etat du cardinal Granvelle, t. in., docum. 30.

xx. Mezeray, Abbrege". chron. t. n., p. 504. Paradin, Hist, de Notre Temps.

xxi. Margaret Walker Freer, *The Life of Jeanne d'Albret, Queen of Navarre, Vol. I,* London: Hurst and Blackett, Publishers, 13, Great Marlborough Street. London1855. P.37

xxii. Ibid. p. 42.

xxiii. Ibid. p. 48.

xxiv. Ibid. p. 49.

xxv. Ibid. p. 51.

xxvi. Ibid. p. 56.

xxvii. Ibid. p. 60.

Book 2.

xxviii. Papiers d'Etat du cardinal Granvelle Testament politique de l'empereur Charles Quint, p.508

xxix. Margaret Walker Freer, *The Life of Jeanne d'Albret, Queen of Navarre, Vol. I,* London: Hurst and Blackett, Publishers, 13, Great Marlborough Street. London 1855.p.64.

xxx. Ibid. 69.

xxxi. Ibid. 72.

xxxii. Ibid.

xxxiii. Ibid. 75.

xxxiv. Ibid.

xxxv. Ibid. 77.

xxxvi. Ibid. 80.

xxxvii. Ibid.

xxxviii. Margaret Walker Freer, *The Life of Marguerite d'Angoulême, Queen of Navarre, Duchesse d'Alencon and De Berry. Vol. 1* Cleveland: Burrows Brothers Company, Publishers — 1894, Elliott Stock, London , p. 350.

xxxix. Margaret Walker Freer, *The Life Of Jeanne d'Albret, Queen Of Navarre, Vol. I,* London: Hurst and Blackett, Publishers, 13, Great Marlborough Street. London1855.p.85 .

xl. Ibid. 86.

xli. Ibid. 87.

xlii. Ibid. 89.

xliii. Vauvilliers, Hist, de Jeanne d'Albret, p. 38. Cayet. Vauvilliers, Hist, de Jeanne d'Albret, p. 374, 1. 1.

xliv. Margaret Walker Freer, *The Life Of Jeanne d'Albret, Queen Of Navarre, Vol. I,* London: Hurst and Blackett, Publishers, 13, Great Marlborough Street. London1855.p 95

xlv. Ibid. 97.

xlvi. Ibid. 102.

xlvii.   Inventaire general de tous les meubles du chateau de Pau, pour le roy et royne, &c, fait par messieurs l'Ev£ques d'Oleron, et de Lescar, et autres. Le — jour de — 1561. M.S. Bibl. Imp. F. de B&hime — Inedited.

xlviii.   Margaret Walker Freer, *The Life of Jeanne d'Albret, Queen of Navarre, Vol. I,* London: Hurst and Blackett, Publishers, 13, Great Marlborough Street. London1855. P.128

xlix. Ibid. 135.

l. Ibid. 140

li. Koenigsberger, H. G. (1987) *Early Modern Europe 1500 – 1789,* Longman, Harlow,ISBN 0-582-49401-X paperback, p. 115.

lii. Margaret Walker Freer, *The Life of Jeanne d'Albret, Queen of Navarre, Vol. I,* London: Hurst and Blackett, Publishers, 13, Great Marlborough Street. London1855.p.167.

liii. Ibid. 169.

liv. Ibid. 172.

lv. Ibid. 176.

lvi. Ibid. 190.

lvii. Ibid. 207.

lviii. Ibid. 209.

lix. Ibid.

lx. Ibid. 213.

lxi. Ibid. 242.

lxii. Ibid. 246.

lxiii. Ibid. 263.

lxiv. Ibid. 292.

lxv. Archives de Simancas, A.B. 6, No. 65. De Juan Martinez d'Escurra, a Erasso, secretario de estado. –Ined

lxvi.   Margaret Walker Freer, *The Life of Jeanne d'Albret, Queen of Navarre, Vol. I,* London: Hurst and Blackett6, Publishers, 13, Great Marlborough Street. London1855. p. 303.

lxvii.   Ibid. 305.

lxviii. Ibid. 310

lxix.   Ibid. 345.

lxx.   Lettre du cardinal d'Armagnac a la royne de Navarre, dat6e de Belleperchc le lOeme d'Aoust, 1563. Olhagaray, Hist, de Foix, Bearn et Navarre. Mem. de Condé, t. rv., p. 594.

lxxi.   Lettre de la royne de Navarre au Cardinal d'Armagnac — Mem. de Conde, t. iv. Olhagaray, Hist, de Foix, Béarn et Navarre.

lxxii.   2 Le Laboureur — Additions aux Memoires de Castelnau, t. I. p. 863.

lxxiii. Margaret Walker Freer, *The Life of Jeanne d'Albret, Queen of Navarre, Vol. II,* London: Hurst and Blackett, Publishers, 13, Great Marlborough Street. London1855. p. 44.

lxxiv.   Ibid. p. 45.

lxxv.   Ibid. p. 48.

lxxvi.   Ibid. p. 56.

lxxvii. Written to the Huguenot troops on September 1, 1568. MS. BiM. Roy. Valiant, Portef. ler.— lnedited.

lxxviii. De Thou, Hist, de son Temps, liv. 36, who gives a minute detail of every circumstance connected with this conspiracy to betray Jeanne d'Albret into the power of the Inquisition.— Memoires de ""Etat de Prance, sous Charles IX.

lxxix.   Margaret Walker Freer, *The Life of Jeanne d'Albret, Queen of Navarre, Vol.II,* London: Hurst and Blackett, Publishers, 13, Great Marlborough Street. London 1855. p. 175.

lxxx.   Ibid. p. 199.

lxxxi.   Ibid.

lxxxii. Ibid. p. 201.

lxxxiii. Ibid. p. 269.

lxxxiv. Ibid. p. 274.

lxxxv.   Ibid. p. 307.

lxxxvi. Ibid. p. 308.

lxxxvii. Ibid. p. 315.

lxxxviii. Ibid. p. 333.

CPSIA information can be obtained
at www.ICGtesting.com
Printed in the USA
FSHW010404311018
53426FS

9 781545 647486